D1012148

Also by Linda Broday

The Bachelors of Battle Creek
Texas Mail Order Bride
Twice a Texas Bride
Forever His Texas Bride

Men of Legend
To Love a Texas Ranger
The Heart of a Texas Cowboy
To Marry a Texas Outlaw

Texas Redemption
Christmas in a Cowboy's Arms

the HEART of a TEXAS COWBOY

LINDA BRODAY

sourcebooks
casablanca

Published by Sourcebooks Casablanca, an imprint of Sourcebooks, Inc.
P.O. Box 4410, Naperville, Illinois 60567-4410
(630) 961-3900
Fax: (630) 961-2168
www.sourcebooks.com

Printed and bound in Canada.
MBP 10 9 8 7 6 5 4 3 2 1

To Jan for always having my back and reading my stories when your plate is already so full it's running over the sides. Your comments, suggestions, and advice are invaluable. We didn't know when we were young and making up stories for our paper dolls that one day we'd still be making up stories—only this time in books. You're my sister, my friend, my partner in crime, and I'm glad we're taking life's journey together. Love you.

One

SOME OLD WIVES SOMEWHERE PROBABLY SAID THAT BLOOD on a wedding day forewarned of things to come. But he didn't have any patience for curses or omens today. Becky Golden was the only girl he'd ever loved. They were perfect for each other.

Nothing would stop him from making a future with her. Nothing.

Houston Legend sucked a drop of blood from the thumb he'd cut on a piece of shattered coffee cup. "Great," he muttered. He'd probably get blood on the highfalutin ascot he was trying to tie. One good thing—it was black.

"Houston, get a move on. You're going to be late for your wedding." His brother's bellow was louder than a snorting, snot-slinging steer on the rampage. The huge stone house that served as headquarters for the famous Lone Star Ranch picked up his voice and bounced it around the walls.

"Hold your horses!" Houston Legend fumbled with the fancy neckpiece that his beautiful bride-to-be had insisted he wear.

The bedroom door flung open and his younger brother Sam poked his head in. "What's the holdup?"

"This damn tie. For two cents I'd wear my normal clothes." Houston shot a longing glance at his comfortable trousers and shirt on the bed. He seldom wore a neckpiece and when he did, it was a simple western tie. "This isn't me. I think it's called an ascot or some such nonsense, but with this thingamajig on, the only ass in the room is me."

Sam strode forward. "You can do anything once, big brother. Becky wants her wedding perfect and you're gonna give it to her. Let me see it."

With a flick of his wrists, Sam had the silk neckpiece tied in nothing flat. "Where's your stickpin?"

Houston handed him the diamond pin. "You're not wearing your sheriff's badge."

"Not on duty." Sam reached for the black cutaway coat and held it for Houston. "Besides, it ruins the look of my suit."

A former Texas Ranger, Sam had given up the job when he married Sierra Hunt and adopted an orphaned boy two months ago. Sam was now sheriff of Lost Point, Texas—a place that until recently had been an outlaw haven. The town was only an hour's ride from the Lone Star, so that made their pa happy. Stoker had said if Sam couldn't live on the ranch, he wanted him nearby. Houston was glad he hadn't gone far. He liked having his brother around.

"Shouldn't need the badge today. At least I hope not." Houston nodded and shot him a grin. "Were you nervous when you and Sierra tied the knot? My hands are shaking."

"Mine shook too the day I wed Sierra." Sam shot him a narrowed glance. "Becky's the right one, isn't she? I mean, you don't have any doubts or anything."

Houston paused for a moment in thought. Although they'd grown up together on different ranches, he knew the exact second he'd fallen hard. Becky was ten and Houston had been twelve. It was right after they'd buried his mother. Although he protested, his father made him go to a barn dance at the Golden ranch. She wore a blue dress that seemed woven from his dreams and the soft lantern light shining on her hair reminded him of daffodils. He knew right then that there would never be another girl for him. Lord, how his heart pounded when he took her in his arms. Becky pushed away the dark shadows of his life with rays of sunshine. He'd known then that she was his one true love for all eternity, and he still knew it now.

"She's the one," Houston assured him.

"I wish Mother was alive to see you," Sam said quietly. "You'd make her proud." He wandered to the window and pushed the curtain aside. "I wonder if Luke will show up."

With one last glance in the mirror, Houston turned. "Hope so. I miss him, you know. I really like having our outlaw brother in the family—it's easier than having a lawman like you, anyway."

Sam moved from the window and flicked off a piece of lint from Houston's shoulder.

Houston slapped his hand. "Stop it. You're not Mother."

Paying him no mind, Sam straightened the ascot. "I worry about Luke out there all alone, searching for the man who framed him for murder. He needs us."

"It's what he chose," Houston reminded him.

Music drifted upstairs from the piano they'd lugged outside for the ceremony. Both bolted from the room. Houston would never hear the end of it if he kept Becky waiting at the altar.

A few moments later, he pushed through the door and stepped onto the wide porch. Though this was a ranch, it was so large that it was more like a town, complete with a mercantile, school, telegraph office, and its own doctor. The early May afternoon was beautiful, with sunshine splashing onto rooftops and whitewashed buildings.

Everything was perfect, and not a cloud in the sky.

He and Sam strode to stand next to the preacher they'd brought all the way from Squaw Valley, the nearest town with a church. Overhead, the Texas flag fluttered in the breeze and the sun caught on the huge bronze star that hung suspended twenty feet away. The brilliant rays passed through the cutouts in each star point, creating a beautiful image at Houston's feet.

Reverend Smith fought a sudden gust of wind that sent his long red hair tumbling, blocking his vision. Remaining ramrod straight, he calmly parted the copper strands in the center like a curtain and peered out. Houston covered his mouth to keep from laughing.

The pianist launched into the "Wedding March" and all eyes turned. Houston's tongue glued to the roof of his mouth. Becky was truly a vision with her golden hair hanging in ringlets from the crown of her head.

How had he landed such a breathtaking woman? Must've been fate. She slowly made her way to his side and took Houston's hand. Crazy with love for her, he stared into her soft brown eyes and squeezed her palm. He mouthed, "I love you for all of eternity."

The sound of a horse whickering outside caught his attention. Guests had been arriving all day. When he glanced up, he spotted his brother Luke, standing apart from the rest next to his black gelding. He'd made it after all. Their gazes met and he nodded to Houston. Houston nodded back, happier than he'd ever been in his life.

Just as the good reverend opened his mouth to speak, a single shot rang out. It happened so fast, no one had time to react. As if in a daze, Houston heard Becky cry out, watched her collapse. He caught her in his arms before she hit the ground.

Blood oozed from a hole in her chest and stained her beautiful blue dress.

Two

CHAOS ENSUED. GUESTS SCREAMED. SOME DROPPED ONTO their bellies while others ran for cover. Mothers shielded their children with their bodies.

In shock, Houston stared as Luke whirled and fired faster than a man could breathe, aiming toward the corner of the house. Sam leaped over bodies, racing to capture the shooter.

Shrugging off his coat, Houston placed it over his bride. Her eyes were open and filled with pain. A gurgling came from her throat, freezing Houston's heart.

"Someone get Doc Jenkins!" he shouted as he focused on his bride. "Dearest, hold on. Doc will be here in a minute. He'll fix you up and you'll be fine. Just don't go to sleep. Please don't close your eyes. Look at me and don't close them."

Houston's hand trembled when he brushed her hair back from her face. This couldn't happen to the woman he loved.

She had to live. They had so much happiness ahead of them.

Please, God, don't take her. Take me instead.

The gurgling worsened. She went limp as life drained from her body.

Doc Jenkins knelt beside him and felt for a pulse. Sadly, he shook his head.

How long Houston held her to him, he didn't know. His father knelt beside him. "Son, you have to let her go. Becky is gone. You can't do anything else for her. Let us take her into the house."

"I can't, Pa."

"Yes, you can. Just let her go."

"I love her." The deafening cry that sprang from Houston's mouth sounded like it came from some wild animal. He met his father's stricken gaze. "Why? Why did this happen to Becky of all people?"

"I don't know, son." Stoker laid an arm across Houston's shoulders. "We're going to find out, though; you can damn sure bet on that."

"I hope they catch the bastard and that he's alive."

"I only know Luke's bullet struck him. I haven't heard how bad it is."

"Good that they caught him. I hope he doesn't bite the dust before I can talk to him." Houston would do a damn sight more than talk. He'd rip the man apart piece by piece and take deep satisfaction in the pain he inflicted.

"Houston, let these men have her so they can take her into the house, away from curious eyes," Stoker said gently.

Houston slowly released his grip.

Fighting crushing pain, Houston watched as men carried his love into the Lone Star headquarters and out of sight. Nothing made sense. How could Becky be dead? He accepted his father's hand and put weight on legs that seemed made of wood.

Only one thing penetrated the shock and horror—he'd lost the love of his life, and someone would pay. He'd take great pleasure in making sure the murdering bastard never hurt another woman. He knew ways to get the shooter to talk.

Oh yeah, lots of ways, and all of them very painful.

❧

How much time had passed Houston couldn't venture a guess, although something told him it must've been quite a while. He sat next to Becky's cold body in the dim parlor. Seeing her on the sofa so silent and still, he couldn't believe she was dead. Piercing pain ripped through him and he had to force himself to breathe. He was glad someone had pulled the thick drapes that blocked out most of the sunlight. The dim shadows let him grieve in private. He just wanted to be left alone in the darkness of his soul.

In the shadows, he could pretend it was all a dream and she'd wake up. Sobs erupted around him, reminding him that he wasn't alone as he wished, but he paid them no heed. He was lost in a thick haze, where little thought could penetrate. Though he felt sympathetic mourners touch his back, he didn't turn to acknowledge them.

Why couldn't they leave him be with the woman he loved?

He unclenched his fist and stared at the bloody veil he gripped. He couldn't let go of the last thing his bride had worn.

Wailing echoed through the walls of the huge house that was still filled with wedding guests. He'd briefly spoken to Becky's parents but they, like him, were grief-stricken and in shock.

How the hell had this happened? How could the love of his life lie stone dead? It couldn't be possible. Houston still felt the weight of her in his arms as she fell. Still heard the gurgle as life drained from her body. Still smelled the stench of death.

How would he be able to live without his Becky?

Stoker Legend pressed a glass of whiskey into his hand. "Drink this. It'll brace you for what you have to do."

Houston took the offering but didn't drink. "Why, Pa? Why did someone have to shoot her? She never hurt a fly, nor spoke ill of anyone."

"I don't know, son." Stoker dropped heavily into the chair next to Houston. "But you can damn well bet we'll find out, even if we have to rip the killer apart."

"Sam and Luke really caught him? There's no mistake?"

Houston's thoughts were so muddled. Words refused to penetrate his brain, or maybe they were rebelling like him, refusing to believe what had happened.

"Yes, your brothers did get the bastard. Doc Jenkins is treating the wound where Luke shot him." Stoker emptied his glass in one gulp.

Houston stared down at the bloody veil.

Becky was gone and he didn't know how he could live without her.

❦

Daylight had begun to fade and Houston still sat with Becky in the parlor. The room was quiet and he had such a frightening stillness inside. Houston gripped the glass of whiskey but had yet to take a sip. He hadn't heard his father leave.

Maybe when the bullet took Becky's life, it had taken his hearing too.

Footsteps sounded on the hardwood floor and Sam sat next to him. "Luke and I locked the murdering varmint in the basement, where no one would hear him yell. Doc removed the bullet without benefit of anything for pain."

"Did the sorry bastard say why he did it?" Houston met Sam's eyes. "I hope you waited for me."

"We did, but he's saying plenty without prodding. He says Becky belonged to him, and he couldn't let you have her."

"She wouldn't let some cur dog think he had a chance in hell at her heart." Becky wasn't that sort of woman.

She would've made a wonderful mother for their children. The house he'd built for her just past the schoolhouse would sit empty forever.

The cry that tore from Houston's throat made a sound he'd never heard before. Rage built higher and higher until he shot to his feet and hurled the still-untouched whiskey glass against the wall. It shattered, sending shards everywhere and amber liquid running down the expensive wallpaper like tears. "I want to hear that from his lips, see his eyes. I want to taste his fear. I want him to choke when I put my hands around his damn throat."

Full of blinding fury, Houston stuffed Becky's wedding veil into his pocket and stormed from the room with Sam trailing behind. The crack of his boot heels against the floor sounded like rifle shots all the way down to the basement door off the kitchen.

In seconds, Houston stood over the rotten bastard who'd viciously stolen his bride. He recognized him from the handful of times he'd seen the man on the Golden Ranch. Ernie Newman lay on a blanket on the dirt floor with Luke guarding from a nearby crate.

Cold, sullen eyes glared up.

Overcome with a rage unlike anything he'd ever felt, he grabbed Newman by the shirtfront, lifting him off his feet with one hand. Houston slammed a fist into the man's face.

When he drew back to hit him again, Luke grabbed his arm. "Beating him senseless won't change the facts, brother."

Houston flung the man back to the blanket. "You're lucky my brothers are here or I'd kill you. I want answers and I'll know if you're lying. For each lie, I'll hit you again."

Hate flashed from Newman's eyes as he dragged his sleeve across his bloody mouth.

"How well did you know Becky?" Houston yelled.

"She always came to me when she needed her horse saddled or the wagon hitched. Then she came to find me just to talk. No woman ever gave me the time of day until I met her."

"Prove it."

"Whatever you want, *Mr. Legend*. I watched from a window when you gave her a ring and asked her father for her hand," Newman spat. "I watched it all. She was having a child—mine."

"You're a lying sack of shit!"

"We planned to run off together but she couldn't do that to her parents. She knew it would've killed them. Doc Jenkins can provide proof of the babe."

Houston turned to Sam. "Bring Doc down here. We'll find out the truth."

Sam nodded and left. Houston leaned against the basement wall to wait. He cast daggers at Becky's killer. No one spoke—not Luke, Houston, or Ernie. It didn't take long for Sam to return.

"What can I do for you, Houston?" Doc asked.

Houston shoved away from the wall. "Tell me about Becky. Tell me she wasn't with child."

"I can't do that." Doc glanced at Newman. "Becky came to me with her secret, begging me not to tell you or her parents. I urged her to come clean, but she said she couldn't. I'm sorry, son." Doc hesitated a moment, torn by whatever he saw on Houston's face, turned, and climbed the stairs to the kitchen without another word.

The air left Houston. It was true. Everything Newman said. Houston wanted to pound something. Anger sat thick and bitter on his tongue.

"Why in hell would she agree to marry me, then?" Houston thundered. He grabbed Newman and slammed his fist into the bastard's jaw. "Why?"

Newman's cold eyes glittered. "Becky was desperate for a name for the babe and her parents wouldn't let her marry me. I wasn't good enough for their daughter. And apparently Becky shared their views. We had a terrible fight this morning. She told me you could better provide for the babe and, when it came, she would tell you it came early."

"So I was nothing but a means to an end?"

"You get the picture. For a smart man, you're really slow, *Mr. Legend*."

God. Houston's stomach revolted, sending bile into his mouth.

Stupid.

Stupid.

Stupid.

He tightened his hands around the man's throat. "Why did you have to kill her? And the babe. It was your flesh and blood, you worthless bastard." Houston could kind of understand the deception and Becky's desperation to some degree. But putting a bullet in her—she hadn't deserved that, no matter what she'd done.

Newman gasped for breath. "If I couldn't have her, no one would. You Legends, with your power and land, think you can have whatever you want. I showed you. Killing her was the only way."

"The only way?" Houston's yell sprang from the hole left deep inside that nothing would ever fill.

"I wanted you to live in hell. When you came to call, you always walked by me like I was some bug crawling on the damn ground. I was beneath the powerful Houston Legend!" Newman shouted.

Houston pushed his face into the man's. It was possible he could've slighted Ernie Newman without even knowing it. On visits to the Goldens, Houston's mind had been on Becky and stealing a kiss, not on making friends with the hands. Still, he didn't think he was ever rude.

"You did this for what? Revenge?"

"In part. I did love Becky, but she wanted what I couldn't give. I hated you and wanted you to suffer." Newman clawed at Houston's hands.

Something glittered, catching Houston's attention. He released Newman's throat to grab his hand.

On the bastard's little finger winked the family heirloom Becky always wore.

Memories danced around Houston's fury. Becky had said the ring had belonged to her great-grandmother. When it disappeared from her hand, he bought her claim of losing it but noticed how she avoided his eyes. Loving her, he'd silenced the whispers in his head.

A guttural sound of pain sprang from Houston's mouth. He was such a fool. When he kissed her, how could he not have felt her pulling back?

But—he had. He'd simply blocked it. Truth was, she'd sidestepped his kisses and dodged passionate embraces.

Most times she'd distracted him with teasing conversation. He'd put down her reluctance to shyness and not wanting to make a show of affection. How could he have been so blind? She'd never once spoken words of love.

The truth hit him.

Becky had never loved him.

"God have mercy on your poor, pitiful, pathetic soul." Houston hurled Newman away and stalked to the stairs. He never wanted to see the man's face again.

From this moment on, he'd never speak Becky's name or allow it to be spoken in his presence. He'd never trust *love* again.

Houston jerked the bloody veil from his pocket. Wadding it into a ball, he dropped it to the dirt floor and climbed the stairs.

❦

Dawn splashed through the windows of Houston's bedroom. Staggering, he rose from the chair where he'd sat all night. He unbuttoned his blood-soaked shirt and launched it into a corner, frowning at the red stains on his skin. Pouring water from a pitcher into a porcelain bowl, he scrubbed away every trace of Becky. His chest was raw by the time he finished.

In the early morning quiet, Houston forced back memories that crowded his mind. Too many, and all brought jagged pain. He strode to the dresser drawer, selected a clean shirt, and thrust his arms into the sleeves.

Betrayal still shook him to the core.

Last night, he'd helped carry Becky's casket and load it into a wagon for the journey home. People would wonder at his cold distance and refusal to accompany her parents. Let them.

A low knock sounded at the door. "It's open," he barked.

His brothers entered. Sam spoke. "We were worried."

"I'm fine. You can head right back out. I'm in a hell of a mood."

"You wouldn't be normal if you weren't," Luke replied.

"But you're still here." Houston buttoned his shirt and tucked it into his pants.

Sam dropped into a chair in the corner. "We have a suggestion."

"I don't need coddling like some child, Sam. Go tend to your wife and son." Houston put on his hat and snatched his gun belt from the bedpost. "I'm not going to blow my brains out. Just need to be alone. Alone as in *by myself*." He gave them a pointed glare.

"Sierra and Hector are still asleep." Sam folded his arms. "We want to help. You're in shock."

"Yeah, well, I'll live." Somehow or other.

"A good hard ride up to the ridge is what you need."

Damn, Sam wasn't giving up. Houston let out a long sigh. Much as he loved his little brother, Sam's mothering irritated the hell out of him.

"Fresh air is exactly what you need." Luke threw in his two cents. "Besides, I want to talk to you both about something."

"I'm in no mood for this. I just want to be alone." Houston's patience hung by a thread.

Sam sighed and softened his voice. "Remember where we went when our baby brother, William Travis, and Mother died? When Pa dove headfirst into a bottle and couldn't remember he had scared boys who needed him? When Pa started gambling recklessly? Each time we sought comfort on the ridge above the Red River. It'll help you now."

At last, Houston threw up his hands. "You win." He did need to clear the smell of blood and betrayal from his nostrils, and he'd go crazy if he stayed here listening to his brothers yacking at him. Somehow, he'd pry the worst day of his life from his head.

Houston buckled his gun belt and strapped it on. Reaching for his hat, he strode to the corral with them, where they saddled their horses. A short time later, he galloped with Sam and Luke across raw, uneven ground, letting the wind blow Becky from his mind.

After riding full-out for five miles, Houston reined to a stop on the high bluff overlooking the mighty Red. The water was as murky as his thoughts, and moved just as fast. The hard truth of loving Becky was the part that hurt the most. While he'd been giving his whole heart and soul to her, she'd been slipping around with another man.

Dammit to hell!

He dismounted and sat, letting his feet dangle off the cliff edge. Sam and Luke dropped down on either side of him. No one spoke for a long while. The quiet was good.

Finally, Houston shot Luke a glance. His brother had a thousand-dollar price on his head for robbery and the murder of federal judge Edgar Percival. The tangled mess of Luke's life was even worse than Houston's.

Maybe talking about someone else's problems would take Houston's mind off his. "You said you wanted to talk about something, Luke."

"My problem is a name taken from one of Beadle's dime novels—Ned Sweeney. The man using it is the one who really murdered Judge Percival." Luke swung to stare into the distance. "Find him and I clear myself of that. Ever hear of anyone going by that name?"

"Nope." Houston absently watched the water below. Had Becky ever truly cared for him, or had she just pretended all these years? He wished he could talk to her once more. He'd ask why she hadn't been honest with him. Why she hadn't been able to tell him about Newman. And why she'd let him fall so deeply in love with her.

"I never heard the name mentioned," Sam said. "How do you know he's the murderer?"

With his thumb and forefinger, Luke pulled his hat lower on his forehead. "I ran into a man, Joe Calderon, down in San Antone, and he told me Ned Sweeney is the one who pulled the trigger. I tried to get Joe to tell the sheriff but he said Ned would kill him."

"Somehow, somewhere, you crossed paths with this killer before," Houston said.

Luke sent a stone zinging out into the water below. "Must've. But don't know where."

"Can you trust this Joe guy?" Sam asked. "He might've fed you a load of bull."

"I've had a few dealings with him. He's always been honest," Luke said.

"How can we help?" Houston asked.

"You and Sam can get access to things I can't. I thought if you could send out some telegrams to different people and see if they've heard of anyone using the name Ned Sweeney, we might find a clear direction for me to go." Luke paused. "I won't ask you for more than you feel comfortable with."

"We'll be glad to help, won't we, Sam?" The wheels in Houston's brain were already turning. A fight might just calm him down. He was angry, and it would feel good to haul off and hit something. Anything.

"I've still got ties to the Texas Rangers and my old boss, Captain O'Reilly," Sam said.

Luke threw three stones down below in rapid succession. "Thanks. Like I said, you have access to people and places I can never have."

"Turnabout is fair play." Houston laid a hand on his outlaw brother's shoulder. They wouldn't have caught Becky's killer if not for Luke. "We couldn't have whipped Felix Bardo and that outlaw mess that had dug in over at Lost Point without you. Your ability to fit in with them and gain their trust saved the people of that town. You made this part of Texas safer. Sam sure wouldn't be here either if you hadn't cut him down so fast after Bardo hung him."

They owed Luke a hell of a lot more than a few telegrams.

"Sierra's and my wedding sure wouldn't have happened. Felix Bardo would've killed her and certainly meant to," Sam said quietly. "I'll be glad to help in any way."

"Appreciate it." Luke seemed lost in thought. Something more was bothering his brother, but Houston knew better than to ask. One thing Houston had learned about Luke was that you didn't push him. Anyone who tried found themselves full of regrets. "What are you going to do now, Houston?" Luke asked.

"Go on like I always have."

"That's no damn plan," Sam hollered. "You're going to have to deal with what happened sooner or later."

"Sam, it's my problem and I'll handle it," Houston grated out. "Now, if you don't mind, I've got some thinking to do."

"Fine." Sam rose. "By the way, you might like to know that Ernie Newman is gone. Pa and some of the ranch hands have carted him to Fort Worth to stand trial."

"I hope he swings for what he did." Houston wouldn't waste one ounce of pity on him.

Luke got to his feet. "I'm leaving at first light. Don't let this gnaw on you, Houston. A man only has so much flesh. Take it from me."

An ache filled Houston's chest, a space he'd thought couldn't hold any more pain. He didn't know what it was like to be hunted like Luke. He'd always known the safety of the ranch. But after yesterday, he knew death could always find him, no matter where he was.

"When you're out there, don't forget you're a Legend, even if you refused to take the name. And that you have a home and people who care for you," Houston reminded him gruffly.

They had an unbreakable bond.

They were brothers.

They were Legends.

Houston watched his brothers mount up and gallop off. His thoughts turned back to Becky. As much as he'd tried to prevent it, she *would* gnaw on him.

It would take a lifetime to forget the woman who'd ruined him.

Three

IN THE YEAR FOLLOWING THE SHOOTING, HOUSTON THREW himself into work with a vengeance, trying to forget Becky and her stinging betrayal. His heart was nothing more than a piece of raw meat that had been stomped and left in the hot sun to wither. He knew he'd let himself descend into darkness, but it was there he found solace…and escape.

Though he tried to resist, he lost the battle, and most nights found him hugging a bottle of whiskey. He turned a blind eye to the looks Stoker, Sam, and sometimes Luke gave him when he briefly swung by. When they said anything, he snapped that he was doing his best.

On a Monday morning in May, Houston pored over the books in the office of Lone Star headquarters and frowned at the figures. The tally didn't make sense. They were four thousand dollars down from where they had been last week. Sure, the ranch had been in trouble for a while, but the steady decline had turned into a free fall off a cliff.

And if he didn't know why, he didn't know how to stop it.

Long-term trouble was coming from the size of their ever-increasing herd and not enough grazing land, even with four hundred eighty thousand acres. Though they'd had a little rain, this year had brought a drought, and the cattle were starving. A ranch in North Texas was always between hay and grass anyway, never flush with either. Simply the hard truth. The only solution for the cattle surge that would bring a little relief was taking two thousand head or more up the Great Western Trail to Dodge City. He'd already given the hands the order to start rounding them up and branding them. He hadn't told Stoker yet. Didn't want an argument.

Having almost a hundred employees to pay didn't help. In addition to the cowboys, they had to support and look after the new schoolteacher, Doc Jenkins, and Jim Wheeler, who operated the telegraph. They also went halves on stocking merchandise for the mercantile, but the store owner kept nearly all the profits.

Houston rubbed his bleary eyes and glanced up as his father entered. His pa didn't appear in any better shape than Houston. His pale-green eyes were bloodshot and his clothes had been slept in, if he'd slept at all. Stoker Legend gave a deep sigh and slumped into the leather chair opposite the desk.

The ladies around the ranch would say Stoker Legend was a handsome man for fifty-eight years old. Only a smattering of silver streaked his dark hair and he didn't have an ounce of fat on his tall frame. Stoker was a man who'd lived hard and carved out the famous Lone Star spread from nothing. He'd cut his teeth on men who'd tried to take his land, and had made plenty of enemies along the way. Not that he gave a damn about any of that. Today, he looked exhausted.

Stoker sighed again.

"Something bothering you, Pa?"

"Had poker games all weekend, but last night's lasted until dawn."

Houston chuckled. "Pa, everyone in the whole blame state knows about your poker games. They're legendary. That must be why you look like you've been dragged behind a horse. I take it there was a good bit of drinking involved?"

"Can't play cards without it, son. The two just go together." Stoker ran a finger along the edge of the desk. "I won a few. Lost a few. There's something I've got to tell you, son."

"Start at the beginning and let it fly," Houston advised. "That's what you'd tell me."

Stoker rose and stared out the window. "It's about... Perhaps I can shed some light on the problem with those books you've been studying."

Houston's stomach clenched. This sounded worse than losing a couple of hands of poker with friends. "The ranch is in a pretty tight bind right now, but tell me how much you lost and we'll cover it. I take it that's where the huge deficit in the books went."

They couldn't take many more losses like that. How many times was Stoker going to wager his life's work away?

"It is." Stoker gave a curt nod. "But that's only a small corner of the problem. The truth is...the ranch has been cut in half. Yours, Sam's, and Luke's—your legacies have shrunk considerably."

Everything inside Houston stilled: his heart, his breathing, his ability to swallow. He couldn't stop anger from flaring. "What do you mean cut in half? What have you done, Pa?"

"It's gone."

"What's gone? Are you talking about land, money, or what?" Houston slammed the receipts register closed. He dreaded telling his brothers their father had finally lost it all.

"You know how I have a standing poker game every Saturday night."

For Stoker to repeat himself meant he couldn't even bear to say the words.

"Quit stalling, Pa. Yes, for as long as I can recall, you, Max Golden, and Kern Smith have cut loose on Saturday nights. You lost half the ranch to them?" That might not be so bad. They were longtime friends. Maybe Houston could persuade them to let the wager go for a drunken mistake and they'd all have a good laugh. After all, they were reasonable men. Kern's wife once came to ask that Stoker return money they needed for ranch expenses.

"Not exactly." Stoker looked away. "We had another rancher join us. New to the area. Name's Till Boone. He bought the spread adjoining ours to the south that's lain idle for thirty years. Till now owns two hundred forty thousand acres of our ranch where it adjoins his."

"Damn it, Pa! That's where all the grass is. What were you thinking?"

Stoker plowed his fingers through his thick hair. "I had a little too much bourbon."

"Pa, you promised to slow down."

His father whirled and leaned over the desk, pointing his finger. "I don't need a lecture from you. I will when *you* will. The main thing is that we can fix this."

"How? I've never known you not to honor all your debts, even the ones made when you were soused. I can't believe this." He didn't see a way in hell of keeping the ranch together. None whatsoever. What was he going to tell Sam? Or Luke, who'd just started to feel a part of the family?

Fire flashed from Stoker's bloodshot eyes. "There's only one way and it'll be up to you. I need you in on this, Houston."

Fury crawled up Houston's spine. "So I'm supposed to fix the mess you've made?"

"You're the only one who can, son."

"Stop talking in riddles, Pa, and get on with it." Houston could barely contain his fury. He didn't like having hard feelings for his father, but for Stoker to expect him to fix a stupid blunder like this stretched their relationship to the breaking point.

"Till Boone's daughter needs a husband. Boone said if you'll marry his Lara, he'll forgive my foolish wager. And we can keep the land."

"What? This is your idea of fixing things?" Houston exploded in a single word: "*NO!*" He leaped to his feet so fast it sent his chair toppling. "You're crazy to even think I'd consider this."

Houston couldn't marry again. He hadn't slept a full night since his first disastrous wedding and only whiskey could silence his demons. He carried festering wounds that hadn't even begun to scab over, and to ask him to marry another would throw him right back into that pit with no way to crawl out. He hadn't been able to trust Becky and he'd known her forever. How could he bind himself to a perfect stranger and not expect more of the same?

"Boone gave us twenty-four hours to think about it." Stoker crossed the space to him and laid a hand on his shoulder. "I know it's asking a lot."

"Hell yeah, it's asking a lot. How about asking me to give up the rest of my life? Asking me to live with a stranger, sleep in the same bed, pretend to care for someone sitting across from me at the supper table? The answer is no. And all that aside, I leave on the cattle drive in three weeks. I don't have time to deal with this." Houston shrugged out from under Stoker's hand. He strode for the door, putting some distance between them before he hauled off and hit his father.

"There's more." Stoker's words stopped him in his tracks. With narrowed eyes, Houston whirled. "How much worse can it be? What else is Boone wanting? The marriage license signed in blood? Tacking my hide to the barn door? What?"

"His daughter, Lara, has a child. A little girl. In return for giving us back the land, Boone is asking you to give her child a name and raise the girl as your daughter."

The air left Houston in a big whoosh. This was like Becky all over again. She had needed a name for *her* child. Was he never to be anything more than a tool for someone to use for their own ends? What about his wants? His longings?

Becky had wanted to foist Ernie Newman's child off on him. He wondered if he would've known, if he'd have seen the man's resemblance in the babe. Would it have mattered?

he wondered. He'd loved Becky so fully and completely. If she'd survived, would he have forgiven her and have a child he loved as his own even now?

And what of *this* girl's innocent babe?

Houston's brother Luke came to mind. He'd been raised a bastard child and it had turned him into an outlaw. People had called him the devil's spawn. What would the slurs do to an innocent girl? Could Houston live with people calling her and her baby all manner of names, looking down on them, when he could have done something about it?

"How old is the child?" Houston asked quietly.

"A babe…not quite a year."

Houston met Stoker's green gaze. "The child's father is dead?"

"He will be when Boone finds the bastard. He forced himself on Lara. The babe needs a real father. She can never know the truth of her birth."

Damn! Stoker had him over a barrel, and he knew it. First there was the land, and then this. And Houston would be the bastard of the year if he didn't help a woman in trouble.

"Boone needs an answer quick, Houston."

Everyone needed something and right away. What about his need for a heart that wasn't scarred and pitted? "You'll have your answer in the morning. Until then, leave me be."

Houston had lots of thinking to do and a hefty decision to make.

All Lara Boone needed was his name. He could do that much. Couldn't he?

No one said he had to love her. Or sleep beside her. Or share secrets with her.

Besides, what else did he have to look forward to in his life? Pretending he cared, pretending pain didn't rip through him every time he breathed—pretending he lived.

❧

Dawn rose on Tuesday with a whisper and Houston had not once closed his eyes. A fist gripped his heart as he got to his feet on the bluff overlooking the mighty Red. Stone-cold sober, he'd spent the night gazing up at the star-studded sky. There, alone, he'd made up his mind about what he had to do.

For years he'd envied Sam, who lived his life as he wanted. Houston had resented him for always riding off to chase adventure as a Texas Ranger. For always leaving big brother with the obligation to run the ranch and try to corral Stoker.

Just once, Houston wanted to see what it was like to wake up to snow-covered mountain peaks. Just once he wanted to taste the salty ocean air. And just once he wanted to get on a ship and sail to some faraway place.

When he was a boy, he'd entertained notions of riding the Butterfield Overland Mail stage all the way to the California gold fields. He'd wanted to pan for gold and put his feet in the Pacific Ocean.

But after his mother died and Stoker took to drink and gambling, Houston had been forced to quash those dreams of adventure. Because he was the oldest. Because Sam had washed his hands of the ranch. Because someone had to stay behind. That someone was Houston.

Hell!

Others' wishes *always* seemed more important than his. When would it be *his* turn? Would it ever?

◈

The Lone Star was beginning to wake up when he reined in at the corral.

As he dismounted, the day's brand-new rays bounced off the huge bronze star that hung next to the headquarters, suspended by heavy chains between two poles.

"I should've slept under that blasted star," Houston muttered. A local legend said a man would learn his true worth if he slept under the Texas star. Of course, no one knew for sure what that meant, exactly. The "Texas star" could refer to the bronze one, the ones overhead, or to the Lone Star Ranch itself. Sam had talked about sleeping on the ground beneath this bronze star to see if that would help him, but then he'd found his worth deep in the depths of Sierra's blue eyes.

Maybe one day Houston would find his worth and know the man he was. If he lived long enough.

As he strolled toward headquarters for breakfast, two ranch hands hoisted the Texas flag up the tall pole that stood at a corner of the two-story, white-stone house. He stopped for a moment to watch the breeze unfurl the fabric, the banner that sported one large star. His chest swelled with pride. Stoker told him that he'd lost his father and every one of his brothers in the Texas War of Independence. They, plus thousands of other men, had died so Houston, Sam, and Luke could live free.

Even though he yearned to see other places in the world for a spell, he had no desire to live out all his days anywhere but here. This was his home, his roots. He loved this wild state and the land where he'd been born and lived his whole life. He'd do anything to keep the ranch in one piece.

Even take a wife sight unseen.

With long strides, Houston entered the house and went straight to the kitchen. Stoker silently glanced up. His father's eyes held the question that his tongue would not ask.

Houston gave him a curt nod and poured a cup of coffee from the granite pot sitting on the table. "I've made my decision, Pa. But before I tell you, I want to say that this is the last damn time I'm bailing you out of anything."

Stoker's face flushed as he snapped, "I'm not a boy in knee britches. I'm your father, dammit."

"Then act like one," Houston snapped back, and took his seat. He lifted his cup for a sip of hot brew. It warmed the outside but did nothing to melt the layer of ice inside his chest. "I don't intend to have this conversation ever again."

Silence spun between them as fragile as a piece of hand-blown glass.

Finally, Houston spoke. "I'll marry Lara Boone and give her baby daughter my name. I'll raise her as a Legend." He paused then added, "But only if you put this ranch in all our names, and sign over the land you wagered to me and my brothers."

Stoker's face darkened. "Those are your terms?"

"They are. I don't think they're unreasonable."

His father studied his coffee cup for a minute. "I'll agree—if you tell no one, and I'm still the boss."

"Deal. I'll put aside my life for Lara Boone." Houston finished his coffee and set down the cup. "If anyone ever speaks ill of her child, they'll answer to my fists."

"And to mine," Stoker said firmly, slamming his hand down on the table, jarring the coffeepot. "One thing I won't abide is someone being mean and spiteful to a child. I know I've hurt Luke real bad, and damn, that tears into me. If I'd known he was my son, I'd have claimed him in a heartbeat. I can only imagine the names people called him. But they're not going to do that to Lara's child if I have anything to say about it."

At least they were in agreement on this. But the hot words Houston had spoken sat on his tongue like a sour persimmon. To have to fix another one of his father's careless mistakes stuck in his craw. In Houston's almost thirty years, he'd never once had his father apologize for anything. And Stoker sure didn't look like he was going to start now.

Releasing a loud sigh of frustration, Houston rose and sauntered toward the door. "You'll let Boone know?" he asked without turning.

"I'll send a message," Stoker replied.

"The sooner I get this over with the better."

"Son?"

Houston still didn't look at his father. "Yes, Pa?"

"Thank you." Stoker's voice cracked, leaving the words hanging in the air.

"I'm not doing this for you. Even with the ranch split in half, we could recover, given enough years. I'm doing this for a woman and her child who don't deserve the rotten deal they got."

"All the same, I'm sorry I put you between a rock and a hard place." Stoker let out a long sigh. "I miss your mother. She had a way of keeping me in line." He seemed lost in a memory. "She made me toe the mark more than once. That's what a good wife does. I hope you can find it in your heart to give Lara Boone a chance."

Without answering, Houston went to arrange for a preacher. The ceremony would likely take place by the weekend.

What did Lara think of this hurried wedding? Was she happy? As shocked as he had been? It would be nice to meet his bride beforehand. He wished he could talk to her, or even see what she looked like. Was she pretty? A blond, brunette, or redhead? Short, tall, slender, or rotund? Did it even matter?

Fury so strong it made him tremble swept through him. Even though he had no answers to his questions, he already knew he'd protect her and her daughter with his life. Any decent man would, and one thing Houston could hold onto was that he was a decent man. And if he ever crossed paths with the man who'd raped her, he'd kill him without blinking an eye and feed his rotten carcass to the coyotes.

Four

THE WEDDING TOOK PLACE EARLY SATURDAY AFTERNOON,
exactly six days after Stoker and Houston had struck the
deal. An hour before the ceremony, Houston dressed in
the house he'd built for Becky but had never slept inside the
walls. A group of ranch wives had volunteered to clean the
dwelling that had sat empty for a year. The rooms now
smelled fresh and all the cobwebs were gone. On Tuesday,
he'd ridden over to talk to Tillman Boone. Though
Houston hated being roped into a loveless marriage, he
found the man cordial.

A widower, Till Boone was a big, barrel-chested man.
Except for his ruddy complexion, he could've been Stoker's
brother. Tangling with him would be like wrestling a grizzly. Houston assumed—maybe wrongly—his bride would
share Boone's sandy-colored hair and brown eyes.

"Treat my Lara right and we'll get along fine," Boone
had said, his dark eyes drilling into Houston. "You don't,
and I'll be all over you like stink on a gut wagon. Her
happiness is more important to me than my own. I won't
stand for anybody treating her as less than a lady. Do you
understand me?"

"Yes, sir, I do. I'll provide a home for her and the babe
and always show her respect." Houston had paused to stare
into Boone's eyes. "But don't expect me to speak words of

love." They might as well get that straight from the start: love wasn't part of the deal. Though Boone's face had hardened, he'd nodded.

Upstairs in the new house where Houston would bring Lara following the ceremony, he drew on a clean work shirt and buttoned it. He wouldn't, couldn't wear the fancy suit he'd worn to his first wedding. He'd already instructed the preacher to strike the "love and cherish" part from the vows. Time would tell about "for better or worse."

The mood he was in, he wouldn't place any bets.

Houston tucked in his shirt and glanced around the bedroom at the things he'd moved from headquarters. The word for the space was modest—no frills, with just enough room to sleep. That's all he'd need. When he'd built the house for Becky, he'd intended this to be their child's room.

An ache filled his chest. He'd had such grand plans. He'd thought they'd live happily ever after. Then those dreams, the plans, the future had all come crashing down.

He winced, dragging himself from the painful thoughts. The dream of having his own child had vanished like smoke in mist. There would be no further children with Lara Boone. She and the baby would occupy the large bedroom and he'd stay here. He didn't yet know their needs, but all she had to do was tell him. He'd see to their comfort.

As the only daughter in a houseful of boys, it stood to reason that Lara's brothers and father had spoiled her. Houston had met the family the day he'd visited. At fourteen, her baby brother, Henry, spoke with a thick tongue, but he'd had a bright smile for Houston. He was slow but friendly.

The sixteen-year-old twins, Virgil and Quaid, had worn matching scowls and looked as though they wanted to shoot him. Clearly, they doted on their older sister, and Houston suspected they'd make him sorry if he failed to measure up.

Lara was the only one he hadn't met that day. Houston had left with the disappointment of not knowing what she looked like. But he'd provide for her. He'd promised.

A man always kept his promises no matter how difficult it became.

Footsteps sounded on the stairs and Stoker entered the bedroom, wearing a vest and waistcoat that showed off his still-lean figure despite his fifty-nine years of living. "You about ready, son?"

"My tie is all I have left." Houston lifted his western tie from the top of the dresser. "You look nice, Pa."

"Just because this isn't a normal wedding is no reason not to put on my best. Need help with that?"

"Nope, but I appreciate the offer." Houston finished tying it, remembering how Sam had helped him with the ascot a year ago.

Stoker handed him an envelope. "I forgot to give this to you when you thought to wed Becky. I know it doesn't feel like it now, but Lara Boone may change your life for the better."

Better than what—purgatory?

Houston took the envelope and removed a piece of parchment paper, recognizing his mother's flowing script. A wedding letter no doubt, similar to the one Sam had received when he wed Sierra Hunt. A mist filled Houston's eyes. He'd been only twelve when they'd buried Hannah Legend, and the loss still hurt.

> *Dear Son,*
>
> *You came into this world scrawny and frail and I remember the moment I first held you in my arms. Although you were so tiny, I saw how fiercely you fought to live. You have the soul of a fighter, just like your namesake, and it won't ever let you give up. I've watched you care for Sam and your staunch determination to guard your brother against hurts. As you take this woman to be your wife, I'm confident she'll find a protector unlike any other. Love her, Houston, and allow her to love you back.*

Kiss her, wipe her tears and always make sure to soften your words.

Unable to read more, Houston carefully returned the letter to the envelope to finish later. He cleared his throat. "Thanks for keeping this all these years, Pa. It's like she's here, in a way."

His father squeezed Houston's shoulder. "I think she is here, and she's been watching over you boys through the years." He sat on the bed. "Got a telegram from Sam. He and Sierra send their best. They'd be here if they could. Luke would too, I'm sure."

"It's better to keep this small. Lara doesn't need a bunch of gawking people. Me either." Houston picked up his coat. "Let's go."

He might as well meet this stranger who was to be his wife, and prayed that she wouldn't make his life hell. If she was kind, that's all he'd ask and it would be enough.

⊰⊱

Upstairs in one of the many bedrooms in the Legend house, Lara Boone tried to calm her mass of nerves. She stared at herself in the mirror, putting finishing touches to her hair, pulling it high and securing it with two combs. The rest of her mass of copper curls cascaded loosely down her back.

Her hands trembled. What would Houston do when he discovered what he'd gotten? It was a given that he'd be angry, that he'd feel cheated. Any man would. She was not only damaged goods but so broken inside that she didn't know if she'd ever be whole again.

When he'd come calling earlier in the week, she'd peered at him through her bedroom curtains. His size had made her breath catch in her throat. He stood well over six feet and was hard muscle. How handsome he was, with hair the color of dark coffee beans. The deep lines around his mouth indicated a worrier. His bronze tan and the crow's feet at the corners of his eyes said he spent a good deal of time outdoors. Probably squinted into the sun a lot.

Even from the distance at which she'd spied on him, she'd sensed anger in his movements. And who could blame him? She was furious as well, even though she knew it was best for her baby girl. Still, she felt like a piece of property to be sold to the highest bidder. She'd wanted to speak to him and explain that it wasn't her idea, only her father wouldn't let her. More than likely, Till Boone had been afraid she'd take pity on him and call off the marriage. The deal their fathers had made must grind as much on him as it did on her.

No one liked being forced into something.

Lara chewed her lip. It asked a lot of him to take on another man's child and raise her as his own. Would Houston resent her?

From her father, she'd heard about the tragedy of his previous would-be wife, Becky, and how she'd gotten shot as she'd stood in front of the preacher. Houston must've loved her and her death must've devastated him. She couldn't imagine what that would do to a person.

A knock sounded at the door and she opened it to her father.

"Are you ready, Lara? It's time," her father said.

"Help me with my veil, Papa?"

With a nod, he took the thick, white veil and put it over her head, pinning it snugly in her hair. She was grateful it hid her face, though Houston would be even angrier when he saw what had been kept from him.

"Your brothers have the baby. She'll be fine until after the ceremony." Her father took her hand, soothing her. "You're like a chunk of ice, Lara girl. Don't be so terrified. When the cards turned my way, it was providence. It's all going to work out."

"Is it? What's going to happen after you all leave and I have to face Houston's anger alone? He's going to be furious," she whispered miserably.

"If he lays a hand on you, he'll answer to me."

Lara had learned that anger came in many different forms—silence, coldness, yelling. Taking her forcibly. A man didn't always have to hit.

She shot him a glare, then realized he couldn't see her clearly through the veil. "And then what? One of you might end up dead. All because of me." She couldn't live with that on her conscience. She wasn't worth men killing each other over. Her quick hand silenced a sob. "Promise me you won't meddle in this marriage. Promise me, Papa."

"I need to protect you," Till protested.

"No. You've been heavy-handed enough. Because you gave the man little choice, I'll have to repair the damage. The rest is up to me." *And Houston*, she added silently. "I'll make this marriage work." Somehow.

"Fine. I'll stay out of it for now, but I don't like it one bit," her father finally conceded. "We'd best go now."

❧

Unlike twelve months ago, this wedding would take place inside Legend headquarters. Houston turned at the whisper of fabric at the parlor door. Like him, the girl in the doorway wore nothing fancy. Just an everyday dress of Wedgwood blue, and oddly enough, a thick, white veil.

Besides the preacher, only Stoker, Boone, and Lara's three brothers were in attendance. The twin named Virgil held the baby. Houston was grateful for his wife-to-be's choice to keep this affair private. This marriage was certainly nothing to celebrate. For him it seemed more of a funeral, burying what was left of his hopes and dreams. From now on, he'd work from sunup to sundown. That would help the ranch and reduce the time he had to make conversation.

He also had the cattle drive that would take him away for months.

As Lara took her place beside him, Houston stared at the heavy veil that concealed her features. He hated that he couldn't see her eyes. Eyes revealed what was in a person's heart. He wondered what he'd see in hers. Was she happy, sad, indifferent?

The top of her head didn't reach his chin and he could tell she was slender, a tiny little thing. He reached for her hand and found it icy and shaking. He realized she was scared to death.

"It's going to be all right," he whispered. "We'll make this work."

Lara didn't reply. He heard her take in a deep breath as she faced the preacher, and it hit him—they'd forced her into this marriage also. She'd given up every dream *she'd* ever had, the night she'd been attacked. Before today, he'd thought only of himself. But it wasn't just him and never was.

Houston relaxed his scowl before he scared her even worse.

The ceremony went quickly. He spoke the vows, then Houston slipped Lara's mother's ring on her finger. When that was done, the preacher asked him to kiss the bride to seal their union.

A peck on the cheek would suffice, he decided. She wouldn't want a real kiss any more than he. Houston lifted the veil and his heart stopped.

Dear God!

A long scar ran down the right side of her face, marring what had once been true, delicate beauty.

Anger raced through him. No one had to tell him the rapist bore responsibility. How could any man do that? Something shifted inside him. Then and there he knew—he wouldn't rest until he hunted down this animal and made him pay for what he'd done. He would avenge Lara the Legend way, fierce and lasting.

Surely the young woman carried great wounds, not only outwardly, but inside as well. Houston knew he had to choose his words carefully. What he said now would forever affect the rest of his life.

Lara's eyes, the color of green stones at the bottom of a silent pool, met his in a challenge. Her chin tilted at a defiant angle at his hesitation.

He saw strength, determination, and something else…hope.

All of a sudden, he was glad Lara Boone belonged to him, and he to her. He would help her heal. And maybe somehow along the way, she could heal him too.

Houston bent his head and chose to kiss the cheek that was scarred, feeling the raised ridge under his lips. "You're beautiful. I'm a very lucky man, Mrs. Legend."

He allowed a smile, realizing the words sprang from his heart. He hadn't lied.

"Thank you," she whispered, gratitude sparkling in her eyes.

As soon as he lifted his head, Stoker wormed in, moving Houston aside. "Come here, daughter," he boomed, drawing her into a hug. "Welcome to the family. You're like a warm ray of sunshine after a cold spell. You're going to brighten up this place."

When Lara shot Houston a nervous glance, he winked, realizing she'd never met Stoker either. His father could be intimidating, but he was glad Stoker had risen to the occasion as only he could.

Abruptly, Stoker shifted, meeting Till Boone's eyes. Houston watched his father-in-law nod. He took that to mean they'd squared the deal. The land went back to them.

Lara's gaze took in both Legend men. "You're all so nice. Thank you for making me feel…welcome. I didn't know what you'd think of me."

Stoker patted her hand. "We think you're a very beautiful, very exceptional young lady and we're proud to have you in this family. You'll bring a level of grace and dignity that I've long missed. I want you to call me Stoker."

Before she could reply, her brothers gathered around. Virgil handed her the baby. Houston watched how she tenderly gathered the child and hugged her to her chest. Such a pretty little angel. As Houston noted her reddish-blond curls and big, blue eyes, a fierce protectiveness wound through him. She would never learn the circumstance of her birth, and he pitied anyone who hurt her. This child of his would be loved and always wanted. He briefly wondered about the babe's name and decided to ask at the first opportunity.

Houston reached out with a hesitant finger to touch a golden curl the texture of corn silk.

"Would you like to hold Gracie?" Lara asked softly. "She won't break."

He wasn't so sure about that; she looked so small and delicate. Before he could decline, Lara transferred the child to his arms. He was amazed at how light she was. A sack of meal probably weighed more. Gracie gave a soft sigh and snuggled against him. Houston gazed down at her, this little person who now bore his name.

Gracie Legend.

As the babe stared up at him with her bright eyes, her hand closed around his finger and a smile curved her small, bow mouth. She looked like a little angel.

His vision blurred and a lump filled his throat.

He was a father.

Suddenly, the gold fields of California, the Pacific Ocean, the dream of being free to live as he desired all disappeared.

Though they'd come into this marriage very differently than most couples, they would be a family. He'd see to it. Lara and his new little angel needed him.

Five

THE MAGNITUDE OF HOUSTON'S SITUATION SUDDENLY overwhelmed him. Unable to speak, he handed the baby to Lara and went in search of a strong drink. Though a couple of ranch wives were serving punch in the dining room, that wouldn't numb the panic and fear crawling up his spine. This called for hard liquor.

Outside in the hallway, he found himself blocked by Lara's kid brother Henry. The fourteen-year-old stepped in front of him and shook his finger under Houston's nose.

"Be nice," Henry warned. "If you ain't nice, I'll give you a black eye."

Seeing as how his young accoster would have to stand on tiptoe to do it made the situation border on the ridiculous. The whole thing would've been comical if not for the glisten of tears in Henry's eyes and his quivering lip.

"What are you talking about, kid?"

"My sister. A man hurt her and gave her a baby. If you give her a baby, you'll be mean too." Henry stuck up both fists. "I ain't a-scared o' you. I'll black your eye."

"I can see how protective you are of your sister," Houston said calmly, wanting to reassure the boy. He wouldn't give Lara a baby because they wouldn't be sleeping together, but there was no way Henry would understand that. "She's lucky to have you stick up for her. I won't ever be mean to Lara. How about you and me getting some punch to wet our whistles?"

Henry shrugged and dropped his fists. "Okay."

Just like that, the anger and their impending tussle was forgotten. Houston draped his arm across Henry's shoulders. "Do you know that I once drank a whole bowl of punch?"

"Wow! Really?" Henry's brown eyes grew as round as saucers.

"Yep. My brother Sam dared me, so I had to do it." Houston grinned, remembering the outdoor party so long ago. "And you know what else?"

"Nope."

"It made me sick. I had to run behind a tree and throw up."

"Did you get in trouble?"

"Sure did. My pa sent me to bed. Without supper." He hadn't been in any shape to eat it anyway, but he had to make it dramatic for Henry's sake. "And you know what else?"

The boy shook his head.

"I dared my brother to kiss a horned toad."

"Ewww! Did he?"

"Yep. And it spit blood in his eye." Houston grinned. That had felt real good. It was the last time he'd gotten payback for something over Sam.

They reached the table with pies and cakes laid out on one end and a big punch bowl on the other. He stared longingly at the liquor cabinet standing against the wall, but he sighed and dipped Henry a glass of the sweet, red liquid that still made his stomach queasy. Then he filled a glass for himself.

Henry took a big drink and burped. "I think I like you."

"I'm glad we're friends. I would've hated to have you black my eye. You've got a wicked-looking fist there." Houston noticed the other two brothers, the twins, striding through the door and making a beeline for him. He wondered if a glass of punch would work for them too. It didn't look it.

"A private word, Legend." Virgil Boone's clipped request sounded more like an order.

"We can talk in the office." Houston set down his glass and led the way.

When Henry tried to follow, the other twin, Quaid, stopped him. "Go back, Henry. This is man business."

"I'm a man." The boy stuck out his chin. "Mr. Houston already told me he would be nice."

"That's good. But I think I hear Pa calling you," Quaid answered. "Best go see what he wants."

"Oh, all right." Henry trudged off.

Houston opened the door of the study and ushered the Boone boys inside. "What can I help you with?"

"This won't take long," Virgil said.

"Care to sit?" Houston motioned to the sofa and chairs.

"We'll stand." Virgil's gaze scanned the room, lingering on the bookshelves lining the walls. Unless Houston missed his guess, the boy liked to read.

"Suit yourselves." Houston took the chair behind the mahogany desk. "What's this about? I've already had your father and Henry lay down the law. I'm guessing it's your turn?"

Virgil glanced at Quaid before answering. "Lara's our only sister and she's been hurt real bad. We mean to make sure it doesn't happen again. We know our pa had you over a barrel or you never would've married Lara."

"You're probably pretty mad," Quaid threw in.

"We just want you to know that we're gonna watch you," Virgil finished. "Make Lara cry, and there'll be hell to pay."

Houston held up his hand. "I understand that my wife is your sister and Gracie your niece, but I'm not an ogre," he said gently. "I'll work hard to keep Lara happy. I'll protect her and the child. With my very life if necessary."

"That's not all we wanted to say." Virgil lowered his voice. He was mostly grown, it looked like, and stood almost as tall as Houston. "Don't let down your guard. The guy is still out there somewhere and he's gonna come to finish the job. He's threatened before that he intends to kill her. Gracie too. He's as mean as they come. I wounded him that night but he managed to get away. Pa lit out after him but lost the bastard in the brush. We've been looking ever since."

Anger charged through Houston. "What's his name?"

"Pa hired him on for a while at the ranch when we were short. Calls himself Yuma Blackstone," Virgil answered. "It's a fake name or I'm a porcupine."

Probably so. Men on the run from something often hid in plain sight by taking on new names. Houston would do some digging. Something told him he wasn't going to like what he found.

"What does Blackstone look like?" Houston's voice was stone-cold and as sharp as flint. He'd kill the man with his bare hands for what he'd done.

"He keeps his head shaved bald but he can't be that old. I'd put him late twenties. Has a thin mustache and missing half of his left ear. Heard a rumor someone shot it off. Has real strange eyes that make you shiver. Almost white, kinda silvery-like." Virgil gave his strawberry-blond hair an impatient toss when a strand fell near his eye. "Fancies himself a ladies' man and was always twirling one of his twin pearl-handled pistols like he was itching to use it. Our ranch hands steered clear of him."

"Those eyes of his gave me the creeps," Quaid added quietly. "When the light shone on them just right, I thought he could see inside me."

Houston filed away the description. He'd have no trouble recognizing someone like that. Big egos always tripped up men like Yuma Blackstone, and it sounded like he had a huge one. Besides, Houston had an ace in the hole, with a former Texas Ranger for a little brother. They'd find Blackstone, and when they did...

"Thanks for telling me." Houston liked Lara's brothers. Virgil would be someone Houston would love to have next to him in a fight. He sensed this tall brother would never back away from trouble.

"Least we could do," Quaid said. "Seeing as how we can't protect our sister now."

"I'm not going to let anyone hurt her again," Houston promised. "You can count on that. Are any of you married?"

"Naw," Quaid drawled. "We're waitin' for the right girls. 'Sides, we gotta finish growin'."

Houston smothered a grin with his hand. If the boy grew much more, he'd have to go through doors sideways. "Don't wait too long. Not many girls around here."

Virgil gave a solemn nod. "Pickin's are a mite slim."

"I don't know. They're around if you look hard enough. I've got to get back to Lara," Houston said. "Make yourselves at home, boys. You're welcome on the Lone Star anytime."

Stepping from the office, he heard lowered voices in the room across the hall. One belonged to Stoker. He guessed the other to be Till Boone. He would have kept going, but the next words he overheard held him tight.

"Lara seems to accept the situation," Till said. "She doesn't suspect a thing. How about your boy?"

"Our plan worked, Till," Stoker said. "Houston was madder than a bull culled from the heifers at first, but I saw his face when he got a glimpse of Lara. He's going to do right by her. I hated having to make him think I'd gambled away our land, but he didn't leave me much choice. He was wasting away, a shell of who he once was. I couldn't let him destroy himself."

"My Lara wouldn't have agreed either," Boone said low. "She's a proud woman, like her mother."

Hell and be damned!

Stoker had manipulated him like a puppet on a string. Houston had half a mind to barge in on the two meddling matchmakers and wring their necks.

Except the memory of Lara's horrible scar and a babe's tiny fingers curling around his stopped him.

Maybe there were worse things to have happen.

Let these two think they'd put one over on Lara and him. But this was the last damn time.

Something deep inside tugged against his heart. No matter how it had happened, he was theirs now and they were his, and he wouldn't go back on his word for anything.

❧

Lara glanced up when Houston slipped back into the parlor. It hadn't taken much to put two and two together after her brothers had gone out right behind her new husband. Her heart warmed that they still felt the need to protect her, even though at twenty-one she was very much the oldest. If not for them, she'd have gone crazy after that horrible night. Despite their age, they'd stepped up, even taken turns helping her care for Gracie after she was born.

But now she had a husband and, except for that slight hesitation when he'd lifted her veil and stared in shock, he seemed to accept her appearance. The anger she'd expected hadn't shown.

At least not yet. But what would happen when they were alone?

Lara raised her chin. She'd bow down to no man. And no one would ever force her to do anything against her will, ever again. Not even her new husband, the towering Houston Legend, who was probably very accustomed to getting his way.

He strode toward her with confidence, his body radiating strength, and she knew he would have no trouble dealing with men like Yuma Blackstone. And yet something told Lara he would never hurt her. She stilled her rapid heartbeat, the thunder that sent blood pumping through her veins. Her husband appeared ten times the man of any she'd known…except for her father.

But would he truly be kind to her when no one was around? That remained to be seen.

"You getting tired, Lara?" he asked when he reached her side.

She hadn't realized how much until now, and the starch

seemed to go out of her at his question. But then, worry had kept her awake all night. A clock somewhere in the Legend house chimed four o'clock. It was time to see the place that was now her home.

"Yes. And Gracie needs to lie down. The poor thing is exhausted from all the excitement."

Houston followed her gaze. The seven-month-old had crawled into a corner, curled up, and was sucking her thumb. He walked over and picked her up then sauntered back. Lara's chest tightened. There was something special about a hard man like Houston gently holding her baby in the crook of one muscular arm.

"Let's get you both home." He put an arm around her waist and they moved to the door.

Lara loved the protective weight of his arm as they escaped the white-stone headquarters, the walls that glistened in the afternoon sun. She paused for a moment, staring up at the Texas flag fluttering in the breeze.

She bore a kinship with that flag. Both sometimes got ragged and torn, but somehow they bravely kept flying.

"Are you all right?" Houston asked.

"Just thinking." She turned and they strolled past the businesses. "I'd heard your family built a small town here, but I thought it had to be a joke."

Houston chuckled. "No one was pulling your leg. Except for a few items, we have most everything a person needs."

His deep voice seemed to vibrate through her, and she found it very pleasant.

"I'm sure you're wondering where our house is," he said.

"A little," Lara admitted as they walked down a path.

He pointed to a two-story, whitewashed clapboard straight ahead. She liked the small house. It looked comfortable, but one never knew until they tested the fit.

"No one's ever lived in it." His words were clipped.

Embarrassment heated her cheeks as reality hit and she remembered Becky Golden. He'd loved her, and he'd built this house for her.

"I'm sorry, Houston. Today must've taken a huge toll on you. I can't imagine how hard it was. And to be saddled with an utter stranger to boot. For what it's worth, I begged Papa to find another way." She struggled to say the right words. "When I was younger, I hated to see signs of spring each year, because my father would line us kids up, hold our noses, and give us each a big dose of castor oil."

Till and Stoker had done the exact same thing to Houston—forced his mouth wide and shoved a double dose of castor oil down his throat. Then held his nose until he swallowed.

"It wasn't right forcing you into this, forcing us both." When he didn't say anything, Lara's stomach clenched. She mounted the steps leading to the entrance of the house the two strangers would share. He held the door for her and, with Gracie still nestled asleep in the crook of his arm, he ushered her inside.

The coolness of the downstairs rooms welcomed her as she slowly turned, taking it all in. The small parlor that opened to the right off the entryway had large windows that allowed light to flood in, but it had no furniture save for a sofa.

"I haven't had time to furnish the house yet," Houston murmured. "A year ago, I didn't expect to ever live here. In fact, I tried to set fire to it. Stoker stopped me." Pain made his voice sound tight.

"Please, don't apologize. Whatever we have is fine." She'd vowed he wouldn't see her as needy and she meant to keep to that.

"All the same, you deserve better."

"Houston, I didn't expect you to have everything in place," she said softly. The urge to rest her hand on his muscle-corded arm was almost more than she could resist. She turned to retrace her steps back into the entryway before she gave in to the impulse.

He followed. "I want to make it plain that this house is yours. Buy whatever you need. Browse through the catalogs in the mercantile and order whatever you see fit. Or we could take a trip to Fort Worth after I return from driving a herd of longhorns north to Dodge City. I probably should've mentioned that I'll leave as soon as possible."

Her swift whirl was a mistake and sent Lara into the hard wall of Houston's chest. She stared up into his coffee-colored eyes. Heat crept up the back of her neck as she took a step back from the mass of solid muscle and power.

"Sorry, I didn't mean to do…" Unsure of what to say exactly, she left the sentence unfinished. "You surprised me. Isn't May too late to take cattle north?"

"Probably," Houston admitted. "If I had a choice, I'd wait until next spring. But I don't. How do you know about cattle drives? It's not a subject most women care to discuss."

Lara smiled. "You're forgetting I grew up in a man's household. It's all my brothers talk about. Virgil and Quaid begged Father to let them join one of the cattle drives going through here, but he wouldn't relent."

She wandered across the hall into the dining room and gave a soft cry. The room was bright and cheery, with a curved bay window along the west wall. It would be perfect for catching the sunset in the evenings. The dining table and chairs were of beautiful mahogany and shone in the light. "I love this room," Lara exclaimed. "It's perfect."

"I'm glad you approve." Houston stood so close behind her she felt his breath ruffling her hair. "It's the one room I took pains with."

"Well, you did a wonderful job. Houston, I wasn't trying to second-guess your decision with the cattle, or tell you what to do."

"Never thought you were." He took her shoulder and turned her to face him. "You're a breath of fresh air. I'm pleased to have you take an interest in ranching and glad I can talk to you."

Lara searched his gaze and knew he was sincere. "I'm relieved that I didn't overstep my bounds."

"I set no boundaries. I always want your opinions. The

only reason I would start out now is that we're already right here on the Red River, so we have a huge advantage. Snow doesn't generally start flying until December or January. We'll be back by late September."

For some reason, the idea of him being gone so long filled her with loss. Maybe it would be good, though. They could adjust to marriage without the pressure of seeing each other every day.

With a nod, she said, "Four months should be plenty of time even if you run into trouble. How soon until you're ready to leave?"

"Two weeks. That'll put us at mid-May," he answered.

Before she could say more, wagons piled high with her belongings pulled to a stop in front of the house, amid the jangling of harnesses.

"They're here. You hold Angel while I go help," Houston said.

Angel? The warmth of his voice at the nickname banished some of the coldness from her chest. If he couldn't find it in his heart to love her, at least he seemed to love the child that had been conceived in a horrific act of violence.

As they transferred the sleeping babe, his hands brushed hers, sending a series of little aftershocks charging through her. Still tingling, Lara watched her husband open the front door and hurry to help her father and brothers unload.

Lara touched the puckered scar ruining her face and her eyes filled with tears.

She wished she was pretty and unsoiled. And that Houston Legend wanted her because he was utterly and hopelessly in love with her.

With a shake of her head, she came down to earth. Such fantasies were useless in the face of harsh reality.

Lara could curse the day Yuma Blackstone had ridden onto their ranch, but she couldn't change who she was.

Six

LARA STOOD ASIDE AND WATCHED HOUSTON AND HER family cart in her belongings. Pain swept through her at the sight of the battered, old trunk. Her mother had brought that to Texas in the back of a covered wagon. Knowing what the trunk held sent Lara's mind tumbling to the night almost a year and a half ago when her life had been very nearly taken from her.

Deep in the very bottom of the trunk, hidden in a corner, was the locket with a broken chain, left that way when Yuma had ripped it from her throat.

The necklace had belonged to her grandmother and she'd loved it once. Yet, she couldn't bear to look at it now. She lowered her gaze to Gracie asleep in her arms. That a precious life could have come from such an evil monster astounded her. God willing, the child would never learn who her father was.

Houston came through the door with her rocking chair. A smile curved his mouth and melted a bit of the ice gripping her heart. "Do you want me to leave this in the parlor or put it up in your bedroom?"

At the mention of the bedroom, fear shot through her. It must've reflected in her face, because Houston murmured low, "You and Angel will have the large room." He set down the chair and lifted his hand as though to touch her, before letting it fall. "You have nothing to fear from me, Lara. I'll never enter your sanctuary unless you ask me."

The surprise announcement wound through her like some kind of trailing vine. She hadn't expected respect like this from a man who'd been given no way out of their arrangement. Her father and Stoker may as well have marched him to the preacher at gunpoint.

Lara found her voice. "Put it upstairs then. I like to rock her at night."

"I can always bring it down if you change your mind."

Gracie stirred and opened her eyes. She gazed at Houston for a moment then smiled shyly, ducking her head into the curve of Lara's shoulder. It appeared her daughter was already taken with Houston Legend. But then, he did have that effect on the ladies.

"She's a real beauty." Houston's deep voice sent a vibration through Lara and she loved the warm tingle that danced up her spine. "I 'spect I'll have to beat the suitors away from our door in a few years."

Without saying more, Houston went upstairs, and Lara's gaze followed him with amazement. He carried the sturdy rocker with one hand as though it weighed nothing.

She wandered into the dining room and set Gracie on the spotless floor to crawl. Henry quietly joined her.

"Gracie likes it," he said, grinning. "No shadows here."

Lara smiled and put her arm around him. "Nope, no shadows, Henry. Only sunlight spilling in the windows." Ghosts couldn't follow. She'd left them behind. Maybe she could finally heal and grow strong again with this fresh start and forget the past. Or at least find a way to live with it.

"Don't get too tired, little brother." Lara ruffled Henry's hair. "You know I love you, don't you?"

The boy nodded. "Yep. I ain't never gonna let anybody be mean to you again."

"I know." But who would stop folks from being mean to *him*? Waves of sadness rippled over Lara. Henry was unprepared for the cruel things people would say and do.

Her mother always said that Henry was a special gift from God and Lara knew that to be true.

When the men came down and announced that they were finished, Henry rose from playing with Gracie and put his arms around Houston. If Houston thought it strange for a fourteen-year-old boy to embrace him, he didn't let on.

Houston ruffled his hair. "Still thinking of blacking my eye?"

The boy grinned up at him. "My pa said you're a brother so I gotta be nice."

"That's right." Houston draped an arm across Henry's shoulders. "Do you remember our secret?"

"Yep. I ain't never gonna tell that you made your brother Sam kiss a horny toad."

Houston threw back his head and laughed, even though Lara knew he probably felt far from it.

Lara's heart swelled, and Houston's kindness raised him quite a few notches in her estimation. She had nothing to fear from a man who could be kind to Henry, win a smile from shy little Gracie, and give her the biggest bedroom all to herself. Lara gazed over the top of Henry's head and mouthed, *Thank you*.

Before she realized it, she was telling her family goodbye. The silence they left behind was deafening. For a moment, Lara wanted to snatch up Gracie and go with them. But her place was with Houston now.

She had a new life to build.

"Would you like to see the upstairs?" he asked. "You can get settled in while I go take care of the stock."

Lara nodded and picked up Gracie. Houston's light touch at the small of her back made her feel safe. And cherished. Except she knew the last to be false.

If he would simply tolerate her messing up his life, that would be enough.

They went up the stairs and he drew her through an open door. Like everything below, the bedroom was light and airy, wallpapered in soft green with a pretty scroll design. A lovely quilt covered the bed. It reminded her of her mother and Lara could almost feel warm arms around her. One of the men had set up Gracie's crib beside it, the rocker that had belonged to her mother nearby. A dressing room stood at one end and her clothes were already hung. He showed her a bathing room and the hot running water amazed her. It was sheer heaven.

"Lara, this door has a lock." Houston met her eyes. "Use it if you need to. I'll not have you terrified in your own house. Not of me or of anything."

She wanted to tell him that she already felt as protected as she'd been in her home with her father, but she couldn't get the words out. Maybe she could find ways to show her gratitude in the days ahead. And learn to somehow live with Becky Golden's ghost that filled every corner.

As he turned toward the stairs, she found her voice. "Where will you sleep?" At his raised brow, she felt her face grow hot and added quickly, "Just in case I need you during the night."

When he opened the door directly across the hall, she smothered a cry at the tiny, sparse room. She couldn't let him give up everything for her. "You barely have space to turn around."

"It'll serve my needs. It has a bed and a washstand." His voice seemed a little gruff, like he was angry. But Lara didn't know why. Was it because she was there—a bride he didn't want? Or maybe she'd reminded him of the bride he *had* wanted. The one he'd built the house for.

With an aching heart, she watched him stride down the stairs in that confident way of his. After seeing the small space where he would sleep, she expected that he would find excuses not to come home. Or maybe he'd seek out some other woman for the needs she wouldn't relieve. There were always lonely women on a ranch—widows too.

A mist clouded her vision as she held Gracie tight against her breast. All she'd asked for was a name…and dear God, that summed up exactly what she'd gotten.

Houston closed the door of the house behind him, not knowing where he was going. He jerked off his hat and ran an impatient hand through this hair. He would've gone mad if he hadn't gotten out of there.

How was he going to make this work?

One big problem was what to say to a woman he'd never met before today. And each time his gaze lit on the long scar down her face, dark anger welled up with such force that it took all his strength to control it.

Lara Boone Legend was a gentle soul who needed someone to love her, to hold her in the darkness, and to kiss away the sadness that clouded her beautiful green eyes. That man wasn't him. He'd fulfill all other obligations.

But he'd never open his heart again.

Another problem was living in a house where Becky's presence loomed, reminding him of everything he wanted to erase. Oh God, why had he thought he could do this?

With his jaw resolute, Houston strode toward the corral. Halfway there, a thought struck him. He'd left Lara and the baby in the house without a morsel of food. *Damn!* Only an uncaring fool would ride off without making sure they had something to eat. Where was his head? The evening shadows had already begun to fall.

Spinning around, he set a course for the ranch headquarters and went straight to the kitchen. A short time later, he returned to the white clapboard house that now had light shining in the windows. Juggling a large wicker basket under his arm, he opened the door. Lara jumped up from a chair at the empty dining room table, wiping her eyes. Gracie played at her feet with some spools that once held thread.

Houston pretended not to notice Lara's wet lashes. "I brought enough food to get us by until Monday. I'm sure you're hungry."

A look of gratitude crossed her features as she took the basket from him. "In the hectic flurry of the day, I forgot to eat. I would've gone for these things, except I didn't know where exactly to head. Everything's so strange and new. I didn't want to disturb anyone."

He followed her into the kitchen. "In the future when I'm not around, go to the main house. Stoker will help you."

"I'm sure he will," she said softly, unpacking the wicker basket. "But like I said, I didn't want to start off my life here bothering people."

"You're never going to be a bother, so get that notion out of your head." He watched her sort the basket contents out into piles, and her eyes lit up when she removed the fresh apple pie.

"Since it's getting late and I haven't eaten today either, I thought we might scramble the eggs and fry some of the ham," he suggested, seeing her indecision.

"I haven't checked to see if we have pans to cook with."

"We do." The cooking utensils were left from a year ago when he thought…

"That settles it then. I might not know much about the workings of this ranch, but I'm an expert cook." Lara's hand collided with his when they bent to push aside a small curtain that covered the lower shelf. She froze. An awkward silence filled the room.

At last, Houston quietly said, "Let me get the pan for you."

She nodded and moved back. "I should check on Gracie."

Houston retrieved the skillet and set it aside. He stood staring out the window, cursing his incompetence as he bumbled his way through the strange maze of his life with this woman. They hadn't even made it through one day. What would a week, a month, or a year be like?

At the sound of baby babbles, he turned to watch her sit the child on the floor. Making up his mind, Houston went and gently took Lara's hands. "We have to find a way to coexist. I can't live with you frightened of my every move. We can't occupy the same house without touching or bumping into each other on occasion. It'll get easier as we go. But for now, can you trust me?"

"I do, Houston." Her vivid green eyes held misery. "It's just that I don't know what you expect of me."

Her statement caught him by surprise. What *did* he expect? Certainly not a proper wife, given they were utter strangers. But not a cook and housekeeper either. That wasn't right. No wife of his would ever fill the role of a maid to be at his beck and call.

Hell! He yearned for a stiff drink.

"A friend." His answer surprised him probably more than it did her. "I expect you to be a partner. We both have things to forget. I need someone who'll stand with me in good times and bad."

Lara's smile transformed her face. Again, her beauty struck him. He felt the urge to let his fingertips brush her delicate cheekbones and drift along the curve of her jaw.

"I can use a friend," she said. "I'll try not to ever make you sorry for your decision."

"You won't." The words came out gruff and he didn't know how he could say them with such confidence.

Yet, somehow deep in his being a calm surety settled, like disturbed silt gliding back to the bottom of a riverbed.

He felt a tug on his trouser leg and glanced down. Gracie had crawled to him and gripped the fabric in her tiny fist. He picked her up.

They would face lots of ups and downs but they'd survive. For no other reason than the little girl giving him a toothless, slobbery grin.

The babe needed a father. Lara, a husband.

And Houston desperately needed some reason to keep living.

Seven

OVER THE FOLLOWING WEEK, HOUSTON SPENT ALMOST every waking minute getting the cattle ready to take north. Only two hours a morning were free, and he filled those helping his brother. As had become his habit over the past year, he pored over wires from all over the state that Jim Wheeler brought him from the telegraph office. Each dawn, Houston prayed someone had information about Ned Sweeney. Someday the identity of the man using the name from the Beadle's dime novels had to turn up. The letters kept trickling in—a few leads, a handful of new sightings, but the bastard remained elusive. That only made Houston more determined. If he could find the one who'd framed Luke for Judge Percival's murder, his brother would no longer have to hide in the shadows.

Otherwise, the days were long, and it was often late when Houston got home. No matter how tired he was, he made sure to spend time with Lara and Gracie. Talking about the cattle drive had relieved a good portion of the awkward tension. His wife had a good head on her shoulders, and he'd discovered she made sense about a lot of things.

On this Friday morning, they were at the kitchen table finishing breakfast. Houston's belly was so full he thought he'd burst. He'd never eaten like this until Lara came into his life.

"My father mentioned when he stopped by yesterday that he'd come to talk to you about something," Lara said, sitting Gracie on the floor.

"Came about the cattle drive. I asked Till to let your brothers come along. It would provide valuable experience." At the tug on his trousers and the accompanying grunt, Houston lifted Gracie into his lap. "It took some doing but he finally agreed."

"Good. Even Henry, I hope."

"Yep. Your father flatly refused at first, but Till finally came around when I assured him Henry would serve as the cook's helper and stay out of danger."

Lara refilled Houston's coffee cup. "Oh, I'm so glad. I've argued for years that he does my brother no favor by coddling him."

"I just can't bear the bitter disappointment that sometimes fills Henry's eyes." Houston let out a deep sigh. "The boy needs to be encouraged, not put in a box. He wants to be a man like his brothers, and just needs a chance."

"Thank you for giving him that." Lara stood and began gathering the plates. "Would you like to take a biscuit for later in case you get hungry?"

Houston groaned. "Woman, I'm going to get so fat I can't get through the door. But you twisted my arm. Wrap one up."

Her smile came easy, not forced like in the beginning. Maybe she was starting to trust him a little.

Early that afternoon, he stood beside a chuck wagon, watching cowboys stock it with supplies for the drive that would begin in two days' time.

"I'm real sorry, Mr. Houston," said Albert, the grizzled old man who had been the bunkhouse cook on the Lone Star since Houston was a boy. "I won't be able to go. My Bessie has taken a turn for the worse an' Doc Jenkins says she cain't last more 'n a few weeks." Tears filled Albert's rheumy eyes. "We've been married for forty years. I just cain't go off an' leave her. She's all I got."

"I understand." Houston laid his hand on Albert's shoulder. "I'll find someone else. If there's anything my father or I can do, let us know. Whatever you need, you'll get."

"I jus' hate lettin' you down." Albert wagged his head and limped toward the small house he shared with his wife.

Now where was he going to find a cook on such short notice? A wagon rolled to a stop and Houston glanced up to see Sam, Sierra, and their son, Hector. As Sam jumped down, the sun bounced off the sheriff's badge on his shirt.

"Hey, little brother," Houston called. "What brings you?"

"Heard about your cattle drive." Sam lifted Sierra to the ground. "Wanted to come see."

"Hi, Houston." Sierra kissed his cheek and grinned. "I want to meet that new wife of yours. Time we got acquainted and compared notes on you wild Legend brothers."

"We're not wild, are we, Sam?" Houston wiped sweat trickling down his face.

Sam grinned. "Not us."

"You're just in time to meet Lara—here she comes now." Houston took in his wife as she stepped out into the sunlight. His breath caught. The rays kissed her hair, setting the copper strands aflame. Her beauty struck him by surprise, as it often did. Indecision crossed her face and her footsteps lagged. He knew she wanted to join them but wasn't sure she'd be welcome.

He went to meet her and took Gracie from her arms. "Come meet my brother and his family."

"I don't know if I'm ready, Houston. Maybe I should…"

"They will love you, I promise." Houston slipped a protective arm around her and drew her forward.

After the introductions, Sam drew her into a bear hug. Then Sierra took her turn. Hector murmured something and ran to the corral where cowboys were working.

Sierra took Gracie from Houston. "Sam, Lara and I are going to chat a bit over some hot tea while I spoil this precious little baby."

"You go ahead, darlin'. Houston and I have some

things to discuss. I don't mind riding herd on Hector."
Once the women had gotten out of range, Sam turned to
Houston. "If you're not going to hunt down the man who
cut Lara's face, I'm going to. The scum doesn't deserve
to live."

"My feelings exactly," Houston replied. "I know the
bastard's name and I know what he looks like. The minute
I get back, I'm making that a priority."

"Pa told me he forced you into marrying her to save the
ranch," Sam said.

With a snort, Houston explained. "He pulled the wool
over my damn eyes. But I overheard him and Till Boone
talking after the wedding and found out they were in cahoots
the whole time. The two were nothing but matchmakers."

"Hell! I never believed Pa had it in him."

"Don't tell him this, but I would've done it anyway."
Houston focused on the distant horizon. "It's an odd feeling, though—marrying someone sight unseen and living in
the same house. We're two strangers bumbling around in
the dark, neither one of us knowing what to do or say. I suspect she'll be relieved not having me around for a while."

Sam leaned against the chuck wagon. "Maybe the distance will be good."

"Maybe so. Did Pa share the terms of the contract?"

"Nope, but I'm sure you had some stipulations. I can't
believe he came up with that whopper. Especially after what
Becky put you through."

"Stoker's a wily one. Don't turn your back on him for
an instant." Houston chuckled. The rough start of finding
his footing with Lara had smoothed to where the low trick
had lost its sting. "But you, Luke, and I now own the two
hundred forty thousand acres he supposedly gambled away.
And all our names are on the rest of the ranch also."

Sam laughed. "I'd say you must've had him by the
short hairs."

"Well, at least I thought I did. Turned out to be the
other way around." Houston took a match stem from his

pocket and stuck it between his teeth. "This is changing the subject, but do you know where I can find a chuck wagon cook on short notice? Albert just told me his wife won't last until he gets back."

"I'm sorry to hear that. Albert and Bessie were good to take us under their wing after Mother passed away." Sam paused in thought for a second. "I don't know anyone with experience who can take his place. Sorry."

"I hope I find someone by the time we roll out at daybreak on Monday."

"Houston, I came to warn you to be careful." Sam's face set in hard lines. "I got a telegram from a US Marshal up in Indian Territory about a large group of outlaws attacking drovers and stealing the herds."

Great. As if driving two thousand bawling, snot-slinging cows to Kansas wasn't hard enough.

"Thanks for the warning. I'll keep my eyes peeled and my rifle handy. Have you heard anything from Luke?"

"Nope. Every time the telegraph operator brings me a wire, I fear it's from some lawman saying he's arrested our brother."

"Me too," Houston murmured. "Luke's living on borrowed time. Things might crash down around him before he gets to clear his name."

And their brother wasn't the only one. The last year had walloped Houston pretty good too. Sometimes in the dead of night, as he lay in his small bed with his feet sticking off the end, he listened to the thunder of his heart and wondered about the why of it all.

Why had Becky done what she'd done?

Why had Lara gotten the rotten deal she had?

Why did Luke have to keep running and fearing the bullet that would eventually find him?

He had no answers to any of it and doubted anyone else did—even preachers who were supposed to know the whys and wherefores of everything.

"What about that group of women Luke kept supplied

over at Deliverance Canyon? Have you gone to check on them?"

"I go once a month," Sam said. "They're a tough bunch. If I went with anyone they didn't know, Tally Shannon would put a bullet through our hearts without blinking an eye."

For a woman to wear a gun belt like a man would be something to see.

"Can you blame her?" Houston moved the match stem to the other side of his mouth. "Lord knows what they went through in that insane asylum. Especially since they weren't crazy at all. People who do that to someone they want to get shed of don't deserve to take up elbow room on this earth." Houston shuddered, thinking about the mark—a tattoo—put on their cheeks by the overseer, making it impossible even to go into towns. Lara probably felt that way also. He'd never thought about how difficult her life was, living with that long scar.

Sam nodded. "I keep them fed and well. Sierra wants to bring them here to the ranch."

"So do I," Houston admitted. "It's not right them being out there all alone with men scouring the country looking for them."

"Every time I mention it to Tally, I don't know if I'll make it out of that canyon alive."

Houston had thought of riding out to try to talk sense to the desperate women but Sam wouldn't let him. Said it was too dangerous for them. All it would take would be for the wrong person to be watching and follow. People would do anything for that bounty on their heads.

He thought again of Lara's scar. He'd kill any man he caught abusing a woman. Or child.

And when he found Yuma Blackstone... Houston clenched his fist. He'd take his time killing him.

⁓⁓⁓

The afternoon was drawing long by the time Sam and his family left. Houston and Stoker waved until they were out of sight. The visit seemed to have done Lara good. She and Sierra had become like sisters already, their relationship easy and natural.

Stoker turned to him. "Got everything ready for the trail drive, son?"

"Just about." Houston shared that Albert wasn't coming. "I guess I'll have to make one of the men do it."

"You'll likely have a catastrophe on your hands too."

"Maybe so, but I don't know what else to do." Houston had thought about it so much his mind was tied in knots. He wouldn't put off the trail drive until next year—they needed to get the cows sold before they either died of starvation or the cold winter. Blue northers could be brutal in this part of Texas, especially on weakened cattle.

"I'm sure you'll think of something." Stoker leaned against a post and gave Houston a pointed stare. "How are things with you and Lara?"

"Fine." Houston's eyes narrowed. "Why?"

"No reason. Just curious is all."

"Are you supposed to give Till a report?" Houston casually asked, watching his father.

Stoker jerked and stood up straight. "Why would I?"

"Pa, I overheard you and Boone talking the day of the wedding. I know what you two cooked up."

Stoker's face reddened. "What were we supposed to do? His daughter was in a living hell, worried to death about her baby growing up labeled a bastard. And you. You weren't eating, your clothes were falling off, and you'd taken to the bottle. You were nothing but a hollowed-out stump. I spent a lot of sleepless nights worrying about you."

A flash of anger washed over Houston. "You could've come to me."

"Like hell. I tried. Over and over. You told me to leave you the hell alone." Stoker laid his hand on Houston's back. "Son, you wouldn't listen."

The truth struck Houston hard. He couldn't deny it.

"All the same, I'll be obliged if both of you keep your noses out of our marriage."

Even if his wife was unhappy, she'd keep silent. Houston had learned that about her in the short time they'd been married. Lara wouldn't tell anyone if he spent all his time drinking and never went home. But he wasn't doing either. It was funny how he seldom thought of whiskey these days. He wasn't as miserable as he'd predicted. Lara was easy to be around.

He didn't deserve a woman as fine as her. She was beautiful and caring and a wonderful mother. The house was always clean and he'd never seen a better cook. Her fluffy biscuits melted in his mouth. Last evening she'd made fried chicken, and he'd eaten so much he'd come near to exploding. But her talents weren't confined to the kitchen. She'd whipped up curtains for the upstairs windows and the parlor, and made the house more homey, not just a place to sleep and eat.

Houston sighed. There was a lot more to Lara than skill in cooking and sewing. She constantly surprised him with all she knew—about ranching and other things too. For instance, she was familiar with overgrazing and equally knowledgeable about planting crops and treating sunburn. She was funny too, with a good sense of humor.

He could've done worse. Yeah, a lot worse than Lara Boone. Any man would be lucky to have her. Even a broken man like him.

If so many unwelcome memories didn't inhabit the house, it would be a great place for them. As it stood, he could barely walk through the rooms. And sleeping—he didn't get much.

Houston turned to his father. "I mean it, Pa, no more meddling. I'm drawing the line."

"Well, that sounds mighty ungrateful. If you're determined to be disagreeable, I'm going home," Stoker declared. "I might scrounge up a game of checkers with Doc Jenkins."

"Sounds like a good idea, Pa."

Stoker tilted his head and squinted. "If my son was worth his salt, he'd invite me to come for supper. I'd like to spoil my granddaughter."

"Soon, Pa. I won't spring unexpected company on Lara. She's still getting used to us." His father's rough talk and ways wouldn't help the situation. Lara reminded him of a skittish mare that required a gentle hand.

Houston parted ways with his father and headed home. His mouth watered, wondering what Lara was fixing for supper.

A moment later, he swung the door open silently and stepped inside. A faint smacking noise in the parlor sent him in there. Lara sat there, nursing Gracie. She glanced up, her eyes wide with alarm.

Eight

"OH, I'M SORRY." HOUSTON QUICKLY RETREATED INTO THE entry. "I didn't know…"

He'd never before witnessed a mother feeding her baby. Hadn't given it any thought.

"It's all right, Houston," Lara called. "You startled me. I hadn't expected you so soon. I'll be through feeding Gracie in a minute."

"Take your time. I'll just…" Stand there red-faced.

After Houston regained his composure, he called, "I'll just go into the…uh…kitchen."

Making a lot of noise so she'd know where he was, he clomped off in search of some coffee. The stirring image of the love on Lara's face as she held her baby girl clung to his mind like a stubborn cocklebur. Mother and child shared a bond so deep it shook him to his toes.

The need to protect Lara—them both—rose up so strong it lodged in his throat.

He had to rethink his role in all of this. How long could he remain an impassive bystander in this marriage? Even if he was afraid to open his heart again.

Maybe Lara was just as torn. After what had happened to her, she probably never wanted another man to touch her. Her prison could be even darker than his own. The thought troubled him. This arrangement didn't affect only him. He felt something soften a bit inside.

By the time he had coffee made and sat down with a cup, she bustled in with Gracie. The wet circle on her bodice where milk had leaked drew his gaze before he quickly lowered his eyes.

"If you'll watch the baby, I'll tend to supper," she said.

"Sure. Come here, Angel." Houston reached for her.

Gracie grinned and waved her arms excitedly. She grabbed his nose and pulled it, babbling something that sounded an awful lot like "Pa Pa Pa Pa Pa."

He'd signed on for the job but wondered if he could actually fill the role. He knew from watching Stoker and Sam that it took more than words on paper. But then, wasn't that also true of a husband?

Houston shot Lara a glance and felt his face grow hot, deciding it was time he went outside. "Want to go see the horsie?" he asked the babe. "Lara, do you mind if I take Angel for a short walk?"

Lara's smile was full of warmth. "She would love that. Horses seem to fascinate her."

He returned her smile. "That's good, since her father is a rancher. I mean...uh..."

"I know what you mean, Houston. You are her father now. You're the only one she'll ever know." A look of pain crossed Lara's green eyes.

Unsure of what to say, he nodded and told her they'd be back soon.

The short walk to the corrals took a while because of having to stop and let ranch wives coo over Gracie. All were in agreement that she was the prettiest baby they'd seen.

Finally, he joined Stoker, who was watching a wild mustang race around the enclosure. He'd been brought in bleeding from one leg, and Doc had sewn up the gash yesterday.

"Hello there, little darlin'." Stoker reached for the babe. "Grandpa needs to spoil you."

"Be careful. She'll try to pull off your nose or gouge

your eyes out," Houston warned. "She's got a grip of steel in those little hands."

"Maybe she can break this stallion." Stoker jabbered some baby talk to her, and the next instant he hollered for Houston to do something when Gracie grabbed two fistfuls of hair.

It took some doing, but he finally managed to pry her hands open. "Now keep her away from your face and head, Pa."

"You've got quite an excitable child, son. She grabbed me before I knew what was happening."

"I tried to tell you." Houston watched her bright eyes as she followed the mustang's movements. He wondered what she was thinking. "I may have a horsewoman in the making. She hasn't taken her attention off that mustang."

He couldn't help but wonder how Gracie would turn out.

"Yep," Stoker said. "Gracie is going to be quite an amazing horsewoman. She seems to have Till Boone's fine blood in her."

Houston rested his forearms on the rail of the corral and spoke of the worry he'd been too ashamed to admit to himself. "Don't forget her rotten father. Who knows what the bastard tainted her with. What exactly have I committed myself to?"

Stoker's voice seemed husky. "Just a sweet babe. It's how you raise a child that matters. Show her love and you'll get love in return."

That still weighed heavy on Houston's mind thirty minutes later as he carried Angel back to the house.

Maybe Pa was right. He hoped so. Still, he'd heard about outlaws whose boys followed down the same path of robbing and killing without ever knowing their kin. It had to be in the blood a little. But when the little darling gazed up at him with that slobbery grin, his heart did a somersault and all worries vanished.

After finishing the supper dishes, Lara sat in the parlor with Houston. He'd brought her rocker from upstairs and she enjoyed the comforting creak of the wood as she pushed the chair back and forth with her feet.

This time of day was her favorite. Except for Becky's ghostly presence and sorrow that oozed from every corner of the house, she found her new life with Houston easy and smooth.

She let her gaze drift to him and how he tenderly held Gracie in his lap. This stranger she'd tied her lot to looked every bit a father and the baby adored him. Lara was worried, though. Just as they were settling into a routine, he would be leaving on the cattle drive. They'd have to start from scratch upon his return. What would his absence do to Gracie? Children were resilient, but her daughter already watched the door for her papa to come home. The separation would deeply affect her.

And what about her own relationship with Houston? What if he found someone prettier? Someone who'd jump into his bed.

Someone without a hideous scar.

Gracie yawned.

"She'll go to bed soon," Lara said. "Her eyes are starting to droop."

"I 'spect," Houston agreed. "Won't be long for me either. My belly's full and all I want to do now is go to sleep. I've never tasted better beefsteak and potatoes in my life. And then you had to tempt me with that fresh, hot bread and gravy. I made a glutton of myself."

"I'm glad my cooking pleases you." At least one thing did.

A sound rumbled in Houston's throat before he growled, "It does a damn sight more than please. I grew up with cooks that put a lot of memorable spreads on the table, but everyone pales next to you."

Unsure what to say, Lara gave him a smile and let his deep voice curl down past the hurt and settle upon her weary soul.

"This day has been one trial after another," Houston continued, "but you make every setback disappear."

"I'll listen if you want to tell me what happened."

Houston sighed. "This cattle drive is about ready to start but Albert can't come. I don't know how in hell I'm going to find another cook on such short notice."

"Can one of the other men do it?" she asked.

"None of them want anything to do with cooking. I'm afraid I'll have a rebellion on my hands if I don't get some decent food into my drovers."

"You can't expect them to put out such grueling work without feeding them solid meals," Lara agreed.

"It takes someone with experience to do the job right. I can't just point to one and say they're the new cook." Gracie sagged in Houston's arms as she gave up the fight. He smiled and leaned to kiss her cheek.

His tenderness made Lara's heart flip over. If only there was a way to keep them all together.

Abruptly, she stopped rocking and leaned forward. "I'll go. I'll be your cook."

"No. It's out of the question."

Lara raised her chin. "Why not? You need a cook and I'm offering." It would solve everything.

"For one thing, you're a woman and a pretty one at that. You'll distract my men from their job. And you'd need more privacy for…" He flushed. "Well, you know. Besides, you're my wife. The first time I caught one of the drovers looking at you, I'd haul off and knock him sideways. Then he'd quit and leave me shorthanded. If a bunch did…Lara, I can't handle two thousand longhorns by myself with only your brothers to help."

"Those are excuses. What is the real reason?"

"There's the baby. What would you do with Gracie?"

"I'll take her. I'd never leave her behind. She'll be fine. We both will. We won't ask for any special favors. You'll treat me like one of your drovers." And it would solve this tension. Despite how peaceful things were between them, she hated living in this *house* and she knew he hated it too. Reminders of what he'd lost were everywhere. Getting away would be good for all three of them.

Except, Houston didn't seem to share her enthusiasm.

He scrubbed the back of his neck. "It's hard work. I'm not sure you know what you're getting into. You'd have to get up long before the others and won't get to bed until late. It can take a toll on you."

"This drive will take a toll on you too," she pointed out. "I heard my father speak about a woman, Margaret Heffernan Borland, who drove a herd of cattle up the Chisholm Trail from Victoria with only her two sons, five hired hands, and a cook. Her nine-year-old daughter and six-year-old granddaughter went along."

"Yes, I know the story. Folks are still talking about that…and how she checked into a hotel in Wichita and promptly died." Houston reached for her hand. "Gracie needs a mama."

Lara's hand tingled from Houston's warm touch. Her fingers curled boldly inside his. "She has one and will continue to. Just because Mrs. Borland died doesn't mean I will," she said softly. It felt nice to have him concerned for her. She could tell he meant his words. "Mrs. Borland wasn't the only woman to take the trail. Granted, it's not very common, but others have as well." Lara could see him weakening. "What other choice do you really have?"

"I could call it off until I get things all squared away." Houston's smile flickered then faded, leaving her wondering if she'd imagined it.

"By then it would be too late." She leaned forward. "You're already driving them late in the season, and this is a very narrow window. If you miss it, can you afford to wait for next spring?"

"No," he answered honestly. "The ranch is floundering. I've got to trim our herd before winter. With so little grass, they get weaker by the day."

"Do you think they can endure the rigors of the trip?"

"There's good grass up north, I'm told. I'll stop for a week or two and let them graze. They'll make it." He met her gaze.

Lara yearned to smooth the worry lines from his face. But she couldn't. Not yet. Maybe one day soon she could touch her husband without thinking about Yuma Blackstone, and the pain he'd taken joy in inflicting.

Without realizing it, she tugged free of Houston and ran her fingers across the scar.

"Does it hurt?" Houston asked quietly.

Lara jerked her hand away. "Sometimes it pulls. I'm fine. No cause for concern."

"I admire you in so many ways." His penetrating brown eyes studied each angle of her face. She squirmed under his gaze. "That scar is nothing to be self-conscious about. The only people without scars are the ones who never fought for anything. You fought to live and you survived pure hell to do it—it's the mark of a survivor. Hold your head high, Lara."

She'd never thought about her ordeal that way. Survivor. She liked that.

"You're a kind man, Houston. You gave up a lot for me and I hope one day I will be worth the sacrifice."

Houston's eyes blazed. "I don't want to hear you talk like that. I didn't give up a bit more than you. You're worth ten times all other women. And if you need to prove it to yourself, then I guess I won't stand in the way. How soon can you get ready for this trail drive? I'm taking you with me."

A smile broke across Lara's face. "I'll be ready by morning. After breakfast, I'll go over the contents of the chuck wagon and see if I need to add anything."

As though on impulse, Houston laid his hand on her knee, sending warmth through her. "I hope I don't regret this," he said, though he sounded like he was teasing.

"You won't."

"You know I've hired Henry as the cook's helper. Do

you think between the two of you, you can drive the chuck wagon? I don't think I can spare anyone for that."

"Don't worry, Houston. My brother and I will be just fine. I've been around horses and wagons my whole life. When we moved to our current ranch, I drove a team of four the whole way by myself...with Gracie. I had no trouble crossing the rivers. Even the mighty Brazos."

"I don't think I've heard where you moved from." Gracie stirred in his arms. He removed his hand from Lara's knee to give a soothing pat to the baby's small back. She loved watching him with the baby. His immense size seemed to swallow Gracie, yet he was always gentle and had taken to the role of father with greater speed than she'd dared imagine.

"I lived at Amarosa."

"Isn't that south of here near Abilene?"

"Twenty-five miles." Lara's mind drifted.

Gossips in the town had made it impossible to stay. The women had looked down their noses and blamed Lara—for the attack, and for her precious baby. The talk had been vicious until Lara gave up on going into town at all. Finally, her father had pulled up stakes.

"If you don't mind my asking, why the move?" Houston asked.

"It was just best that..." Laura got to her feet. "I think it's time I called it a night. Will you carry Gracie up?"

"It would be my pleasure."

He turned down the wick in the oil lamp and followed her up the stairs. His tall presence was reassuring. Without a doubt he had questions and one day she'd have to tell him what had happened.

Only one thing remained unclear. Would she tell him the part no one knew?

Or could she keep that secret buried?

Nine

Almost as though on cue, the sun peeked timidly over the horizon and blinked hard at the same moment Houston waved his arm, signaling the start of the long trek to Kansas.

He breathed the Monday morning air, taking in the pink glow that spread across the sky like a young girl's blush. But when his gaze swept to Lara, inching the chuck wagon forward behind the long line of hide and horns, knots twisted in his stomach.

Houston prayed he hadn't made a mistake. If she or the baby got hurt or killed, he'd never forgive himself. Nor would he go home to face Till Boone. Death would wait for him on the Lone Star, because Till would surely kill him. If Lara's brothers didn't finish the job first.

Tugging on the reins, he turned his Appaloosa and rode toward Lara and Henry.

"We'll go upstream to Doan's Crossing and ford the river there," Houston explained. "I'll be close in case you have a problem. And if you need help with the baby, I can take her for a while." He winked. "I'll make a horsewoman out of her yet."

The rising sun caressed her face, tilted up beneath the wide-brimmed hat, and for a moment, all Houston could think about was kissing her. The golden rays softened the angles of her features and he had to strain to see the scar.

Although it was impossible, the jagged gash appeared to fade a little more each day.

"Relax, Houston. I appreciate your care of me, but at this rate, you're going to worry yourself to death before we even leave Lone Star land." The slight breeze lifted a copper curl and laid it across Lara's emerald eyes. He felt the urge to smooth it back. To lean and touch her. Again, to kiss her.

"I just don't want anything to happen to you," he said.

"Out here, Henry and I are two of the hands. I don't expect any special treatment." She brushed back the bothersome tendril of hair. "If I hadn't thought I could do the job, I wouldn't have come."

"Sorry." Houston rubbed the back of his neck. "I don't think I'll ever see you as one of the hands."

"You'd better." She grinned. "If you start harping on that again, I'll take my frying pan to you."

"Yes, ma'am." Houston grinned back. "I get the message…Cookie. How's that?"

"Better. If you can't remember Cookie, call me Short Stuff."

Henry leaned forward. "I'm Bones."

"Bones? Where did that come from?" Houston grinned. "Are you a pirate?"

"Nope. I'm a cowboy. It's my made-up name."

"I see. I like it, Bones." Houston loved hearing the boy's laughter, and it didn't take much to bring it on. He made a vow to give Henry more reasons to laugh. Sometimes the smallest things could make such a big difference. "Just make sure no one buries you."

With the boy's laughter taking flight in the breeze behind him, Houston rode forward. He had a job to do, and while he couldn't totally forget the woman who drove the chuck wagon, he was able to direct his focus to getting the cattle over to the Great Western Trail and make the Red River crossing.

Quaid Boone rode drag at the end of the herd. As Houston leaned his elbow on the saddle horn and watched,

Quaid took out after a runaway steer. The stubborn animal seemed to want nothing to do with going to Kansas.

After a minute or two, Quaid got the miscreant going in the right direction. He handled his horse well and kept an eagle eye on the stream of cows, always keeping them in line, watching out for troublemakers and pushing the lollygaggers forward. Houston admired his ability.

Midway of the herd rode Virgil. Houston had no trouble spotting the other Boone twin, with his reddish-blond hair. Virgil rode swing position behind the tall point man, Clay Angelo, who had worked on the Lone Star just shy of a year. The mysterious man had appeared one early morning asking for a job. The secretive look said he was running from a checkered past, but that hadn't stopped Stoker from hiring him. Despite his short tenure, Clay had proven his worth many times over. Houston knew him to be a quiet man who kept to himself, but he trusted him completely. Some said he'd lost his right eye during the Civil War, but no one knew for sure. The only thing glaringly apparent was the black eye patch Clay wore. To a kid, he was a scary sight. Except to Gracie. The child adored him.

The mysterious man and Virgil made a good pair. Clay had plenty of patience to offer a young cowhand willing to learn.

After watching the brothers work for a minute, Houston heaved a big sigh of relief. Though lacking experience, they knew their way around horses and cattle.

Yes, he'd chosen wisely. This group of eighteen would give their all and pocket a goodly sum upon reaching Dodge City. He'd known cowboys who'd bought their own spread with money they made driving cattle north. He'd like to see that for each of these brothers. They were smart as whips. In fact, Virgil and Quaid reminded Houston of him and Sam. They yearned to prove themselves, to follow their own path wherever it may lead.

He just hoped it led to good health and prosperity. That was about all a man could wish for.

∽

Toward sundown, with miles to go yet before they reached Doan's Crossing where they would spend the night, a dry storm sprang up. Houston felt the shifting nervousness of the cattle. Longhorns were notoriously skittish. A silent warning made the hair on the back of his neck rise.

Once, the sound of a man striking a match had set off a stampede. He knew about the danger and there was nothing he feared more. He'd seen seasoned men get trampled to death under the heavy hooves.

Desperate to try to contain the cattle, he galloped toward the front, wanting to be near the lead steer until the storm passed. Before he reached midway, a horrendous thunderclap shook the earth and deafened him in the bargain.

Two thousand spooked longhorns bolted.

The ground trembled violently under the force of thundering hooves. Houston cursed, scanning the sea of cattle for his men, praying they'd come through this alive.

If only he could get to the front, he stood a chance of turning them. If not, they'd have to run themselves out, and he couldn't hazard a guess as to how many animals they'd lose. The likelihood of it being a good many was high.

With his focus riveted on his goal ahead, he stifled the urge to look back for the chuck wagon. He told himself that Lara and the baby were safe, praying he wouldn't be wrong. He couldn't bury their broken bodies so close to the Lone Star.

No, it wouldn't happen. He'd vowed to keep Lara safe.

As he passed Quaid, the young man's horse stumbled. Quaid tumbled from the saddle into the midst of the churning, mindless beasts.

Houston's heart stopped. Thank goodness his Appaloosa kept going, running toward the downed man. Drawing near, he reached down and yanked Quaid from certain death. Grunting, Houston heaved Lara's brother onto the back of his horse. Quaid was none the worse for wear, but in saving the young man, Houston had lost precious ground. He now had no hope of reaching the front.

Dust billowed up in huge clouds, blocking his vision. His Appaloosa stumbled and went down on one knee. As though by some miracle, the horse picked himself up and kept running.

The bawling longhorns' eyes rolled back in their heads. They couldn't see or hear anything except the madness inside their brains.

Quaid's fingers dug into Houston's skin in an effort not to lose his seating for a second time, and they galloped for what seemed like an eternity. Finally, through a break in the dust, he saw that Clay and Virgil had managed to get to the head steer. The two turned the cattle in a wide arc to the right— exactly as Houston would've done. In his experience, that was the best method for stopping a stampede.

With the big hook beginning, he knew Clay and Virgil had the upper hand and slowed his horse.

Only then did he search for the slow-moving chuck wagon. But it was nowhere in sight.

His heart leaped into his throat. Had it turned over, buried Lara, the baby, and Henry underneath? Houston's mouth went dry.

As the cattle began to slow, Houston pulled on the reins and headed back the way he'd come. When he reached Quaid's horse, Houston let him off then rode toward whatever lay in store.

Please let me find them alive.

He followed the crushed vegetation, remembering a stampede ten years back, the smashed wagon with broken bodies underneath. Fear gripping him, onward he rode until he crested the top of a small hill.

The chuck wagon sat intact thirty feet away. He released a deep breath and charged forward. When he neared, Lara walked from the back. Houston bounded from the Appaloosa before it even came to a stop. With a cry, he raced to Lara and lifted her off her feet. Her hat flew to the ground.

Hugging her to him, he buried his face in her hair. "Thank God you're all right."

"Everyone's fine." She pulled back and stared in alarm. He was mesmerized by her long, dark lashes that brought out the startling green of her eyes.

"Sorry. I went a little crazy when I couldn't find you," he explained. Before he realized it, he'd settled his lips to hers. The minute their mouths touched, a spark flared and sent little offshoots through him.

He hadn't meant this to happen, none of this, and it surprised him.

The unexpected kiss was full of the kind of heat that joined metals. His stomach flipped upside down as the feeling that this was right raced through him. Confusion warred with the pleasure winding around his heart. He let her go and stepped back.

But then he noticed how still she was. Oh God, he'd scared her. He couldn't stand the fear written on her face, her breath that came in gasps. And the sounds she made in her throat that sounded like a small, cornered animal. What should he say—or do—now? Should he touch her? No. That probably wasn't wise. It might scare her even more. Maybe he should just talk.

"I'm real sorry, Lara. I shouldn't have done that." He called himself every name he could think of and wished he knew what the hell he was doing. If only she'd slap the daylights out of him or yell.

Lara's eyes were wide, her hands trembling.

Hell. Houston yanked off his hat and crushed it between his hands. "I was just so happy to find you alive and... I didn't mean to frighten you."

She glanced up. "I know. Please, it's all right. You simply startled me."

"It won't happen again," he murmured, watching a fiery tendril blowing in the breeze. He imagined it felt like silk. Unsure of what to do next, he talked about the stampede and told her how far the cattle had run before they could get them stopped. He knew he wasn't making much sense but he rattled on. If only he could take her in his arms. But that would make everything worse, of course. He felt like a bumbling idiot.

Just as that thought crossed his mind, she moved a little closer to him. "Though I've never been in a stampede, I knew to stay back. Did my brothers survive?"

"I think they're all okay. Quaid fell from the saddle but I managed to pull him to safety before he got trampled."

She laid a hand on his arm and the warmth seeped down to banish the cold that filled him over his stupid mistake. "Thank you, Houston. If anything had happened to him, I don't know what I'd do."

"Where are—" Houston was interrupted when Henry poked his head from the opening of the thick muslin that formed the domed top and Houston relaxed. The boy held Gracie. "There you are, Bones. I was wondering where you got off to." He might not know what to do with Lara, but with Henry he found sure footing.

"Hidin'."

"Smart man." Houston grinned. "I felt like doing that myself."

"Mad cows are scary." Henry dragged his sleeve across his eyes.

"Yep, they are." Though Gracie held out her arms to him, he told her to stay with Henry. "Let's go find the rest." He helped Lara up into the wagon box, tied his horse to the back, and climbed up beside her. He'd drive to the place where they'd camp for the night.

They rode in silence across the vast land. Henry had crawled back into his den, leaving Houston alone with Lara, who appeared to have recovered.

At least so it seemed. He still didn't know what to say to her and he didn't want to make things worse. A glance showed that she'd unclenched her hands in her lap. He took that as a good sign.

"Lara, I want to talk to you about something. I

should've brought this up before we left, but frankly, I forgot about it. Tell me if I ask too much and I won't bring it up again." He took a deep breath. "On a cattle drive, the men notice everything. They get bored and look for things to talk about."

"Like what?"

"They're going to think it very odd if we don't act at least a little bit married." Houston rubbed the back of his neck. This was out of his field and he knew he was making a mess of it. "What I'm trying to ask is…would you kiss me each night before you turn in?" He angled on the seat to look at her. The delicate curve of her cheek and the set of her chin gave no hint of her thoughts. "I won't have them talking about you."

If they did, Lord only knew how fast he'd light into them.

The horses' hooves striking the ground and the rigging clanking broke the quiet.

"A kiss?" Lara met his gaze, her voice still quiet.

"One kiss. Unless it's something you simply can't do. If so, I'll make up something to tell the men." He watched her turn to stare straight ahead, her back stiff, and wished he could read minds. *Dammit to hell!*

He forced himself to remember the hard lesson he'd learned. Besides, Lara wanted nothing from him but his name. Why then had it felt so right kissing her? He hadn't imagined that. She'd even leaned into him just a bit. He knew he was dumb about fragile women, but he hadn't imagined that for one second. Maybe he hadn't messed up too badly.

Still, theirs was a bargain struck—a deal made. This marriage was nothing more. For either of them. They were *friends*.

They lumbered along in silence with Houston calling himself every name he could think of for even suggesting a nightly kiss.

"I wouldn't mind." She met his gaze. "You ask for so little. And I think it might be…nice. And, Houston?"

"Yep?"

"Don't be so hard on yourself. You're doing the best you can. The problem is me. And, Houston, just so you know— the feel of your lips on mine felt real good."

A sudden smile curved his mouth. He glanced at the vivid blue of the sky to hide the unexpected happiness shooting through him. Despite doubts that had invaded his bones, life was good.

A long way from perfect, mind you. But good all the same.

Ten

ONCE THEY MADE CAMP THAT NIGHT, LARA SET TO WORK. The men were dirty and hungry and dead-tired, so she would fill their bellies with wholesome food that would lift their spirits.

Instead of the quick meal she'd planned, she decided to make mounds of hot biscuits, gravy, and the freshly killed prairie chickens Houston had brought her. Apple dowdy for dessert. While she and Henry prepared the food, Houston took Gracie with him. Her heart swelled and a mist blurred her vision to see him prop her little daughter in front of him in the saddle and ride off. How had Lara gotten so lucky? Houston amazed her with his patience and kindness.

She closed her eyes for a second, remembering their kiss earlier that arose out of relief to find her safe following the danger. The way his firm but gentle mouth had gently pressed to hers floated across her mind. Her lips tingled. No one had ever kissed her that way before. His tender touch had made her feel special, almost cherished even.

Maybe he wouldn't be so gentle the second time. Sighing, she nervously brushed back a tendril of hair that had slipped from her braid and told herself she'd seen no anger in the man she'd married. Putting her doubts aside, she turned her attention to the meal.

The minute she had everything ready, Henry rang

the bell to call the men. Because of the cattle stampede, no one had eaten since breakfast before dawn. Amid the darkening shadows, they came running. Houston rode up a few minutes later, bathed in the dusky twilight. Clutching Gracie in one arm, he swung down. The lines around his mouth looked much deeper. When he reached Lara, the smell of sage, saddle leather, and man engulfed her. She loved the different fragrances that spoke of a working man. He bent and brushed her scarred cheek with his lips. The preference appeared to send a message—that her scar didn't bother her.

She handed him a cup of coffee, smiling shyly. "I imagine you can use this."

"Yes, ma'am. I sure can." His fingers curled around hers as he took the cup. "It's been a long day, Mrs. Legend."

"One to be grateful to survive." Flustered, Lara stepped back.

His coffee-brown eyes pierced her. "I never take the lives of my men—or family—lightly."

Lara watched him turn to his drovers and admired the easy way he had with them. She held Gracie as each man tipped his hat to her and said thanks before reaching for a plate. But her eyes never left one tall Texan who wore honor and strength like a second skin.

With night pressing around her like a cloak of soft wool, Lara hummed while she washed the dishes and put everything away.

The men were fed and they'd loved what she'd served. Houston sat on the ground with Gracie. Her gaze touched him as he leaned back against his saddle and laid the babe on his chest, one hand patting her small back. She didn't have to see Gracie's eyes to know that soon she would be in dreamland.

Houston caught Lara looking and winked as boldly as

some scoundrel. Heat rose to her cheeks. She lowered her gaze and made quick work of the dishes.

Maybe she could get out of kissing him. He didn't appear the kind to force his attentions on her. But before she took a step, a yearning to feel his lips on hers again pushed all that aside.

She *wanted* to discover more of the pleasure that had wound through her earlier.

Stowing everything in the proper bins and crates, she placed the tongue of the chuck wagon to the north as her father had explained was customary. That way, in the predawn hours, the trail boss would always know which way to head.

"Do you want me to take Gracie to her bed?" Lara asked, joining him.

"That would be a good idea, if you can pry open her fist to get my vest out of it. For such a little thing, she's sure got a grip on her."

Lara laughed, bending. It wasn't easy, but she finally freed Gracie from him. The child had hung on for dear life. Maybe she feared he'd leave and not come back.

Houston was so near, his soft breath fanned Lara's cheek. Her pulse raced. This man she'd married invaded her every thought. He'd shown her kindness and caring and brought hope back from the grave where she'd buried it.

"I'll lay her in her bed," Lara said.

"Good. She's tired." Houston laid a hand on her arm. "You'll be back?"

"Yes. I won't be long."

A rider materialized from the darkness. When the horse moved closer, she recognized her brother Virgil. He looked dead on his feet. He untied his bedroll from behind the saddle. No doubt he'd be asleep in half a minute.

"I'll be here for just a little while," Houston said, yawning. "Have to spell the others." At her questioning glance, he explained, "Everyone shares guard duty, me included."

She nodded and hurried to lay Gracie in her crib beside

the chuck wagon, lingering a moment to make sure the child didn't wake.

With her precious daughter sleeping soundly, she returned to the fire. As she'd predicted, Virgil was fast asleep, but Houston was nowhere to be seen. Her heart sank with disappointment. She'd missed him, missed their good-night kiss.

Then she heard him calling quietly from the deep shadows. "Over here, Lara."

Following his voice, she discovered him leaning against a dead mesquite tree. Rays from the full moon lightened the dark-brown strands nestling against his collar, adding glints of silver. His gaze met hers.

"I didn't want the comings and goings to interrupt, so I walked out here," he explained.

Lara wet her lips. "I thought you'd changed your mind." That he didn't want to kiss a woman so scarred.

"Not a chance, lady."

Others had spoken of Becky Golden's beauty. Houston had loved her and still did. Lara had been forced on him. No matter that she was beginning to warm to the idea of feeling his lips on hers—of *wanting* that intimacy—Houston may not feel the same. It could really all be playacting for his men, so they wouldn't gossip. This was a mistake. She turned to go.

"Please wait." He pushed away from the tree. "I won't hurt you. I'll never hurt you."

No, he would never lay a hand to her, and that surety, plus the earnest note in his voice, stopped her from leaving. Her steps were hesitant as she moved slowly to him. When he opened his arms, she walked into his embrace as though it were a door and safety awaited there. Inhaling the scented air, she laid her head against the hard wall of his chest.

Houston lightly rested his chin on top of her head. "I'm real glad you came on this drive. Nights can get lonely out here."

His deep voice vibrated inside her. It was like he'd become part of her. "I'm glad I did too. Even though I had to work to convince you."

"Yeah, well, I'm a stubborn fool."

He put a finger under her chin and lifted her face. Without a word, he lowered his mouth. The instant his warm lips touched hers, Lara had to clutch his arm to keep from falling. Her heartbeat pounded as though trying to keep up with the blood racing through her veins.

A hot, demanding achiness swept over her. She needed this man. At this moment, she didn't think she could live without him.

Nor did she want to try.

With a low cry, he placed his large hands under her jaw and deepened the kiss, sending a series of quickenings into her stomach, similar to the ones she'd felt when Gracie curled in her womb. Maybe these stirrings signaled life, much in the same way her baby's movements had, to let her know she was alive and couldn't wait to be born.

Maybe she was being reborn.

Maybe she could forget the past and start fresh.

Maybe this was what she'd waited so long for.

As she leaned into him and gripped Houston's vest, pleasure like she'd never felt swirled inside her. She clung to him, afraid if she let go, he'd vanish and she'd discover it was a dream.

Could this be tiny stirrings of love?

Lara suddenly pushed away from him. No, it wasn't love. She refused to even let that thought enter her head. Love didn't exist, not for her. It was too dangerous to believe there could ever be anything more than what she had.

Houston was in love with a ghost, and she…

"What's wrong, Lara?" He gently pushed back her hair. "Did I do something to upset or frighten you? I shouldn't have grabbed you like that. I forgot."

"No, you did nothing wrong." It was her. *She* was all wrong. "I'm sorry," she murmured brokenly.

Through tears, she stumbled back to the light of the campfire, escaping all that brought pain.

The past.

Herself.

An impossible future.

Escaping everything. If only it were that easy.

As she stood beside Gracie's crib, Houston lightly touched her shoulder. He'd followed her. "Tell me. Talk to me. I want to understand."

She owed him some explanation. Impatiently dashing away the tears, she turned and let anger spill. "It's not you, Houston. It's me. I'm broken. Too broken to fix. You can't repair something that's missing the pieces. Blackstone took a lot more than…" She paused. "He stole…"

"Your soul," he supplied quietly. "Mine was stripped away also. I don't know exactly how you feel—I couldn't possibly—and I'm sure it will take a long time to work through. But…we can try. If you're willing."

His hand tightened on her shoulder, and the shadows couldn't hide the muscle working in his jaw. She saw caring in his eyes and felt it in his gentle touch.

"We're both trapped by the past. I don't know if I can ever find peace. I don't know if I can ever be a wife," she murmured, looking out into the darkness that hid waiting evil. It always waited there, just beyond the light. "Sometimes I still see his sneering face, hear the hate in his voice, feel his hands on me," she whispered. "I haven't slept a full night through since. Not once."

"I can make no promises that this will work out, but I will try my hardest. I want to help you. Just tell me how."

She raised her eyes to his. "I may not ever be whole again. Are you prepared for that?" No matter how difficult she found it, she would always be honest. He deserved that at least.

"I am. I'll never forsake you." Houston pulled her to him slowly, giving her time to break away if she wanted, and smoothed back her hair. "I'm not going anywhere.

We'll work this out together. We have mountains in front of us, and Lord knows you have one of the tallest, but no one can tell you when or how to climb. I'll help you figure it out and, if I can't catch you, I'll pick you up when you fall."

This was the first genuine conversation about their relationship they'd had since the day they pledged to stand by each other in sickness and in health. Maybe it meant they were making progress. Or maybe it was nothing more than meaningless words for a poor woman who had little to offer.

And yet… "Don't ever pity me," she warned. "I will accept anything but that."

"It's not you I pity," Houston assured her in a cold voice edged with steel. "It's Blackstone. I'm going to make him very, very sorry he was ever born, and you can bet on that."

"If you find him."

"I'll find him, all right. I'll dog him to the ends of the earth if I have to. There's no place to hide that I won't find him. I'll turn over every rock, look in every hole. He won't be able to take a deep breath, because I'll be there."

His cold voice, coupled with the bitter words, scared her a little. She feared for anyone who hurt his family. Houston Legend would kill without batting an eye. That much was crystal clear. He was barely able to contain his rage now— what would he be like without restraint?

Though she truly believed deep down his promises to never hurt her, she didn't wish to see that rage directed at anyone. Anger terrified her. It made men do horrific things.

She didn't want to see Houston in that state. If she lost him, what would she do?

Lara yearned to touch his hard jaw where a muscle still twitched, but she'd already pushed him away. Laying her hand on him now would only confuse the issue. She wasn't going to be someone who was hot one minute and cold as ice the next.

"Houston, I'm not asking—"

"I know that. But it's something I have to do. For you

and for me. The crime can't go unpunished. If we don't have justice, what will the world become? This is an unforgiving land full of lawless people, and they have to pay for the evil they do." His expression told her he'd go all the way to hell and beyond to make their world safer.

But still—Yuma would kill him as soon as he got the chance. Terror froze her blood.

"And that duty falls on your shoulders, Houston?"

"Mine and every man with a desire for law and order. It's going to take every single one of us to tame this wild land." He jerked off his hat and shoved a hand through his hair. "I hope I live to see the day when we run the evil men out of this state." He crushed his hat in his large hands before jamming it back on his head. "Reckon I'd best take my turn at singing these cows to sleep."

Houston took two steps before Lara caught his arm.

"Do you think you could kiss me once more?" she whispered.

Firelight revealed a surprised but pleased smile. "Anything for you, Lara."

Lara searched his eyes. "Does it mean that much to you?"

"I didn't expect it to, but it does. It really does."

Her heart hammered when he dipped his head and laid his lips to hers. Instant heat flamed, along with something else—a dream that one day she could give her husband the kind of wife he deserved.

As he drugged her with a slow, scorching kiss, she did something she'd never done before. Lara melted into his arms and slid a hand around his neck into his soft hair.

What they had was far from a normal marriage, but this seemed a start.

Maybe, just maybe…she felt a tiny flicker of hope curling through her. Maybe making a life together was like starting a campfire. You had to begin with small pieces of kindling and let the flames take hold.

And maybe eventually, they'd find a way to the peace they both sought.

Eleven

A TWISTING, RUSHING CURRENT GREETED HOUSTON UPON reaching the mighty Red the following morning. He pushed back his Stetson and surveyed the river. The Appaloosa stamped his feet impatiently.

"She'll give us a tussle," Clay said, wiping his face with his neckerchief. "But we should cross it here just fine."

Houston grunted. "I agree. This is the shallowest part."

He wasn't worried about the cattle or the men that much. The ones that concerned him most were Lara, Gracie, and Henry. Even though Lara had reminded him again that very morning that she was just one of the drovers, try convincing his heart.

Small chance.

She was his partner. His friend.

Hope lodged in his heart that they could heal and grow into this marriage. One thing about him—when he'd decided to take her for a wife, it had been for keeps. There were no half measures either. Despite his past problems, he couldn't ask her to trust him without being committed.

Maybe he could still give her a happy life without letting her into his heart…and without being allowed into hers in return.

The feel of her slightly parted lips against his still burned in his memory, along with the fragrance of roses that had wafted around his head, making her impossible to forget. Despite being dog-tired, when he'd crawled into his bedroll in the wee hours, sleep had evaded him. Trying to figure out how to act around her was making him crazy. How could he touch her without frightening her to death? What could he say that would put her at ease? When would this awkward stage pass?

"Let's get these snot-slinging bunch of dogies across, Clay," Houston said, dragging his thoughts to the job at hand. "I want to help Lara during the crossing, so the biggest portion of this will fall on you."

Clay shot him a glance out of his good eye, grinning. "Don't worry. I'm up for the job."

"Sort of figured that out a while ago," Houston answered softly. "Thanks for never bellyaching. You're a good man, Clay."

"Always figured complainin' was a pure waste of time." Clay's grin spread. "Besides, I need all the air I can get for breathing."

Virgil Boone rode over to them. "Houston, any special instructions?"

Houston eyed the kid. "Don't get killed."

"I don't plan to. Anything else?"

"Keep an eye on your brothers. Help them if they need it." Still the kid stayed, as though he wanted to say something. Houston waited.

Finally, Virgil spoke. "You'll look after my sister?"

There it was. The worried look in Virgil's eyes hurt Houston's heart. Lara was precious to countless people and he doubted she knew exactly to what lengths they'd go to protect her. Guilt was a hard thing to handle, and the Boone boys had it in spades.

"Count on it, Virgil." Houston tugged his hat lower to hide the unease that must show in his face. Whatever, whoever, sought to steal her would have the fight of his life on his hands.

Lara Legend had him to stand beside her in sickness, in health…and in crossing this dang river.

❦

The water rose higher and higher. Lara gripped the reins, trying to remain calm and let the team feel her confidence. She could do this. She had to.

Houston rode beside the wagon, adding a level of security. He'd wanted to tie the Appaloosa to the back and drive, but she refused to relinquish the reins.

This was her job and she needed to do it—for her self-worth, her need to prove she could, and for her baby girl. Lara had to show Gracie that she should be strong and not wait around for someone to always get her out of difficult situations. Being independent was crucial for a woman in this wild land.

On the plains, a woman needed good wits about her.

Now, as they began to cross the mighty Red, she found herself grateful that Houston hadn't gotten angry and ridden off. Having him near was a comfort. One thing she knew—if anything should happen and she couldn't figure out a way past it, her husband would make it right again. He could fix almost anything.

Lara glanced at his rugged profile: the squared shoulders, the set jaw and the hard lines of his face that now seemed carved in granite. Never before had she known a man like Houston. Why hadn't she met him before that horrible night when the world stopped turning and she had prayed to die?

Back when she could've loved a man.

She gritted her teeth and brought her attention to a task she could do something about.

New buoyancy told her when the horses started swimming, and the floating chuck wagon followed behind. Slow and steady. Relieved that everything was going well, she took a deep breath and relaxed her hold on the reins.

"You're almost there," Houston called. "I'm proud of you. You're gonna make it."

His praise sent a happy glow through her. She gave him a

smile. Just a little more and she'd have the river behind her. They floated slowly toward the bank where her brothers all stood.

"You're one tough lady," Houston said, riding beside her. "In fact, I'd say you're a match for your Margaret Heffernan Borland."

The kindness in his deep voice seeped into her bones. Never had anyone shown such gentle caring, not even her papa and brothers who had nursed her back from near death.

"You're not still doubting my abilities?" she asked.

"Nope."

The hard edges Houston Legend wore were deceptive. He could be kind and gentle and encouraging. He could even be sweet.

However, something told her that for anyone who harmed his family or men, he would be someone to fear.

After seeing the chuck wagon safely on dry land, he turned his attention to the others. Her gaze followed Houston's tall, muscular form. She loved watching him work. Confidence oozed from him. Though she was still learning his ways, she hadn't seen any task he hadn't measured up to. Even marry a woman he didn't know to give her child a name. Sharp pain filled her. He'd given up everything for her and Gracie. And now he wanted to go after Yuma Blackstone.

Fear froze the blood in her veins. When he caught up with the man—and she knew it was only a matter of time— one of them would die.

She took Gracie from Henry and absently fingered her reddish-blond curls. They both needed the man who had just come into their life. The fear riding inside her like the black shadow of a vulture sharpened the brittle hardness that had formed during her recovery. If Yuma put Houston into a grave, she'd go after him herself—and deliver the vengeance that burned inside her like the fiery pit of hell. Except then it would be exacting retribution for two murders—one for Houston and one for the death of her spirit and self-worth.

Yes, Yuma Blackstone would pay. But at whose hand was the question.

Henry propped himself beside her. "I was scared. Were you scared, Lara?"

"No, Henry. Water is nothing to be afraid of. Remember that Virgil and Papa taught you to swim. Do you recall that?"

"Oh yeah." He grinned. "I can swim like a doggie."

"That's right. Besides, with all of us near, you'll never have to be afraid." She just prayed her brother would always have someone near to save him. Lara hugged his arm. "Thank you for taking such good care of Gracie."

"I didn't want the river to get her."

"You're a good uncle to the baby."

"An uncle?"

"Yes, you're her uncle. Remember?"

"But I'm the brother."

"No, honey," Lara corrected in a gentle tone. "You're *my* brother but you're Gracie's uncle."

"Who's her daddy? Can I be the daddy?"

The question caught Lara off guard. She'd cut out her tongue before she spoke Yuma's name.

"Houston is her papa."

"Oh yeah. I forgot." Henry grinned then turned to watch the men. "I'm hungry. Can I eat?"

"Not yet. Soon, though."

Gracie looked up at her and babbled something. The child was so pleasant and hardly ever cried. Lara prayed she would grow into a beautiful, caring woman. All Gracie needed was a chance. "Yes, sweetie," Lara crooned and kissed a dirt-streaked cheek. "Whatever you said is right. I love you too."

She imagined Gracie was getting hungry. Dismay filled her. She didn't want to nurse her in front of the men—she'd never even fed Gracie in front of her brothers. Hopefully she could have some privacy before they started moving again. If not, she didn't know what she'd do.

Houston rode over. "It'll take a while to get all these

cattle across. Stretch your legs if you want." He leaned to touch Gracie's chubby cheek, his gaze meeting Lara's. "I imagine she's getting hungry. I'll rig up something so you can feed her in private before we roll out."

That he clearly guessed Lara's dilemma astounded her. He didn't miss anything. "Thank you, Houston. I didn't want to ask."

He leaned back in the saddle. "What kind of man would I be to leave you exposed to curious stares?" he asked softly. "You can always ask me anything. You know I'll move heaven and earth for you, Lara."

"I know." Sudden tears sprang into her eyes. "I don't deserve you."

"Hush with that nonsense. You deserve a good deal more than my feeble efforts," he murmured low. His words seemed to have a double meaning, almost as though he apologized for not loving her.

Some kind of private message wafted between them. Frustration rose that she was too dumb to read it.

"I'm hungry too," Henry announced loudly, breaking the spell.

Houston swung his attention to him. "Well, I can't have my cook's helper being hungry." Houston dismounted. "Let's see what we can find in the back of that wagon."

Houston climbed up and they disappeared through the opening.

Lara's heart swelled for the tall man and the boy full of hero worship who yearned to be just like him. Houston didn't know it, but he'd already made such a difference in all their lives.

And the quickening inside her was getting stronger and stronger.

A few minutes later, Henry crawled from the back, munching on a cold biscuit and a piece of jerky, saying he was going to watch Virgil and Quaid with the cattle. She warned him to stay out of the way.

"Lara, I made a place for you." Houston reached for Gracie.

Surprise washed over her when she saw the cozy place he'd prepared. He'd moved the large barrels of flour and sugar to one side and had made her a low stool from a crate to sit on. A folded bedroll lay on the floor of the wagon for Gracie when she napped.

"This is perfect. Thank you." She gazed into his face, wishing she was bold enough to smooth away the deep lines that bracketed his mouth. Maybe one day when she knew him better and the pain of losing the woman he loved wasn't so strong, she could touch this man she'd married and he'd not wish she was Becky.

"I also have this curtain of sorts you can pull across once I'm out." He showed her the piece of burlap he'd tacked up.

"You've thought of everything." The private little space was all Lara needed and Houston had fixed it up just for her. A pleasant warmth stole over her. But her insistence that she was one of the drovers crossed her mind. He was already treating her differently. She placed a hand on his broad chest, trying not to notice the beat of his heart beneath her palm. "Now go. You have your men and the cattle to see about. Gracie and I are fine."

Hearing her name, the baby girl began to babble excitedly.

Houston laughed. "One day Angel is going to lay down the law to both of us and in a language we'll have no problem understanding."

"I expect so."

Still Houston stood as though needing to say more.

"Is something bothering you?" she asked.

"Lara, don't walk on eggshells around me. I'm not going to get mad or start hollering if you say or do things. This marriage is only going to work if we relax and be ourselves." Houston touched her cheek with a finger. "I'm not an easy man to live with. I know that. Sometimes I might forget to soften my voice. But it won't mean anything against you." He released a deep sigh. "I have far too much of Stoker in me and that's a fact."

She took Gracie from him. "I understand what you're

saying. Trying too hard is just as bad or worse than not trying hard enough. I'm going to be a work in progress, though."

"All this is going to take time."

Lara just wondered if their life together would always be crowded with Becky's ghost. Or would Houston one day see Lara instead of the woman he wished she was?

"I'm glad we're having this conversation," Lara said. "I need to get something off my mind. Let's make a vow that if either of us wants out of this marriage, we can leave with no questions asked."

He jerked in surprise. His voice was quiet. "Is that what you want, Lara? Do you wish to go back to your father?"

"No." She was only giving him a way out if he grew to find her too lacking. "I like being here away from the memories. I like being with you."

"I like being with you too." He appeared relieved that she wasn't asking out of the marriage.

Or had she only imagined that?

Saying he needed to see to things, he left. Lara watched him through the canvas opening, admiring his lean figure and broad shoulders. He swung into the saddle as easily as stepping from bed and rode to help his men.

She would never leave him. Somehow, unexpectedly, he was becoming her life and this was starting to be her home.

Twelve

Someone is trailing us.

The hair rose on Houston's neck as he lifted a spyglass for another look and adjusted for the morning sun. Four riders. Too far away to make out more than that. Yet, they were always there. Always just barely in sight no matter how fast or slow the cattle went. Always keeping a safe distance back. His gut clenched into a knot.

He'd first noticed them yesterday and cautioned his men to be on alert. They could be the outlaws Sam had warned about. Or rustlers.

They'd traveled three days into Indian Territory, which put them beyond range of any law. The raw, untamed land was the perfect place for an attack, with hundreds of hills, ravines, and canyons for a group of no-accounts to hide in. To the east, the peaks of the Wichita Mountains rose. He'd have to double up on guard duty.

Houston put away his spyglass and galloped toward the chuck wagon that lumbered along behind the cattle now snaking across Cherokee lands. Several Indian groups had ridden close in the past two days but hadn't spoken. The men weren't hostile. Maybe a little curious, maybe guarding their land, or maybe just extending friendship. Here on the short-grass prairie, they knew exactly where hidden dangers lay and had other beneficial advice.

He slowed his horse to ride beside the chuck wagon. "Is everything all right?"

Lara smiled, the sun brushing her face beneath her hat. "Going fine."

Their nightly ritual of kissing had left him in a sorry state. He loved feeling her warm lips beneath his, and that was fine in the beginning, but he wanted to touch the softness of her skin.

Last night while he'd held her in his arms, he casually tugged down the collar of her dress and pressed his mouth to the hollow of her throat. She hadn't pushed him away. And the wild pulse beneath his lips had been enough to keep him awake most of the night. Maybe tonight he'd try that again, or do something more daring if she seemed like she wanted him to.

Though she was coming to trust him more, he had to go slow. The wrong move could send him back to the beginning in a heartbeat. Lara remained—what she called—broken inside. Like he was a year ago. Maybe with time, two broken people could become one strong piece of steel that could stand any test.

Houston shoved away his thoughts. "Glad you have everything under control, Lara. Anything I can do before I ride to the front?"

From the security of Henry's arms, Gracie started jabbering furiously and reaching for Houston. He had a feeling she was baby-cussing him for ignoring her. "Mind if I take Angel for a spell?" he asked. "A ride would do her good."

Lara's smile faded into worry. "Houston, you can't take care of a baby on horseback. You have things to do."

"And I'll do them. Angel can help." When he saw his wife soften, he rode to the other side, plucked Gracie up, and settled her in the saddle in front of him. "I'll take good care of her, I promise."

"I know you will. Bring her back when you get tired of her."

As Gracie snuggled against him and looked up with her

big blue eyes, Houston grinned. That would never be. "I 'spect I'll see you when she gets hungry."

Sudden laughter that sprang from Lara's mouth surprised him. The sound reminded him of the silvery tinkle of a bell. He liked it. They seemed to be relaxing and drawing closer. With each kiss, a little more of the barrier between them crumbled. Who knew what would happen by the time they reached Dodge City.

Sudden memory of her talk about leaving crowded his mind. He'd fought tooth and nail against this but now the idea of her walking out brought deep pain.

"She'll pee on you," Henry yelled as Houston began moving away.

"Then I'll bring her back to you, Bones," Houston yelled back.

The boy hooted with glee. Houston glanced up at the big blue sky and winked at God. The big man had brought joy into his life in ways he was still discovering. It seemed a lot like peeling an onion and uncovering all the many hidden layers. Some were thin and some a little thicker, but they all comprised a rich wholeness he'd never had.

He moved near some straggling longhorns, and Gracie began jabbering excitedly and shaking her finger as though scolding the animals for not sticking with the herd.

"You tell 'em, baby girl. Get on up there, you hide-covered bag of bones, and be quick about it."

Gracie giggled. The sound drifted past the worry that he wouldn't measure up as a father and settled deep in a private place in his heart. Whatever he'd gone through had been worth it, to get to this point. If he could help shape this tiny little girl into a beautiful young lady, he'd be happy. He thought of her more and more as his daughter. A mist sprang into his eyes and a lump rose in his throat.

He turned the Appaloosa out of range of the dust clouds and skirted some five-foot-high juniper. To be on the safe side, he removed the bandana from around his neck and tied it across Gracie's nose. She stared up at him, her blue eyes twinkling like stars.

"You look like a pint-sized bandit, little one. Ready to take to the outlaw trail, rob a bank or two?"

She babbled something and laughed. That she didn't try to yank the cloth off as most babies probably would appeared a miracle. He guessed she liked being a bandida. He could imagine the wanted poster hanging with her picture on it as she looked now. The words beneath might say: *Desperada on the loose! Disarming and dangerous heart stealer.*

Lara's brother Virgil chased after a runaway. He got it back into the herd and rode over.

"Hi, Gracie. You herding ornery ol' cows?" Virgil asked.

Sharp jabbering seemed to scold him for mistaking her for a common drover.

Virgil threw back his head and laughed. "I guess I got told."

"Yep, in no uncertain terms," Houston agreed. "She's got no shortage of sass." He groaned. "Already."

"She does know how to lay down the law. Well, I guess I'd best get back to work." Virgil waved to Gracie and turned to focus on his job.

He noticed Clay speaking to a group of Cherokees in their language and joined them. Two Indian women and three small children were among the band numbering close to two dozen.

"These people are telling me things to watch for ahead," Clay said low. "They said water is scarce. Not much until we reach the Canadian River."

Houston searched each of their faces, saw the pride reflected in their eyes. He nodded and smiled. "Tell them we're grateful for their help and ask them to join us for supper. Why are they in the area?"

"They're protecting a small herd of buffalo in a nearby canyon from hunters. There's a sacred white one among the herd," Clay replied. "We need to detour around the animals."

"Of course. I don't want to cause a problem for them."

Gracie gave excited jabbers and yanked off the bandana.

One of the women, who looked to be in her middle years, noticed Gracie and came near. Sadness oozed from her. Her clothes were simple doeskin but she walked as tall as a queen. She smiled. "Pretty smile."

"Yep, she can rival the sun, all right," Houston replied, standing the baby in front of him. "Her name's Gracie Jewel."

"Blessed one," she said. "Important. Healer."

She took Houston aback. Maybe they were just empty words to make small talk, but somehow he didn't think so. "I hope you're right." Maybe Gracie could heal her mama. She seemed to have already started. From what Lara's brothers had said, she was in bad shape at first, not eating or sleeping and startling at the slightest sound. Houston turned to Clay. "Tell them they're welcome in our camp anytime as honored guests."

Clay grinned and gave him a curt nod. "Be my pleasure."

After relaying the message, the woman who'd spoken to Houston asked him to lower Gracie. When he complied, she handed the child a carved wooden wolf that was painted red.

"Keep safe. Men follow."

Houston swung from the saddle. "What are you saying?"

"They come. Evil." Without more, she turned and rejoined the others, marching off toward some barren, low-slung hills.

"Hey, wait. I want to ask about the men." Houston stared helplessly after her. He needed more. What did she know about the men trailing them?

Hell and be damned! But clearly he'd get nothing else from her now. When she came with the rest later, he'd take the woman aside and ask. He had to know what she meant. How could he protect his people if he didn't know the threat?

His heartbeat thundered in his ears. He couldn't lose what he'd found.

He'd fight the devil with his own pitchfork first.

Or with a bullet from his Colt.

Lara put the finishing touches on the evening meal. She wanted everything to be ready for their guests. These people had given them useful information, according to Houston, and she wanted to repay them.

The food was simple—beefsteaks, fried potatoes, red beans, and sourdough bread, with peach cobbler for dessert. As she stirred the potatoes, she thought of the haunted look that had been in Houston's eyes when he brought Gracie back. Her husband was uneasy and it didn't take a fortune-teller to know he kept something from her.

Everyone around her thought keeping quiet and not raising an alarm was doing her a favor. But danger had stalked her during one of those times. Her father and brothers hadn't wanted to frighten her, so they'd kept their suspicions about Yuma to themselves.

When people kept secrets, no one was safe.

Danger stalked her again now, and what terrified her most was not knowing from which direction it would come.

She cast Houston a glance as she cooked. He stood talking with her brothers and several of the other drovers. And of course Gracie was in the middle of it. They passed the babe around like she was a piece of penny candy they'd bought at the mercantile, and the little stinker loved every bit of attention she could get. You'd think she was starved for love the way she carried on, but from the moment she took her first breath of air, she'd been coddled. Someone was always lugging her around. She wouldn't be worth two cents when she was older, if something didn't change.

Lara let out a chuckle, remembering how Gracie had looked with Houston's bandana tied around her nose when he brought her back. She'd sat so straight in front of him on the horse. So serious. Just like a little outlaw.

And Houston's big grin, the kind that made the lines at the corners of his eyes fan out, had made her wonder which of them had the best time.

With her eyes on her husband, Lara saw the group of Cherokees enter her line of vision. Houston went to greet them. She stirred the potatoes one last time and set them off the fire.

Wiping her hands on her apron, she moved to Houston's side. "Welcome. I'm glad you came to join us," she said.

Houston put his arm around her. "Meet my wife, Lara. She makes very good food." When he rubbed his belly and rolled his eyes, they laughed and nodded. Her husband, the comedian. But then, he'd put them at ease. Hunger was a universal language, understood by all.

Though they gave her curious stares, they didn't move toward her. She shrank back a little, thinking they took in her scar as did everyone she met. One man, evidently the spokesman, stepped forward. "We come."

"Welcome. We're honored." Houston waved his arm toward the food. "Eat."

She stood aside as everyone filled tin plates and sat down. No one, not cowboy or Indian, spoke much. Maybe they didn't know what to say to each other. She filled her plate and joined them, Houston making room for her on his blanket. Gracie sat inside the circle of his arms, gnawing on a piece of bread.

"You have a big heart, Houston Legend," Lara murmured beside him.

"Shhh!" He winked. "Keep that quiet. I wouldn't want it to get out."

She noticed his gaze scanning the group as though searching for someone. "Who are you looking for?"

"A Cherokee woman I met today. I wanted to talk to her."

"You don't see her among them?"

"Nope." He forked a bite of steak into his mouth. "You outdid yourself tonight, Lara. This is delicious."

"I'm glad you think so. My resources were pretty limited but I wanted something a little more festive than our normal fare." Lara put a bite of potatoes into Gracie's mouth and watched her brother, Henry, taking a plate of meat around, asking if anyone wanted seconds. "What did you want to speak to the Indian woman about, if you don't mind my asking?"

"Oh, nothing really. She said our daughter was blessed."

While Houston's explanation was plausible, Lara caught him glancing into the darkness as if expecting to see something beyond the black shadows. He wasn't telling the whole truth. Cold fear gripped her.

Houston was keeping something secret.

Thirteen

SOUNDS OF THE NIGHT SETTLED AROUND LARA AS SHE cleaned the dishes and readied things for morning. Cattle lowed, drovers on watch sang soft tunes, and farther in the distance she heard the lonely howl of a coyote. It would appear peaceful, if not for the unease strangling her like a gloved hand.

The gloved hand of Yuma. A shiver passed through her. She knew what that felt like. His grip had tightened around her throat, squeezing, blocking off her air, silencing the screams.

An arm came around her and she let out a yell, whirling with a raised fist, dripping soapy water.

Houston blocked the blow. "Lara, it's just me."

"You scared me. I thought—"

"I'm sorry. I didn't mean to frighten you." He pulled her close, wrapping his arms around her. "You're trembling. I'll never do that again. If I bend over, will you kick me in the rear? I deserve it."

She clutched his vest. "No. I was locked in a nightmare and didn't hear you come up. It's my fault."

He held her until she stopped trembling, rubbing her back. She'd never seen a gentler, more caring man.

"I'm so ashamed," she whispered.

Confusion rippled in his eyes. "Of what?"

"All of it."

"No, darlin', you have no need for that. You've done nothing wrong. Exchange the shame for anger. Get good and mad and wallop the daylights out of me, out of something. I guarantee you'll feel a lot better."

"I hit you."

"Yeah, but you didn't mean it." He let a hint of a smile flicker across his face before he turned solemn again. She wished he'd smile more often. He was a handsome man, this tall Texan she'd married. "I'm glad you have fight left in you. Before this is over, you may need it."

She searched his eyes. "Houston, it's time to spill what you're keeping from me. What's wrong? I have to know."

"Darlin', it's little more than a gut feeling right now. I need you to trust me. Two days ago, I noticed some men trailing us. Don't know who they are or what they're after, but they'll have to kill me to get to you or Gracie." He brushed back a tendril of hair and kissed her forehead. "I'm on watch and so are the men. You're in good hands."

The thought that he might give his life for her brought a tightening to her chest. Lara swallowed hard and nodded. "I do trust you, Houston. More than any man I've ever known, except my father. You have honor and courage and goodness. I know without a doubt you'd die before you let anyone hurt me or Gracie."

"I'm glad you can see it, because I would." Houston brushed her lips in a light kiss. "Nothing means more to me than your safety."

"One day I'll be the kind of wife you need. I just can't do it now. Please forgive me." A sob caught in her throat.

"Nothing to forgive. Not one damn thing." His voice was husky.

"Kiss me, Houston. Drive away the shadows that press close."

Without a word, he placed his hands on each side of her face and brought her lips to his. The kiss soothed the ragged edges of her soul and allowed peace to settle around her.

Lara prayed that if a bullet ever ended Houston's life, she'd die also.

He was the answer to a dream she hadn't even known she'd had. Their marriage meant a lot more than giving Gracie his name, and if he should choose to walk away and end it, Lara would know total devastation.

In the short time she'd been his wife, she'd known deep peace and contentment.

Why then hadn't she told him?

And why did she withhold her heart from him?

∽

Houston stood in the darkness, holding the carved red wolf the Indian woman had given Gracie. He'd taken it from the child before returning to camp, because she wouldn't keep it out of her mouth. Everything she got went right into her mouth. But he was glad he'd tucked it out of sight. He didn't want to frighten Lara more than she was.

Why did Gracie need protecting? Who would harm such a sweet child? So many questions, and answers to none.

Cloaked in the night shadows, Houston let his gaze follow Lara as she finished the last of her chores before crawling into her bed.

This wife of his moved with grace and ease. He loved watching her work. No movement was wasted. Her beautiful long fingers worked with efficiency. The last few days he'd had such a longing for her to touch his face, smooth his hair, undo the buttons on his shirt.

Confusion swirled inside like a storm of some kind. He couldn't seem to remember his vow to never let any woman in his heart. But how could he trust himself to know that what he felt was right? What he'd known of love had been false. He hadn't known anything about anything before. Maybe he was just as thick-skulled now.

But he was sure of two things. When Lara was near, he

just wanted her closer. And she was nothing like Becky. He found deep peace and contentment in Lara's gentle ways.

But, again he didn't understand why she'd spoken of leaving. Had she meant it as a warning?

The lady didn't know the hole she'd leave behind. Still, if she wanted out, he'd release her no matter the devastation it would bring.

Houston pinched the bridge of his nose and turned his attention to the band of Cherokees and his disappointment that he hadn't been able to speak to the old woman again.

Her warning suddenly sprang up, circling in his head. *They come. Evil.*

What in the *hell* had she meant?

She'd warned him, and then she'd just vanished. When he'd had Clay ask one of the others in the group why she hadn't come with them, the man said she was doing her work, whatever the hell that meant.

For God's sake, he needed more from her!

With one last look at Lara, he tucked the carved wolf into his shirt and turned to his horse. He had to find his head drover. He'd be gone only long enough to relay orders.

Clay glanced up as Houston rode to him. "Hey, boss." Clay tucked his small bag of Bull Durham into his pocket and reached for a match. "You look worried."

"I am." He told Clay what the Indian woman had said. "I don't know what the devil she meant and she didn't come with the others. I need to know what the men following us want."

"Who the hell knows? Maybe the Cherokee woman was just spouting some stuff." Clay lit his cigarette and blew smoke rings into the air. "One thing for damn sure...if those trailing bastards want blood, we'll give 'em so much this land will run red with it." He took another drag on the cigarette. The lit end burned crimson, showing the hard lines of his face. "If they think they're gonna hurt Gracie or her mama, they'd better bring a damn army. I'll fill those bastards so full of holes their own mama won't know 'em."

"For damn sure," Houston growled. "But I rode out here to ask you to spread the word among the men. And to say that I won't take a shift guarding the herd. You're in charge of arranging guard duty. I'll be protecting Lara and Gracie."

"Goes without sayin'. I'd do the same. Miss Lara is sure a mighty fine woman and she's been through pure hell, faced more pain an' misery than the lot of us. An' that little one is a heart-stealer." The top man took another drag on the cigarette. "Leave this part out here to me. You concentrate on them."

The seasoned cowboy's staunch words brought a lump to Houston's throat. He couldn't buy loyalty like that.

With only a nod, Houston rode back to camp to find that Lara had already set the wagon tongue pointing north and gone to bed. Deep disappointment burrowed into his chest. He walked quietly to the edge of her blanket and sat down. Gracie turned over in her crib, gave a whimper, and went back to sleep. Houston tugged the collar of his jacket up around his neck.

No one would get them. He'd stomp evil all the way back to the gates of hell.

One by one, he watched the drovers ride up and fall onto their bedrolls with the change of each shift. As some came, others left. Clay was doing a heck of a job. He'd make sure to add a bonus to his pay at the end of the trail.

About midnight, he crawled under the chuck wagon and lay close to Lara. Shutting his eyes to soak up the feel, he caressed the fabric of her skirt peeking from the blanket. She slept so near but an ocean away. Finally, he withdrew his hand and put his Colt between them within easy reach.

Her breathing was as soft as a whisper. The fragrance of the soil drifted around him. She reminded him of the earth. Lara was a bit ragged, and though the winds shifted the sands, she stayed rooted. Like the earth, she provided all the necessary elements that made things grow and thrive and be everything they could be, people included.

He tried to force himself to relax but found that he couldn't until he rested his fingers on the edge of the blanket that covered her curves. A strong yearning rose for the day when he could draw her slender body against him without panic filling her eyes. A day when she could trust.

"Sleep well, my beautiful lady." He barely breathed the words that ached to be said. "I'll never leave you."

At the sudden rustle of brush that the cattle had beaten down, he raised his head to listen, reaching for his Colt.

Someone tiptoed, doing his best to avoid detection.

Houston scanned the small area he could see, searching for a pair of boots. The person moved closer and paused.

He silently cursed the fact that he was trapped under the wagon. He glanced around. He had to hurry. Only one thing to do, but would he have time?

A pair of worn boots moved to Gracie's crib. With fear blocking his air, Houston quietly inched out the other side and stole around. Darkness hid the intruder's features and he couldn't tell much other than he wore a gun in a low-slung holster. The man touched Gracie's blanket and that aroused Houston's fury.

With a growl, Houston stuck the barrel of his Colt between the man's shoulder blades. "Raise your hands real slow, mister."

The man stiffened. "Houston, that you?"

"Yep." Houston turned him around. The moon shone on Virgil's face. "What are you doing sneaking around? I could've shot your fool head off."

Lara peeked from under the wagon. "What's going on?"

Dandy, just dandy! Houston shoved his Colt into the holster. "Go back to sleep, darlin'. Didn't mean to wake you."

Now why in hell had he called her that? He hadn't meant to. Or had he? It came natural.

With a yawn, she lay back down. Houston and Virgil moved to the low campfire. Houston tossed another stick of wood onto it and watched the fire flame up.

Virgil spoke first. "I was only checking on Gracie. Heard

about the warning. Figured you'd be close by, but still wanted to see for myself if they were all right."

Houston shoved a hand through his hair, wondering about these Boones, and let out a measured breath. "I told you their safety is my priority. You can trust me just a little."

"I didn't take Yuma seriously enough and look what that got us," Lara's oldest brother snapped.

"There's a damn sight of difference between me and Yuma." Houston glared. "I give my word, I keep it. I said I'll protect them and protect them I will."

"Sorry," Virgil murmured. "Old habits die hard."

"So they do, son. So they do." Houston's anger faded.

He wanted to say that the biggest reason for his anger was how close he'd come to killing the young man. Houston's finger had been on the trigger and he was about to draw back. One more moment and they'd be burying Virgil. Then Lara sure wouldn't have anything to do with the man with whom she'd cast her lot. That's what made him mad enough to swallow a horned toad backward.

"Get some sleep, Virgil. Be morning soon." Houston pushed aside the anger and squeezed his shoulder. "I'll be on watch."

"Thanks," Virgil murmured and stumbled toward his bed.

Houston moved back to the wagon but stayed by Gracie's crib. That's what being a man was. Sacrifice and diligence.

❧

Lara rose before dawn to find Houston sitting on the ground beside Gracie's crib, with his gun in his hand.

"Morning, Houston. What on earth are you doing?"

He ignored her question and rose, putting his gun away then stretched the kinks out of his tall frame. "Did you sleep well?"

"For the most part." She wanted to ask why he'd felt the need to stand guard over her and Gracie last night, and not over any of the others, but she knew it would be a wasted effort. He wasn't ready to talk about whatever was gnawing a hole in his gut.

She watched him light her lantern. One thing a blind woman could see…he was plenty worried about something.

For some reason he'd thought the men trailing them might come into camp. And do what? Fear inched up her spine like a creepy-crawly. She could feel its hundreds of tiny legs and the fine hairs brushing her bones.

Don't be silly. Maybe the riders were only after the cattle, looking to make some quick money. Unease settled over her. To get the herd, they'd have to kill men. Houston. Her brothers. Everything came with a price. How many graves would they have to dig? Only…Houston hadn't been out with the longhorns. He'd been here. With her. She fought the implication.

"You'd tell me if there was reason to worry. Wouldn't you?" she asked, lifting her apron.

He sauntered over and laid his large hands on her shoulders. Lowering his head, he kissed her cheek. "The very second I know, I'll tell you to put your worrying cap on. But that isn't today. Can I help you get breakfast started?"

Henry stumbled to the fire, rubbing his eyes. "I'm the helper, not you."

"Sorry, Bones." Houston shot him a grin. "I'll keep my hands off. Don't want to get my eye blacked."

"Good." Henry got a pail and trudged after water at a nearby spring.

"What's wrong with Henry?"

"He hates being confined to helping his sister." She let out a sigh. "He wants to be there with you men, working with the cattle. Says this is woman's work."

"I'll see what I can do after breakfast. Maybe give him a small job. Just promise you won't breathe a word to your father—I sure don't want to get on his bad side."

"I promise. Thank you, Houston." She turned back to dipping out flour for biscuits when she noticed an Indian woman and a child standing at Gracie's crib. She hadn't seen her at supper last night. "Good morning," she called. "Can I help you?"

The woman, somewhere in her middle years, came near. Two long braids hung down the front of her dress, and her calm, passive face gave no clue to her thoughts.

Wearing relief on his face, Houston stepped in front of Lara. "I was hoping you'd come. You're welcome to eat breakfast with us in a bit."

The Cherokee thrust out a small deerskin bag. Lara peered around Houston at the bag he opened and saw some kind of gooey salve inside. The woman muttered a few words in her tongue before reaching into the bag and drawing out the salve with her fingers. Then she proceeded to rub it onto her face. She pointed to Lara's scar and held up two fingers.

What on earth did she mean? Frustration wound through Lara that she couldn't speak Cherokee. She ran to the wagon and rummaged around for a little rag doll she'd made Gracie. She returned and handed it to the little Cherokee girl, along with a smile. The child's face lit up as she shyly clutched the toy to her.

Houston swung to Lara. "Darlin', she's telling you to put this salve on your scar."

"What a sweet gift." Lara reached for the woman's thin hands only to find a frown etched on the woman's face. Lara guessed she shouldn't touch her and let her hand drop. "Thank you. But I don't have anything for you." Lara relaxed to see Clay riding into camp. He could speak the language, she remembered.

Houston called him over. "Ask what this salve is made from and why she brought it."

After several moments of talking in Cherokee, Clay turned. "Ma'am, she says this is a gift for you to repay us for the two beeves we let them have. Best I can tell it's made from cactus, aloe vera, and oil from the marigold plant."

"What a thoughtful gift," Lara said, deeply touched. "Please thank her."

The woman spoke again and Clay translated. "You're

supposed to put it on your scar every morning and night. She says it'll help it fade."

Lara moved around her mountain of a husband and smiled. "I will do that."

Houston turned to Clay. "She can speak limited English but not enough for what I want. Ask her what she meant yesterday about the men following us."

After doing as Houston bid him, Clay said, "There are four riders—which we know—but she said they raided some Cherokee encampments, killing and burning."

Cold fear swept over Lara. She clutched Houston's arm. "What does this mean to us?"

"Not sure yet." He turned to Clay. "Find out why she came again with the warning." ·

For a minute, the two spoke in the strange tongue, then Clay's face hardened. "She said she had a vision while the others were here eating with us. These men want to kill them and us too. She saw the color blue in the flames and said it spelled trouble and defeat. Gracie's blue eyes drew her yesterday, and the medicine woman knew she had to offer the talisman to protect the child as she protects her own granddaughter."

A talisman? This was the first she'd heard of it. Had she given Gracie a symbol of some kind? Why hadn't Houston mentioned it?

"Evil!" The woman suddenly spat in English. "Keep safe."

Lara watched fury fill Houston's eyes and heard his low oath. Something told her this was what worried him deep down into the marrow of his bones. But was this all? Or did he hide many other things as well? The cold that had invaded her turned to ice.

How could she trust him when he kept secrets from her?

Fourteen

HOUSTON STARED AFTER THE MEDICINE WOMAN AND CHILD as they disappeared from sight after delivering one last message—that others would join the evil men and they'd make war. Well, they'd find him waiting. If a fight was what they wanted, that's what he'd give the murdering bastards.

Lara grabbed Houston so hard he winced. "She was concerned about Gracie. Exactly what kind of talisman did the old woman give her? And why didn't you tell me yesterday?" In her frantic need to know, her voice had risen shrilly.

In the face of Lara's panic, he knew he had no choice. "Come. We need to talk."

Once he'd seated her on a barrel, he took out the carved wolf and handed it to Lara. She stared at the red, carved wood. "This is supposed to ward off trouble," he said. "Hell, I don't know if it works but we won't lose anything by trying it."

"That explains why you stood guard over us all night." She turned the charm over. "Please don't keep things from me. Not even when you're trying to protect me."

Houston wiped his weary eyes. "I don't want you to fret. Let me do the worrying—I'm real good at that. You have your hands full taking care of Gracie."

"Promise to tell me if you see those men following today." She grabbed his hands. "Promise me."

"All right." But he knew he wouldn't. What good would it do to feed her fear more? Not a God-blessed thing.

Clay filled a tin cup with coffee and walked off a little ways. Houston saw him staring toward the south, looking for the riders. Darkness hadn't yet given way to the dawn, so the effort was useless.

Lara went back to her breakfast chores and Houston got up and filled his cup with the hot brew. He wandered down to join Clay. "I've made up my mind."

"What about, boss?" Clay looked fierce in the blackness, with that eye patch peeking from under the brim of his hat.

"I'm going to backtrack while you push the cattle forward. I'm going to see exactly who's behind us."

Clay met his eyes. "Need company?"

"Not yet. I think we should keep everything as normal as possible. I'm just going to look, not take any action." Houston paused then ground out, "Unless they force my hand."

His gaze lit on Henry as he cracked prairie chicken eggs, and he changed the subject. "Clay, I want you to find some small job for Henry when we leave here. Something that he won't get hurt doing. I told Lara I would." Houston didn't like the frustration in the boy's eyes. "Maybe he can help with the remuda. Just don't let him do anything dangerous."

"Be glad to. He's a good kid." Clay finished his coffee and poured the dregs onto the ground. "Better get this day started. Good luck. If I hear gunshots I'll come runnin'."

"Thanks." Houston noticed Gracie wiggling around in her crib, Lara too busy to see to her. He set his coffee on the pull-down table of the chuck wagon. When he reached Gracie, she gave him that toothless grin that made his heart lurch. "Hey, Angel, how are you this fine morn?"

Houston picked her up and gave her a kiss. As usual, she was wet, so he grabbed the small blanket that was in the crib and wrapped it around her. She snuggled against him as though he were a soft pillow. It astounded him that she hardly ever cried. True, he had limited experience with babies, but he'd never seen one so pleasant. Not even when wet or hungry did she raise much of a fuss. A strange wish rose inside that he'd been her real father, heard her first cry, witnessed the first time she sat up, crawled, or smiled.

But he hadn't and the missed milestones were all in the past, witnessed by her mother alone. He took heart in the fact that he'd be there for all the others. That would have to be enough.

Henry rang the cowbell and cowboys who weren't already by the fire came running. Each had a word for Gracie, a tip of the hat and a smile for Lara, before filling their plates.

Houston looked them over. He had a good crew. Without them saying so, he knew they'd stand and fight to protect his family, each other, and the herd. Not one, young or old, would run when trouble came. They rode for the brand and would give their lives if need be.

God, he prayed he wouldn't have to ask that of them.

Gracie seemed to sense his dark mood, for when she glanced up again there was no silly grin. Her blue eyes held solemn weight and she patted his leather vest with her little hand.

Houston pulled her up. "Okay now, none of that. You need to be happy and let me do the worrying."

His daughter jabbered something and pointed in the direction they'd come. He wished he knew what she was saying, what went through that head of hers.

"It's a sad day when a baby gives the orders around here," Virgil said, grinning. Eggs, potatoes, salt pork, biscuits, and gravy loaded his plate to the brim. A mess of hot peppers sat on top of it all. The kid must have an iron stomach.

"Sometimes I think you're right," Houston agreed. "Her gibberish makes a whole lot more sense than I do most days."

Clay laughed. "Maybe you can try that next, boss."

Quaid Boone walked by. "We're used to her laying down the law to us."

Houston flashed him a grin. Hard work must be good for

him. The young man had slimmed down some, he believed. Not that the size of his heaped plate was any indication of trying. Despite his light-brown hair, Quaid bore a remarkable resemblance to his sister. Both had expressive eyes and a determined chin. Virgil took more after his pa, with his quiet determination and steely stare. The brothers still had some growing to do, but Houston could see the makings of fine men.

Lara came forward. "I'll take her now. You need to eat."

The slight breeze lifted a tendril of red and laid it across her eyes. Houston longed to brush the hair back, but wouldn't with all eyes on them. She didn't want to be a spectacle. That's all that kept him from it, though.

"I'm sure the little angel's hungry." Their hands brushed as he transferred the babe. A slow fire burning inside tried to flame high. "I'll bring a seat for you behind the wagon."

At her nod, he grabbed a barrel and rolled it around out of sight.

"Thank you, Houston." Lara touched his arm. "I won't take long. I know you'll want to get the cattle moving soon."

"Take your time," he said gently.

"I don't want to hold up anyone."

"You should know by now that everyone respects yours and Gracie's needs. The rest can go ahead anytime. I'll stay and help if you need it." Houston breathed the air that was laden with the fragrance of sage…and hope.

Reality slammed into him like a two-by-four. He wanted this woman.

Not only wanted, he *needed* her.

"All right. But first I need to change her."

He left Lara replacing the soaked diaper with a dry one and went to fill his belly.

Raising his gaze to the blue sky overhead, he paused, praying he could find out who followed them before dark and wishing Dodge City was over the next hill.

❧

Every nerve stretched taut, Houston lay in clumps of sagebrush and wild grasses, listening, waiting, barely breathing.

Several hours into the day and the sun had heated up, promising to be a scorcher by noon. Sweat trickled into his eyes, making them sting. Raising a hand, he brushed it away in an effort to keep his vision clear.

In front of him, partially hidden by juniper, cholla cacti, and rock, sat the riders' camp. So far nothing had moved in the ten minutes he'd been here. He finally decided no one would double back and rose. The cold fire told him they'd long gone. Empty tin cans, burned up cigarettes, and other trash lay among the leavings. It could've been a hundred campsites left by countless travelers, though none as careless as these.

He knew the men who meant to kill them had slept there. He *smelled* their evil. Strange that he hadn't seen them during the ride out. Where had they disappeared to? Or had he ridden right past them without knowing it?

A scrap of paper, held down by a rock, fluttered. He picked it up.

> *Waiting ahead. Hurry. Gotta job.*

The instructions had to be meant for others coming to join the four bushwhackers. No doubt the job referred to stealing the herd. But was that all? The Cherokee woman predicted there'd be more.

Who were these men, dammit? But he saw nothing to indicate a name.

He'd give anything to have Sam and Luke with him. When these reinforcements arrived, who knew how large a force they'd have to face.

He laid the note into the cold ashes, took out a match, and watched the paper flame. After making sure not one word remained, he gathered some good-sized rocks. He arranged them into an arrow that pointed in the wrong direction. "That should buy some time," he muttered to himself.

Standing, he dusted off his hands and strode to the Appaloosa. It made him nervous that he'd missed the riders. He mounted up and set out at a gallop. Something told him not to dawdle. When a snake was on the loose, you moved fast before it could strike.

The horse ate up two miles in nothing flat. Up ahead, the chuck wagon had stopped. What was going on? Why wasn't she moving?

And where were the others?

A bloodcurdling scream rent the air, chilling his bones.

Fifteen

HOUSTON LEAPED OFF THE HORSE BEFORE IT COULD SLOW. "Lara!"

He reached for his Colt when he saw her standing alone where the team of horses should have been. She held Gracie in her arms, but her heartrending sobs tore into him.

"What is it, Lara? Please, God, tell me what happened."

She handed him a thin cigarette paper. "He was here!"

"Who?"

"Read this."

He glanced down at the words:

I could've killed the brat. Next time I will.

Deadly quiet settled over him. When he spoke, the words were harsh and raspy in his ears. "Where did you find this?"

"Lying next to Gracie. It's him, Houston."

"Yuma? Did you see him?"

"No, Henry did." Her voice was cold and full of fear.

He glanced around. "Where is Henry?"

"Hiding inside the wagon. Yuma terrified him."

And her too. Houston put his arm around Lara's trembling body. "You're safe. I'm here. I told you I wouldn't be long. I'm not going to let Yuma have you or Gracie."

Gracie whimpered and looked at him with wide eyes. She might not know what to be afraid of, but she knew fear. He kissed her, then wiped away Lara's tears. He kicked himself all the way to the Rio Grande and back. He should've been here.

Why the hell had he left?

But she had been with the others when he rode out—he'd made sure of it. The wagon was rolling alongside the cattle, but now there was no sign of the longhorns.

"I need to find Henry, and then I want you to tell me everything."

At her nod, Houston climbed up into the wagon box and glanced inside the interior where they kept all the supplies. "Henry, it's me. You can come out now. No one can hurt you."

The fourteen-year-old poked his head from between sacks of meal, flour, and sugar. Tears streamed down his face.

"Can you come out and talk to me?" Houston quietly asked.

The boy shook so hard he could barely crawl over the wagon seat. Houston helped him to the ground.

"Is he gone?" Henry asked, looking around.

"Yes, he's gone. Did you see him?"

"I was afraid. I hid," Henry said, his voice full of raw emotion and shame. "I didn't save the baby. He took her."

"No, Henry. Lara's got Gracie. See?" Houston led him around to prove he spoke the truth. When Henry saw Lara, he stumbled to her, saying over and over how sorry he was for being a coward.

It took Houston several minutes to get everyone settled down. "Now, tell me everything and don't spare one detail."

"I was with the herd, exactly as you told me," Lara began slowly. "We crossed that small creek back there and I stopped to refill the water kegs because they were low. Quaid and Virgil were with me."

"Good. That's what I told them to do."

"We heard gunshots and I told my brothers to go see

what was happening. Henry and I finished up and got going again, but the harnesses snapped on the horses and they ran off. I only saw afterward where they'd been cut. Yuma must have done it. I walked a little ways, trying to find the horses, and left Henry with the baby."

With effort, Henry gathered himself. "I sat Gracie on a blanket. I started to go help. The baby cried." He began shaking.

"That's okay, Henry. What happened next?" Houston gently prodded.

"I saw him."

"Yuma Blackstone?"

"He was holding Gracie. I'm sorry. I'm sorry." Henry began rocking back and forth, his tears leaving tracks in the dirt on his face. "I'm sorry."

Houston put an arm around the boy's neck and pulled Henry to him. "It's all right, son. You didn't do anything wrong. No one blames you. You love that little girl."

"I was scared."

"I know, but you don't have to be scared now," Houston said.

Lara put her arms around Henry. "I don't blame you, little brother. I love you."

Henry pulled back and cried, "No. I'm a coward."

Clearly no one could reason with him in his distraught state, but Houston needed answers. He took a deep breath. Maybe getting him back to the story would help. "Tell me what happened next, Henry. Can you do that? I need to know so I can keep Yuma from coming back. When you saw him holding Gracie, what did he do?"

"I yelled."

Houston strove for patience with the boy. "And then what?"

"He put that paper on Gracie and dropped her. She cried. He laughed and called me stupid. Said I was a dummy. Pointed his gun."

A muscle worked in Houston's jaw. Blackstone was awfully brave when faced with a mere boy. Let him face a grown man. Then they'd see how much guts he had. The urge to put a bullet between his eyes burned hotter than the fires of Hades.

Without a doubt, Blackstone was the evil that the Cherokee woman had said followed them. Although it was pure conjecture, Blackstone and his men must've raided the Indian camps.

Houston forced himself back to the present. "Then after you ran and hid, he rode away?"

Henry sniffled and nodded.

"Were other men with him?"

"Nope." Henry turned and trudged away, probably back to his safe hiding place.

The others must've created a diversion to draw Virgil and Quaid away while Yuma went after Gracie and Lara. Only Lara had left by the time he arrived. But what if she'd been there when he came? What would Yuma have done to her? Would he have killed her this time? Cold fear spread through Houston.

Hell and be damned!

He was thinking about the wisdom of leaving the chuck wagon to look for the horses, when Virgil and Quaid galloped up. He quickly told them about Yuma and the cut harnesses.

"We'll find the team," Virgil said, wasting few words.

"What were the gunshots Lara and Henry heard?" Houston asked, praying that no one had been hurt.

Quaid wiped sweat from his forehead. "Three riders came out of nowhere and took two horses from the remuda. We shot at 'em but they got away. Now we know why they attacked us." He paused before adding, "I wish we'd have killed 'em!"

"Yep." Virgil spat on the ground as though he had a bad taste in his mouth.

"We will." Before this was over, Houston would see them all dead. Only now he knew more were on the way, and how many was anyone's guess. "Go round up the horses so we can get Lara moving. From now on, no one leaves her. We've got to stick closer together."

"Yep," Quaid echoed his brother and both mounted up.

As they rode off, Lara grabbed Houston. "Our baby isn't safe. Please help me stop Yuma from getting her."

"I'll see to it that he won't harm Gracie. I'll keep you both safe. I promise."

But could he keep that vow? Fear of how easily Yuma could've succeeded if he'd wanted put chunks of ice in Houston's veins.

"Did I cause this because I didn't have the talisman on Gracie that the Cherokee gave you?" Lara's voice was but a whisper, as though speaking too loudly would draw back the evil.

He'd asked himself the same question. Living a stone's throw from Indian Territory, he knew a lot about the culture, and though not specifically, the importance of their symbols and charms. The woman had given it to them to protect Gracie, so it seemed to him they needed to somehow put it on her...for now.

Until he could chop off the head of the snake and feed the sick bastard's carcass to the buzzards.

Even now, Blackstone could be watching from a hiding place in the huge rocks five hundred yards away. Houston scanned the area but nothing moved.

"You're not to blame, Lara. Who's to say if it would've made a difference?" He wrapped his arms around her and their child. Gracie squirmed between them and he realized he held her too snugly. Yet it felt as though he didn't hold her and Lara tightly enough.

He wanted to draw them inside him where no one could get to them. But that wasn't possible. "We're going to get through this, Lara."

"How did he find me? How?"

Good question with only one answer. "He had to have been watching you for a while. When you came on this cattle drive, he saw his opportunity."

"But Papa and my brothers searched for him high and low after that night. If he was near, they'd have found him."

"He's slippery, Lara. But one day his luck will run out."

Lara's pretty green eyes stared up at him. Her gaze was full of torment. "I know why he wants to kill me. But why Gracie? She's his own flesh and blood. She's innocent."

"Yes, but she represents what he did. He can lie to himself about the whole thing but Gracie is living proof of his evil deed," Houston said quietly.

As though sensing they talked about her, Gracie began to wail.

Lara stepped out of his arms to comfort her, while Houston watched helplessly. He bit back a curse and shot a glare toward the rocks. One minute with the man who'd caused it. That's all he asked. But the boulders stared back in silence.

Why in hell hadn't he left them safe on the Lone Star?

Calling himself every name he could think of, Houston stalked to his horse and lifted the flap of a saddlebag. He took out the extra pistol and walked back to Lara. "Keep this with you at all times. If Yuma catches you alone again, shoot him."

Lara stared at the gun. "I hate these things. They hold such destructive power."

"They're supposed to. I need to know you have some way of defending yourself."

"But—"

Houston brushed her cheek with a finger. "Humor me on this."

"All right." She stuck it into a pocket in the fold of her dress.

Gracie set up a new round of wailing, and while Lara comforted the babe, he moved toward the wagon.

For an hour, Houston worked fixing the harnesses. Step by step, he taught Henry. The boy's quickness in picking up the technique surprised him. Henry struggled to saddle a horse, but yet found the harness repair easy to master.

Houston made a mental note—there were always things to be fixed, and a man on the trail never knew when he'd need to repair something. Henry could easily be given more duties of this nature.

They had just finished up when Virgil and Quaid returned with the runaway team, and it took no time to get moving. Houston let Henry ride the Appaloosa while he drove the chuck wagon. He wasn't going to let Lara and Gracie out of his sight again.

As they rolled slowly along over the cattle-trampled earth, Houston slipped an arm around Lara and she seemed to move closer to him. Although he might've imagined that last part. No words needed to be said.

Sixteen

"WHERE DO YOU WANT TO START, BOSS?" CLAY ASKED AFTER bedding the cattle down for the night. He ground out his cigarette with the heel of his worn boot. "Let's find the rotten bastards and kill 'em."

Houston had told Clay about Yuma's notes and the possible reinforcements, and watched his face harden. Clay was like a pool of still water—at first glance you couldn't tell how deep it went. Over the last few months, Houston had found that Clay's resolve went all the way to his bones.

Virgil and Quaid squatted on their heels in this meeting. Every so often they'd cuss a blue streak, but mostly they listened.

"Gotta find them first," Houston reminded Clay. "They're cunning, and that makes them all the more dangerous. For now, keep pushing the herd hard toward Dodge. Make sure the men remain on guard and we'll all watch out for Lara and the baby."

"I never was too happy with her being at the back of the herd. To escape the dust, sometimes that wagon fell back quite a ways." Clay swatted at a fly buzzing around his head.

"Something we've got to fix," Houston admitted, tugging his hat down on his forehead and pulling on his gloves. He glanced toward the chuck wagon where Lara prepared supper. She seemed to have regained her strong spirit, but he knew she was still worried. "From now on, the chuck wagon travels alongside us. If Lara needs more time, we'll slow. Or stop altogether."

"Damn right." Clay turned to his horse and swung into the saddle. "Anytime you want to backtrack, holler at me. There's nothing I'd like more."

Virgil stood. "Count me in."

"And me," Quaid said. "We're both a fair hand with a gun."

Houston met their gaze. "Have either of you ever shot a man? It's a lot different shooting something that can shoot back."

"I winged Yuma the night he…did what he did." Virgil's face reflected his hate. "I'd have no trouble putting a bullet between his eyes. Or anyone else's who threatened my family. Some things a man's gotta do if he wants to be a man."

Quaid nodded. "And this is one of 'em."

"I'll give you both the second shift," Clay said as his gelding danced, anxious to be off. "If you hear or see anything strange, fire a shot and we'll come running."

"We will," Virgil assured him.

Houston watched Clay Angelo ride toward the milling longhorns, and the Boone twins hurry to help with Gracie. He'd never seen such close-knit brothers, or ones so committed to their family. When the bullets started flying, they'd be in the thick of things.

After a long sigh, Houston murmured into the wind, "Just try not to get killed. Till Boone will whip me all the way to kingdom come and back."

Damn, if only Dodge was closer.

A last glance showed Gracie in Virgil's arms, with a group of hardened drovers crowding around. They acted downright silly in an effort to elicit one toothless, slobbery grin. Satisfied the child was cared for, Houston mounted up. He'd have time to inspect the area before supper.

He pulled his Colt from the holster, flipped open the cylinder, and twirled it to make sure a bullet filled every chamber. A muscle in his jaw quivered. Reassured, he replaced the gun, and with a light touch of his spurs, the Appaloosa moved out.

After a sweep of the rocky ravines, windswept canyons, and thick brush that offered the most likely hiding places, he turned back. He'd long heard the clang of the bell calling everyone to dinner and knew they'd likely be finished eating. Guilt rose that he kept Lara from finding her bed, so he set the horse into a gallop.

Though Lara rose hours before everyone else and got to sleep late, she never complained. She wasn't afraid of hard work, and proved it every single day.

Pride filled Houston, but it wasn't just that. When they kissed and touched, his stomach did this funny little thing. And when she came into his arms and looked up at him with those big green eyes, he wanted to draw her inside and hold her there where trouble couldn't find her.

What he felt was a little like it had been with Becky Golden, except this went far deeper. Down into his heart and soul.

Lara made him feel all man, a man who knew what he had and was desperate to keep it.

But mostly, she made him realize he wanted her, hungered to touch her skin, to know her deepest thoughts. At odd moments of the day, he found himself thinking about making love, and no matter where he was, his gaze always searched for her.

For a moment he let Becky drift across his mind. Had they married, she wouldn't be here on this drive. She craved comfort. And if she had by chance come, she'd complain about the dust, the heat, the smell—sleeping on the hard ground.

Funny, now that he let himself recall her, he remembered how nothing was ever quite right. Becky had complained about everything. And when they'd talked, the conversation was all about inconsequential things.

Why hadn't he noticed? He was such a fool.

A sudden thought jolted through him. The excuse

Becky had given Newman for not running away with him or marrying was her parents. She'd flat lied. Mr. and Mrs. Golden built their lives around making Becky happy. Whatever she wanted, she got. They would never have kept her from making a life with Newman—especially since she was with child.

Becky hadn't married Newman for the simple reason that he couldn't keep her in the manner to which she was accustomed. That right there explained why she was going to marry Houston. He could've given her the things she wanted. The materialistic woman never loved him—she'd used him for her own gain.

Houston inhaled the sage-scented air, glad he'd dodged a miserable life. Not that he was glad Newman had killed her. Not that at all. He'd never have wished that on her. But he couldn't have been happy with her—she was no Lara.

Lara. He couldn't wait to see her. She was worth twenty of anyone.

If only she wanted him for more than just his name. He'd give anything for her to see him for the man he was. Hope rose. Maybe one day.

As he came within sight of the campfire, he sat bathed in the darkness for a while. His gaze caught on her, held by her beauty and grace. Watching her, his heart did that little dip-and-whirl thing. She stirred around, setting the camp to rights and readying for bed, reminding him to hurry.

For a second, he forgot that she didn't love him and probably never would.

For a second, he could pretend that Lara welcomed him with open arms.

And for a second, hope rose that she'd find a place in her heart for him.

At the sound of him riding up, she turned and hurried to meet him almost before he swung from the saddle. The glistening in her eyes hadn't come from smoke and he realized he'd caused her tears. *Hell!*

"Houston, I was worried. I thought Yuma had…"

"Come here, darlin'." Houston gently pulled her close. "I'm sorry I caused you to fret. I never want to cause one second of worry in your pretty head."

Lara snuggled against him. He prayed that the moment would last forever.

"I saw you ride out and knew you'd gone to look for him." She smoothed his leather vest. "If you were to die—"

"I won't." Houston tightened his hold and pressed his lips to her temple. "Only one of us will need a grave and I can assure you that won't be me. I'm afraid you're stuck with me, lady." The last part came out husky, because the words had to squeeze through his constricted throat.

✑

Lara shifted in his arms so she could stare up into his eyes. She couldn't bear to hear him speak of dying. She needed Houston Legend. The thought shook her. He'd become so much more than just a stranger she'd married. He filled her with happiness and crowded out the face she'd tried hard to forget.

Oh God, if anything happened to him, she didn't know if she'd have the strength to go on.

And if he died because of her—she couldn't let that happen. She couldn't have his death on her hands. She had to keep him far away from Yuma Blackstone.

"I like being stuck with you." Lara clutched his vest. "I can't live knowing you died because of me. This may sound strange in light of everything, but what if we try to talk to him?"

"Men like Blackstone only listen to one thing—bullets." Houston lifted a tendril of hair. "Talking won't change the course Yuma's set. You know that."

"Can we just try before someone dies?"

"Some things a man can't let go. This is one. Lara, the time for taking the high road has passed," he said gently. "He's stalking you and Angel. Even if I could let it lie, can you?

After the threat he made today? I could kill him with my bare hands just for touching Gracie." He forced himself to swallow his anger. "I won't trust the bastard—not even for you."

He was right. They couldn't look the other way. As terrified and jumping at every noise as she was, she couldn't forgive the man who'd stolen so much from all of them. He would not get their lives too. She had to believe that Houston would come out on top when they came face-to-face. And she couldn't stop that from happening no matter what she did or said.

"Thank you," she whispered. "I needed the reminder. Gracie and Henry are lucky to be alive."

"And you." Houston brushed her cheek with his lips.

She let out a troubled sigh. "What are we going to do?"

"Fight." The word came out harder than he'd probably intended, but it summed up everything and tied a bow around it. "We fight. We hold our ground. We don't give an inch, not even when the white flag comes out. Not even when Yuma Blackstone cries for mercy, for there will be none."

"These drovers didn't ask for this," she cried.

"Neither did you or Gracie or Henry." He softened his tone and added, "I couldn't hold these men back, your brothers included, even if I tried. Shoot, Clay is fighting mad and wants to make the land run red with their blood. You're the wife he never had and Gracie *his* child. Down to a man, you're worth fighting for. You're family. Lady, the best of you isn't over. In reality, your life is only beginning."

His statement jarred her and she realized he spoke the truth. She'd finally begun to live and she wasn't about to let anyone steal that from her.

He kissed the tip of her nose and chuckled. "Besides all that, you're their cook and nobody messes with the lady who puts grub in their hungry bellies."

She smiled at his poor attempt to joke.

"They tip their hat and offer a grin before they take a plate but I never knew they thought of me that way," Lara said.

"Well, now you do."

When she tipped back her head, Houston placed his large hands along her jaw and pressed his lips to hers. Tingles raced up her spine as she lowered her eyes and drank like a desert wanderer drawn to water.

The instant their mouths touched, a wildfire spread through her, devouring her as it swept along. Overpowering hunger rose up in its wake, and for a moment, she didn't know if she could rein in this heated desire flooding over her.

Or if she even wanted to.

But another woman lived in Houston's heart, she reminded herself.

Trembling, Lara broke the kiss and pressed her face into the hollow of his throat. Maybe this was all they'd have—a few stolen moments in his arms. Moonlit kisses and heated touches would have to suffice.

His breathing was ragged. "I don't know what to call this thing between us," he murmured at her ear. "Maybe it will grow into something lasting. Lara, would you tell me what you want?"

If she could speak of this strange desire filling her, what would she call it? She had no idea, but prayed it was permanent. She couldn't do temporary.

"I want to make a life with you, Houston." Lara breathed in his scent, feeling safe in his arms even though trouble stalked them. The familiar lowing of the cattle, the horses nickering, and the cowboys' voices filled the night. She lost track of time as he held her close, not moving a muscle, barely breathing.

One thing was clear to her—they needed each other. Maybe this was what marriage meant. Being there in whatever way she could, giving of herself in whatever way he let her. And taking whatever he was willing to give.

"But you love another and I have no right to—"

"Wait right there," Houston said, stopping her. "Who do you think I love?"

"Becky Golden. Don't you?" She stared up in confusion. Was there someone else?

"We need to clear up some things." He took her hand. They walked to the firelight and the barrels they used for chairs and Lara sat down.

Surrounded by the crackle and pop of the fire, she listened as Houston spoke. "Becky and I grew up together, and we just kind of fell into an easy relationship. I think our parents might've pushed us into the idea of marriage more than anything. Looking back, I can see that she didn't share the love I thought I felt. I don't think I could ever have made her happy. After she was shot, I found out she was in the family way with another man's baby. I felt betrayed and angry, but then I came to see that we'd have been absolutely miserable together." He lifted a loose strand of hair and gave her a wry smile. "Truth is, I confused deep friendship with love. I was simply in love with the thought of having a wife and children—a home." He brushed her cheek with a finger. "I have everything I want and more."

Her heart ached for him. Becky had tried to destroy this good, decent man.

Another thought froze her. She'd done much the same thing to him. He was raising someone else's child. *Oh God, what had she done?*

"Houston, I didn't realize exactly what we asked of you. To raise Gracie, a babe that's not yours…" She put her hands to her mouth.

"Stop." Houston stroked her cheek. "There hasn't been a day since we married that I think of Gracie as belonging to anyone but me. She's mine. Do you get that? She's my daughter. And I don't regret that for one single minute. I never knew it was possible to love any child the way I do her."

Lara stood and touched his face like she'd dreamed of doing. She stared into the brown depths of his eyes and brushed his cheeks and jaw with her fingertips. "I see the man inside and he still has much to give. You can't let her define you. You define yourself. You alone decide your future. I'll be grateful if it's with me."

Houston kissed her fingers. "I like to see fire flashing

from your eyes and hear the anger in your voice. As I rode in tonight, I saw everything about Becky clearly and I feel free for the first time since the shooting."

"Good." Lara gave a sudden gasp. "You haven't eaten. You must be starving. I put some supper aside for you. It should still be warm."

"Whatever you have is fine. Don't fret about me."

"If not me, who? Who'll care for you, Houston?" Everyone needed to matter. Lara knew she'd always be there to fill the job. For as long as he wanted her.

∽

A jolt raced through Houston. Who *would* care? His dad, Stoker, of course, and his brothers, Sam and Luke. But he hungered for a gentle woman like Lara to warm his bed. Someone to stand beside him when times got hard and the cold winter winds blew and burrowed down into his soul. He'd been by himself too damn long. Dare he hope Lara would truly come to care for him?

Houston turned toward the shadows to hide the wanting that must show in his eyes. The depth of the raw emotion would frighten her.

Sam had spoken once of seeing a reflection of himself in Sierra's eyes. Just for a second, Houston longed to see that in Lara's pretty green ones. But her scars ran too deep. He was a fool to wish for something that could never be.

"You have far more things to worry about than me," Houston finally managed through the thickness clogging his throat. "I'd better eat so you can go to bed. Don't want to keep you."

With an arm around her, he walked to the chuck wagon. Though saying little, she sat with him while he ate. Around a mouthful of food, he asked about Gracie and urged her to go to bed.

"I'll wait for you." Lara worried with the hem of her apron. "You might need something."

"If I do, I can find it. I'm pretty self-sufficient."

Out of the blue, Lara asked, "Does my scar embarrass you?"

Houston stilled and laid his fork on his plate. He met her troubled gaze. "No. I'm proud to be seen with you. You're a beautiful woman. Few have your rare beauty, the kind that makes folks stop and stare. Why would you ask?"

Lara shrugged. "I've seen how people lower their eyes and turn away—as though I only had one leg, or was missing an arm."

"They're fools," Houston snapped. "Did any of my men do this? If so, tell me who."

"None here. But it was why we had to move from Amarosa. It became too hard on Papa and my brothers. I don't want to make things difficult for you too."

Houston took her hands in his and was shocked by how cold they were. "The only thing that would make it unbearable for me would be if you left. I hope you're not thinking of doing that."

"No." Lara's smile lit up her eyes, just the way the campfire danced in her copper hair and made it flame.

They sat silent while he finished eating. Cowboys came and went and Lara gave a sudden yawn that she tried in vain to hide behind her hand.

"I think it's your bedtime," Houston said, rising. He took her hand and pulled her up from the blanket on which they sat.

As he passed the cold dish pan, he slid his plate into the water. When she tried to stop to wash it, he pulled her away. "Nope. I'll wash it after I tuck you in."

"But it's my job."

"Not tonight. I caused this by being late. I'll fix it."

A few more steps took them to the shadows beside the wagon. "Now, to continue what I started a little while ago."

Slowly lowering his head, he claimed her softly parted lips. His kiss sprang from a desperate need to feed the hunger blazing inside. His hand splayed across her back in order to leave not a fraction of an inch between their bodies. Her curves fit snug against his hard frame.

Lara's nearness aroused him. Made him yearn for the impossible.

The stirrings that had begun the minute Houston rode into camp became insistent and he fought to make his body behave. But dammit, it was doing what the hell it wanted. Still, he was reluctant to step away from her.

The pull was too great and he'd been a monk for too long.

With his big hands under each side of her jaw, he deepened the kiss. Her fragrance swam around his head, rivaling the scent of sage and wildflowers. He wanted her, no denying, and felt immensely grateful she didn't push him away.

A tiny mewling sound escaped as she slid her hand into his hair. To know his wife didn't find him objectionable heartened him. Then she surprised him even more. Lara unfastened two buttons on his shirt and slid a palm onto his warm skin.

He inhaled a quick breath. She was timid, but her touch burned like heat from a mighty forge.

Something had shifted tonight, but damned if he could figure out what. Was it fear for him that had sparked it?

Or had he finally made her see that he would never hurt her?

God help him! His heart was cracking open. The trust he thought he'd lost forever was alive and well. Lara was different—much different.

Whatever had taken place, he welcomed the progress and prayed that the foundation upon which they'd built was solid and lasting.

Seventeen

LARA'S BREATH HITCHED. THERE WAS SOMETHING SINFUL about being here in the night shadows with Houston, even though she reminded herself that this was what husbands and wives did.

She loved kissing him and pressing against the hard planes of his body. Surrounded by the crisp air, she found something wild and carefree about running her fingers across the expanse of his chest beneath his shirt. The fine hair wasn't crisp as she'd imagined.

Living in a household of boys, she'd often seen her brothers without shirts. Something told her that Houston would be much different from what she was accustomed to. Houston's body had filled out, his powerful muscles rippling under her touch. He projected a sense of danger—a sleeping rattlesnake whose strike could be lethal if awakened. Men who crossed him should take heed.

With great daring, she let her fingers feel their way across his warm skin until she reached the hard pebble of a nipple.

Houston's quick breath whistled through his teeth. Lara jerked her hand back.

What had made her touch him like that?

A soft chuckle caught on the breeze. "I didn't mean to scare you, Lara. That felt nice."

"I shouldn't have done that." She turned toward a rustle

in the brush. Her face flamed. What if someone had seen her just now? They'd think… Houston would think…

Her mind flew back in time. She knew how little it took for a man to get ideas. A perceived glance, a flicker of a smile. That was all it had taken for Yuma Blackstone to rip off her dress and throw her down. She hadn't touched his chest. In fact, he hadn't taken his shirt off. And cruelty and pain had been the result.

"Lara?" Houston laid a gentle hand on her shoulder and brought her around to face him. "I don't know where you went just now but come back so we can talk. You can touch me."

"No." She kept her eyes lowered. "It causes men to do bad things."

"Blackstone, you mean. Never, ever confuse the two of us." Houston snatched off his hat and plowed his fingers through his hair.

When she dared to glance at him, she saw a grim, tight mouth and hard lines that appeared carved from a piece of granite.

"It's all I have to go by," she whispered brokenly.

"Then I'll have to give you some new examples." Houston jammed his hat back on and folded his arms around her. Lara felt warm and safe as his honest, fresh scent washed over her. He carried the essence of the wild land, be it Texas or Indian Territory.

A few minutes passed in silence before he spoke again. "Darlin', just touching me as you did won't release some savage beast. I'll never make you do anything you don't want to. I promise you that."

His deep voice settled like comforting warmth in her heart.

"But—" she began.

"No buts. None," he said firmly. "You can feel safe and trust me." He buried his face in her soft curls. "If it takes me a lifetime, I'll replace every bad memory with a good one until nothing remains but light and happiness. All right?"

Lara sighed. "I don't mean to make your life harder."

"You're not. We're going to get through this. Now, I think you need to get to bed, darlin'. I'll be nearby watching over you." Houston turned toward the fire.

She watched him take two steps before she spoke. "Wait."

He stopped. "What is it?"

"This." Lara moved in front of him. Rising on tiptoes, she pressed her mouth to his.

Currents of something strange flowed through her. She didn't know what it was but she liked it and wanted more. When she was a girl, she used to stick her face against the windowpane when lightning shook the ground, and the thunder would send waves through her. Kissing Houston felt that way.

It was wonderful and strange and she seemed alive again.

His arm came around her, enveloping her. She realized suddenly that he was her lighthouse, like the one she'd once seen in Galveston. He was her beacon in the night on a storm-tossed sea and he'd never steer her toward rocks.

She was breathless when they ended the kiss. "Now I can sleep."

"If not, I'll be here any time you need another." From the big grin on his face, you'd think he'd found gold.

She didn't know about him, but could vouch for herself. What she'd found meant more than all the gold on earth.

She'd found a man who could shine a light on the dark places and make her heart sing.

And he already belonged to her.

Two days later, Lara was serving the men breakfast. Houston had grabbed coffee and a biscuit and ridden out to talk to Clay. Virgil sat Gracie on a blanket on the ground to get in line. She smiled at how fast her daughter crawled, chasing a small beetle. Before she could go after her, Henry picked up a hot pan.

"Ow! It burns!" he cried, dropping the skillet. "Hurts bad. Help."

Lara quickly dunked his hand into a bucket of cool water while she looked for her tin of ointment. By the time she took care of him, she went in search of Gracie and found the babe clutching leaves of a trampled plant in both fists. Her heart froze.

Deadly jimsonweed.

"No, Gracie!" Lara grabbed her up and frantically ran her finger around the inside of the babe's mouth, bringing out small bits. Maybe she hadn't swallowed any. Minute particles would sicken but not kill her, but Lara's doubt wouldn't let hope rise.

The scourge was every rancher's worst nightmare. Cattle died from eating it.

If it killed a hefty cow, dear God, what would it do to someone of Gracie's size?

Please, God, let me have caught her in time.

In the midst of the chaos, Houston arrived at a full gallop. He strode toward her with his chaps slapping his legs, and his face reflected her fear.

"How much did she eat?" he asked.

"I don't know. She had some in her mouth. Maybe I caught her in time. I washed her good and flushed out her mouth." But they both knew better. Already Gracie's eyes were heavy and her head slumped against Lara's shoulder.

Houston picked up the babe. Lara watched him desperately trying to rouse her, but she slipped further and further into a world where they couldn't follow. Worry etched the faces of each silent cowboy who gathered around them. Lara knew how much this little girl meant to each of them.

"Is there anything we can give her?" Lara asked. She'd never known of treatment but that didn't mean none existed.

"I don't know of anything." Houston's dark brows crimped together. "I've never heard of a person eating the weed, only cattle and the results…" He left the rest unsaid.

"I have to do something. I can't just stand here." Lara balled her apron between her hands. The urge to scream rose.

"A doctor might help, but…"

"How far would we have to go?" She refused to voice the doubts in her head. She'd seen the vast land, and so far, Cherokees were the only living souls they'd come across. If this territory had towns within riding distance, they'd be isolated. She reached for Houston's hand. She needed his warmth to melt some of the ice floating in her veins.

Just then, Gracie stiffened and began to jerk uncontrollably and her eyes rolled back in her head. Houston cradled her to him, rubbing her back. No sooner had the convulsions stopped before the child vomited up bits of green.

Lara sobbed so hard, she didn't realize that Clay had joined the circle until he spoke. "The map shows a town called Chimney Rock not far. I'm sure it's small. Might not have a doc."

"How far?" Houston barked.

"An hour's ride more or less," Clay answered, scratching his head. "Nearest doctor could well be Fort Supply, though."

That was weeks away, and they might not even have an hour. Gracie's skin had turned red and her pulse raced as fever ravaged her body. She didn't seem to see them through her half-closed eyelids or know they were near.

Lara stilled. "We have to try."

Houston pulled her into the circle of his arms. "Whatever needs doing, we'll do. I won't let Gracie die." Houston kissed her cheek then glanced down at the unconscious babe. "Let's find a doctor."

Before Lara knew it, cowboys put her on a pretty little mare and she and Houston set out at top speed. They seemed to ride for days, time slipping by unnoticed. At times she wondered if they'd lost their way. When she asked, Houston assured her they'd be at Chimney Rock soon.

But would the town have what they needed?

She couldn't lose her baby. Gracie was her reason for

living. A glance at the babe in her arms showed her barely breathing. Her eyes were closed and her chest barely rose and fell. Tears ran unheeded down Lara's face.

A gurgling noise alerted her. "Houston, she's going to throw up again."

He grabbed the mare's headstall and stopped the mount. Lara held Gracie over in the nick of time. When she'd emptied her stomach, Houston wiped her little mouth very tenderly. A shimmer of tears filled his eyes and Lara realized that this big, strong husband of hers, who always appeared in control, wasn't.

"We're going to make it," Lara said firmly. "We're going to find a doctor in time."

He nodded. "Let's ride."

Lara almost screamed with impatience, but soon Chimney Rock came into view. The small town nestled in a little valley like some place that time forgot. The buildings were in a sad state. Lara's hopes sank as they rode down the single street, only a few businesses on each side. They passed the saloon, the mercantile, the barber, and all the rest without seeing a doctor's shingle swinging in the breeze.

Houston stopped in front of the mercantile and dismounted. "I'll go in and ask. Just don't lose hope. Often doctors don't hang out a shingle when they operate out of another business."

"All right. But please hurry."

A glance at the sun told her several hours had passed since she'd found Gracie. What kept Houston? A small group of young men sauntered around one of the buildings. They saw her and came forward. Lara pulled her hat low, hoping to hide her face.

The one with a hawk nose and a protruding tooth in front touched her dress. "Don't recall seeing you around. Me an' the boys can show you a real good time if'n you're needin' a man."

"Leave me alone," Lara answered through gritted teeth. "I have a man and he'd make twenty of you."

His friends hooted and one said, "Zeb, she seems a mite uppity to me. Bet you can take her down a notch."

Zeb leered up at her. "Got a long scar on her face. Don't have anything to be uppity about. Fact of the matter, she's as ugly as lye soap."

"I'm warning you." Lara kicked at him. "You'll be sorry if you don't go about your business."

"That so? I'm shakin' in my boots." Zeb threw back his head, howling with laughter. The next instant, he grabbed her foot and yanked her sideways in the saddle.

Lara clutched Gracie and clung to the saddle horn. Her heart hammered in her chest as panic swept up her spine.

Boots pounded on the wooden steps leading from the mercantile, but Lara was too frightened to look. She recognized Houston's growl, though. He grabbed Zeb and tossed him like a matchstick.

Caught off guard, Zeb hollered, scrambling for his gun. Lara's heart stopped when the despicable young man pulled out a .45 and pointed it at Houston. "You just dug your grave, mister."

A muscle quivered in Houston's jaw as his hand hovered above the handle of his Colt. When he spoke, his words were hard and brittle. "That woman is my wife and I should shoot you for touching her. But if you pull that trigger, son, I guarantee you'll regret it."

"That so? I'm not your son either. I'm no one's son. Listen, I'm going to make this a fair fight, pops. Just so everyone will know who's faster." Zeb got to his feet and returned his gun to the holster, keeping his hand an inch above the handle. "Tell the devil Zeb killed you."

Frozen in fear, Lara held her breath, afraid to blink. Her tongue worked in her dry mouth, trying to form words to stop the bloodshed. But none came, leaving her to watch in silent horror.

Houston was all that stood between her and these horrible ruffians. If they killed him…

Lara watched in horror as Houston moved to square

himself, his feet spread apart, his body braced for whatever came. She just prayed it wasn't a bullet.

Suddenly, as if realizing exactly how much trouble he'd walked into, Zeb sent his friends a silent plea to jump into the fight. He didn't appear that enthused about taking on Houston alone. But his friends shook their heads and stepped into the roof's shaded overhang. She understood Zeb's dilemma and his companions' reluctance, because Houston's large shadow could put fear into any man. Having watched him on the cattle drive, she knew he wouldn't back down from anyone.

She'd heard her father speak of men like Houston, saying that no one could whip them. They had a mental advantage and size to match.

With her eyes shut, she jumped at the sound of gunfire, listening for the sound of Houston's body hitting the ground.

Please let him be all right.

When she opened her eyes, relief flooded over her. Zeb's shot had missed Houston.

In a lightning move, Houston slid his Colt from the holster. She cringed at the powerful boom and watched orange flame burst from the end of the weapon.

Eighteen

THROUGH THE THICK SMOKE, HOUSTON SAW THAT HE'D wounded his opponent in the shoulder. Part of him, still trembling with rage, wanted the brash young man dead.

He swung to the others. "Anyone else want to try me?"

They shook their heads and one spoke up. "No, mister."

Houston moved to the lickspittle who looked to be only a year or two older than Henry. On the way over, he kicked the boy's gun out of reach, and knelt down. Zeb glanced up at him with pain-filled eyes. The wound didn't appear to be bad. Houston directed his words toward the boy's friends. "Take care of your friend. If I see or hear any of you so much as touching my wife or saying a word to her, I'll put a bullet in you."

Without waiting for a reply, he turned to Lara. "Darlin', there's a doctor down the street."

"Thank God." She sagged with relief.

Mounting up, Houston followed the clerk's directions to the last house before the town gave way to barren, unforgiving land. Seconds later, he stood with Lara on the porch and knocked on the screen door.

A cigar-smoking woman appeared, wiping her hands on her apron. She wore a strange necklace that appeared to be made of bullet slugs. "Can I help you?"

Houston removed his hat. "We have a sick baby, ma'am. Need a doctor bad."

"Come in." She opened the screen door. Houston's spurs jangled as he and Lara followed her into a room filled with cabinets full of vials and bottles. A bed stood next to a window. "Lay the baby down and tell me what happened."

Houston twisted his hat in his hands. "She got into some jimsonweed."

"She must've eaten a leaf because she had some in her mouth, and then when she twice vomited, I saw a small amount of green." Lara's voice broke. "I only left her for a short while."

"We don't have much time. It might already be too late." Houston glanced around. "Is the doctor in the house?"

"You're looking at her. I'm the only doctor for a hundred miles. Folks call me Dr. Mary. Excuse me while I get rid of this cigar."

When she walked from the room, Houston exchanged worried glances with Lara and shrugged. He'd never seen a woman doctor. In fact, he'd never heard of one. Had she even gone to a school of medicine? Could they put Gracie's life in her hands?

But what choice did they have? It was this or nothing.

Dr. Mary's skirts rustled as she hurried back into the room. "Smoking is a filthy habit. Now let me see how I can help this sweet little thing."

"We'd be obliged for any help, Doctor." Houston put his arm around Lara and watched the woman fly into action. She looked into Gracie's mouth and eyes, scowled when she checked her pulse and listened to the heartbeat.

Finally, Dr. Mary turned. "Our only chance is first charcoal, then washing out her stomach. It's not going to be pretty. Is that okay with you?"

"Yes." Lara spoke without any hesitation. Though she appeared calm, Houston felt her trembling beneath his hand.

"Whatever you have to do…just save our daughter," Houston added.

Dr. Mary reached for a bottle of black liquid on a shelf and a piece of tubing. "I could use your help."

"Tell me what to do," Houston said.

"Tip her head back a little so I can run this down her throat and into her stomach."

Houston did as requested. Gracie's eyes remained closed and she didn't move a muscle as the doctor inched the rubber tube very slowly down the babe's throat.

Dr. Mary then attached the container of charcoal, held it up and let it slowly run in. Once the bottle emptied, she removed the tubing. "We let that sit a while, then I'll wash out the stomach, give her a laxative, and get some fluids back into her."

"Will that be enough?" Houston asked.

"All I can do." The doctor stared down at the child. "We wait and see. If you know how to pray, I suggest you do it."

Lara smothered a little cry with her fist. Fear colored her pretty eyes black as night as she leaned over to touch her baby.

"Thank you for your efforts, Dr. Mary." Houston fingered Gracie's blond curls. He needed to see those mischievous blue eyes. So did her mother. He placed an arm around Lara.

"It's Dr. Marguerite Leona Cuvier, for long." The woman doctor bustled about, putting her things away. "I'll leave you with your child for a while."

Houston barely heard her leave the room. His attention was locked on the life appearing to ebb from his Angel. He blinked hard, clutching Lara tighter. "It's not enough. Nothing ever seems enough."

This hard land often beat a man down regardless of how he tried not to let it. The damn land just took whatever it wanted. He was so tired. Little sleep and days in the saddle had simply exhausted him.

Lara touched his arm. "This will be," she said firmly. "You have to have hope and believe that our prayers will be answered."

About two hours later, Houston still stood with his arms around Lara, watching the lady doctor spoon small amounts of water into Gracie's mouth. Most dribbled out. Through all the procedures, the babe had yet to twitch a finger.

"When will she open her eyes?" Lara moved from Houston and patted the small back.

Houston wished like hell he could do something. This waiting was getting to him. But it had to be far worse for Lara. It was a wonder she hadn't lost her mind with worry.

"Hard to say," Dr. Mary replied. "If the treatment worked, we'll know soon. But I'm also concerned about you, Lara. Your breasts must be painful. How long since the baby nursed?"

Houston saw Lara's struggle to remember. Both had lost track of time. Then he watched embarrassment stain her cheeks to talk about such a personal thing in front of him. "Would you have a cup of coffee, Doctor?" he asked quietly.

"Keep a pot on the stove all the time. Help yourself."

Lara seemed relieved, and Houston strolled to the kitchen. Everything was neat and tidy, so he had no trouble finding a cup. He filled it while glancing around the small room that seemed to have been added as an afterthought. The good doctor must not cook much. Besides the wood stove, there were two shelves made from crates that held three plates and a bowl, and a rough plank table with four chairs. Only a little sideboard completed his inventory. He took a seat.

The minutes dragged. He downed two cups of coffee, then guessing the women would need more time, went out to take the horses to the livery, and get some feed into their bellies.

The short walk back to the doctor's house let him clear his head. He entered the room to find Lara fastening the last button of her bodice. A bottle full of milk sat on a table and nearby lay an odd contraption. Clearly, Lara had somehow sorted out the problem. He didn't want to know anything more.

Houston held his hat, shifting his weight. "Is everything all right?"

"It is now." Lara raised her eyes to his. "I feel better and Gracie has milk, which we've already begun spooning into her mouth."

Dr. Mary glanced up from patiently dribbling life-giving fluid into Gracie. She gave both him and Lara a steely-eyed stare. "How long since either of you ate?"

"Nothing since breakfast at dawn, ma'am," Houston answered, glancing out the window. Must be around three in the afternoon, long past lunch, though he doubted he could stomach anything.

"The town doesn't have a café. In fact, Chimney Rock has little to commend it." Dr. Mary sighed. "I tell you what. I'll fix a bite and you can tell me what you're doing out here in the middle of Indian Territory."

Lara wearily wiped her eyes and glanced up. "Only if you'll let me help. I need something to do or I'll go crazy."

"Deal. I confess I'm a lousy cook. Just do enough to keep some weight on these old bones. Your man here can sit with the babe." Dr. Mary patted Houston's arm. "You're a little white around the gills, cowboy. How about a shot of whiskey to brace you?"

Houston yearned for something to dull the ache squeezing his heart. "I could use one for sure."

He pulled a chair to the bed and laid his hat on the floor. A minute later, she returned with a good portion of whiskey. The amber liquid reminded him of Stoker and he wished his pa was there. Though Houston was thirty years old, he still needed his father sometimes. Stoker always knew what to do and how to handle situations. It killed Houston to see Gracie lying so still and white. And the fear darkening Lara's green eyes tore off a piece of his soul.

How much more could she bear? The level of pain and suffering she had already borne would drop a lesser woman to her knees. If Gracie didn't make it, he doubted Lara would ever recover. The heartbreak would finish her off.

Though he wasn't a religious man, he laid his large hand on Gracie's chest and, in a bumbling way, prayed that God would spare her.

He didn't know how long he sat there before Lara touched his shoulder. "Houston, the food's ready. I'll sit with Gracie."

"What about you?" He stood and brushed back a strand of her copper hair, seeing her exhaustion.

"I'm not hungry. I can't eat while Gracie is so sick."

And he didn't want to eat without her. "I'll move the table in here, if it's all right with Dr. Mary, and maybe you can take a few bites."

Dr. Mary spoke from the doorway. "I was going to suggest that very thing. The table is small and I'll help you move it."

Within a few minutes, they all sat down. Lara had fried some potatoes and ham and added green beans from the doctor's garden. He filled his plate.

"Lara tells me you're from the northernmost part of Texas," Dr. Mary said with a faraway look in her eyes. "I always wanted to see what Texas looks like. Doubt I'll ever get a chance."

"Why not?" Houston forked a piece of ham into his mouth.

"Can't make a living down there. No one much will let a woman practice medicine. I came here because folks were so desperate they overlooked that little flaw of mine. Coffee?" At Houston's nod, Dr. Mary filled his cup. Her strange necklace caught the light with her movements.

Houston laid down his fork. "Mind if I ask you something?"

"Depends. But go ahead."

"What is that necklace made of? I've never seen one like it."

"And you won't. A friend of mine made this necklace from bullet fragments I've dug out of patients over the years." She removed the odd jewelry and handed it to him.

He fingered the various pieces of lead. Some were flat,

some round, and some still bore the markings of the maker. "It's an unusual thing for a lady to wear. Can I ask why you had it made?"

Dr. Mary snorted. "Dug out so many I could've made ten necklaces like that. Threw most away. But as for the reason for keeping them... I wanted the next shot-up man seeking my services not to expect an easy treatment. I want the jackasses to suffer. A lot. Then maybe they'll think about what's waiting for them the next time they pull a loaded gun."

The explanation made sense. And no bigger jackass than Zeb, who'd made a losing play outside the mercantile. Houston wondered why he hadn't come to let the doctor to treat his wound. Or maybe her attitude explained it and the kid didn't want the lecture.

"Now, it's time to answer a question for me." The doctor refilled Houston's cup. "Have you two been married long? The babe is five months shy of a year and yet I get the impression you're newlyweds. Call it a woman's idle curiosity."

He didn't say anything about the attack—that was Lara's story to tell. Houston told about their fathers' matchmaking, leaving out the rest.

Mary roared with laughter. "That beats all I ever heard."

Lara glanced at Houston in surprise. "Why didn't you tell me? I didn't know that's what happened."

"Never got around to it, darlin'. We were busy. You with settling in and me with getting ready for this cattle drive." Besides, he didn't see much point. It had all worked out. Or almost, anyway. He glanced at Gracie lying so still and swallowed hard.

"You can bet I'll have a talk with him when we get back. I'm not some puppet to place at will. Neither are you," she said angrily.

Houston had halfway thought she'd been in on the scheme. He was glad she wasn't and that manipulation wasn't part of her thinking.

"I want to talk to you about my scar." Lara directed her words to Dr. Mary.

"It was a nasty cut, I'm guessing."

"Yes. It bled for weeks and weeks. A doctor tried to stitch it up but he didn't have your skill. A few days ago, a Cherokee woman gave me some ointment and told me to rub it on twice a day. She said it would make it fade some." Lara looked at Houston but addressed the doctor. "I've been using it faithfully but I don't see any change."

"Darlin', I never see that scar when I look at you. Only your beautiful eyes and the spirit shining through." Houston covered her hand with his. "You fret too much."

"My appearance matters to me," Lara said quietly. "You saw what happened when we arrived."

"They're fools. You can't let men like that bother you."

"It does. I can't help it. Doctor, will the ointment help?"

Houston's heart ached that he couldn't make her whole and restore her face. When he looked at her, he truly didn't see it.

"What's the salve made from? And how long have you been using it?" asked Dr. Mary.

After Lara told her, the woman nodded. "I've used a similar treatment and it will work, but it takes time. You can't expect change to happen overnight. Keep using it, my dear. You'll start to see results by the time the season changes." Mary paused then added, "I'm sure it's a source of embarrassment. No one wants to stand out when they really yearn to blend in. People can be quite cruel."

"See, Houston? Dr. Mary understands." She turned to their hostess. "Thank you for easing my concerns."

Just then, a voice yelled from beyond the screen door. "Come out, yellow belly. Face me like a man."

Houston's heart stopped. He didn't need this. He just wanted to be left alone. Besides, the kid was barely old enough to shave.

"I know you're in there," Zeb hollered. "Quit hiding."

Dr. Mary went to the door. "Go home, you little fool.

This man's baby is deathly ill. He doesn't have time to mess with the likes of you."

"Then he'll just have to make time, 'cause I ain't budging."

Houston sighed and pushed back his chair. This must be what his brother Luke had to live with every single day. Never knowing who'd challenge him next. Never knowing when a bullet was going to find him. Never being able to live his life as he wanted and be normal.

"Please don't go." Lara got to her feet and clutched his sleeve. "He might kill you."

"He's not going to let this lie. If I don't face him, he'll shoot us in the back when we leave. I won't put you and Gracie at risk." His tone was gentle. She'd lived with so much violence and he knew how it twisted at her insides. He pulled her close. Lowering his head, he kissed her moist lips and held her for a long moment.

The loud ticking of the doctor's clock filled the room, seeming to warn of death beyond those doors.

Dr. Mary came back, shaking her head. "I apologize. Zeb's got a brain the size of a gnat. Not a week goes by I don't pull another slug out of him. He's desperate to make his pa proud, but that won't ever happen, because his father's a drunk and a poor excuse for a human being."

"Not your fault, Doctor. Lara, stay in the house no matter what happens." Houston put on his hat and moved past Dr. Mary. His spurs clinked loudly as he strode for the door.

Laying a hand on the screen, he fought the urge to turn around, to kiss Lara and Gracie once more. Just in case he didn't make it back. Air left his lungs in a big whoosh. Then he squared his shoulders and stepped toward his fate.

"Thought you'd see things my way," Zeb crowed when Houston stepped out. A crude bandage circled his shoulder. The boy's friends had evidently come to watch again. They stood off to the side, silent, still.

Houston's gaze swept over them before turning to Zeb. "You know this is stupid, don't you, boy?"

"I ain't no boy," Zeb screamed.

"Acting like one. A snot-nosed one at that. How old are you?"

"Eighteen. Plenty old enough to blow you to kingdom come. I aim to get satisfaction." Zeb pointed a finger at him. "You shot me an' now you're gonna pay."

Houston's eyes narrowed. "You tried to assault my wife, in case you don't recall."

"Any woman with a face that ugly needs to stay home or else suffer the name-callin' 'n such. Where'd you find her anyway? A whorehouse?"

Anger rose. He stared at the pimply faced boy, digesting the bravado in his young opponent's voice. "I really wish you had time to grow up and understand what life's all about. Makes me sad that you aren't going to get a chance. If I don't put you in the ground today, someone else will."

"Boohoo! Tryin' to scare me?" Zeb taunted.

Was there nothing that could frighten some sense into him? "Have you ever killed a man before? Ever watch the light go out of his eyes? Ever smell the stench of death?"

"Sure, plenty of times." But the way the kid glanced over at his friends said he lied.

"We don't have to do this," Houston said, praying the words would get through Zeb's thick skull. "You can go home and I can return to my sick baby. There's no shame in that." Dammit, he didn't want to take this young fool's life. But the kid was out for blood. If Houston turned and walked into the house now, a bullet would slam into his back. Or in Lara's.

"Pa says I'm a good-for-nothing coward. I aim to prove him wrong. I ain't a coward. I ain't."

"There are other ways to prove it. But not this. Let's shake hands and let me help you," Houston pleaded.

"This gun is all the help I need. *Pops*."

"All right. Talkin's over, boy." His voice held a cold, deadly edge. Zeb was deaf to his advice. "Let's see what you're made of."

Indecision filled Zeb's eyes; he probably realized he'd come too far to back down. His bony Adam's apple bobbed in this throat as his hand hovered over the gun. He licked his lips.

A bead of sweat trickled down Zeb's face. Houston knew the inside of his mouth must be as dry as a sun-baked riverbed.

Don't do it, kid.

Please don't draw, Houston silently begged.

Don't pull the damn trigger.

From the corner of his eye he saw Dr. Mary steal up behind Zeb with a raised skillet, evidently aiming to knock him out. His heart stopped. His stomach clenched with the need to cry out and stop her, to send her out of danger.

Before he could, Zeb whirled and turned his gun on her.

In a split second, Houston drew and fired.

Nineteen

THE DISCHARGE WAS LOUD IN HOUSTON'S EARS. HE rocked back on his heels but didn't feel any burning pain. That appeared to be a good sign. He slid his Colt back into the holster.

Dr. Mary caught Zeb as the force of the blast sent him into her arms. She lowered the kid gently to the ground, showing the gaping hole he now had in his chest. Houston stumbled to him and knelt. A bloody hand fumbled for his. He took it and looked into Zeb's distant eyes.

"You were…right. Stupid," Zeb mumbled. "I wish…"

Houston knelt beside him. "I didn't want to do this. I tried…"

"No choice," Zeb mumbled as blood gushed from his mouth in a final gurgle before his head rolled to the side.

"I wish I could've saved you, boy," Houston murmured brokenly. He wished to God Gracie hadn't eaten the jimsonweed and brought them to the town of Chimney Rock.

He cradled Zeb's lifeless body, not caring that blood soaked his shirt.

Even after Zeb's friends gathered 'round, Houston wouldn't let go of the boy. He was back at his first wedding day, with Becky, his mind full of how he'd gripped her body to him and the helpless feeling that had washed over him. Horrible loss, deafening silence, and disbelief filled him.

He couldn't save her then, and he couldn't talk sense to this boy now. Damn Zeb's father! If he just could've shown the boy some kindness, none of this would've happened.

Dr. Mary laid a hand on his shoulder. "You did all you could, Legend."

"I should've tried harder to talk him out of it."

"You could've talked until you were blue in the face and it wouldn't have changed a blooming thing. The boy left you no choice. Zeb was on a runaway horse heading for a cliff from the minute he was born."

"Did he have a mother, any family?" Houston glanced up.

One of the friends who'd come to watch spoke up. "Only his pa. Ma died a long time ago. Mostly Zeb lived alone on account of his pa never finding his way home."

Deep sorrow fell over Houston. What a wasted life. As Zeb's friends carried him away, Houston staggered to a well at the back of the doctor's house to wash and collect himself before he went inside to Lara.

In the cool of the trees, Houston released his frustration and anger. He pounded on a large tree trunk until his knuckles were raw and bleeding.

Dammit!

Exhausted, he slid down the trunk to the grass and laid his hat next to him. He didn't know how long he sat there. It could've been a few moments or a day or more. He didn't know. He wasn't aware of anything until Lara's arms penetrated the numbness.

"It's all right, Houston," she murmured, pulling his head to her breast. "You couldn't have stopped him. No one could've."

"I tried. I couldn't let him shoot the doc."

"I know." She kissed his hair and smoothed it back. "And it's because of me your lives intersected. I caused this."

"No." Houston shook his head vigorously. "Don't consider that for even a second. Not one speck of this was your fault."

Her soothing touch was a balm for his ragged soul. He wanted to stay in the coolness of the trees where trouble couldn't find them.

"The blood." He jerked away from her. "I'm covered in blood. You'll get it on you."

"If you think I care about little things like that, you don't know me very well." She ran her fingers across his jaw. "Blood washes off. What stains your soul...that's what stays. You're hurting and you'll probably never be the same. Taking a life has to be unimaginable."

"You have no idea of the misery that fills a man. Zeb was just a kid." Houston scrubbed the back of his neck. "If I had to kill, I wish it had been Blackstone."

"I wouldn't want you if killing didn't affect you."

That she did want him came as a surprise.

Houston touched her flawed cheek. "I don't think I told you my brother is a gunslinger. He's constantly called out by men who want to become known for killing the famed Luke Weston. I always wondered how he can stomach taking so many lives."

"Living by the gun would destroy something deep inside. Death must lurk around every corner," Lara said.

"It does, but I never understood what it must be like for him until today." Houston stood and pulled her up. "I need to wash so I can see Gracie. Any change?"

"She's breathing easier. That's a hopeful sign."

"Sure is." He brushed a kiss across her lips. "Go back in to her and I'll be along."

He watched her move slowly toward the house. He loved watching her walk. Her soft curves flowed like a stream of water—smooth and constant. His wife had a natural grace and a heart full of compassion.

He glanced down at his bloodstained hands. He'd brought more violence to Lara's life. Why had he let her come with him?

The answer was clear.

Because he was a selfish bastard.

He'd taken Lara from the safety of the ranch, and now Gracie lay at death's door.

How was he going to look at himself in the mirror again?

The shadows had grown long by the time Houston finally entered the doctor's house. His boot heels struck the wood floor and his spurs clinked loudly, disturbing the quiet. He removed his hat and went straight to the room where Gracie lay.

Dr. Mary stood at the window looking out, her head down and shoulders curled, one hand gripping the necklace made of spent bullets. Her fingers were trembling and he thought he heard a sniffle, though he couldn't be sure. Zeb's death seemed to have affected her deeply too.

Someone had shoved the small kitchen table aside. Lara glanced up from the babe's bedside and reached for him.

"How is Gracie?" He laid his hat on the table and took her hand.

"Showing tiny signs of coming around."

Dr. Mary turned and spoke in terse sentences. "Though she hasn't opened them yet, her eyes are twitching. Heartbeat is slowing some, pulse is stronger. I think she's going to pull through but I caution against moving her from here today. The danger hasn't passed, Mr. Legend."

"I didn't see a hotel when we rode in." Was there anywhere suitable here for Lara? He could always sleep in the loft at the livery or on the floor here, but his wife needed more comfort.

"We don't have one," Dr. Mary said.

"If you can put Lara up, I'd be obliged. I'll find a place for myself."

"No need, Mr. Legend. Both of you will stay here. I'll not argue about it either. By all rights I should be dead. Your quick reflexes saved my life."

"Call me Houston. I'm glad I was there, although…" He could still smell Zeb's blood, see his sightless eyes. And he could still hear the last words the boy had spoken.

"I'll fix supper." Lara rose and laid a comforting hand on his arm. "By the time we eat, it'll be dark."

Houston noticed her indecision about leaving Gracie. "I'll sit with her, darlin'. At the slightest change, I'll holler."

When Dr. Mary and Lara went into the kitchen, Houston sat down next to the bed and lifted his Angel into his lap. The tiny fingers got lost in Houston's large palm. She was so small and fragile, yet the girl had such a mischievousness about her. He'd give anything to have her sit up and scold him again.

Tired of fighting the weariness, he closed his eyes for just a second. He must've dozed off, because he jerked when Gracie's finger closed around his. His eyes flew open and he found the baby staring up at him with a shy grin.

"Lara, come quick!" Houston sat the babe up, propping her with his arm.

"What is it? Is she worse?" With her hands dripping water, Lara ran into the room.

"See for yourself," he answered, filled with relief.

Gracie reached for Lara. When she took the child, Gracie patted her mother's cheeks then laid her head on Lara's shoulder.

Happy sobs broke from Lara's mouth as though she could no longer hold them in check. "I can't believe it. It's a miracle. I simply can't believe it."

Dr. Mary beamed and wiped her eyes. "Moments like these are why I'm a doctor."

Houston blinked hard. A glorious sunset burst through the window in a blaze of deep oranges and purples. It seemed God had painted the magnificent view just for them. In a day full of tragedy, death, and worry, Houston took comfort in the breathtaking picture. Maybe this was a message of some sort.

Or could it be a reminder that a man could lose his way if he didn't pay close attention?

A reminder that not everyone rejoiced pierced him. He thought of Zeb and the fact that Houston had taken his life today. Somewhere in Chimney Rock, sorrow filled the hearts of Zeb's friends. Maybe a few others as well.

"Houston, I need to finish seeing to supper," Lara said, holding Gracie out to him.

He shook his head. "Dr. Mary and I will prepare the meal." He wasn't sure how much help he'd be, but he could take direction well. Most times, that is. "You try to feed Gracie."

"All right." Lara settled into the chair and positioned the babe in the crook of her arm. Dr. Mary handed her a light cloth, and she covered herself and let Gracie nurse.

Houston stood in the doorway, watching his family for a long moment. The sight brought a lump to his throat. He saw the love of a mother shining in Lara's eyes. She might not ever be able to show him love, but he knew she did care for him, at least as a friend. Maybe that was a start and it would grow from there. That's all he could hope for. He turned toward the kitchen.

After eating and washing the dishes, Houston rolled down his shirtsleeves and collected his hat. "I'm going to step out for just a bit, Lara. Sit here with Dr. Mary and talk. You don't often have a chance to be with other women."

Worry wrinkled her brow and her voice filled with panic. "Do you really need to go out? You might run into trouble. Stay here with us."

The pleading in her voice pierced him, but he wouldn't be able to live with himself if he didn't go.

"Don't worry, I won't be long. I need to check on your mare." He bent to kiss her then walked the short distance to the livery.

Five minutes later, he tied the Appaloosa to a hitching rail. He stood in the evening breeze for a second then swung toward the noise of the dimly lit saloon.

Heads turned and the piano player's hands froze on the keys when Houston entered the local watering hole. He scanned the room and sauntered up to the polished bar.

"What can I get you, mister?" the barkeep asked.

Houston pitched him a silver dollar. "Information."

The slender man caught the coin and bit it to verify that it was real. He wore a jaunty green derby, and red garters edged in black on his upper arms kept his sleeves in place.

"Never sold words before." He grinned. "This is a first."

"I'm looking for Zeb's father. Don't have a last name."

"Oh, you mean Jubal Flanagan." The barkeep jerked his head toward a man puking in the corner onto the sawdust floor. "Good luck."

"Obliged." When Houston strode toward Jubal, the piano player resumed pounding out his tune and conversation returned to a loud din.

Jubal finished retching and glanced up at Houston. "What the hell are you lookin' at?" He wiped his mouth on his sleeve.

Gray bristles covered the stout man's face, testifying that he'd not shaved in God-knows-how-long. His beady dark eyes glittered wildly in deep-set sockets, reminding Houston of a possum. Jubal seemed to have a surly attitude. No wonder Zeb turned out the way he had.

"Came to pay my respects and offer condolences."

"For what?"

"For your son," Houston said.

"Good riddance." Jubal hiccupped. "Zeb was nothing but a disappointment. Always whining about food an' the cold an' why I never came home. Worse than his damn ma. He should've died when she did."

Thin-edged anger rushed over Houston. He grabbed Jubal Flanagan by the shirtfront. "His death is on you, you sorry bastard. If you'd been a real father, he wouldn't be dead now."

"Never wanted a snot-nosed kid in the first place." Jubal twisted free. "Leave me alone less'n you're buyin' the next round."

Houston grabbed the man's arm and propelled him toward the swinging doors.

"Hey, you can't do this!" Jubal glanced around at the other patrons. "Stop him. He's gonna kill me just like he killed my boy."

No one stirred. They shot him one disinterested look and turned back to their whiskey and card games.

Out in the darkness beyond the lamplight, Houston threw Jubal to the ground. "Where's your horse, Flanagan?"

"Where the hell do you think?"

Several horses stood next to the Appaloosa at the hitching rail. "Which one?" Houston hauled Jubal to his feet and pushed him toward the animals. Of the three unfamiliar horses, one was in poor shape. He dragged the drunk to it. "This yours?"

"Yep. What are you gonna do?" Jubal slurred his words.

"Something that people should've done a long time ago." He boosted the man up into the saddle and held the reins while he climbed onto his gelding. He glanced up and down the street, wondering which direction to go. Luckily, a man emerged from the saloon.

"Mister, do you know where they took Zeb Flanagan's body?"

"You'll find him at the Mitchells' next to the schoolhouse." The man glanced at Jubal and shook his head.

"Thanks." Houston turned the horse's head in that direction.

"Say, aren't you the one who shot the boy?" the man asked.

Houston winced. "That's right. He didn't give me any choice."

"He never gave anyone their druthers. Jubal's fault sure enough." The stranger moved down the street, muttering to himself.

"Where are you taking me?" Jubal screamed.

"You'll see soon enough."

When he stopped at the house, Houston dismounted and yanked Jubal from the saddle. Gripping a fistful of shirt, he marched to the door and knocked.

"Yes?" A woman said through the opening.

Houston removed his hat. "Sorry to bother you, ma'am. I was told this is where Zeb Flanagan's body is laid out."

Jubal clawed at Houston's arm, trying to get away. "You ain't gonna take me in there!"

"The boy's here." The woman stared hard at Jubal. "They brought him to me because they didn't have anywhere else to take him." She held the door. "Come in, Mister—"

"Legend, ma'am. Houston Legend. I won't take up much of your time."

"It's no bother. I'm Mrs. Mitchell. I fed Zeb and tried to keep him out of trouble." She wiped her eyes with the hem of her apron. "I'm afraid I didn't do a very good job. He wasn't a bad sort. Just needed direction and to be loved, something he never got from his father." She cast Jubal a look of reproach.

"No! Let me go!" Jubal yelled as Houston propelled him into the house by the nape of the neck.

She led them into a small parlor where a half-dozen boys Zeb's age sat stiffly. Houston nodded to each one then shoved Jubal toward the roughly hewn box.

"Get a good look, you sorry bastard." Houston held Jubal's face nose to nose with Zeb. "Look at your son. See what you did. You bear the responsibility for this. He wanted to make you proud of him for the first time in his life. Your need for whiskey was stronger than the love for your son. Take a good long look." Anger made Houston tremble. "You threw him away like he was slop for the pigs."

Jubal sobbed. "It wasn't my fault."

"You make me sick," Houston spat. "You're a pathetic, miserable excuse for a human being." He shoved the smelly drunk from the room and spoke to Mrs. Mitchell. "I apologize for interrupting, ma'am." He took some money from his pocket and pressed it into her hand. "To help with expenses. Give Zeb a good send-off."

"Thank you, Mr. Legend. I'm glad you forced Jubal to see him."

"Doubt it'll make any difference but it had to be done. The boy deserved to have his father weep over him." Houston put his hat on.

With the lamplight catching on her chestnut strands, Mrs. Mitchell stared up at him with a piercing stare. He didn't know if she was about to lash out at him or not. "You're nothing like I imagined, Mr. Legend. When I saw Zeb's body, I hated you and wanted to give you a piece of my mind. Then I heard you had to kill the boy to save Dr. Mary's life... That changed things. How's your sick baby?"

"Better. She woke up. Good night, ma'am, and thanks." Houston touched a finger to the brim of his hat and turned to Jubal. "Outside."

Jubal rubbed his hand across his slack mouth and tried to stumble off to the saloon.

Houston grabbed him. "Oh no, I'm not finished with you yet."

"What are you gonna do now?"

"You'll see."

Moonlight illuminated the path to the gate and they mounted up. Stopping only to refill one water canteen, amid lots of squawking from Jubal about going back to the saloon, they headed out of town.

Jubal Flanagan was about to get a lesson he wouldn't soon forget.

Twenty

IT WAS NEAR MIDNIGHT WHEN LARA GLANCED OUT THE window. What kept Houston?

Was he alive or had someone killed him? That boy's friends—or his father—might have shot Houston, making him pay for sending a bullet into Zeb. They had reason to want her husband dead.

Every noise sent Lara to the door. If he didn't return, who would she go to for help? The town had no law. Would anyone help her find him?

One thing was for sure: she wouldn't leave without her husband.

How could she begin to go on if he'd met his end here in this lawless town in the middle of Indian Territory? She remembered how he'd defended her. Despite all his previous reassurances, she'd always believed he'd only tried to make her feel better. Until now. Now she knew for sure her scar truly didn't bother him.

Lara moved to look out the window again. If he wasn't back by sunrise, she'd turn the town upside down looking for him. Someone had to know what had happened to him.

He was her life now, her hope and her future. Houston Legend held her dreams in his hand.

Dr. Mary stood in the doorway, clutching a shawl around her nightgown. "Can't sleep?"

Lara turned. "Did I wake you?"

"No. I wanted to check on Gracie. Any sign of that husband of yours, dear?"

"Afraid not. I'm really worried. I can't imagine what might be keeping him." Lara swiveled to the window to hide her trembling lip.

"Is he a drinker? Drinking men often lose track of time." Dr. Mary moved to one of the chairs at the small table still in the room and sat down.

A drinker? She'd only seen him take a glass of whiskey with his father twice since they'd married, and then only a little.

"No, Houston isn't one to drink. Or gamble." But she hadn't known him that long. Was that another secret he had been hiding from her? Anything was possible. Still, she wasn't going to jump to conclusions. When he got back, he'd have a logical explanation for his long absence. Instinct told her it had something to do with that boy he'd killed. She'd never seen him so hurt.

Should they by chance survive this visit to Chimney Rock, she vowed to double up on the salve for her scar. If she was pretty, Houston wouldn't have to shoot anyone else because of her.

"How about I make us some hot tea while we wait?" Dr. Mary said. "Houston will probably be here any minute."

Lara pressed her cheek to the cool windowpane. "Tea sounds good."

But what if he wasn't back? What if she never saw him again?

❧

Beneath a thin slice of moon, Houston stopped his horse. They'd ridden at least a good ten miles from town, and his companion had sobered up during the ride.

"Get off your horse, Jubal."

The man's eyes grew wide. "What're you gonna do?"

"This is the end of the line for you." Houston dismounted. "You're walking back to town. Get off the damn horse."

Jubal clutched the reins tightly. "You cain't leave me out here in the middle of nowhere. It's inhumane. I'll die."

With a yank, Houston dragged him from the saddle. "You won't die…unless you get snakebit. I want you to have a lot of time to think about every possible way you failed your son. And to dry out. You're pickled. By the time you walk back, I hope you remember how you saw him tonight and never get Zeb's face out of your head." Houston handed him the water canteen. "With luck, it's branded into your whiskey-soaked brain."

The man began to whimper then cuss. Houston glanced at the man's shoes, debating whether to add more to Jubal's punishment. After a second, he decided against it. The soles of his shoes had big holes. That was misery enough.

"You're a poor excuse for a human being, Flanagan, and it's high time something jarred you to your senses. Change your ways. Give up whiskey. Learn how to be a man, for Christ's sake."

"What you ask is too damn hard." Jubal sat down. "I might as well die here."

"Your choice." Houston swung into the saddle and gathered the reins of Jubal's horse. "You haven't even taken care of your horse in weeks. If you make it back to town, you'll find him at the livery. I'm going to pay someone to feed him and help him recover from your mistreatment."

"You're a coldhearted son of a bitch, Legend," Jubal hollered.

"You might have a point, but at least I don't abandon my family." Houston glanced down. "I'm going to pass through here on my way back to Texas. I'd better find you sober."

"Most likely dead, or do you care about that?" Jubal asked sullenly.

That was the problem. Houston cared too much. Though he didn't tell Jubal, he was going to tell Dr. Mary where the man was in case he didn't show up in town in a day's time. She could either come looking for him herself or send someone.

"Remember what I said. You'll answer to me if you're not sober when I come back." He turned to his horse and rode to town.

It was a little after midnight when he made it to the doctor's dark house, bone-tired. He'd returned the horses to the livery and walked the short distance. After removing his spurs and laying them on the porch, he tiptoed into the house and turned into the room where Gracie and Lara were sleeping.

Lara sat with her head on her arms. She jerked at the sound of his footsteps. With a cry, she ran to him, knocking off his hat when she threw her arms around his neck. "Thank God, you're back. I was so worried."

"Sorry I was gone so long." He stared deep into her eyes, thinking he'd never seen anything so pretty. "Hadn't meant to be."

She fingered the strands of his hair. "I sense a story."

"Let's go out on the porch so we won't disturb the sleepers." He picked up his hat and took her hand. They sat on the stoop, with shoulders touching. In the thin moonlight, he told her about Jubal Flanagan. Even in the telling, his anger flooded back.

"What you did showed the depth of your caring." Lara leaned into him.

"Yeah, well. Jubal had a different opinion, I'm afraid."

"No one likes taking their medicine but sometimes they have to."

"I just hate that it took me away from you. Come here." Houston put his arms around her and pulled her against him, kissing her long and deep.

The flames that were always just beneath the surface flared as soon as their lips met. He would always hunger for this slip of a woman who had already consumed his life, his thoughts, and his heart.

He thought of what Zeb Flanagan had yelled—that she

was as ugly as lye soap. The boy had been too crazed to see what was in front of him. Houston knew without a doubt that Lara was the most beautiful woman he'd ever seen. And she belonged to him.

As he deepened the kiss in an effort to draw her inside him, she gave a little cry and gripped his shirt, pressing closer.

"Lady," he said against her mouth, "you make me crazy with need. One day, God willing, I'll make you hunger for me too."

She pulled back just far enough to meet his gaze while she toyed with the hair at his temple. "I like you touching and kissing me. Maybe if you take it slow and let me get used to you in small bits, I can get over this unease. I know you must tire of being saddled with a wife who won't sleep with you. I'm trying. I want to lie beside you and be what you need."

"Darlin', I'm not saddled with you, as you put it. I'd want you regardless of everything that's happened. I found a diamond when you raised that thick wedding veil. I will never pressure you. We'll go at your speed for as long as it takes." He lifted her hand to his mouth and kissed each fingertip. "You'll find me a very patient man."

Lara's eyes were dark and full of hunger. "That's one of the things I appreciate about you. You never make me do anything."

He nibbled her mouth. "I don't believe in forcing anyone, least of all you. This marriage is give and take. We have to strike a balance to make it work."

"I haven't done much giving." She slid a hand around his neck and curled against his chest until their hearts touched. Houston swallowed hard and folded his arms around her. "All I seem to do is take," she whispered as though afraid someone would hear her confession.

"You give more than you think, and I have no complaints."

"That's kind of you to say, but I'm stronger now, and here with you tonight, I feel as though the past never happened. I only see the future and it's golden."

Houston nuzzled her ear. "You're a different person from when we met…what is it now…three weeks ago?" He loved seeing this change. Each day she gained strength.

"Almost a month." Lara pushed back from him to meet his eyes. "Houston, I think it's time to take our relationship a step further."

His heart nearly leaped from his chest. "I'm always willing to try anything you want."

"For a place to start…I sort of have a plan. Unfasten a button of my dress now and add to that each time we kiss good night in private. Maybe by the time you get them all undone, I'll be over this crazy fear. That is, if you're willing."

It took great effort to steady his racing pulse. "I'll be grateful for the chance to show that you can trust me," he assured her. "But are you sure you're ready?"

"I am positive." Her green eyes glittered, along with her blinding smile.

"Anytime you get uncomfortable, I want you to tell me and I'll stop."

"Oh, Houston, I don't deserve you." She blinked hard then lowered her voice to a whisper. "Will you start now?"

"Anything for my lady."

Houston pulled her onto his lap and nibbled her neck and behind her ear. He felt her hands on his chest, felt when she slipped her fingers inside to touch his skin. And felt her lean into him.

Placing his lips on hers, he kissed her, a searing kiss that made his body heavy and warm. Molten desire pooled low in his belly and spread through him like a raging wildfire. Maybe this wasn't such a good idea. He was in danger of losing control, and that would send Lara running scared, back to her father.

He closed his eyes and focused on his breathing. *Inhale in. Exhale out.* He forced his thoughts to the cattle drive, to the obstacles that lay ahead, and to the men stalking them.

When he'd slowed his heart rate, he released the top button of her dress. Leaving a trail of kisses down her neck, he pushed the fabric aside and pressed his lips to the hollow at the base of her throat, where her pulse beat wildly.

Lara trembled beneath his lips and he knew the tremendous courage it took to let him do this. He was so proud of her for taking this tiny step toward getting her life back. Slowly but surely they'd get there.

Houston did her dress back up. "Thank you, Lara. You don't know what your trust means to me. And how nice to have someone to share my problems with."

"Just don't keep secrets. I can take anything except that. We're partners."

With a light kiss, Houston smiled. "Yes, ma'am." He tweaked her nose. "Miss Partner, I think we'd better get a little shut-eye. It'll be daylight soon and we'll have to ride."

"What about my mare? Will she be able?"

"No galloping and she'll be fine." He stood, sweeping her up into his arms. They'd crossed a wide chasm tonight. He maneuvered through the door with her and strode to where Angel slept. Lara curled up beside the child and Houston pulled a blanket over his girls.

"I'm happier now than I've ever been in my whole life, Houston," Lara murmured. "I'll always cherish this private time. I don't know what's going to happen with Yuma and his riders, but you give strength to fight. We're going to win, aren't we?"

Shadows darkened her green eyes to near black as she gazed up. He brushed her hair with his fingers, undone by the fierce need to keep her and Gracie safe. A lump grew in his throat and he had hell swallowing.

"Yes, darlin', we'll win," Houston finally managed. "Get some sleep." Before he gave in to the hunger to lie down beside her, he reached for a folded blanket at the end of the bed and moved into the parlor, where he dropped into an overstuffed chair.

But sleep didn't claim him. His thoughts went to Lara in the next room. She was a constant surprise. She tried so hard to overcome her fear of a man's touch, and had made giant strides tonight. He could see how desperately she yearned to be a wife and to free herself from the memories. Somehow, he'd force himself to be patient. The prize was worth the wait. Her quiet strength amazed him and he wanted no other by his side.

Hell yes, they'd win this fight! Houston clenched a fist so tightly the muscles in his arm knotted.

Yuma Blackstone would get what was coming to him—and more.

Like Virgil Boone had said, there were some things a man was willing to die for.

Twenty-one

OVER BREAKFAST THE NEXT MORNING, DR. MARY LEANED back in her chair. The butt of a cigar rested beside her plate. She absently fingered her bullet necklace. "I have something to speak to you about."

Houston forked a bite of flapjack dripping with molasses into his mouth. "Shoot."

She told them about a young couple in Chimney Rock whose kin, every last one, had all been stolen by cholera. "Nick and Caroline Vincent are young newlyweds, no more than kids. He gets a kick out of telling everyone he got an older woman because she's a year older. They live in a rickety wagon around the bend." Dr. Mary propped her elbows on the table. "This is no place for them. Would you consider taking them with you to Kansas to Nick's distant uncle outside of Dodge?"

"I'll be glad to talk to them. Won't make any promises, though." Houston laid his fork on his empty plate and wiped his mouth. He didn't want Nick to wind up in a grave along with Zeb, but he couldn't offer them safety either, and he'd make that clear right off. They might be exchanging one place rife with trouble for another.

Lara stood and gathered the plates. "I'll go with you, Houston. Gracie needs to take a nap before we head out anyway."

A half hour later, they walked the short distance to the old wagon that sat in the shadow of a tall mountain that was bare of vegetation. A trickle of water running from large rocks at the base sparkled like diamonds in the early morning sun. Houston took in the shape of two horses nibbling at some wild rye, approaching to get a better look. Surprisingly, he found both in excellent condition. On the other hand, Dr. Mary had been right about the poor shape of the wagon. One of the wheels leaned at an angle, just barely attached, and the rigorous rocking by the occupants inside made the planks groan and threaten to collapse.

Houston tried to hide a grin. Lara sent him a questioning glance from the cold fire, and he averted his gaze. Damn, he hated to interrupt.

Finally, he cleared his throat and hollered, "Hello the wagon."

The rocking immediately ceased. He heard a flurry of activity and loud whispers.

A male voice finally mumbled, "Be right there."

"Are they fighting?" Lara asked low.

Far from it. He chuckled and put his mouth next to her ear. "Starting a family."

Color flooded her cheeks. "Oh." She turned and picked at a loose thread of her shawl.

A head finally poked from the canvas covering the wagon and a lanky, barefoot man climbed out. His shirt was askew with the buttons in the wrong holes. He struggled to stuff it into his pants then gave up in defeat, leaving the fabric half-in and half-out. His dark hair stuck up in all directions. "It's a little early for callers. You lost, mister?"

"Nope. Sorry to bother you." Houston introduced himself and Lara, explaining that Dr. Mary had sent them. "We'll let you ride along and feed you in exchange for some work."

A hefty young woman squealed and jumped from the back of the wagon. "You're a godsend, Mr. Legend."

"Now, Caroline honey, I told you this old wagon won't

make the trip," Nick scolded. "Besides, the husband is supposed to do the talkin'."

Caroline put her hands on her rounded hips. "Says who?
I'll not bite my tongue when I have things to say." She
paused then added in a tone that dripped sugar, "*Sweetheart*."

The young couple's wedded bliss appeared to be a work
in progress. Houston glanced at Lara out of the corner of
his eye. She inched toward Caroline, evidently taking the
girl's side.

"I got all excited at the prospect of finding your uncle,
sweetheart." Caroline pouted, running her hand along
Nick's arm, then down his back, before resting at his waist.
She was a beauty, with golden hair that sparkled in the
early sun and curled around her shoulders. She turned to
Houston. "We have land waiting up north. We'll make
a home in Kansas for us and the children we'll have."
Caroline sent her husband a stubborn glance even as she
kept touching him.

Nick couldn't keep his hands off her either. He caressed
her hair, her shoulders, down his wife's back. No telling
what would happen if Houston and Lara weren't there.

"My Caroline likes to think she's the boss, but I know
how to handle older women," Nick said with a big grin.

"I do declare, Nick Vincent, stop saying that." Caroline
playfully slapped his arm. "I'm only one year older than
you, so don't make me out to be your mother's age. And
you have another think coming if you think you're gonna
boss me around."

Houston quickly covered his laughter with a cough.
Caroline was bound and determined to have the final
word. If young Nick thought to make her biddable, he'd
best reconsider.

"Then we'll get you to that home you want," Lara said,
putting her arm around the girl. "Won't we, Houston?"

No use hesitating. He knew he'd give in anyway, no
matter how much a better wagon would cost. "Certainly,
dear."

Caroline beamed, ignoring Nick's scowl.

"I can't let you go into this blindly," Houston added. "There's something you ought to know first. The trip won't be without danger." He told the couple about Yuma Blackstone and his men, then ended with, "I can't guarantee your safety."

The lanky new husband stood up straight, crossed his arms, and spoke in a strong, quiet tone. "Mr. Legend, Caroline and I found out early that life never comes with any promises. Both our folks died a month ago and there's no future for us here in Chimney Rock. At least we have hope in Kansas. I heard it's good land up there. We'll go with you and I'll kill anyone who tries to harm Caroline."

The boy's firm convictions and way of speaking touched Houston. Though lacking in years and experience, Nick looked to be a man in the ways that counted.

"Pack your things." Lara patted Caroline's shoulder. "We'll buy another wagon and be back. You can help me do the cooking on the trail. It'll be nice having a woman to talk to."

Nick sighed in defeat and shrugged his shoulders helplessly. "Go see the blacksmith. Heard he had one to sell."

"Thanks." Houston stepped to Lara.

"Wait," Nick called. "Make sure you get one with sturdy springs, Mr. Legend. Caroline and I… Well, we… Never mind." Red splotches crept up his neck as he seemed to decide he'd said too much.

Houston put his arm around Lara and they walked back to Dr. Mary's. Apparently Caroline's chatty bug had bitten his wife because she talked the whole way, like she'd found long lost relatives. Houston didn't mind. He just loved listening to her voice.

All too soon he left her with Dr. Mary and strode to the blacksmith. He found a good used wagon and hitched Lara's little mare and his Appaloosa to it for now. He'd switch them out later with the young couple's horses.

The telegraph office caught his attention. He pulled up

next to it and sent a telegram to Stoker, telling him about Yuma Blackstone. Houston wasn't sure why he felt the need—there was nothing Stoker or his brothers could do to help. This fight was his. Some of the weight lifted from his shoulders just the same.

In no time, he returned to Dr. Mary's to fetch Lara and Gracie, said their good-byes, then rolled to collect the newlyweds. They heard the racket before they rounded the last bend in the road. The rickety wagon seemed to be getting another workout. Whatever differences Nick and Caroline had sure didn't pertain to lovemaking.

This time Houston pulled to a stop and jumped down, pretending to check the harnesses. He didn't have the heart to interrupt them a second time. According to Dr. Mary, they hadn't been married but two weeks. Even so, at this rate, he'd have to give them plenty to do or they'd be so slow on the road they'd never make it to Kansas.

Lara's laughter surprised him. He fought back laughter of his own and climbed up onto the seat with her. While they waited, they spent the time talking about their life together.

"Do you realize we haven't discussed where we're going to live when we return from this trip?" Houston asked. "Where do you want to live? Tell me and I'll make it so."

"The Lone Star is your home. I want it to be my home too." She met his glance unflinching. "Except not in the house you built for Becky. Even though she never lived there, I feel strange, like I'm filling a dead woman's shoes."

"Then I'll build one just for you. Truth is, I don't like living there either." He lifted her hand. "I own a section of the ranch away from everyone. I'll build a castle if you say the word."

"No, nothing grand. Just a comfortable house where we can raise Gracie. I've never put on airs. I'm a simple woman with simple tastes."

He begged to differ on that. Lara Legend was anything but common or simple.

"I want to set aside a certain time each day, even if it's no more than fifteen minutes, to talk," Houston said. "We'll only have one rule—not to mention the past during this golden time."

"I'd like that. I want to know the man I married." She brushed his jaw with her fingertips and warmth spread over him.

"I propose we set this time for after you put some grub in the men's hungry bellies. We can get someone to watch Gracie for a bit and you won't have to worry about her until bedtime." He'd paid attention to Lara's routine and seen her begin feeding the little angel bits of table food at suppertime, reserving her milk until she rocked the babe to sleep.

"That will work. I'm glad you had this idea."

Houston chuckled. "You'd be surprised at the things I think about." But the look she gave him said she wasn't surprised in the least.

"I daresay you would find my thoughts surprising as well." Lara smiled.

"That right?" His voice turned teasing. What was she trying to tell him? "Care to elaborate?"

"The men are starting to talk about why we don't sleep together, Houston." She gave him a sidelong glance.

That was news to him. He hadn't heard a whisper of this. The thought crossed his mind that she was using the drovers as an excuse. "Go on. What do you propose we do about this vexing problem?"

"I want you to sleep beside me at night." She chewed her bottom lip. "On top of the covers for now. Can you do that?"

Excitement and hope flooded over him. That she felt strong enough to take the next step was beyond his wildest dreams.

"Your wish is my command. From now on, I'll lie beside you at night...fully clothed. I promise nothing will happen unless you want it."

Lara stared deep into his eyes. "I just don't want to cause any talk."

Houston brought her palm to his lips and pressed a kiss on the smooth flesh. He had to work hard to hide his grin. "No, me either. I don't deserve you. I hope you never regret hitching up with me."

This stolen time couldn't come soon enough. And tonight he'd get to unfasten one more button on her dress.

Another button toward making her his.

And then he'd lie next to her—the one place he wanted to be.

Twenty-two

HOUSTON, LARA, AND THE VINCENTS CAUGHT UP WITH THE cattle drive about noon. Flat, arid land fanned out in front of them as far as the eye could see. A mesa over to the right rose up from the inhospitable landscape, and clouds of thick dust coated Houston's tongue. He prayed they'd make it to the Canadian River without losing any cattle, grateful to have the Cherokees' assurance there was water in it.

After leaving Lara and Gracie at the chuck wagon, he put Nick on horseback and located his number one man in charge.

Clay grimly pushed back his hat and used his shirtsleeve to wipe the sweat running down his face. "Mighty glad you're back. How's sweet pea?"

"Sassier than ever. All the way from Chimney Rock, she pointed her finger at every bird, blade of grass, and rabbit, scolding them for crossing her path." Houston grinned. "Personally, I think that woman doctor put something in her water."

"Could have," Clay agreed after Houston described Dr. Mary and her necklace. "Sounds like my kind of woman."

"What are you talking about? Every woman seems to be your kind. A word of warning...don't mess with this one. She knows a hundred different ways to hurt a man." Houston thought about how easily Zeb could've shot the doctor, and grew serious. He introduced the young man beside him. "This here's Nick Vincent. He and his wife are riding along to Kansas. Put him to work."

Clay told the young man to help with the remuda until he had time to break him in as a drover.

"Anything happen here?" Houston asked after Nick had ridden off.

"Other than the disaster at breakfast with Henry, it's been pretty quiet." Clay reached in his pocket for a match to light his rolled cigarette. "Only, the riders following are getting bolder. They don't seem to care if we see them; they just keep coming. I've never seen them this close."

Houston let out a curse. "We're sitting ducks."

"The worthless bastards," Clay Angelo spat. "Ain't fit for buzzard bait. Makes me skittish. What do you reckon they're waitin' for?"

"For their friends to catch up. The bastard wants to stack the deck first," Houston answered. He really must've sent the rest of the gang on a wild-goose chase when he burned the note Yuma had left at his campsite. His glance swept to the drovers. Good men, and he'd put them up against anyone. "We can't outrun them, but hell if we're going to make it easy. Push the herd faster. We've got to drive them to the limit."

"The pace will kill a bunch. You ready for that?"

"My people mean more than this herd. We can always raise more cows. The men and my family have to come first."

Clay's black eye patch lent extra danger to his wary face. That, combined with the dark whisker growth along his jaw, made him look downright formidable. He took a drag on the cigarette and let the smoke curl from his mouth. "I've worked for plenty of ranchers who valued the almighty dollar over their men. You're different, Houston. So is Stoker."

"It's the way we see things." Houston leaned forward to pat his horse's sleek neck. "You mentioned Henry."

"The poor boy tried, but burned everything." Clay

wagged his head in sympathy. "Felt sorry for him. His brothers finally took over and got a little grub into the hungry bellies at least. Miss Lara will be a sight for sore eyes."

Houston glanced back at the chuck wagon where he'd left Lara and Gracie, praying Caroline Vincent would prove a big help. "She'll have things running smoothly now."

"You ain't lyin'. You were right about Henry being good at fixing things. Every time he got upset, I'd take him something broken—even broke things on purpose—and that settled him right down."

"That's good to hear. Henry can get agitated sometimes."

Virgil galloped up. "You're back. Is everything—"

"Gracie's fine, son."

"What happened was my fault." Virgil glanced down but Houston saw the slight quiver of his lip. "I never meant to leave Gracie…to let…"

Houston squeezed his shoulder. "She's a handful. No one holds you responsible."

"I do. Because of me she could've died." Virgil's voice was raw with emotion and self-loathing.

"Could've is a far cry from did," Houston reminded him quietly. "She's alive and well and that's what's important. I'm sure you learned a valuable lesson."

Virgil's gaze rose to meet Houston's. "Yes, sir, for a fact."

"Okay, then let's get these cows to Dodge." When Virgil gave him a quick nod and rode away, Houston turned to Clay. "I'll go to the rear and protect our backside if you have things in hand up here. The way the hair is standing on my neck, we'd best stay alert."

"I never stop, boss." Clay pointed his horse north and hollered some orders.

Protecting his men, the women, and the herd would call for strength, commitment, and nerves of steel. Stoker had instilled all three in his sons. Now, Houston finally understood the tough lessons his father had taught.

"Come on, you sons of bitches," he growled low. Turning, he kept an eye on the dust devil swirling behind them, like a giant brown beast ready to grab them in claws of sand and wind. That swirling tower of sand seemed to have been created by Blackstone himself, to slow them.

He galloped past the long column of bellowing long-horns that surrounded the chuck wagon. "Lara, keep in the middle of the cattle. Don't straggle behind and if riders attack, try not to panic. Whatever you do, keep moving."

"Where will you be?" She seemed calm and collected. His wife had a good head on her shoulders, now more than ever. The days in Chimney Rock had helped her settle into a newfound confidence.

"Stopping them," Houston answered.

"Do you think an attack is coming?"

Damn, he wished she hadn't asked that. She'd made him promise to tell the truth, though. After letting out a long sigh, Houston said, "I do."

Henry leaned around Lara. "I have a rock. I'll hit him."

"Keep it handy, Henry." Houston didn't tell him that they'd need more than a rock against Blackstone. "Do as your sister says and don't argue. She knows what's best."

"I will. But you forgot that my name is Bones."

"Indeed it is. Thanks for the reminder, Bones." As Houston was about to touch his spurs to the horse's flanks, Gracie reached for Houston and babbled something. "I'm sorry, Angel, but I can't take you with me. Not this time. Remember what I said, Lara."

Gracie started bellowing when Houston galloped off to tell Caroline the same thing. It didn't sit well to break his little girl's heart.

Hell!

Before his horse had gone three lengths, gunshots burst from both sides. Riders emerged, two on each side, from behind the cover of some juniper that stood beside the trail.

His Colt .45 filled his hand and he returned their fire while jockeying for the best position. With the two-thousand-strong herd being fifty to sixty feet across, the safest place was in the middle, so that's where he headed, praying all the while that the gunfire wouldn't stampede them.

From the corner of his eye, Houston watched the wagons speed up. He breathed a sight easier when they were out of the direct line of attack. Now they had to keep Blackstone and his men too busy to go after the women.

The drovers were quick to double back to help, and Clay and the others were in the thick of the chaos in an instant. The blasts of gunfire, frightened screaming horses, and bellowing cattle deafened Houston.

Blackstone was smart; Houston gave him that. He and his men kept constantly moving, making it difficult to draw a bead on them. They'd run at them in a charge on two fronts, then quickly retreat. Over and over they repeated the strategy, dividing the drovers' focus. That told Houston the man had to have been in the military at some point.

When Houston's Colt ran out of bullets, he yanked his rifle from the scabbard and kept shooting. One of the attackers' horses stumbled and went to its knees. Houston aimed and fired. The rider flew from the saddle and landed facedown on the ground, and the horse got to its feet and galloped away.

Satisfied that the rider wouldn't get up, Houston turned his attention to the other three attackers.

A drover fell from his horse to the dirt in the middle of the moving cattle. Houston didn't have time to check on him, as the next bullet zinged past his cheek.

Saying a prayer the drover wasn't dead, he turned and fired. Painful screams filled the air as the hot metal shredded the attacker's shoulder. He slid halfway out of the saddle and hung there as his horse disappeared into a dry wash.

Houston turned in time to see a man riding straight for him. When the rider was a few lengths away, he tumbled from the saddle, where he lay unmoving on the ground. Houston stared in disbelief. He knew he hadn't shot him. But who had? Clay was too far away and had his hands full with the others, and the rest of the drovers were chasing the one who'd ridden into the gully.

A loud cry penetrated the noise. "Retreat! Retreat!"

The two remaining riders galloped hell-bent for safer territory, leaving behind their two fallen comrades. While Clay and the drovers gave chase, Houston dismounted and ran over to the man who'd mysteriously fallen from his saddle.

"Help," came the faint cry. "Please help."

Twenty-three

Just please let it be Blackstone, Houston prayed.

With their leader out of the picture, the rest would probably give up the fight. He quickly reloaded his Colt then kept it trained on the fallen man as he turned him over. The reddish complexion didn't match Yuma's description, and this one had no missing half of his left ear. Still, it could be a trick of some kind.

Fear darkened the eyes staring up at him. "Please help me, mister. I beg you."

Houston kicked a fallen six-shooter from reach. "Who are you?"

"Frank. Frank Farley."

No blood, not even a drop, was visible. "You injured, Frank?"

"Nope. I'm begging for your protection. I'm surrendering."

What the hell? None of this made any sense. Enemies didn't just give themselves up out of the blue.

"If you think I'm going to buy this cheap trick, you must've fallen off a turnip wagon and cracked your fool head," Houston snapped, grabbing Frank Farley's shirt and yanking him up. "The minute I turn my back, you'll put a bullet in one of us."

The outlaw wearily rubbed his eyes. His voice shook when he spoke. "I realize I've given you no reason to trust me, but I swear on a stack of Bibles I won't bring you any harm. Yuma has gone mad and I just want far away from him. I'll tell you anything you want to know. Hell, tie me up and take me to Fort Supply."

"Don't worry. That's exactly where I'm taking you, Frank." Houston searched his prisoner. Strangely, other than the side arm he'd kicked away, he found nothing. "What does Blackstone want?" he asked. "What does he hope to gain?"

"Your wife. He wants Lara Boone."

"To kill her this time?" Houston feared the answer.

Frank wiped his mouth. "No. In his mind, she belongs to him. He put his mark on her face and figures that makes her his property."

Houston let out a curse so bad it blistered his tongue. "He'll have go through me to get her, and he'll discover that's a pretty big chore."

"Any mention of the baby sets him off. He hates her. Says that's not his child. Claims the babe belongs to someone else."

Anger danced along Houston's spine. "He had a chance to end the babe's life. What stopped him?"

"Two reasons. One, to taunt you. He hates your guts and wants to kill you too. Another reason was the simple boy. Yuma thinks he's devil-possessed." Frank's mouth quirked up at the corners. "I told you he's crazy as a loon."

"I'm beginning to get the picture." If only they could tap into those delusions somehow. But to do so, Houston would have to learn to think like Yuma. He didn't know if he could.

"He also means to put you in a grave and take your herd. Has plans to sell them and use the money to take Lara far away. The man talks out of his head all the time. Scares me because I never know what he'll do."

"Why didn't you just ride away?" Seemed simple enough to Houston.

"Kept me tied up at night. Yuma threatened to put a

bullet in my back if I ran. One other thing," Frank said. "The last thing Yuma said before we rode here—he'll kill one of your men a day. I'd take him very seriously."

Houston's blood ran cold. The threat spun inside his head like a roulette wheel. He just prayed the marble going round and round didn't land on red. A man a day—when would it start?

"Which of us is first?"

"Whoever gets in Yuma's way. Plans to start whittling until you have no one left."

The strategy would work. Two men could inflict deep wounds—a bullet from the darkness was something you couldn't defend against when you were in open, desolate country as they were. Hell and be damned! He turned at the sound of riders and saw Clay leading the returning drovers.

Disappointment wound through him at not seeing Yuma Blackstone with them. "Any luck, Clay?"

"Lost the other two. Seemed like a hole opened and swallowed them. They went behind some rocks and just disappeared." The head drover rested his arm across the pommel.

With a tight chest, Houston glanced at his men. Most were hurt and bleeding. "How much damage did the riders do?"

"Bullet caught Quaid Boone's leg." Clay dismounted. "One creased Emmett's head, horse fell on Joe but I think he's okay, and Virgil… He insists he doesn't need doctoring."

"Nothing but a flesh wound." Virgil's tight voice held pain.

Houston pushed Frank Farley to the head drover. "Clay, watch this man and shoot him if he moves. Emmett and Joe, go see my wife. The rest of you check on the dead man lying over there." Houston strode to Quaid and Virgil to assess their injuries. Lara wouldn't be happy he got her brothers shot. *Damn!*

For all the pain of a bullet in the leg, Quaid seemed unfazed, if his wobbly grin was any indication. Houston inspected the wound and saw the bullet was still inside. If they got the slug removed right away, the boy should be all right. He moved to Virgil.

"It's nothing," Virgil insisted as he dismounted, though blood soaked his sleeve.

"Let me be the judge of that." Houston tore the shirt away for a better look, but Virgil was right. The bullet had just grazed his upper arm. Houston used the sleeve he'd torn away as a bandage, wrapping it tightly around the wound. "Ride forward and let Lara clean it. And take care of your brother."

"I'm fine." Virgil turned his attention to his rifle.

"I'm not asking, son," Houston said quietly but with enough authority to let Virgil know he was boss and expected his orders to be obeyed.

"Yes, boss." The young man angrily turned to jam his boot in the stirrup.

Houston could see the steam coming off him as he mounted. He hated to make him mad, but Virgil had to learn that on a cattle drive someone had to be in charge and his word was law. He'd try to smooth things over later.

"Who's our prisoner?" Clay asked.

"Frank Farley, one of Yuma's men. He wants our protection."

"The hell you say! This is a first for me."

"You're not alone." Houston swiveled to yell to the drovers who stood over the dead man. "Is it Yuma Blackstone?"

"Not unless he has a big black mole on his jaw," Emmett O'Brien answered.

"*Hell!* The bastard's too mean to die." Clay shifted his rifle to the crook of an arm, keeping it ready for trouble in case Frank decided to give them some.

Houston grunted in agreement. Grabbing their prisoner, he pushed him forward. "Tell us who the dead man is."

"I told you I'd help any way I can," Frank answered. "Don't have to look, though. Slim is the only one with a big mole."

"Make sure anyway. Then I want to know exactly where

Yuma's camp is and I want to know about this other group of desperados who are coming this way." Though Houston had many unanswered questions, a clear picture emerged of what they were up against.

A den of reptiles, but which one would try to inflict the first bite?

Relief swept over Lara to hear the absence of gunshots behind her. Only now, the wait had begun. It seemed she'd spent her whole life marking time for one thing or another. Waiting for Gracie to be born, for people to forget, for her scars to fade. But this seemed more excruciating because Houston was part of her life now.

Before the shots had rent the air, she'd been lost in the memories of how Houston had kissed her and opened the top button of her dress. And how he'd slowly awakened her as if from a heavy sleep. But now, her thoughts tumbled this way and that, as though pushed by a strong river current.

Her mind raced, keeping time with the pounding of her heart. Was anyone hit during the attack? Even now, Houston could lie injured...or worse. Dear God, she'd go crazy if she didn't see him soon.

Lara heard riders coming. She swung around, hoping to see her handsome husband. Worry knitted her brow when her oldest brothers and two of the drovers rode alongside. All four were bleeding, but her brothers' injuries made her heart lodge in her throat. Henry stuck his head out from inside the wagon, where he went when he was scared. Gracie gave a cry, apparently awakened by the noise, and Lara heard him tell the babe it was okay.

"Is the skirmish over?" She stopped the wagon and set the brake, praying Houston wasn't lying dead behind her.

"For now," Joe said with a slow drawl, dragging up a smile. "Hate to be a bother, ma'am, but we need a little patching up."

"Joe, you couldn't be a bother if you tried. But tell me… is my husband all right?" She couldn't help the tremble in her voice.

"He's very much alive, Mrs. Legend. Nary a scratch."

"That's a relief. Let me get my doctoring supplies." Lara took a deep breath and tried to control her shaking hands as she reached through the canvas opening of the wagon for the box of medical necessities. She wasn't that proficient in digging out bullets, but she'd do her best.

"Can I help?" Caroline Vincent pulled up next to the chuck wagon.

"I can sure use you," Lara said, explaining the situation.

Quaid slumped in the saddle as Emmett and Joe hurried to help him. Lara stifled a sob as she accepted Emmett's help to the ground and rushed to them. One look at Quaid's bloody thigh and she struggled to swallow.

With a grimace, Joe turned to her. "We'd be obliged if you'd take care of Quaid and Virgil first, ma'am. Miss Caroline can doctor us."

The wounded cowboy's unselfishness made her chest tighten. "Thank you. We'll have you fixed up soon, Joe." Lara glanced at the anguish written on her brother's face as she spoke.

"The kid's a mite scared," Emmett said, breathing heavily. The man tried to grin but the effort evidently proved too much. "I'll soon be righter than rain. Too ornery to die."

Caroline jumped from her wagon and raced to them. "My mama taught me a lot about doctoring. We'll fix you up before you can think of a good cuss word, Quaid."

Lara admired the down-home way about her and the gentle touch that put the injured men at ease. Emmett and Joe lifted Quaid into the back of the Vincent wagon and Lara crawled inside, trying to calm her heart that thundered in her ears. Virgil followed and sat beside his twin. Henry leaned next to them, holding Gracie.

"Virgil, hand me the scissors." Lara smoothed back Quaid's sweat-soaked hair.

Quaid jerked up on an elbow. "Huh-uh, you're not cutting off my britches."

"Then how in the blessed name of our father do you think I'm going to remove this bullet? And don't you dare tell me to leave it in there. You'll get gangrene and die."

"Virgil can take them off, won't you? Just one leg," Quaid pleaded.

"I'll try." Virgil moved closer.

But Quaid wasn't ready. "Sis, turn your head."

"I swear to goodness!" Lara threw up her hands. "I've changed your diapers and now I can't see your naked thigh?"

Color crept up Quaid's neck and flooded his face. "Christ, sis! Hush about the diapers!"

Looking on, Henry made things worse. "Babies wear diapers, Quaid."

"Shush, Henry." Quaid hid his eyes and groaned.

"Can you go get some water and clean cloth for me, Henry?" She heard him scurry off. Lara waited with scissors ready in case Virgil couldn't get the wounded leg out, but put them down when he managed, much to Quaid's immense relief.

When Henry returned with water, she carefully cleaned the wound, relieved the bullet hadn't gone deep. She grabbed hold of it with the tweezers and pulled it out. Covering the hole with ointment, she wrapped a bandage around his leg. Quaid watched during the whole process.

"There, we're all done," she said.

Quaid grinned like a fool and slapped Virgil's palm as though in victory.

"What on earth? Both of you just got shot. Why are you grinning?" Lara asked.

"Yeah, we got shot," Quaid answered. "We're men now."

"Good heavens! I don't know what the good Lord gave you for brains." Lara shook her head at the silly boy. He didn't know that character was the sign of a man. He and Virgil became men when they rescued her from Yuma, and in the way they helped care for Gracie.

Confident that Quaid would make a full recovery, she turned her attention to Virgil and told him to sit on the tailgate. His grin had faded and he wore a black scowl. He shoved a lock of sun-bleached hair from his eyes. "Don't get all weepy or anything. It's just a scratch," he said.

"Let me decide. You bled an awful lot for something small."

"I'd still be there with our men but Houston ordered me to come find you." He let out a frustrated snort. "He treats me like I'm some kid in short britches without a lick of sense. I should know when I need doctorin'. But not according to him. Won't even listen to me."

Henry poked his head around Lara. "I listen to you, Virgil."

"Thanks, Henry." Virgil blew out a big breath when she prodded the wound.

"Believe it or not, Houston knows what he's doing." She poured some water into a metal bowl. "Besides, he's the boss, and if he thinks you need doctoring, then you do. Personally, I agree with him."

"You would," Virgil huffed. "I think it's a law or something that a wife has to take her husband's side."

Henry leaned forward to watch. Gracie pointed her finger and babbled.

Lara allowed a smile. Virgil had so much to learn. "I thought you liked Houston."

"I do...when's he's not bossing me around."

"Sometimes you get too big for your britches," Lara scolded.

"Does it hurt, Virgil?" Henry asked.

"Like a son of a..." He glanced at Lara, swallowed hard, and muttered, "Yes."

"Are you gonna cry?" Henry shifted Gracie and reached for his brother's hand.

Virgil jerked away. "Stop it. And no, I'm not a bawl baby. Men don't cry."

"If I got shot, I'd cry." Henry sniffled, trying to muster up a few tears to demonstrate.

Lara reached for a clean cloth and put it into the pan of water, watching her brothers. Two trying to prove themselves as men and the other just wanting to be included.

Very gently, she washed the blood away. Once she could see clearly, she sided with Houston. Though not serious, it was more than a scratch and required attention. She doused some cotton with iodine.

"This might sting," Lara warned, dabbing it on his arm.

Virgil jerked and muttered an oath. "Good Lord, sis! That stuff burned a hole clean through me. Might as well light a match and stick it my skin. Wouldn't hurt no worse."

She ignored his ranting and reached for a roll of gauze. "Houston is a good man and knows his business. Whatever he says goes and I don't want you arguing with him. He cares about you. About all of us. You don't know the load he carries on his shoulders."

"Aw, I know. I'm just out of sorts because I wanted to stay. I want to see Yuma dead, the sooner the better."

"Tell me what happened." She wrapped a bandage over the gauze and tied it. "And don't leave out anything."

Virgil started with the gun battle and how they'd shot one rider from the saddle. "He just lay on the ground. I don't know if he's dead or wounded or who it is. That's why I wanted to stay. I need to know that we got Yuma. I want to make you and Gracie safe from the likes of him."

"Thank you, I appreciate that." What a relief it would be if they'd killed the man who stalked them. She wanted him out of her life forever and the people she cared about safe.

"I didn't get to see if we got him," Virgil complained. "And we caught another one alive. Houston called him Frank something."

Good. She hoped they caught them all.

"You're free. Go find out." She gently shoved him toward his horse. "Find out for both of us."

When Quaid struggled to get his leg back into his pants, she stopped him. "Not you, buster. Lie still."

Virgil stuck his boot in the stirrup then paused. "Sis, I'm sorry I let you down and almost killed Gracie."

"She's good as new. That was a lesson for us all. Now go see what you can learn."

"Bye, Virgil," Henry hollered, waving.

Lara put her arm around her red-headed brother and watched Virgil gallop off. "You know I love you, don't you?"

"Yep," Henry said, laying his head on her shoulder. "I miss Papa, but I miss my mama really bad."

"Me too." Sometimes unbearable longing filled her.

"I wish she didn't go away. My heart is crying. I need her." Henry looked up with tears in his eyes. "Will you be my mama?"

"Sure." She kissed his cheek but didn't point out she'd been that for a long while. "I've got to help Caroline. Can you watch Gracie a bit longer?"

At his nod, she joined the young woman and injured drovers.

Caroline turned. "These two were easy. Cleaned Emmett's head, and Joe only has a sprained foot and knee."

"You're a lucky man, Joe." Lara gave him a smile. "Why that horse didn't break every bone in your body I'll never know."

The man winked at her and laughed. "I live a charmed life."

Lara laughed. "You must."

Despite reservations, she relented with Quaid and the men rode out. She helped Caroline set her wagon to rights. Though she tried, Lara couldn't help giving the narrow bed a glance. It didn't really have enough room for two people, yet Nick and Caroline appeared to spend a lot of happy time in it. She wondered how it would be to lie next to Houston.

Though she expected fear to crowd her mind, instead, anticipation filled her. Somehow, it was going to be all right. She trusted him.

In the wagon box of the chuck wagon, Lara held

Gracie, waiting for someone to come and tell her whether to go or stay. Worry deepened on Henry's face. She wondered at his unease. He'd been very quiet when Virgil talked about Yuma.

Lara draped an arm around him. "What's wrong, Henry? Is something bothering you?"

"I don't want you to die and leave me."

"Oh, honey, I'm not going to die."

Tears bubbled in his eyes. "If Yuma kills you then who'll take care of me?"

There it was. She was her brother's anchor to this world, the one who kept him grounded. The thought of having to navigate alone scared him half to death. Everyone needed security. Though she was better equipped at dealing with life, she couldn't bear the thought of losing what she'd found.

Another gunshot blast made her jump.

Twenty-four

HOUSTON SLID HIS COLT INTO THE HOLSTER AND GLANCED at the dead steer. The animal had broken its leg during the gun battle and there wasn't anything else to do except kill it. A shame they couldn't salvage some of the meat, but they had no way of keeping it from spoiling.

Houston turned to Clay. "I'm going to ride over to that rock formation Frank told me about and scout around."

"Want me to come with you?"

"Nope. Take the men and push the herd as fast as possible. Don't stop until full dark. From now on, we need to make double time. I've taken Frank's weapons, but keep a close eye on him."

"I'm not sure we can trust him yet," Clay agreed.

"Exactly." Houston's chaps flapped against his legs as he strode to his horse. "And, Clay, tell Lara not to worry."

"Will do, but I might as well tell the moon not to rise." Clay grinned. "Women are real good at frettin' over stuff."

"Guess you're right." Houston glanced at Virgil's sullen face. It bothered him that the kid hadn't said two words since returning. Houston softened his voice. "Walk with me."

With a nod, the sixteen-year-old fell into step. After they'd taken ten strides, Houston stopped and faced the young man. "I'm sorry we got crossways. But I promised your dad I'd bring you safely home. Being a father myself now, I know how I'd feel if someone took Gracie off and brought her home hurt or dead. I'd want to kill them."

Virgil blinked hard. A little of the anger left his eyes but his body was still rigid.

Houston went on. "You're a big help to me. I trust your instincts. You have the best instincts I've seen for someone your age and you're more man than some grown men I've known. You're a brother to me and when that bullet found you…" Houston rubbed his eyes, hoping to take the tremble from his voice. "I wish it had hit me. Maybe one day you'll understand why I overreacted. Do you think you can help Lara until I make it back to camp?"

"Absolutely." Vigil relaxed his stance. "Houston, just so you know…you're all right. I'm proud to have you in the family. And thanks for caring about us Boones."

"Anytime." They walked back to the horses, where Clay and Emmett waited. Virgil mounted. Houston watched the three ride to catch up with the herd before he focused on his task.

The saddle creaked as Houston swung into it, and he rode toward the distant rock formation rising up from the inhospitable landscape, the place where Frank said they'd camped last night. With his partner's arm shredded by that bullet, Yuma would be focused on patching him up. He wouldn't want to let another die. Now was the time to strike.

He reached into his pocket for the note left on Gracie. The words stared back at him.

I could've killed the brat. Next time I will.

Anger bubbled to a fine froth all over again. For the bastard to threaten a defenseless baby set his blood boiling. Through a narrowed gaze, he stared at the distant rock formation.

The Appaloosa snorted and tossed his head back and forth as his nostrils flared. Apparently, the horse shared his hope. Maybe this would end here and now.

The jutting boulders Frank had pointed to were jagged and sharp. Houston decided not to risk injury to his horse and dismounted. Besides, he could be quieter on foot. Frank said that Yuma never slept in the same place twice, but he didn't want to get sloppy. He might have only one chance, and he wasn't about to ruin it.

Sliding the Colt from his holster, he picked his way over the obstacles. Frank had described a hollowed-out area in the midst of the rocks where they'd bedded down.

After thirty minutes of treacherous going, Houston decided Yuma Blackstone was part goat. Every so often he'd pause and listen, but he heard only the sighing of the wind and chirps of an occasional bird. Still, he pressed on. Just as he'd decided Frank had lied about it all, the rocks opened up into a secluded clearing of sorts. There lay the remains of a campfire, with empty cans strewn about.

Houston's boot kicked a drained whiskey bottle and sent it rolling. Blackstone left a mess wherever he went. Sliding his Colt back into the holster, he scanned the rubble. Spying nothing of benefit, he made his way back to the Appaloosa.

The light of the distant campfire became a beacon drawing him forward. In his mind's eye, he saw a vision of Lara, cooking supper. Firelight softened her features and danced in her hair. In his mind, she turned toward his horse with a big smile. Running, she kissed him, pressing her curves against his body and letting her hand drift below his gun belt.

He shook his head and muttered to himself, "You're getting as crazy as Yuma, you fool."

But still, he couldn't stop thinking of her. Soon it would be their golden time…his heartbeat thrummed.

He'd lived another day. Tonight he'd kiss Lara senseless and then…then he'd undo two buttons on her dress.

His mouth went dry just thinking about touching her again.

❧

Lara stood at the edge of darkness, listening to the night sounds. But she didn't hear the one thing she longed for—Houston's horse.

Supper was over and done. She'd washed the dishes, put everything away, and set the wagon tongue to the north, and still he wasn't back. She pulled her shawl close, refusing to let her mind dwell on any of the disasters that could've happened.

Houston *was* coming back to her, she told herself firmly.

In the distance, thunder rumbled as a storm brewed. Rain would make the drovers' work miserable. Lightning spooked cattle and could start another stampede. Lara prayed not. Houston needed one good night's sleep.

And he'd vowed to do it next to her.

Her glance swept to the Vincents' wagon. No doubt Nick and Caroline were curled up on that narrow bed, doing what married couples did. Lara envied their bliss and the love that put such a glow on their faces. She'd give anything for it to be that way for her and Houston.

Turning, she put on a pot of coffee for the men coming and going. The drover named Joe sat on a bedroll nearby. He reached for his harmonica and began to play. She couldn't place the song, but the melancholy tune settled over her like a sodden blanket.

Joe stopped and glanced at her. "He'll be along directly, ma'am."

"I know. But with trouble lurking about, I can't help but worry." She clutched her shawl together against a sudden chill.

Another drover, Pony Latham, propped himself on an elbow with his legs stretched out in front of him. He had a ragged playing card stuck in his hatband. "Houston's tough. His old man taught him well. I've never met anyone who can put the fear of God in me like Stoker Legend." Pony barked a laugh. "I think he took lessons from General Sam Houston himself."

How odd to hear that. Lara had never seen anything intimidating about Stoker. She'd seen the side of him that welcomed her as a daughter, despite her scar. Stoker, like Houston, saw her with his heart, not his eyes.

While the coffee brewed, she listened to Joe and Pony tell stories about the Legend family. The one about rustlers hanging Sam drew a shiver. How horrible! But then being saved by an unknown outlaw brother, that story touched her. She couldn't wait to meet Luke Legend, although he went by the surname Weston. She found it very admirable that he refused to take the Legend name until he straightened out his life. The Legend brothers shared many common qualities—honor, courage, and toughness, all bound together by deep caring for each other.

By the time the coffee was ready, she understood a little more about the storied family she'd married into.

Pony Latham rolled to his feet and reached for a cup. "Better get some of this before that storm rolls in."

"Gonna be a long night for sure," Joe agreed, moving toward the pot. "Who's going to roust that new guy from his bed?"

"If you mean Nick Vincent, it ain't gonna be me." Pony stretched and yawned. He was tall, with the most bowed legs Lara had ever seen. The cowboy could put a barrel between his legs and have room to spare, and his friendly smile made him easy to like.

Joe sighed. "Not me either. Young Nick is one lucky man to have a willing wife and a warm bed."

Both men glanced toward the Vincents' wagon and laughed at the vigorous motion.

Pony poured the coffee. "One thing about it, those springs must be made of iron."

"Yeah, but at this rate, they'll be plumb wore out soon."

Another cowboy who'd been asleep through it all stirred. She didn't know his name because he kept to himself. "Only fair way is to draw straws," growled the cowboy. "Whoever gets the short one has to roust him."

Joe snorted. "Don't trust you, Pete. You'll rig it somehow."

"Aww, Joe, you wound me." Pete sat up with a yawn.

Though she kept silent through the exchange, she had to agree. Nick and Caroline were very…passionate.

"Should be against the law having that much fun while we sleep on the hard ground in all kinds of weather, wishing for a woman next to us," grumbled Pony. "We got needs too."

"Well, one of us has to pull Nick out of there before Clay sees him missing from guard duty." Joe grabbed some sticks from the dirt, broke them into pieces, and closed his hand around them, leaving the tops sticking out.

Pony drew a long one and gave a whoop. Pete took a turn, then Joe.

Joe let out a mild oath when he got the short stick. "Should've known."

"Be gentle now," Pete cautioned.

Grumbling, Joe marched to the Vincents' wagon and hollered, "Time to go to work, Nick. You won't like it if the boss has to drag your rear out of there and throw you on a horse."

"Hold on a minute. I'm coming," Nick yelled.

A few minutes later, Lara smiled at the young husband as he emerged, pulling on his boots as he crow-hopped to the campfire. She held out a cup of hot coffee and refilled the others.

While they drank the brew, she moved back to the edge of the night to wait. She heard them mount up a short time later, but she didn't turn from her vigil.

❦

Lara ran to put things away an hour later as the wind began to whip the canvas top of the wagon. After everything was secure, she stood next to Gracie's crib, watching and listening. Finally, she heard the clop of hooves and knew Houston was back. Excitement swept through her. He rode in from the darkness like a black avenger, an image of strength and granite hardness. She made out the outline of his strong nose and jaw, but the profile otherwise appeared to blend with his Stetson and jacket.

Her breath caught in her throat at the sight of this man who could make her grow weak with a single glance.

Saddle leather creaked when he swung down. He looked utterly exhausted. She slipped an arm around his waist under the heavy denim jacket he wore. Her husband was solid and lean against her touch, and she was met with the heat of his body. A current danced just under her skin in anticipation of having him lie down next to her where she could feel him anytime she wanted. She was getting bolder and bolder after the visit to Dr. Mary's. Not surprising, though. One by one, his silent, feathery touches were helping her heal.

"I'm glad you're back." Her words came out breathless and whispery.

"Me too." His deep voice wound through her the way woven threads created a warm winter blanket. He draped an arm around her shoulders and kissed her temple.

Lara pressed against his side, inhaling his scent of leather, sage, and horse. "I missed you."

"Frank Farley told me where Yuma and his men slept last night. I went to try to find them."

Lara gave a cry. "Why did you go alone? They could've killed you."

"There's only two of them left, and one is hurt bad." He said it as though men who'd committed horrible, unspeakable crimes were no worse a threat than a bull gnat. "No better time to capture them. Besides, I ordered Clay to push the herd hard and fast."

"Yuma and his man still have guns and bullets," she reminded him with a frown.

He glanced up at the dark sky as a peal of thunder rumbled. "Storm's coming."

"It'll be a miserable night for everyone."

"Yep. I'll have to head back out soon. All hands have to be on deck in a storm."

"Oh, Houston, I was hoping you'd get to grab a little sleep. Do you at least have time for a cup of coffee?"

Houston leaned to whisper in her ear. "Maybe more than coffee if I play my cards right."

"I can deal you all aces if it'll help," Lara teased.

"Play cards, do you, Mrs. Legend?" He grinned and plopped his Stetson onto her head.

Lara loved this playful side of him. Most of the time he was far too serious.

"What else is there, living with three brothers?" Breathless, she glanced up into his eyes, where a fire smoldered. "I got pretty good. Don't mean to brag, but I used to win quite often."

With a long whistle, Houston grinned. "You don't say. I married a card sharp."

In one surprise move, he swung her into his arms. Her heart nearly hammered out of her chest. Was this how women in love felt? Her pulse raced as she rested a trembling palm on his broad chest. If only she had someone to ask. She'd never breathe a word of her ignorance to the drovers, and Caroline was too young. Besides, she didn't want anyone to know she was so dumb.

Houston carried her around the chuck wagon and out of sight before setting her down. Sheets of rain began to fall as the skies opened, but she didn't pay it, or the wet tendrils of hair that clung to her face, any mind.

Without a word, he kissed her eyelids and traced the outline of her lips with his tongue.

She strained for more, as burning hunger spread through her. Whatever this thing was, she wanted it. Had to have it.

"Please, Houston. Please teach me how to love," she begged against his mouth. Summer rain pelted her face and drenched her clothes, but it barely registered.

With a low growl, he crushed her to him, grinding his lips to hers. His Stetson fell from her head as the kiss stole her breath, her thoughts, her sanity. She stood in the rain with thunder shaking the ground beneath her feet.

Swirling wind buffeted her, lightning flashed. But nothing mattered, not the rain running down her face, not the fact her clothes were plastered to her—nothing except Houston and his kisses.

Struck with the realization of just how much she needed this man, she wound her fingers into his wet hair, clutching him to her. The deluge had soaked her to the skin but she didn't care. Lara lost track of time and space and let his kisses take her toward some invisible abyss. Once she'd fallen, she knew there would be no turning back. Something told her that whatever lay in that place would make her a true wife to Houston. Peace awaited there. Peace and healing.

And love? Perhaps all she had to do was reach for it. Could it be that simple?

His mouth left hers to kiss her earlobe and jaw. He trailed kisses down her throat before reclaiming her mouth in the rain. An ache built inside her for lots more.

He ran his hands down her back and sides before coming to rest at her waist. "Lara, I'm trying to go slow but you make it impossible. This fire inside won't allow it," he murmured against her mouth. "Woman, you make me crazy. You're all I think about, all I see when I close my eyes. I'm consumed with hunger for you."

With weak knees that threatened to collapse, Lara quivered in his arms. "I know nothing of tenderness between a man and woman. If you'll show me how… I trust you. I want to be whole."

She could say this only because he'd shown her how a man should treat a lady.

"You will be." Houston held her face in his hands. "I'll show you how, but not here, where danger lurks and someone can stumble upon us."

"Can you hold me longer?"

"As long as you want, darlin'. Besides, I haven't opened the allotted two buttons of your dress yet."

Happiness washed over her that he hadn't forgotten as she thought he must've. She leaned into his strength.

"But first, you're cold. Let me try to shield you from the rain." He picked up his Stetson and plopped it back on her head, then shrugged out of his jacket and slipped it around her.

Rain trickled down his face but he didn't seem to care. Light as a feather, his fingers brushed her skin as he unfastened the top of her dress. He touched her skin once the buttons were open, and she burned with a strange desire. Her stomach flipped with that quickening she'd noticed before as heat spread along her limbs.

Lara closed her eyes and let the sensation carry her toward heaven and hope.

She undid several more buttons to allow him greater access. Wondering at her newfound boldness, she embraced the sweet ache running through her body. She hungered for more of his touch, the brush of his large, work-roughened fingers that were gentle and loving.

This man she'd married drove her to seek more—things she couldn't have unless she reached for them.

Her breath came in gasps as pleasure caressed each nerve ending. She'd never known anything like this warmth that flowed over and through her. It reminded her of fluid honey, sweet and smooth as though it were a part of her. Not something foreign on the outside. This amazing sensation was inside her.

The day of their marriage, she'd believed the attack had rendered her incapable of this kind of emotion, but Houston had thankfully proven that theory wrong. Maybe she *could* know how it felt to love and be loved in the hands of a gentle man.

A powerful need to return what he gave to her weakened her knees. As he caressed her exposed flesh, she unfastened his shirt and stuck her hand inside, like she'd done before. His heart beat wildly against her palm with her fingers splayed across his skin. His body gave off sizzling heat. Slowly, in the driving rain, she began to explore.

Her mother had taught her to play the piano by ear,

when she was eight years old. The trick was learning the keys and which one made the sound you wanted.

She was learning Houston by heart, one stroke at a time. She intended to have not only his moods but his body committed to memory by the time they reached Dodge City. When they checked into a hotel there, she'd know which kind of touch evoked the response she sought.

And Houston was learning her too. Maybe marriage was simply discovering each other and learning what each loved. A smile curved Lara's lips. Already, she knew what made his heart race and breathing hitch.

"Find anything interesting?" Houston rasped as though he had trouble finding his voice.

"Lots." Lara moved aside his shirt and pressed her lips to his heated skin.

"Keep doing that and I'll forget all about guard duty, lady," he said hoarsely.

"Somehow, I don't think you'd mind." Lara buttoned him up. "But you're getting drenched. And you have work to get to."

After setting her clothes to rights, he took her face in his hands, kissing her with a fiery passion she'd carry with her when they laid her to rest.

And she'd always remember the rain-scented night that Houston had held her in his arms.

"Thank you for the gift you gave me tonight," he murmured against her ear when their lips parted. "I'll treasure the memory forever. I won't lie to you—I've been with women over the years, but none equal what you offer. You're something rare that a man seldom finds, and once he does, nothing else will ever do. You, pretty lady, have ruined me."

Happiness wound through her like a persistent trumpet vine. Tonight she'd committed some of the keys to his body to memory. Soon, and with enough practice, she'd have the whole melody.

Twenty-five

HOUSTON SWIPED AT THE RAIN RUNNING DOWN HIS FACE, took her hand, and tugged her toward her bed beneath the chuck wagon. "I have about fifteen minutes. This will be our golden time."

"I thought you'd forgotten," Lara said softly.

"Not a chance." He chuckled. "It's all I've thought about since we spoke of it this morning."

She crawled onto her blanket, laid on the dry ground beneath the wagon, with Houston stretched out beside her. As they faced each other, he put his arm out to serve as a pillow for her head. The other arm went around her, holding her snug against him.

"Warm enough?" he asked, willing her to respond to him, concerned that she held herself stiff.

"Yes. I'm warm."

"Relax," he murmured against her hair. "I'm not going to do anything."

"I know." She sighed. "It's going to take a while."

"I imagine." He shifted, giving her more space. "Tell me what you were like as a little girl."

Lara laughed. "Terribly spoiled. All arms and legs. I loved playing mommy. I had this rag doll my mother made for me out of scraps of material and yarn and I wagged that thing everywhere. One day it fell into the fireplace and I watched in horror as it turned to ash."

Houston loved the sound of her voice and picturing her as a girl in his mind. As she talked, her muscles relaxed and she molded to him so closely he could feel her breasts against his chest.

"My mother offered to make another, but I wouldn't let her."

"Why?"

"I knew I couldn't take the heartbreak if a similar fate befell the new doll. Besides, by then I had live babies to play with that offered a lot more. I learned how to change them and my mother often had me watch Virgil and Quaid while she did her chores."

Houston kissed her forehead. "I'm sure you made a good substitute."

"Until they got hungry." She laughed quietly. "I couldn't do anything for them in that department." She stroked his jaw. "Tell me about your boyhood."

"Mischievous. Always trying to get out of doing my chores. I would sneak away, get on my pony, and gallop bareback across the pastures like a wild heathen, searching for something to explore."

"Did you find anything?"

"Always. With my vivid imagination, it didn't take much. A rusted-out ammunition box became a chest that held pirate treasure. An old, grimy buckle belonged to a desperate outlaw, and once I found a coin that could've escaped from his loot, at least in my mind. Sam was two years behind me, and when he got big enough to join me, we got into all kinds of trouble. What one of us didn't think of the other did. Luke didn't live with us. In fact, we didn't know he existed back then. I wish he had, though. When I was about eight, Stoker decided I'd been a boy far too long and went to work teaching me to be a man." Houston grew somber, thinking about how strict his father became, seemingly overnight. "This harsh land drove him to teach us how to survive in all kinds of situations, knowing he wouldn't always be there."

"You were so young!"

"Didn't matter. The lessons began."

At the time, he hadn't understood. Now he knew a big part of the changes came when his mother's heart had begun to fail. It was about then she'd become bedfast, too weak to get up or walk across the room. Stoker didn't know how to handle the changes. He missed his partner and grieved her death long before she died four years later.

"How old were you when your mother died, Lara?"

"Eighteen. And you?"

"Twelve."

"You were just a boy." Lara brushed a kiss across his lips. "I'm sure you were probably as scared as Henry."

"Yep, but I had to be strong for Sam. He needed me to make sense of things for him, and to fill in for our pa when he went on whiskey binges and we wouldn't see him for days."

"I'm sorry."

Houston shook himself. "Don't be. I got through it and it made me tough." He tweaked her nose. "Next time I'll tell you about the time a big cat attacked while I was out riding. I killed it, but then I had to fend off a pack of hungry coyotes all night until help arrived."

Lara rose up on an elbow. "Tell me now. I'm dying to hear your harrowing tale."

"Nope. That's for next time." A bolt of lightning lit up the sky. "I need to go."

She reached for him as he moved to scoot out from under the wagon. "Wait. I need to talk to you about Henry."

Houston heard something different in her voice. Not fear; deep concern. "Other than this drive being too dangerous for him, what's wrong?"

"I've never seen him this terrified. I think we should send him back."

He brushed her cheek with the pad of his thumb. "How?

Who'll take him? I can't spare anyone. For that matter, I'd like to send you back also."

"I'm staying," she stated bluntly. "So don't get any notions about that. As for Henry…I'll think of a way."

"Let me know when you do." Clothing rustled as he pressed his lips on hers. The kiss settled his jumpy nerves. "I'll be back as soon as I can."

"Be careful."

He crawled from her bed and strode to his horse in the driving rain, wishing they were anywhere but the lawless Indian Territory.

∽

Lightning flashed around Houston as he moved among the herd. Blue flame danced along the six- to nine-foot horns of the frightened animals, leaping from tip to tip. A hissing sound accompanied the eerie sight he'd seen several times on the ranch, the first as a boy. He hadn't believed it possible for the animals to live. Stoker explained that it was electricity in the air and he called it St. Elmo's fire. The only thing Houston knew was that St. Elmo was sure raining flames down on them this night.

In the midst of the midnight summer rain, he scanned the herd, looking for signs of a possible stampede. So far, they were only restless. The biggest threat was always at the beginning of a trail drive. After a few weeks, the jumpy cattle settled into the routine and became acclimated to the noises. Thank goodness for that, or this storm would send them into a panic.

His thoughts tried to return to Lara and he kept reeling them back in. Lives depended on him focusing on the work right now. Everything else would have to wait. He rode around the fringes, speaking soothing words, keeping the animals in a tight bunch.

Harmonica music drifted in the air as Joe rode alongside him.

The song "Beautiful Dreamer" had a calming effect on the herd. One by one they lay down, lulled by the music. Houston breathed a sigh of relief that the danger had passed. He watched the steady drip of water off his hat brim onto his oilskin slicker, wishing he was in a Dodge hotel. After a hot bath with his lady, Lara would curl up next to him with nothing between them but skin.

With what had happened tonight, he had high hopes for the very near future. He still felt her hand brushing his chest and sneaking up under his jacket. She seemed to like touching him and he certainly didn't mind a bit. Whatever she fancied to do was fine with him.

But teach her how to love?

Not a chance. What did he know? He was raised with precious little softness. Stoker was a hard man and he'd instilled that sharp-edged toughness into his sons, leaving no room for affection and sentiment. Houston had been so convinced he had loved Becky, and yet that had proved to be nothing more than a fantasy. The best teaching method was by example and he'd show her tenderness and patience. He wanted more than anything for Lara to know a true husband's love and be treated like the special woman she was.

Clay rode to him. "I think we're all right, boss. These cows sure wanted to raise a ruckus tonight but we talked 'em out of it." A lit cigarette dangled from his mouth. The thing had to be damp, yet somehow it still burned.

"Yep, we did. They just decided to bed down docile-like."

"Want a snort?" Clay pulled a flask from inside his slicker.

"Don't mind if I do." Houston welcomed the bite of the whiskey, hoping the alcohol might make him forget the ache for the woman sleeping beneath the wagon. He took the flask and turned it up, letting the liquid sear a path down his throat to his belly.

"You think Yuma and his varmints will pay us a visit tonight?" Clay asked, taking the flask from Houston.

"Might." Houston glanced toward the chuck wagon and the low flames of the campfire. "It'd be a foolish move."

The storm was the perfect cover, though. All the men were busy and the peal of thunder would drown out any noise.

Clay wore a grim look. "No one ever accused Blackstone of having brains."

"Nope." All Yuma had was a ruthless mind and a heart of stone. "If you have this under control, I'm going to head back. Just want to make sure Lara, Gracie, and Henry are all right."

"Go ahead while these dogies are taking a nap."

Houston turned the horse toward the flickering fire. The camp looked peaceful enough, but he wanted to make damn sure. He wasn't leaving anything to chance. He dismounted at the wagon and looped the reins through a wheel. Thankfully, Gracie was still asleep in her crib beneath a covering of canvas some of the drovers had rigged. He pulled a blanket up over her, then knelt to check on Lara beneath the wagon. At her soft breathing, he looked around for Henry. Not finding him on the ground where he usually slept on a bedroll with his brothers, he checked inside the wagon and there he was. Asleep on a sack of flour.

At last Houston let out a sigh of relief and added a piece of wood to the fire, watching the flames flare and cast sparks. He sat down on a barrel and put his head in his hands.

The rain had slowed to a drizzle, showing signs of petering out. He was glad of that. The storm had turned the summer air a bit chilly. He hadn't felt the cold one bit when he was kissing Lara, mind you. He doubted he'd have felt freezing snow. He grinned. His wife knew how to warm him up.

His wife?

Houston jerked off his hat and scrubbed the back of his neck. How was it possible he'd come to think of Lara that way in such a short time? Yet he did. That's what she'd become, and he found what once seemed impossible to accept now easy to embrace.

Having her in his arms with his heart racing brought a sense of heaven and an all-was-right-with-the-world sort of feeling. Damn, he'd never felt this way before about any woman. Only once in a lifetime did a man meet his soulmate. No getting around it; Lara was truly that.

He settled his hat back on, reached for the coffeepot, shook it, and got up for a cup. One swig of coffee and he'd return to the herd.

Returning to the barrel, he sat down and let his thoughts drift back to Lara. Lying on her blanket, talking about their childhoods had put her at ease. He needed to turn the conversation to more of that. And to their future. He just prayed they'd get back to the Lone Star so they could have a future. He emptied his lungs in a big whoosh. Just then, soft hands touched his shoulder. He turned to find Lara.

"You sound like a cross bear," she said. "Is everything all right?"

"So far." Houston pulled her onto his knee. "I came to check on you. Hope I didn't wake you."

"Nope. I don't know why, but I find it hard to sleep when you're close." Lara laid her head on his shoulder. "I'd rather be up, talking to you."

Houston kissed her forehead. "I feel the same way." His senses heightened each time she came within a hundred yards. It pleased him that he had that effect on her too. She was everything he wanted and needed in a wife, a partner, and a lover.

"Why did you come to check on things? Did you think Yuma might've paid me a visit?"

For a second, he almost lied but remembered he'd promised to be honest. "Thought entered my head. Wouldn't put anything past him. He'll be out for blood now that we killed his man, captured one, and shot up the other. Might've killed that second one too for all we know." Houston drained the cup and tossed the dregs into the crackling fire.

Lara stirred. "You're out of coffee. I'll make another pot."

He tightened his grip, preventing her from getting up. "No need. Have to head out. Go back to bed for a little more shut-eye."

"Are you sure?"

"Yep." Houston slanted a kiss across her mouth. He stood and she walked him to the Appaloosa.

Lara rested her hand on the saddle. "Please don't worry. We'll be fine. Yuma is probably holed up in the rocks, nursing his wounded partner. He's not a particularly brave man…except where women are concerned."

Anger climbed up the back of Houston's neck. Some men loved preying on those who were weaker. Let them face a stronger person and they crawled away with their tails between their legs every time. The thing that worried him about Yuma was that he was mad. Angry men were foolish.

And very dangerous.

"Are you keeping the revolver close?" he asked.

She wrinkled her nose in distaste and pulled it from her pocket. "I hate this gun but I never let it leave my side."

"Good. If you need it, don't hesitate to fire."

"Believe me, I won't." She put the gun away and clutched Houston's vest. "Please be careful."

He kissed her once more, tugged away to untie the reins, and stepped into the stirrup. Before he could spur the animal, a yell rent the air. He took off at a gallop. Clay and the drovers had gathered into a circle when he reached them.

Houston slid down. "What's the problem?"

"Emmett is missing," Clay barked. "I'm organizing a search party."

"Good. Count me in." Houston remembered how Emmett had been calm and collected under pressure during the shoot-out yesterday. The drover wouldn't have just up and ridden off.

"Already did," Clay answered, suggesting he check out a nearby ravine. The second in command turned back to the cowboys. "If you find him, don't fire your gun into the air or it might spook the cattle. Just hightail it back here."

Before the men could scatter, Houston spoke up, "You've all had a miserable night. Just want to say that I couldn't ride with a better bunch of drovers. Thank you for your loyalty."

They nodded, then fell into the search. Houston's area was rugged, a thicket of bramble making the land mighty near impassable. The darkness added to the peril, hiding dangerous drop-offs. He took great care in picking his way down the rocky ravine. One wrong step of his horse and that would be it.

Rocks weren't the only danger either. His gut still told him Blackstone was near. He slid his Colt from the holster and continued.

A shot rang out, the bullet barely missing him.

Houston dove to the ground into some thick brush. His heart hammered as he scanned the area. Where had the gunfire come from?

Nothing moved.

Every rustle of the brush only heightened his senses more. He jumped not only at sounds but shadows. The Appaloosa was skittish too, snorting and swinging his head. Muscles jerked beneath the layer of hide and hair.

He listened to the sounds of the ravine but heard only the birds and the wind through the brush. Houston was beginning to think he'd imagined the shot, when a horse and rider burst past, almost running him down. By the time he aimed his Colt and fired, they'd already disappeared into a thicket. So had his Appaloosa.

Damn! He should've drawn a bead on the rider quicker.

Kicking himself, Houston went to find his horse. Thankfully, it hadn't gone far. He found the animal up against the wall of the ravine and worked to calm him. Finally, Houston climbed into the saddle. He pondered the wisdom of going after the rider, but the man would be long gone by now. He decided to resume his search for the missing drover.

The rain had long stopped but he hadn't removed the bulky gear. He needed the warmth a little longer. The clouds passed, allowing the quarter moon to shine. It didn't give much light but he welcomed what he got.

After the slow going, he finally made it to the bottom and proceeded the length of the narrow arroyo, a space that measured no more than the breadth of six horses across. Small branches from a mulberry tree grabbed him when he rode by, ripping a hole in his slicker. He got off and stuffed it into a saddlebag. The sky had begun to lighten but he saw no sign of dawn.

He rounded a bend and emerged from the small canyon into a little clearing. A dark splotch lay on the ground in front of him. A large animal of some kind? He couldn't tell but he needed to approach with caution. A wounded animal could be very dangerous.

"Whoa, boy." Houston swung down. Gripping his Colt, he crept forward.

As he neared the dark shape he could tell it wasn't an animal at all, but a man lying facedown. Houston turned him over and found the face of the missing drover staring at him. His hands and feet were bound and caked blood had formed around a hole in his forehead. Someone had shot Emmett between the eyes.

Someone had executed him.

Pain and rage ricocheted through Houston. He rocked back on his heels. Emmett had worked for the Lone Star for ten years and given the Legends everything he had. The middle-aged, crusty cowboy had loved everything about riding the range.

A thin cigarette paper sticking from Emmett's pocket caught his eye. Houston reached for it and read the words someone had scrawled.

One a day.

No one had to tell him who'd written the note. He stuffed the warning inside his vest then hoisted Emmett onto his shoulders. He eased the faithful employee across the horse's rump and began the arduous trek back. His mind churned. He had to stop Blackstone. And he had to do it before those expected reinforcements finally caught up, which they would eventually.

How was he supposed to keep driving the cattle, protect the men, shield his family, *and* go on the offensive?

He needed more help, more men. But from where?

Stoker's voice echoed in his head. *When trouble comes, stand proud. Remember you're a Legend. You carry the blood of generations of fighting men who don't know the word quit.*

Damn it to hell if his pa wasn't right!

A Legend could handle a bunch of ruthless outlaws. He'd still be standing when the dust cleared. Blackstone had better find a hole, because he was coming for him, and this was Houston Legend's fight to win.

Twenty-six

HOUSTON FACED A SOMBER GROUP OF MEN WHEN HE walked back with Emmett's body. Pony Latham came to meet him first. "What are we gonna do?"

"Are we gonna sit here and wait for the bastards to pick us off one by one?" Joe's angry voice blended with the murmuring dissent around him. "Emmett was our friend… my friend."

Houston watched his deeply shaken crew. Their questions were ones he'd asked himself.

Clay answered, "He was a friend to all of us. Emmett will be missed, no doubt about it. We ain't gonna sit idle and wait."

"Nope." Houston squeezed Joe's shoulder. "Let's get Emmett in the ground and then we'll plan. This hurts like hell, but we're not whipped. We're going to be a whole lot smarter and twice as cunning from now on. I assure you, his death won't go unpunished." Though he didn't know how they were going to do it yet, surely they could rid themselves of two ruthless outlaws bent on murder and revenge.

"Damn right," Pony spat.

As a rosy dawn broke, someone brought out a shovel. Each man took his turn digging in the muddy earth. When the grave was deep enough, they wrapped Emmett in a blanket and laid him into the hole. Joe brought out his harmonica and played an old hymn. Houston stood at the head of the grave and said a few words.

He felt as old as Stoker standing there. He forced strength he didn't feel into his voice and the only Bible passage he knew rang out across the desolate prairie. He kept his words brief out of a need to get moving.

While the men filled in the hole, Houston walked Lara to the chuck wagon. He was glad for a private moment. His arm tightened around her waist. "Do you have that gun handy?"

She glanced up. A tear poised on the tip of a long lash. "Yes and I'll use it. Don't you worry."

The brittle hardness of her tone was new, and it hurt him to hear. He'd never wanted her to feel unsafe, and yet he'd put her in this situation.

He kissed her upturned mouth. "In a fight, people often get separated and I may not always be able to protect you." That constant fear had paralyzed him and kept him awake.

Lara rested her small palm on his leather vest. "I want to take that worry from you if I can. I'll kill to protect myself and my family. Yuma has taken all from me he's going to. Each one of these drovers is my family now too. I remember how tenderly Emmett held Gracie, as though she was *his* child. He was a sweet, kind man and I'll miss him. Trust me, I'll fight."

Houston brushed the pad of his finger along her scarred cheek, unfazed by the raised flesh. "How did I get so lucky? You're everything I ever dreamed of finding in a woman."

"And I in a man," she said softly. "When all this is over and we reach Dodge City, let's do something special. Just you and me. I think I know just what."

"That's a deal. Want to share what you're thinking?" He nibbled her enticing lips.

"Nope."

"Will I like it?"

"I daresay you will." A smile teased her mouth. "You'll just have to wait."

"I have plans of my own for you, Mrs. Legend." Lots of plans. He'd make her happy if it took a lifetime. "Just keep thinking about our future when you want to give up. Believe me, this fight is going to get very ugly before it's over."

"You're right. I can't help but wonder how many will have to pay the ultimate price for protecting me." Her quivering chin pierced Houston's heart. He saw how desperately she tried to hold back her fear.

He opened his arms and she walked into them. Drawing her close, he kissed her, taking comfort in the warmth that spread through him. He hoped she felt the same. At least a little.

"Darlin', the men are protecting each other, not just you. I wish I could make this trip easier, but I can't control what will happen." Only one thing would help…Blackstone's death. Houston narrowed his gaze, staring toward the ravine where he'd found Emmett. "From now on, you'll ride in front of the herd. Someone will be with you at all times. You'll have to sacrifice a lot of your privacy, but I'd rather have you safe."

If only he could, he'd move heaven and earth to spare her more violence and worry. Lord knew, she'd had enough.

"I told you at the outset that I wanted no special treatment." She stepped from his arms. Putting her foot on the small step, she climbed up into the wagon box beside Henry and lifted the reins.

"When you need to feed Gracie, let the drover or Henry drive," Houston continued. "At night I can't allow you to leave camp alone to take care of personal needs." When she quickly opened her mouth to protest, he softened his tone and went on. "I'll try to make sure I'm available. But if not, you'll have to let someone else come with you. I'm sorry."

Though he saw a second of silent mutiny, she gave him a resolute smile and straightened her shoulders. "I understand. I'll just have to get over my qualms."

"Wish you didn't have to, darlin', but I'm afraid it's necessary for now. Go ahead and roll out. We'll be behind you."

Henry waved excitedly as though leaving on a long ocean voyage. "Good-bye, Houston. I can drive good 'cause we're fam'ly. If you need stuff fixed, I can do it."

"Bye, Bones. I know you can." Houston watched them move forward only to stop and pick up Gracie from brother Quaid, then he strode to his top drover to relay new rules. The words *one a day* beat in his head like an Indian death drum.

Clay glanced at Houston from beneath the brim of his weathered, sweat-stained hat. "Reckon you have a plan."

"I do." Houston told him about putting the chuck wagon out front with a drover whose only job was to protect them.

"Good idea. At least for now." Clay thumbed back his hat. "Blackstone will just change tactics once he figures it out."

"Yep." Then Houston gave the order for no one to leave camp alone. "When we're with the herd at night, the men will ride in pairs. To help recognize each other in the dark, I'll issue a password and countersign each morning. If anyone fails to answer with the correct word, I authorize the drover to shoot him. We won't take any more chances. Keep the herd tight and don't let any get away. If they do, don't chase them down. Let them go. Understood?"

"For sure. Can't afford to let any drover ride alone after a cow an' give the bastards an openin' to gun him down." The saddle leather creaked as Clay leaned forward. "I think we should expect Blackstone's group to multiply any time now."

"I agree." Houston let out a troubled sigh. At least he'd bought them a little extra time by burning the note and sending the bunch in a different direction. He only wished he knew their numbers. He prayed they were small.

A glance at the Vincents' wagon reminded Houston he needed to address that. Caroline was clinging to Nick. She was too young to have to manage a wagon and team by herself.

"Clay, tell Nick to drive their wagon and to stay up front with Lara. We could use him to fill Emmett's spot, but she needs him more."

"They're so young." Clay's voice held a strange quality, as though he was talking about himself. "This unforgiving land makes people grow up too fast. I'll tell 'em." The drover sighed. "I'd best relay your orders so we can get these ornery dogies on down the trail a ways. We're burning daylight."

Houston nodded. "Come nightfall, you and me are going to find the murdering bastard's den."

"I'll consider it an honor, boss."

"We'll find them." Houston mounted up and rode over to Virgil and Quaid, warning them to be extra careful. The last thing he needed was to have to take their corpses back to Till Boone. A shudder ran through him before he turned and galloped over to the remuda. The Appaloosa deserved a rest. He selected a palomino and switched his saddle.

Houston glanced up from the cinch he was tightening. "How's the little mare's foot?" The animal had developed a limp the previous day.

Pete, somewhere in his early twenties, met his gaze. "Doing fine. You got that rock out in time. I won't let anyone ride her for another day or two to make sure."

"Appreciate the fine care you're taking of the horses. I couldn't ask for better."

The young man grinned. "Horses are my life. I hope to start a horse ranch one day."

Something about the love in the man's voice and on his face as he talked about his dream made Houston's throat tighten. Pete was going to go far…if he got a chance to grow up. Houston thought of Zeb Flanagan, dead before he even found out who he was. Maybe happiness was a way station between too much and too little. Only thing was… Zeb seemed like he'd always lived on the too-little end. Houston would try to see that Pete didn't.

"That's a fine dream, Pete. Maybe with what you make

on this trip, you can." Houston tested the cinch and found it good. He stuck his foot in the stirrup and threw his leg over. "Trouble's riding this way. Keep your eyes open and your .45 ready."

"Yes, boss, I will."

Houston rode away feeling guilty. He'd been wrong about trouble riding toward them—it was already there.

"Take your *one a day* and shove it, Blackstone," he growled into the wind. "I'm going to kill you. You're as good as dead."

Twenty-seven

MIDAFTERNOON, LARA SPOTTED A PRAIRIE SCHOONER tilting severely to one side straight ahead, with people standing near it and a tent stretched close by. Alarms sounded in her head.

Pony Latham noticed it about the same time. "Hold up, Mrs. Legend. I'll ride over and check it out. Might be a trap."

He might be right, although the group seemed to be mostly women and children. Who would cross Indian Territory with a bunch of small children if they didn't have to? She glanced at Gracie in Henry's arms and remembered how close she'd come to losing her daughter. But who was she to judge without knowing their circumstances? Maybe they hadn't had a choice.

Henry leaned forward with a frown. "Want I should get my rock?"

"Certainly not. I don't think these people mean us harm."

He shrugged. "Okay. Look at the butterfly, Gracie."

The child pointed, jabbering with excitement, seeming to have returned to normal, thanks to Dr. Mary.

Nick and Caroline pulled up alongside. "Who are those people?" Nick asked.

"I don't know. Pony went to check them out. Told us to wait here," Lara answered.

Caroline craned her neck to see. "I'm so happy to find other women. They'll give us someone new to talk to."

Lara stifled a laugh. Except for preparing the meals, the girl spent all her time in the wagon with her husband. She doubted having others around would make much difference.

Pony had reached the travelers, and Lara stayed alert as he spoke with them. His relaxed body told her he didn't see trouble. Soon he turned and rode back. In minutes, he pulled up beside Lara and wiped his face with a bandana.

"Their wagon has a busted wheel, ma'am," he said. "Boss will probably camp down where they are for the night so we can help 'em fix it, but I'm just guessing on that. Not my place to say."

"I'd say the same, Mr. Latham. My husband won't leave anyone stranded out here." Lara knew that much.

Clay galloped up. "A problem, Latham?"

Pony explained the situation. "We can't very well leave 'em out here with those outlaws trailin' us. Got a bunch of women and little kids."

"We'll help 'em," Clay said. "Go on down and start making camp. I'm sure Mrs. Legend and Caroline will welcome the company of other women for a spell."

That she would. "Thank you, Clay. I look forward to it."

As the head drover rode back to tell Houston, Lara released the brake and drove toward the stalled group. She hoped some of the women were her age. But on the other hand, maybe an older one would know the answer to a question that burned inside her. No matter their ages, they would be a welcome sight.

A short while later, she found the perfect spot near a little stream of water and parked the wagon. Pony Latham went to join a man who sported a long, dark beard. Children ranging in age from about ten down to five ran over, asking Henry if he wanted to play hide and seek.

"I have to work," Henry said proudly, sticking out his chest. "But I can play for a few minutes. Okay, Lara?"

"Go ahead. You've earned some fun." Lara took Gracie

and watched her brother scamper off with them. She knew how lonely he was both on the ranch and out here on the plains. He needed kids to play with. In size, the fourteen-year-old loomed over these small ones, but he matched them mentally, which was more important.

One of the women wearing a prairie bonnet approached her and Caroline as they climbed from their wagons. "Hi, I'm Hannah. It's nice that you folks came along."

Lara stuck out her hand and introduced herself. "I'm married to Houston Legend, the owner of those longhorns coming yonder. We're headed to Dodge City to sell them."

Caroline did the same, adding that she was a newlywed. She appeared curious about the young woman who was clearly in the family way. "Is this your first, Hannah?"

"It is and I'm very excited." Hannah's smile lit up her face. "Time seems to drag its heels, though. I'm getting impatient to have this babe." She tickled Gracie under the chin and set off a round of giggles. "You have the prettiest little girl. Can I hold her?" she asked Lara.

"She's a tad on the rambunctious side, so be careful." Lara handed the kicking child over. "Her name is Gracie. Do you have names picked out for yours yet?"

"Hiram the fifth for a boy, because that's my husband's name, and Abigail for a girl."

"Good names. How much longer do you have?" Lara asked.

"About four weeks." Hannah drew some other women forward. "These are Martha, Sarah, and Ruth."

Lara found the women warm and friendly. The dark-haired Ruth appeared the oldest, judging by a few lines around her mouth. She carried a small toddler who looked to be about two or three years old. He buried his face against his mother.

"What a handsome boy, Ruth. What's his name?"

"Hiram the fourth." Ruth smoothed his dark hair. "I named him after his father."

Caroline asked to hold Hiram the fourth and hugged him to her, a dreamy look on her face.

"But I thought… Hannah, aren't you naming your child the same thing if it's a boy?" Lara thought this was the oddest thing. Why would both use the same name? Maybe it was some kind of competition between them, or perhaps a long-standing joke of some sort. Yes, that must be it.

Hannah jiggled Gracie. "Yes, I just love that name."

"I'm going to name our son Nick when he's born." Caroline put Ruth's baby on her shoulder and patted little Hiram's back, the dreamy expression still glued on. "I can't wait to have a baby. Nick and I are trying very hard."

They certainly were. Lara would give them top marks for effort.

Sarah came forward. "We're so relieved you came along. We've been stuck here for three days. We saw some Indians in the distance but they didn't approach us."

"I'm glad we can help. I just pray we don't bring our trouble to you." Lara explained about the men trailing behind, sparing them the details. That was Houston's place and he may not want to frighten these women if the threat was over.

Standing beside her, Caroline jostled little Hiram, who was grunting and squirming to get down. Everyone else could've vanished as far as the girl was concerned. She was dreaming of motherhood.

Sarah pushed back a stray hair, tucking it inside her bonnet. "Thank goodness your men were able to send them running. We'll warn Hiram."

Houston arrived with the herd, and Lara's gaze followed his tall, lean form as he dismounted near the only man with these women and offered a handshake. For a moment she forgot about these ladies, her attention drawn to the bulging muscles of Houston's forearms just below his rolled-up sleeves.

Her heart raced in anticipation of more stolen kisses. With luck, he'd lie beside her again with night's shadows around them and make her feel like the luckiest woman alive—all safe and protected as though he cherished her.

She prayed one day he could. He'd said she drove him crazy with need, but that seemed only to mean physical. He hadn't said he loved her. Maybe he never would.

If he just treated her with kindness and cared for her, it would be enough.

Yet, in her heart she knew it wouldn't. She needed all of Houston with nothing held back.

Martha appeared shy but she smiled, showing pretty dimples. "Aren't you afraid to go on this trail drive with all these men, Lara?"

"No, I'm not afraid. My husband won't let anything happen to me or our daughter. That's him standing over there." Lara thought Houston looked especially handsome, even covered in a layer of trail dust.

She licked her lips that had gone dry. "But even if my husband weren't here, I wouldn't worry. These drovers are nothing but kind and care about me and the baby." Lara laughed. "You'd think they were all Gracie's fathers the way they carry on sometimes."

Hannah leaned close. "Your husband is very tall with such broad shoulders. He'll give you many more fine children."

Lara's cheeks grew hot. She really should explain about Gracie, but she couldn't. Somehow she didn't think it was important. Houston was her daughter's father and that was that.

As for other children? The thought sent old fear rising up, where earlier she'd felt nothing but excitement. She had to get over that, fighting to tamp it down. Sometimes in the dead of night, she pictured herself lying naked in Houston's arms, feeling the beat of his heart and hearing his deep voice whispering words of love in her ear. Kissing her and…

"Lara?" Ruth asked.

"Yes?" Lara dragged her attention back to the women.

"You were a million miles away," Hannah said. "I hope we're not keeping you from your work. We just wanted to meet you and Caroline."

"I do have to start cooking for the drovers soon." Lara

took Gracie from Hannah. "Oh, I just had a thought. What if we pool the food, share the work, and all eat together?"

Ruth glanced toward Hiram. "We'll see what Hiram says, but it sounds like a wonderful idea." The woman reached for her son and let him down. If she hadn't kept a firm grip, he would've taken off running. Ruth softly scolded the boy, "Oh, no you don't. You have to stay with me, little man."

"He sure doesn't like to stay still." With the toddler gone from her arms, Caroline emerged from her trance at last. "You've probably guessed that I'm very young. I need to find out all about babies. Nick and me are going to be having a whole houseful, so I've gotta get to my learning."

Lara smiled at the young girl's zeal. Caroline didn't know how much work babies were or how fast they could be stripped from you. And she didn't know it took more than a child to make a marriage complete.

"Ladies, there's really no need to eat separately," Lara pointed out again. "And besides, Caroline and I both want to talk to you more before we have to go our separate ways."

Something had to explain the tingles when Houston glanced at her and the way her stomach flipped when they kissed and touched. If she dared, maybe she'd ask the questions that had burned inside for the past two weeks. Surely they could tell her how a woman knew if she was in love.

Or if it would hurt when Houston made love to her.

And if it did…could she hide it from him?

She wouldn't be able to bear the hurt in Houston's eyes if it all went wrong.

Twenty-eight

THE NIGHT AIR MOVED THROUGH THE TALL GRASSES, whispering, warning of death. Such a silent message had often saved Houston's life. Only a fool would ignore it now.

While he waited for Clay, he sat next to the campfire, unable to take his eyes from Lara—her serene look brought a lump to his throat. She and the other women had formed a circle across from him. The firelight flickered on his wife's beautiful face, caressing her cheekbones and dancing in her fiery hair.

He envied her wide smile that came so easy with the women, her conversation relaxed in ways it rarely was with him. Despite having Caroline now, plainly she hungered for female companionship. But then with nothing but men at home and on the trail too, it was little wonder. She had to miss the woman who'd brought her into the world.

Even though his mother had died seventeen years ago, at times the sense of loss became so strong it strangled him and brought tears to his eyes. Mothers were irreplaceable.

But Rachel Boone's death would still be fresh. Seemed he recalled Stoker telling him she'd passed a year or two before Lara's attack, before Lara became a mother herself. There had to be things Lara wanted to talk about, things only women spoke of to each other.

Clay rode up, dismounted, and limped over to take a

seat next to Houston. "Still thinking about hunting for Yuma's camp?"

"Yep." Houston dragged his attention away from Lara to look at his one-eyed drover.

"Good, I'm ready. What're we gonna do when we find it, boss?"

"Depends. We'll have to play it by ear and seize any opportunities that come our way." Houston gulped the last of his coffee. "I'd like to take every drover and wipe those outlaws off the face of the earth."

Force was the only language Yuma understood. Houston looked forward to meeting up with the murdering piece of ant dung.

Lara rose, drawing his notice. She motioned to Henry and walked to the chuck wagon. He admired the flare of her rounded hips and narrow waist. No one in the world moved with such fluid grace. She was a quiet stream with rippling sparkles, sauntering on its way. He watched, mesmerized by her natural grace.

Clay punched his arm.

"What?" With effort, Houston tugged his focus back to his drover.

From beneath his battered hat, Clay followed his gaze. Houston suspected they were about the same age, their faces equally weathered by their time outdoors.

Grinning, Clay shook his head. "You've got it awful bad, boss."

Houston sighed. "I 'spect."

Only that was a lie. No supposing to how he felt about Lara. He *knew* how firmly his wife had lodged in his heart and how he longed to sleep beside her in the privacy of a room. Even if he had to stay dressed to reassure her, he would. As long as he could touch her.

His thoughts returned to the days leading up to their marriage. He'd asked for nothing more than she be kind. Good Lord! That didn't even begin to touch on all she was.

With a low chuckle, Clay stretched out his long legs. "I

was saying that we'll hunt 'em down an' be done with it if you give the go-ahead."

"If I knew where to find them, I would in a heartbeat. But I have more to consider. What if we miss them and they ride into our unprotected camp and put a bullet into the women or, God forbid, Gracie? Or if I lose more men? Or…" He had a million things keeping him from going off half-cocked.

"Get your point." Clay blew out a frustrated sigh. The drover motioned to Frank Farley, sitting apart from them. "Reckon he knows more than he's saying?"

Though they hadn't tied him up, Houston had assigned a man to watch him at all times. Frank couldn't even relieve himself in private, and he slept with a wrist bound to someone at night.

"I questioned him at length and I don't think he can add anything more. My gut tells me he's cooperating."

Lara and Henry returned, carrying a large Dutch oven. "I made cherry cobbler for everyone," she announced.

As people lined up, Houston turned to Clay. "Let me speak to Lara and we'll ride out. That is, if you don't want dessert."

Clay chuckled. "And ruin my girlish figure?"

They rose and went separate directions. Houston weaved among the people in line, finally reaching Lara. He drew her away from the campfire into the deep shadows and told her of his and Clay's plans.

Lara clutched his arm in panic. "Please be careful. You don't know what Yuma is capable of."

He ran his finger across her cheek, noticing the ridges weren't raised as high. "That's just it, darlin'. I do know."

"Come back safe. I couldn't stand it if something happened to you." Her voice broke.

Houston drowned in her pretty green eyes. Putting a hand to her waist, he drew her against him and placed his lips on hers. That kiss was his undoing. The touch seared a path through him, leaving flames and hunger in its wake.

He slipped his tongue into her softly parted mouth and enjoyed the feel of her breasts pressed against the hardness of his chest. He ran his palm lightly down her back and the flare of her hips before resting it at her waist.

His lips and hands did things his body wasn't allowed to do yet. And all without removing a single stitch of clothing.

When he let her up for air, he found that her ragged, tortured breathing matched his own.

"What if I beg you not to go?" she asked.

"Is that what you want?" Houston asked quietly. "Would you rather we sit here and wait for the next person to die?"

"No." She glanced away. "It's just that this fear for you overcomes me sometimes. Often life is fleeting and… we haven't begun to live as man and wife yet." Her eyes returned to his and they glittered like broken glass in the dim light. "Almost losing Gracie, and then finding Emmett's body, made me aware of how fast tragedy can strike."

"Nothing's going to happen. I'm just going to see if I can find their camp. I don't want them sneaking up on us."

"You'll not take foolish chances? You promise?"

He lifted a tendril of hair from her cheek, searching for words to lighten the worry in her eyes. He chuckled. "I promise not to miss a big helping of your delicious cobbler or your biscuits at dawn. You're not getting rid of me." He kissed the tip of her nose, growing serious. "You know I'll do anything in the world for you. If you wanted that moon up there, I'd do everything in my power to rope it and put it in your palm. So yes, I'll even stay alive." He lowered his mouth next to her ear. "I'll do it for you if for no other reason."

Lara traced the curve of his jaw with a fingertip. "You better, cowboy. And when you get back…"

Houston grinned. "I'll kiss you silly, unbutton your dress, and show you how I feel about you, Mrs. Legend." He nipped at her finger.

"I'll stay up for you, no matter how late."

Brushing her lips with another kiss, Houston said, "Clay's waiting."

He found pulling away from her was a little like dying. Lara was growing more comfortable and he loved seeing passion in her eyes. In light of her naivety, she probably didn't even know she'd let her building hunger show. That made it doubly important to take it slow.

Lara needed to come to the decision on her own, not be hurried by him. He'd never force her into anything.

As he walked toward the palomino he'd chosen from the remuda, he turned for one last look. Just in case. Lara stood as he'd left her. She raised her hand to her mouth and blew him a kiss. His chest hurt with the need to go back, to crawl beneath the wagon, to curl up next to her and block out the world.

Houston's eyes burned. He'd give the entire herd for one private night in her arms with no duties except satisfying her.

"Ready, boss?" Clay stuck his cigarette in the corner of his mouth and adjusted his black eye patch.

At last, with a ragged sigh, Houston turned. "Let's ride."

The sooner they got back, the better it would suit him. He had a date with his wife. He'd teach her the finer points of wooing.

In the midst of the summer rain, she'd asked him to show her how to please him.

"I'll show you how a husband pleases his mate, my darling wife," he murmured to himself. "You can count on that."

Houston and Clay rode about a half mile from the herd before they got a break. At first Houston thought his eyes were playing tricks on him, but there it was again.

"See that, Clay?"

"What?"

"That faint flicker of light over there at the foot of that mesa. Campfire maybe?" Houston stood up in the stirrups.

"Damn, boss, I think you're right."

They got off their horses and looped the reins around the branch of a juniper. Slowly, they inched forward, not making a sound. Houston's breath got lost somewhere in his chest.

A babel of angry voices reached them before they spotted their targets. The outlaws seemed to be arguing.

Keeping low in the brush, Houston kept moving. Finally, he saw the camp that butted up against the wall of a mesa. His stomach clenched tight. Their luck had run out.

There in front of them sat at least a dozen or more men around a campfire.

Yuma's group of outlaws had grown.

One terrifying desperado, wearing twin revolvers strapped to his hips and cartridge belts crisscrossing his chest, leapt to his feet. "I say we mount up and ride into their camp with guns blazing. Kill 'em all an' steal the cattle."

Armed to the teeth with angry flames from the fire casting shadows around him, the man looked like a devil rising up from hell. That is if the devil wore guns. He stood nose to nose with a bald man who could only be Yuma Blackstone. Lara and Henry's descriptions had proven true.

Only now, the man had a scalp hanging from his belt. The feathers attached said it'd come from a Cherokee.

The realization of the type of killer Yuma was made Houston's blood run cold.

"I'm the boss of this gang and what I say goes!" Yuma yelled. "If you don't like it, Digger Barnes, you're welcome to leave. Make no mistake. *I* am in charge and *I* make the plans."

Even at fifty yards, Houston could feel tension rippling between the two. Their hands hovered an inch above gleaming pistols. Houston expected to hear deafening blasts any moment.

A giant of enormous height stepped between the pair. "We're all on the same side. We want the same thing—the women and the cattle, with the men lying to rot under the sun."

"Move out of my way!" Yuma yelled. "We'd have every bit of that if Digger had just followed the damn instructions I left behind at that first campsite!"

"If you'd have left any note, I'd have found it!" Digger hollered back. "Crazy bastard."

In a sudden move, Yuma streaked around the giant, grabbed Digger by the neck, and threw him to the ground. The two wrestled in the dirt, trading vicious blows as the rest cheered them on. Houston couldn't tell who was winning. First one was on top and then the other—the pair well-matched in size and ruthlessness.

Suddenly Yuma landed in the flames and caught his shirt on fire. Someone tossed water on him to put it out. He flew into a rage, grabbed Digger by his cartridge belts, and flung him into the rocks.

Bleeding severely, Digger grabbed a whiskey bottle from one of the onlookers and broke it. With a slicing motion, he caught Yuma's arm with the jagged glass, leaving a long gash.

The two continued to punch, kick, and throw each other for several more minutes. At last Yuma stood over Digger and hauled him up by the throat. He slammed a fist into him and the bandit went down, this time for good.

Yuma turned, wiping blood from his mouth. "Anyone else want to challenge me?"

Each gang member shook his head and slowly sat back down.

"We attack when *I* say," Yuma said. "Not anyone else. We'll wait until those Bible-toters have moved on. We need to keep whittling away at Legend's drovers. One by one, we'll gain the upper hand and then we'll kill him, take the woman and the cattle. I want it all."

Frank Farley had spoken the truth. Yuma Blackstone's axle was severely bent and that made him more dangerous than anyone Houston had ever run across.

And Lara had faced the man all alone with no help. He closed his eyes to block out her horror.

"Any questions?" Yuma thundered. When no one

spoke up, he ordered, "Someone pour water on Digger. Take him and ride to the fork in the trail a mile back. I'll join you there."

With a motion of Houston's head to Clay, they carefully retraced their steps. When they reached the horses, Houston spoke low. "We know what we're dealing with at least."

"We've gotta do something, boss," Clay whispered. "If we don't, we'll be at the bastards' mercy."

"I know." Houston glanced up at the night sky as though hoping to see a message written among the stars. But he saw nothing except the fiery tail of a comet. "Ride back and gather the drovers. Get Hiram Ledbetter too, if he'll come. We've got to stop them while we can. Leave a couple of men behind to guard Frank Farley and protect the women."

"Now you're talkin'. We'll show 'em what a bunch of mad drovers can do." Clay jumped on his horse and walked it out of earshot, then galloped toward the camp.

While Houston waited, he thought about the odds. The fight would be fierce. Yuma had fewer men, but they were by far more ruthless. After losing Emmett, Houston had fourteen seasoned men, plus the Boone twins and Nick Vincent. He scrubbed the back of his neck. That was all. It would have to do.

More would likely die. Hell! How many would he have to bury in the desolate expanse of Indian Territory? But wasn't it better than letting Yuma pick them off one by one? He was sure every single drover would agree.

He squatted on his heels to wait, praying his men would soon return. Unless the gang knew of a back way, they'd have to pass by him.

Something suddenly crashed through the brush. He swiveled, but not fast enough.

Twenty-nine

A LARGE, BLURRY FORM FLEW FROM THE DARKNESS AND grabbed Houston by the neck. The attacker pulled back his head to press a razor-sharp blade against his throat. Stinging pain pierced him and a warm trickle of blood ran down his neck, soaking into his collar. Desperate, Houston quickly reached behind him and pulled whoever it was over his head. Before the enormous, dark figure could get up, Houston stood, kicking away the gleaming knife streaked with blood. It clattered into the rocks.

He fumbled for his revolver but never got it out of the holster. The shaggy-haired assailant was on him.

Dear God, he looked like a mountain! Immense height, combined with width, told Houston he didn't stand a chance.

But a Legend never quit. Houston used every bit of strength he possessed to throw the man off him. Finally free, he searched the ground for some type of rock or club.

My boot knife.

Get the knife.

The words echoed in his head as Houston clawed at his pant leg, but before he could yank out the knife, his attacker came at him again.

Shaking his head like a wounded bear, the giant squared his shoulders and tossed Houston like a rag doll. They exchanged blows but, though Houston's knuckles were raw, he didn't appear to faze his opponent at all. He'd never seen any human this large. This beefy man with hands as big as ham bones would stand an easy foot above Stoker.

The taste of blood heavy on Houston's tongue, he fought to stave off the dizziness, to stay on his feet. If he went down, the giant would be on top of him and that would be all.

Blood ran down Houston's face and into his eyes, blurring his vision. He prayed for Clay and the drovers to hurry.

He couldn't best this giant with his fists. He needed an equalizer, anything to give him an edge. Fumbling, he managed to pull out his Colt. Before he could find the trigger, his assailant knocked the gun out of his hand as though it were a toy. Was this a man or some kind of beast? Houston wasn't sure about anything except that he was fighting now for his life.

He backed up against a boulder, holding his hands wide, praying he could grab his foe. If he could just get a hold, he'd pound his head on the boulder and keep pounding until it was a bloody pulp.

They circled each other with their hands held wide, taking the other's measure, each searching for an opening.

So far the man hadn't uttered a word. The only sounds that came from him were grunts and harsh breathing.

"Who the hell are you?" Houston shouted.

When the man didn't answer, he repeated, "Who are you?"

"Ghost."

One word and it said everything. Houston listened for his men but heard nothing. With a loud yell, he lowered his head and rammed into Ghost's stomach, knocking the wind out of him. As the giant struggled to breathe, Houston scrambled behind and applied a choke hold.

"Who are you, Ghost? Tell me."

A gurgle left the man's mouth. Houston tightened his arm around his foe's neck. One swift twist would break him—he just needed a bit more leverage.

As the satisfaction of finally besting this Hercules washed

over Houston, the man tensed his arms. Ghost surprised him with sharp jabs to his ribs, breaking Houston's hold with superhuman strength. The attacker lifted Houston high over his head.

Piercing pain shot through him as he stared at the ground below, steeling himself for the impact that would likely break every bone in his body.

Even if he wasn't thrown onto the rocks, the jarring force of the ground would break him in two and cripple… or kill him.

He closed his eyes as his promise to come back to Lara hammered in his ears.

You know I'll do anything in the world for you. If you wanted that moon up there, I'd do everything in my power to rope it and put it in your palm. So yes, I'll even stay alive.

And so he would—somehow—someway. Even if it looked hopeless. Even if he had to slay every demon. He'd survive even if nothing much was left of him, because he'd promised.

An abrupt, quick succession of shots rang from nowhere and slammed into his assailant's chest, ripping past muscle, bone, and tissue.

The ground shook as Ghost dropped like a giant oak tree.

Thirty

HOUSTON LANDED ON TOP OF THE DEAD MAN WITH A jarring thud. Stunned, he shook his head and pried Ghost's hands from him.

Who had fired?

With smoke curling from the barrel of a pearl-handled .45, Yuma Blackstone stepped from the darkness. Moonlight shone on the scalp dangling from his belt.

Fighting to breathe through the fire in his ribs, Houston rose from atop Ghost's body, staring at the murdering bastard. The image of Lara's long scar with its raised, puckered ridges crossed his vision. Rage boiled. He grabbed for his Colt, remembering too late that Ghost had knocked it from his grip.

Yuma sauntered forward as sleek as a cat stalking its prey. His bald head brought to mind a sun-bleached skull. A cruel smile curled the man's lips below the thin mustache. "I should've let him kill you, my friend."

"You should have," Houston agreed. "Because I'm going to make you suffer every bit as much as you did Lara."

"The stinkin' little whore was good for nothing except a moment's pleasure." Yuma sneered. "You should've heard her moan and cry and beg for more. Lara Boone wanted it."

It took all the strength Houston had to resist the urge to

lunge at him. But the deadly pistol pointed at his heart forced him to show calm. "So why cut her up if she was willing?"

Yuma gave a careless shrug and tugged on the remaining half of his ear. "I always leave my mark on women so they'll never forget who they belong to." Excitement colored his voice just thinking about it. "And you know how it is with them and their teasing ways. First they say yes, then they say no. The whores never know their own minds. What was I supposed to do?"

"Why are you stalking her?"

"To get her back. She belongs to me."

No way in hell. Houston would see that never happened.

Yuma went on. "After Till Boone packed up and moved, I didn't know where she was, until by chance I saw her at the river crossing. She belongs only to me."

Houston's thoughts again went to the knife in his boot. He had to get to it. He didn't need to pretend to be in pain—it was blinding already. He grimaced and gripped his chest before dropping to one knee.

Using Ghost's lifeless body to shield his movements, Houston managed to ease the knife from his boot. "Lara is my wife now and I don't share."

"I see we disagree, my friend."

"Most definitely—in every way." Houston gasped in pain, keeping Yuma distracted. "Why did you kill this man? I assume he was your friend."

"He was going to steal my pleasure. You are mine. I wish to be the one to bring the sting of death!" Yuma thundered, but something else was in his eyes.

"You were afraid of Ghost," Houston said softly as understanding dawned. A searing flame tore through his chest as he pulled himself to his feet, gripping the knife behind him. One chance was all he asked for. "You knew the giant would turn on you someday and take your life. Where's the ruthless outlaw? You're just a coward."

"You're wrong. I fear nothing."

Houston took a measured step. "I see it in your eyes.

You're afraid of Lara's little brother, Henry, and you feared Ghost. You also have at least one other man in your ranks capable of taking your life. From what I saw, Digger might just be man enough to kill you, in the daylight or in your sleep. He's not afraid of you."

With slow half steps, Houston crept toward his rival. A little closer and he would be within arm's reach. He kept his focus on Yuma's glittering, crazed eyes and not on the gun aimed at him. The man's appearance showed him for the sinister bastard he was. From the thin mustache above his lip, to the shaven head, to the shot-off ear—but most of all, the ruthless smile that promised no remorse for killing.

"Ah, yes, Digger." Yuma snorted, smoothing his mustache with one finger. "You must've been hiding nearby. I can handle him. If you stayed for the fight, you saw I whipped him good."

"Always in control, right?"

"That's right, my friend."

"You keep using that word." Houston took another step. "Make no mistake, you and I will never be anything more than enemies."

"I beg to differ." Yuma laughed. "You and me are more alike than you want to admit."

Quiet rage colored Houston's voice. "We are nothing alike. Not now, not ever. Are you going to shoot or talk me to death?"

"In a hurry to die, are you?"

Moonlight caught the flash of the blade as Houston lunged, slashing Yuma's face. He had only one chance to damage Yuma enough so he couldn't see to shoot. Houston quickly brought the knife back and ripped a long gash across the first slice, making a bloody X. The next instant, Houston grabbed Yuma's gun. A bullet burst from the end as he wrapped his hand around the barrel and managed to shove the weapon downward. Though the heated metal burned his palm, he held tight.

Galloping horses burst upon them with the arrival of

the drovers. Houston glanced up for a split second. That was all it took for Yuma to leave Houston holding the .45. The man leapt on Houston's palomino and galloped into the blackness.

Damn it to hell!

"Clay, go after Blackstone," Houston hollered. "He's getting away."

Leading the rest of the drovers, Houston ran toward Yuma's camp, praying the outlaws hadn't left. Thorns and brambles tore at his clothes and face. Pain knifed his ribs with each breath and his stride wasn't as long as it needed to be. He knew he'd be dead now if Yuma hadn't shot Ghost.

Moonlight illuminated the way across the rocks. Tall juniper rose up like silent sentinels, guarding the arid land's secrets. Houston gripped Yuma's six gun, taking comfort in the piece of steel. As battered and stove-up as Houston was, he'd be hard-pressed to win a fistfight. The .45 would do his fighting for him.

Every so often he'd stop to listen, but heard only the haunting silence of the windswept plains and rustle of the grasses.

At last the camp came into view. Houston's heart sank.

They'd already pulled up stakes and lit out. So there must've been a back way after all.

Clutching his ribs and limping, Houston and his men returned to Ghost's body.

"Who is this man, and what happened to you?" Pony asked.

Houston tried to straighten to his full height but the pain was too great. Bent over and gasping for air, he told them about his fight with Ghost and the chat with Yuma. "By all rights, I shouldn't be here."

Virgil put his arm around him. "I'm glad you are. I wouldn't want the job of telling Lara her husband is dead."

Clay galloped up and Houston told the story again.

"Glad you sliced the bastard's face," Clay said. "Let's get you back to camp."

"My Colt. It landed somewhere in the brush," Houston said.

"I'll find it," Virgil said. "Take my horse. I'll ride double with one of the others."

"Thanks." Houston bit his lip against the agony and settled into the saddle. Counting his blessings, he rode slowly toward the herd. With every step the roan took, he let out a string of curses.

He wished to hell he wasn't in so much misery. The need to have Yuma Blackstone dead burned inside a devil's fire.

For two cents, he'd go back and finish the job. *Dammit to hell!*

Next time he wouldn't fail.

❧

Lara walked away from the campfire and stared into the darkness in the direction Houston had ridden, as she'd done so often the last hour. But the expanse remained empty and silent except for Frank Farley's snores. The men had left him bound in his bedroll.

She sighed and drew her shawl tightly around her. Movement at the Ledbetters' tent drew her attention. For over thirty minutes, she watched women traipse back and forth from the high-topped wagon to Hiram, sitting outside the tent. Each would give him a good-night kiss and an embrace.

A light dawned. They were sharing Hiram, of all things.

Lara clasped a hand over her mouth to stifle the giggle. So that's why they named all their boy babies Hiram. He was the father to all their children—all eight. She'd heard her father once speak about a man like Hiram in the town of Amarosa. Maybe it wasn't that uncommon.

She knew one thing—she was not going to share Houston with anyone. He was hers.

It had to be close to midnight, but she wasn't going to

bed until she knew he was safe. She twisted the hem of her apron into a knot, matching the one in her stomach.

Tonight she'd decided to do more than lie in his arms, but maybe her courage had come too late. Maybe he wouldn't come back to her.

Maybe she was a widow. A frightened sob escaped her.

Caroline walked from her wagon to join her. "I couldn't sleep. I'm so worried about Nick. Do you mind if I wait with you?"

Lara put her arm around the girl. "Honey, I don't mind a bit. In fact, I'd love the company."

"Thanks. I just didn't want to be alone." Caroline motioned toward the Ledbetters' tent. "What do you think about that? I've been watching and every last one of those women gave Hiram a kiss and hug before going to bed. And Sarah stayed. The light just went out."

"They don't appear to sleep with him at the same time." A giggle slipped out. "At least I hope not. But yes, I noticed too."

Caroline drew herself up. "I'll kill any woman who tries that with my Nick."

"It must be a very strange feeling to see another woman with your husband. I'm not judging, but I couldn't live that life."

"The only thing I'd share would be my fist." Firelight reflected Caroline's seething anger. Lara imagined the young girl would be quite a handful in a fight.

She drew the newlywed toward the fire. "Want some coffee, dear? We need to make some for the men anyway."

"I'll help you. Gives us something to do besides wait and worry."

"That it does. Seems like I spend half my time suspended between reality and the unknown." Lara opened the coffee while Caroline filled the pot with water.

After nestling the pot amid the low flames, they sat down beside each other.

"Do you think our men are all right?" Caroline asked.

"Yes, I do." Because to let herself imagine the worst would drive her insane. Lara stared out into the darkness, praying no harm would come to the men. She knew those guarding them beyond the light waited as well, hoping for the same thing.

Caroline scooted closer. "I'm glad we have this chance to talk. Do you mind if I ask you a question?"

"I don't mind at all. What is it?"

"How long does it take to get pregnant? Nick and I have been trying night and day ever since we got married and I don't think it's working."

Lara hoped the shadows hid her red face. She had no earthly idea. With her, it had only taken the once. But she couldn't reveal how little she knew—it would kill her to have the young girl know more than she did at twenty-one. She had to sound wise even if the information was false.

"Uh, I'm not real sure, honey." Her face burned with embarrassment. "It seems to depend. Every woman is different. You shouldn't worry. Give yourself three months at least before you start fretting about it. There's no rush."

"Do you think there's something wrong with me? Maybe that's it."

"Absolutely not." Lara patted her hand. "This seems very premature. You just got married. Try to wipe it from your mind. That's the best thing." After a moment, she added, "A watched pot never boils."

"But what if there *is* something wrong? I'll die if I can't have our two boys and two girls."

"Caroline, listen to yourself. Don't borrow trouble."

"I'm trying not to." The young girl moved closer to whisper, "Nick can't last very long. He gets inside and the next thing I know he's already done. Maybe there's something wrong with him. I hate to ask, but is Mr. Legend like this?"

Lara jumped to her feet. She couldn't have this conversation. She couldn't even ask her own burning questions of the Ledbetter women when it had come down to it. Though they'd spoken briefly of love, she just couldn't voice her concerns. How would she know what's common in lovemaking?

"I think I hear something. Do you?" She was desperate to change the subject.

Caroline cocked her head. "Nope."

"Okay. Guess I made a mistake. Want some leftover cobbler? I'm starving." Lara strode to the chuck wagon's drop-down table where she'd left the dessert. She'd do anything to get Caroline's mind off that uncomfortable subject.

"Cobbler sounds good." Caroline rose and joined her.

For the next half hour, they ate their fill of the delicious dessert. Lara gave thanks that the conversation didn't return to pregnancy or lovemaking.

Finally, she caught the sound of horses and men talking low. Minutes later, the group of drovers materialized and her heart lurched.

Something was wrong. Houston slumped in the saddle, and there was no sign of the palomino he'd ridden out on.

With cold fear racing through her veins, she ran to him and touched his leg. "Tell me what happened."

Houston glanced down. She couldn't see his eyes but heard the suffering that rendered his strong voice to barely above a whisper. "Lara, darlin', now don't be mad. Just... stove-up...a bit."

She stood aside while he dismounted then put her arm around his waist and walked him to a blanket. Biting back a low oath, he lay down.

Clay took her aside. "Had a vicious fight with one of them outlaws, ma'am. Might've injured his ribs. Just pretty banged up all over, best I can tell."

"Thank you for getting him back here, Clay. Now excuse me, I've got work to do."

While the men removed Houston's vest and torn, bloody shirt, she filled a bowl with water and grabbed a cloth. She never knew when the drovers left, only suddenly, she was alone with her husband. She ran her fingers over his chest and along each rib. Angry redness and swelling covered one side of his rib cage where a bruise was already forming. It would be as black as coal come morning. Scores of other similar marks marred his skin. Blood that didn't continue to leak was drying everywhere.

"Oh, Houston, you promised." She struggled to still her quavering voice and not let him see her worry.

Houston lifted a finger to her cheek and attempted a grin. "I kept my vow. I stayed alive…for you."

Unshed tears filled her eyes. He meant more to her than her own life. Houston Legend was her North Star that always guided her to safety. Without him, she'd be lost and alone, crashing against jagged rocks.

Swallowing the lump in her throat, she spoke. "I can't feel anything broken but I'm not a doctor. Likely your ribs are only cracked and bruised."

But it was the nasty, still-oozing cut across his throat that made her quickly swallow a sob before it escaped. A little deeper and he'd have died. She'd come so close to losing him forever. She gently cleaned the injury and kissed it, very thankful the cut wasn't worse. He would carry a scar, though, no matter how well it healed.

"Tell me what else hurts."

He raised his scraped knuckles. "Here."

She lifted his hand to her lips and kissed each knuckle.

"Here." He indicated a long, ugly scratch along his bicep.

Lara left a trail of kisses up and down the scratch. She liked playing this game.

"Here." He pointed to his split lip.

Bending, she gently placed her lips to his, being careful not to hurt him.

After a long kiss, she washed blood from his body and tended the multitude of cuts, scrapes, and scratches. He looked as though he'd fought a grizzly and come back a bloody mess. But he was *her* bloody mess.

Bits of her earlier conversation with the Ledbetter wives flooded back.

"A woman in love can't bear to be apart from her

husband. He's all she thinks about," Ruth had told her. "Each time he steps within eyesight my pulse races, heart pounds, and palms become sweaty. You simply know."

Hannah had added softly, "I knew when mine kissed me and stood up for me against spiteful people who spread their hate. I will stand by his side, no matter what comes."

"Imperfections don't matter when you're in love," Sarah had said. "Everyone has flaws. Love is wholly accepting someone."

Suddenly, Lara knew what the strange butterflies, yearnings, and constant thoughts meant.

She was in love with Houston Legend—bruises, blood, and all.

Thirty-one

THE STRUGGLE TO CONTAIN GIDDY LAUGHTER TOOK ALL SHE had as Lara embraced the heated, rosy glow inside.

Houston frowned. "What's so funny?"

"Nothing, sweetheart. Nothing at all." She laid down the wet cloth that was stained with blood. "Just thinking about something those women next to us said."

"What do you think about them?"

"They seemed awfully odd at first," Lara answered. "The idea of four women married to the same man. But they're most warm and gracious."

"Hiram's got it made. Four wives at his beck and call. A different one every night to warm his bed." A mischievous light came into Houston's eyes. "I might try that."

"You do and you'll find me gone, cowboy." She didn't smile.

He ran a finger across her lips. "Do I detect jealousy?"

His liquid touch made her shiver with longing. She leaned toward him. "You belong to me and I don't ever intend to share."

"Whew, that's a relief!" Houston tucked a strand of hair behind her ear. "I don't think I could handle a whole mess of wives. You're the only one I want, the only one I need, not only now but forever. I have this hunger inside that only you can meet."

"Who knows what the future holds, dear." Lara met his smoldering dark eyes. Though she yearned to tell him she loved him, she held back, unsure of how to voice what was in her heart.

"What's that supposed to mean? You're talking in riddles, wife."

She couldn't say more, couldn't offer what might be false hope. Though her heart yearned to fill his needs, her body might rebel.

"I've got to find some cloth strips to bind your ribs. It'll help with the pain," she murmured and climbed up in the chuck wagon. A tingling in the pit of her stomach came with the new awareness that she had to do something soon to quiet this strong need to be his.

The pull of Houston Legend was like a thousand magnets, making him impossible to resist. Running exploring hands over his injured chest in search of broken bones only amplified that. She no longer wanted to hold back. She desired him as she had nothing else in her life.

Only…now he was hurt and in too much pain.

She located the box of medical supplies with her stash of long cloth strips. Grabbing the box, she bustled back to his side, surprised to see Quaid sitting with Houston.

Her brother grinned. "He's going to be all right, isn't he, sis? I poured him some coffee."

Lara's warm gaze drifted over the man she loved. "He's going to be just fine. Appreciate you taking care of him."

Houston grinned. "Not the same as a mess of wives, but I reckon Quaid will do in your stead."

"No more thinking about stuff like that, mister," Lara scolded, shaking her finger.

"Uh-oh! I think you're in big trouble, Houston. I know that tone." The boy got to his feet. "I should've been with you tonight. I grew up with a gun in my hand—all of us did."

Houston glanced up. "You already proved you can shoot, son. I just needed a good man I can trust to watch Farley and stay with Lara. That's the only reason I kept you behind."

Quaid nodded and took a wide stance. Lara could tell how Houston's words pleased her brother. "Guess I'll take my turn for guard duty."

"Keep a sharp eye out," Houston warned. "Don't take any chances."

"I won't." The boy went to his horse.

Lara watched her brother ride away, wishing growing up wasn't so difficult. Like Virgil, Quaid yearned to make his mark, to be a man. This untamed land demanded that of boys. They had to give up childish notions and be tough as fast as they could. Her heart ached for all her brothers. Often boys were cut down before they filled men's shoes.

Both twins had already been wounded. Next time they might not be so lucky.

"I'm worried, Houston." Lara's fingertips brushed his chest as she reached around to get the edge of the strip from behind.

His dark eyes met hers. "Me too. They're coming for us."

"I know." The binding slipped from Lara's trembling fingers. One a day was what Yuma had vowed, and she knew better than most how vicious the man could be. Get in his way and he'd cut you down in a heartbeat. He always got what he wanted.

And God in heaven, Yuma Blackstone wanted her and would kill anyone who got in the way.

What for?

A sob tried to rise as fear traveled the length of her before twisting into knots in her stomach.

"Trust me to protect you." Houston raised her chin with a forefinger and kissed her.

"I do trust you to keep us safe. I do. It's just that I've seen plenty of times when people in the right didn't win. I've often heard that justice is blind."

"Not this time. Have faith and believe that good will win out. Can you do that for me?"

"Yes." Lara touched a muscle that quivered in his jaw. This husband of hers carried convictions lodged so deep inside that seemed to give him strength beyond the normal man. He made it impossible for her not to believe.

What she wouldn't give to be able to spend a quiet day with him. They'd go on a picnic beside a lazy river. Just the two of them with nothing more pressing than when to eat the delicious fried chicken she'd bring. On impulse, she pressed her lips to his. His arms came around her, locking her in his embrace. She didn't care who saw. She only cared about this honorable man who'd struck a bargain and married her sight unseen.

"Watch it, darlin'," he growled when their lips parted. "Keep this up and I'll forget I'm a patient man."

Giddy joy brought a giggle. At this moment, even with the danger and the smell of death in the air, she felt young again and carefree.

With a happy sigh, Lara wound an arm around his neck. This was what she'd longed for since she was a girl with a yarn doll in her arms.

A husband and a babe to fill her heart with love.

But could she keep them? Or would Yuma rip them from her life just because he could?

As though sensing she was in her mother's thoughts, Gracie whimpered and let out a sharp cry.

Lara pushed away. "Let me check on our daughter. I'll be right back."

"I'm not going anywhere."

Hurrying to tend the babe before the child woke fully, Lara prayed this wouldn't take long. She scolded herself for letting Houston distract her from caring for his wounds.

Gracie quieted as soon as Lara patted her back. Waiting a few minutes more to make sure she wouldn't wake, Lara was satisfied and returned to the fire and the man whose heart called to her.

"I think it was just a bad dream." Lara's glance found Houston pulling on the binding, trying to remove it. "Stop that!"

"Forget this blasted wrapping. I've got to see to the men."

When he tried to rise, Lara held him down. "You're in no shape, Houston. Clay and Pony can handle things."

He sat back with a long sigh. "I'm the boss. If something happens to another…"

Lara dropped down beside him and lightly touched her lips to his. "You can't be everything to everyone. You've given instructions down to the letter and they know to follow them." She didn't remind him that he could be right there and still Yuma could take one of the drovers, if he took a mind to. It would do no good to tell Houston something he already knew.

She picked up the edge of the strip. "You know, when I was a little girl, a man lived nearby. His name was Clarence. No matter what anyone needed, he always jumped in and provided it before waiting to see if the person could help themselves."

"Does this story have a moral?" he drawled.

"You can't be everything to everyone. Let your men be men. They're not children. I know Emmett's loss weighs heavy—it does on my heart too—but trust your drovers to follow the rules you've laid down."

He lifted a strand of her hair and rubbed it between his thumb and forefinger. "When did you get to be so smart?"

"Lord knows I'm a long way from that." She tied off the binding and rested her cheek on his chest.

A groan slipped from his mouth. "We need to be alone, my love. Just you and I. Somewhere away from all these watchful eyes and gossiping tongues. These drovers are like a bunch of widow women."

His deep voice rumbled, arousing a slew of excited quivers. Lara captured her bottom lip between her teeth. It was time.

She stood and reached for his hand. "Come."

Thirty-two

HOUSTON'S BREATH CAUGHT SOMEWHERE IN HIS CHEST. HE knew what it cost for Lara to take the initiative. That she did seemed to signal that she'd begun to heal.

He met her pretty emerald eyes that glistened by the light of the campfire. She was the most beautiful woman he'd ever seen. She was the one person in the world meant for him, and he would cherish every second of every day with her. Heart hammering loudly in his ears, he managed to murmur, "Your every wish is my command, darling wife."

A comfortable silence enveloped them as he rose and took her hand. Together they strolled to the bed that awaited. He checked on Gracie and Henry while she crawled onto the blankets beneath the chuck wagon and got situated.

Finally, clenching his jaw against the agony, Houston slid into place next to her and pulled her against him. When their bodies fit together like a pair of spoons, he covered them and let one arm drape across her stomach. He pushed aside her hair and kissed the back of her neck.

She'd come such a long way in so short a time, allowing him to cuddle her in this manner, with her flush against him. Overcome with emotion, he pressed a kiss to her temple. Her curves fit perfectly into his, so much that they seemed to share one heartbeat. He prayed his body wouldn't betray him, wouldn't show the depths of his desire. Yet it appeared determined to show proof despite his desperate attempt to quell the response.

"Thank you, sweetheart," Lara murmured. "Am I hurting your ribs?"

"No," he lied. Truth was, he and pain were old acquaintances. Yet, he'd gladly suffer anything to be close to her. "Are you comfortable? If I'm hogging the blanket, just tell me."

"This feels heavenly." Lara sighed and stroked his arm. "While I waited for you tonight, not knowing if you'd come back or not, it struck me once more how fragile life is and how fast it can end. Each time you go out, I worry that I'll never see you again, but tonight the reality was even more powerful. When I saw you were hurt, my heart stopped beating for a full moment and I wasn't sure it would start back."

"I'm sorry I scared you."

"Clay didn't tell me much. Something about a fight. Was it with Yuma?" Lara twisted to face him, sending knifing agony to his ribs. He bit his lip, drawing blood. Thank goodness for darkness, because he knew his face had to be ashen.

"Partly." He prayed she wouldn't ask more.

She gasped. "You fought more than one?"

Damn, he should've known she'd not let it lie. "Afraid so." He told her about the group of outlaws, and a few details about Ghost.

"That man could've easily killed you!" Lara tenderly kissed him.

Houston sighed. "Except he didn't. Lie back and rest."

She did…for a full second. She rose onto her elbow again. "We've got no choice but to send Henry back to Texas. Since our friends are headed that way, it's the perfect opportunity to keep him safe."

But was that the safest thing? Yuma's words to his men stuck in his head. He'd ordered them to leave the Ledbetters alone and focus on Houston and Lara. So yes, they had to be the best and safest option. Still, misgivings nagged.

"I agree." Houston met her eyes and stroked her hair. "I'll talk to them tomorrow. I'll feel better with him out of danger. Yuma isn't going to bother the Ledbetters. He wants us too bad." Houston debated on sending Lara and Gracie too. But she'd been very firm about staying when he'd brought it up before and it didn't sit well to force her to go. She'd had to deal with too much force in her life. Still, he had to ask one more time.

"I'd send all my brothers if I could. But their wagon is full to the brim." Lara snuggled against him and laid her head on his chest.

"I want you to consider going too, Lara."

"No," she answered almost before he got the words out. "There's nothing to consider. Didn't you hear me say their wagon is full and spilling over the sides? Don't pawn me off on them. Please."

Houston touched the curve of her jaw. "I'll never pawn you off."

"Then, let's talk about something else."

The strong beat of her heart kept time with Houston's. "I've noticed a change in you lately."

"The work, the fresh air, and being with you has made a lot of difference. Thank you for bringing me. It allowed us to get to know each other without the pressure of living in the same house. Out here we go our separate ways through the day and come together for our nightly ritual."

That such simple things helped heal her came as a surprise. He called daily routines living. Maybe that was the secret. Maybe it didn't take any grand scheme to restore self-worth and confidence about yourself. Maybe just fresh air and release from the pressures of being the perfect husband, the perfect wife, had provided enough space to learn what they wanted from each other. He'd discovered he could trust again. He could open his heart to her.

"Lara, I love whatever it was, though I've pondered the wisdom of my decision many times over." Houston lifted a strand of copper hair, rubbing the silk between his fingers. "I brought you and Gracie to a place of great danger."

"You had no way to know Yuma would be out here." She raised her head to kiss the hollow of his throat.

"I sliced his face tonight." The minute the words slipped from Houston's mouth he wished he could call them back.

Silence fell around them. At last she spoke. "I'm glad."

"I made a large X on his cheek. He'll remember this night for the rest of his rotten, godforsaken life."

Lara smoothed the blanket that covered them. "He deserves it. I never told you about the night of the attack."

"You don't have to, darlin'."

"I want to get it out. I've never breathed a word of this, but I need to tell someone. Until I do, it's a festering sore that won't heal."

Houston gently kissed her, savoring their newfound closeness. He would've said that the feeling bursting from his heart was love, except after past experience, he couldn't say. He did know a deep bond had formed with the woman curled beside him.

"If a listener is what you need, then I'm all ears," Houston mumbled against her temple.

"You can fill in most of the blanks so I'll spare you the details," she said. "It's what happened afterward that I can't forget. I've never told another living soul."

"You don't have to do this. Maybe you shouldn't."

She inhaled deeply. "The memory eats at my brain. I have to get it out."

Houston knew about things that ate at you and how they destroyed the fabric of a person until he could no longer recognize himself. He drew her close. "Then I'll listen."

"Blood streamed from my face that night and I couldn't tell which direction to go. I crawled, desperately trying to find help. Find someone to end the nightmare. I had nothing to shield my naked body with, but that barely registered.

"On some level, I simply knew I didn't want to die there with him and feared I might. Yuma laughed and kicked me as I crawled." Her voice broke as she sobbed. "Taunting and kicking and stomping with his boots. The torture, the pain, the temptation to lie down and die was so strong. But I chose to live."

Houston tenderly wiped her tears, folded his arms even tighter around her trembling body. He couldn't bear to hear more, wanted to beg her to stop. But he didn't—because what she said was true. She needed to tell someone so the wound could finally heal. That she chose him spoke of her trust.

And he'd carry her words to his grave.

He rubbed her back and held her as she cried, releasing deep, shuddering sobs that came from the depths of her soul. He didn't know how long it was before she lay spent. He just held her, giving her time, murmuring soothing words, rubbing her back and shoulders.

When she was able to talk, she went on. "I can still hear him, you know? Yuma's laughter, the hateful words. He called me a pitiful, worthless whore. Among other things. There was another man also there that night. And…" Quiet sobs shook her again. "He…took a turn."

Shock and molten anger washed through Houston, blinding him. "Who? Tell me." He'd find the bastard and shove him headfirst in a grave.

"I never knew his name. He was Yuma's acquaintance. He wore twin guns and had these strange-looking cartridge belts coming down from each shoulder, crisscrossing his chest. They dug into my skin."

Digger Barnes. Had to be him. Everything fit. Houston trembled with rage so powerful he tasted the bitterness on his tongue. He had to stop both men from hurting any other women.

This wasn't just about avenging Lara. What burned inside was to see justice done. To hunt down both and let them hang before they hurt anyone else.

Suddenly in the quiet, a thought hit him. Gracie could be either man's child. That sweet babe didn't deserve this any more than Lara did.

A stillness came over him. He had to weigh his next words carefully and make sure he expressed the feelings inside that made him tremble in the dead of night.

"You are without a doubt the bravest woman I've ever known. You survived to give life to our little Gracie." He kissed her fingertips. "I'm sorry you had to suffer through that. I only wish I had been there." He shook with the need to get up right then and ride back to the snake's den. Only now they were gone. Didn't matter. If it took him the rest of his days, he'd find them. And when he did, he'd make sure both men died a very slow and very painful death.

"I wish you had also." She caressed his jaw. "I'm glad I chose to live."

"So am I." What a fool he'd been to waste half his life loving the wrong woman. No, even worse than that: the *idea* of her. He hadn't known her at all in the end—and he hadn't really known love either.

Houston tenderly kissed her forehead, then drifted to capture her lips. His hands moved down her stomach to rest on one flared hip. Finally, he broke the kiss. "Try to forget. Wipe it from your memory. Neither are worth one second's thought. They're already headed to hell."

He'd carry her secret so she could live her life free. The two thought they'd gotten away with their unspeakable crime.

Lara pressed her lips to the hollow of his throat. "I feel a little better already."

"I'm glad. Keep your eyes firmly on the future and all the happiness we'll have making a life together." Houston kissed away the remnants of the tears that poised on the tips of her lashes. "Promise me you will."

"I promise." A shuddering breath ran through her. "Thank you, Houston."

"You have more courage than anyone I've known. I'm proud to be your husband." Houston tucked her against him and held her for a long time, letting the silence spin a healing web around them. He was glad he didn't have to speak, because he didn't know where to begin to find the right words. Maybe there weren't any. Maybe it was better to keep quiet and let his hands do his talking for a change.

Finally, Lara shifted and took his hand. She placed it on her breast, then fumbled with the top button of her dress. "I'd like to feel you touching my bare skin. If you've no objection."

Protest to that? Good Lord!

He moved her hand aside but paused with the button. "Are you sure? If you'd rather wait a while, that's all right."

"I'm certain. But that's all I'm up to for now."

"I understand." Only a fool would complain. With trembling fingers, he unfastened her dress. Her white cotton chemise was all that stood between them. Earthy scents of the night and passion swirled around them as Houston pressed his hand to her bare flesh.

So soft.

So warm.

So intoxicating.

He tried to fill his lungs but instantly regretted it when the pain brought tears to his eyes. He closed them and waited until his ribs eased before letting his fingers glide, caressing the long column of her throat and stopping at the swell of her bosom. Sweat popped out on his forehead. He yearned to move the chemise aside and brush across her breasts, but he wouldn't betray Lara's trust.

Just being with her this way made him feel as though he'd drunk half a bottle of whiskey. His head swam and heat swept along each nerve ending, spreading through his limbs.

He'd been with other women during his life, but somehow this seemed like his very first time. Lara pushed out memories of all others from his brain. Even if someone held a gun to his head, he couldn't recall one detail about them.

They'd meant nothing to him. Nothing at all.

Lara ran her fingers across his lips. "Houston, do you think it'll always be this way between us?"

"Which way do you mean?"

"Easy. Comfortable. Tingly."

"I expect so, darlin'. Only better. What we have now is fresh-made wine. We still have the grapes between our toes. Give us a few years and our relationship will age to perfection. Deeper and more meaningful."

"I can't wait." She stretched to kiss him, and not a quick brush of the lips either. The kiss singed the hair on his chest and lingered, washing over him like a midnight tide. His lady was a fast learner. Houston grinned, placing his lips to the skin laid bare above her white chemise.

Lara gave a moan and threw back her head, allowing him greater access. She slid one hand along his neck and buried her fingers in his hair.

It was worth the pain in his ribs to see the depth of her passion. To feel the wild beating of her heart. And to know she was beginning to find the courage to move on. Lara's strength amazed him, and he nearly burst with pride.

One step at a time. That's what Stoker always said.

Her sweet, intoxicating fragrance washed over Houston. He'd remember this night for the rest of his life.

While they hadn't yet joined bodies, they had already become as one, deep in their hearts where hopes, dreams, and deep commitment lived.

Someone standing beside the wagon cleared his throat. "Boss?"

Lara stiffened in his arms as Houston asked, "What is it, Clay?"

"Hate to bother you, but you'd best come."

"Be right there."

The cowboy's footsteps moved away and Houston quickly did her dress back up.

"I wish you didn't have to go." Her voice quavered with fear.

Houston kissed her. "Makes two of us. Try not to worry. I'll probably be back before you can count all those sheep in your pretty little head."

He knew different, though. Clay wouldn't have come

for him, injured like he was, unless something big had happened. Whatever it was…it was bad.

"Keep your gun close and don't wander from the campfire," Houston said low.

"Okay." Though her hands had turned icy, she remained calm.

Taking care not to move the wrong way and hurt his ribs more, he crawled from his wife's bed. Clay Angelo stood by the fire, staring toward the herd. Houston's gaze swept to the empty bedrolls. Every drover must be pulling guard duty.

"What's wrong, Clay?"

"Gus King's missing. We searched nearby but no luck. Too dangerous to go far."

"We'll have to wait until daylight," Houston said. "Maybe he'll turn up."

"Maybe so," Clay agreed.

Both of them seemed to know he wouldn't. *One a day* Yuma had vowed.

Clay yanked off his hat and twisted it. "Another thing, boss. The men are real jittery. There's talk of leaving while they still can. If you're able, you need to talk to them."

Hell!

Houston couldn't blame them. Their lives were at stake. But how would he get these cows to Dodge by himself? Everything was slipping away—the ranch's livelihood, the herd, and the drovers who had trusted him.

"Hopefully I can say something you haven't," he said.

Clay nodded once, jammed on his hat as both strode to the horses.

Houston rode to try to save the cattle drive. He fought for not only his very life but his family's as well. He found the men in a tight knot, talking low. The group'd shrunk by another drover. Grimacing with pain in his body, along with that in his heart, he threw his leg over and slid from the saddle.

"I heard there's talk of quitting." He looked in each

man's face and saw fear beneath the layers of dirt, sweat, and sacrifice.

"We got no choice, Mr. Legend," Pony Latham said. "It's leave or die. This job ain't worth it."

"I understand, and if you choose to go, I'll pay you right now." Houston paused to let it sink in. "But if you decide to stay and help get these longhorns to Dodge, I'll put an extra thousand in your pocket. Together we can beat Yuma Blackstone and his band of killers. I can't do it by myself."

"You make it hard, boss," Joe said. "I came to ride for the Legend brand way back yonder because everyone claimed the Lone Star was a top-notch ranch. That the family took care of the men who worked for them. I found everything to be true. But this…"

"I couldn't ask for a better group of men," Houston said. "Neither I nor Stoker will hold your leaving against you."

Clay stepped forward and planted his heels. "I came to get this herd to Dodge and no one, not Yuma Blackstone or anyone else, is going to keep me from it. I'll fight 'em to the gates of hell then stab them with the devil's own pitchfork. Boss needs our help. He's treated us fair and asked nothing more than what he's willing to do himself. Almost got killed tonight proving it. What do you say?"

Silence dropped over them as each looked at the other.

"I'll stay and help find Gus," Pony finally said. "After that I don't know. I can't leave him out here in this godforsaken place. He was like a brother to me."

One by one, each decided to do the same. It was better than Houston dared hope. He glanced at Clay. The man surrounded by mystery had proven his worth yet again. Clay was a good man, and maybe that was all anyone could hope for—men you could count on around you and one very special woman.

No one came more special than Lara. He'd watched passion darken her eyes tonight. And it damn sure blazed a path across his heart.

Thirty-three

"WHO SAW GUS LAST?" HOUSTON GLANCED AROUND THE circle.

"That was probably me," Joe said. "I was playin' my harmonica to put the herd to sleep an' Gus sang along. When I finished, he moved north an' I moseyed south. Never saw him again."

"Anyone else?" Houston asked. "Who was working the north?"

Pony stepped forward. "I heard Gus singin', if you can call his bellerin' that, but I never saw him. Whatever happened must've taken place between Joe an' me."

"Did anyone hear anything unusual? Maybe a strange noise?"

Quaid said, "I caught what sounded like rustlin' noises an' a smothered groan. I called out the password—*Taters*—but no one answered back, so me an' Virgil went for a look-see."

"We didn't find squat." Virgil met Houston's gaze. "No hat in the dirt or nothing. Too dark to spot drag marks."

"Thanks, boys." Houston laid his hand on Quaid's shoulder. "We'll have to wait for morning for a better look. Not wise to wander around in the dark. Anyone else hear anything? A cough, or a heel striking rocks? Maybe a cow took off and Gus went to bring it back?"

No one spoke. They had precious little to go on. It seemed as if the earth had opened up and swallowed Gus

King, and right out of the middle of the herd to boot. Houston knew he had only to look in Yuma's direction. He told the men to stay alert, and put his foot in the stirrup.

A woman's sudden scream, followed by a gunshot rent the air, freezing him.

His heart hammering, he scrambled into the saddle. He never felt his painful ribs, not even a twinge. He only knew he had seconds to get to Lara. Nothing else was important.

The roan flew over the rocky terrain. Houston vaguely heard others behind him, but his focus was ahead. The powerful horse ate up the short distance in nothing flat. Able to make out several figures in the light of the campfire, he slid his Colt from the holster.

Had Yuma decided one a day wasn't enough?

Please let me get there in time to stop whatever's happening.

Gracie screamed at the top of her lungs, terrified. He yearned to go to the babe but had to rescue Lara first.

Two men were at the camp with their backs to Houston when he drew to a stop and leapt down. One held Lara's hands above her head while she kicked him for all she was worth. Henry had thrown himself onto the other intruder's back and clamped both hands over the man's eyes. Caroline Vincent was pounding both interlopers' heads and backs with a large spoon. All were so engaged in the fight, they hadn't heard Houston and the drovers galloping up.

"Let go of me, you brute," Lara hollered.

"When you settle down, ma'am. You tried to kill me."

"Pity I missed." Lara's scathing words told of the fight still left in her. "You're going to be very, very sorry."

"Already am, ma'am, for a fact," the man growled. He was awful polite to be a cold-blooded killer. And his voice—

Houston strode into the fray with his Colt leveled on the attackers. "Get your hands off my wife or I'll blow your rotten head off."

The men turned and both yelled at the same time, "What kept you?"

"Luke? Sam?"

Lara, breathless, her hair streaming from a long braid, rushed to Houston. "You know them?"

"They're my brothers." Remembering he still held his gun, Houston slid it back into the holster and tried to slow his breathing. Clay and the drovers followed his lead, putting their revolvers away as well. Oddly, Houston noticed Clay stepping deeper into the shadows, tugging his hat low to conceal his features. A second later, he mounted his horse and rode off.

"You met Sam once at the ranch," Houston said, bringing his attention back to his wife. "Spent time with his wife, Sierra. But I'm sure he looks pretty scary in the dark." He put his arm around Lara and addressed his brothers. "What do you mean sneaking up on our camp? Didn't you tell her who you were?"

"We didn't see anyone around, so we stopped for a minute to get warm by the fire before coming to find you. Helped ourselves to the last of the coffee," Sam said. "Next thing we know, a bullet zings over our heads and we're in the fight of our life. No time for explaining or saying howdy or anything. They could've killed us."

Henry's rapid breathing was loud. "No one hurts my sister. You scared the baby too."

Gracie's screams grew louder and more insistent. Lara pulled away from Houston and hurried to get her.

"How can we make it up to you?" Sam asked.

"By going away." Henry turned and stalked to the wagon. The boy had already dismissed them.

"By all rights they should've killed you." Houston scowled at the two. Both brothers looked done in. Their clothes were ripped and faces bore scratches. Luke stalked to his black hat and picked it up.

"We've got a mess of outlaws killing us," Houston said. "So far, we've had to bury one drover and another is missing. Doubt we'll find him alive."

Lara walked back with Gracie in her arms, the babe still snuffling.

Luke stood, head bowed, his hat in his hands. "I'm real sorry, ma'am. I didn't mean to scare you. Sam and I came to help. We've been riding hell-bent for leather for days trying to get here. I hope you'll accept my apology." He moved toward her, offering a handshake.

"I'm sorry for trying to shoot you, Luke." Lara clasped his palm. "No hard feelings, I hope. I took you for one of Yuma's men."

"How in hell did you know I needed you?" Houston asked.

Sam picked up his hat from the dirt and slapped it on his pant leg. "After Pa got your telegram from Chimney Rock, he got in touch, and here we are. Like Luke said, we rode hell-bent, with little sleep and food."

"I'll fix you something to eat to tide you over until breakfast." Lara handed Gracie to Houston.

"No thanks, ma'am," Luke said firmly. "We'll wait for morning."

With a long stride, Lara moved to stand toe-to-toe in front of him. Her chin jutted at a determined angle. Houston watched the gunfighter take a step back. The brother who could face a man at twenty paces and give him a steely eyed glare seemed unsure of his safety. Houston covered a grin with his hand. Luke was about to learn what tangling with trouble really meant.

"No more of this *ma'am* business. I'm Lara. We're family, not strangers. Got it? That goes for you too, Sam."

Sam jerked around. "What did I do?"

"Nothing yet," Lara said. "That was a friendly warning."

Luke winked at Houston. "I like her. You've got yourself a keeper."

"Don't I know it," Houston agreed. Being on the trail had changed her from a shy, quiet woman to a tigress who didn't mince her words.

"Since you won't take food, I'll make another pot of coffee." Lara grabbed the pot and headed to fill it with water.

Houston's gaze followed her. He wished he was lying in her bed, whispering sweet nothings in her ear and watching her blush. He wanted to press his lips to hers and drink in her passion. To wake in the morning with her in his arms. And God willing, to grow old together.

But now that he'd found what he wanted, was it going to be yanked from reach?

"Tell me and Luke about the vermin who're killing the drovers." Sam's quiet request reeled Houston's attention back.

"Have a seat." For the next half hour, Houston filled in his brothers, starting with when he'd first seen the riders and followed their trail. He ended with, "I have to say I'm mighty glad to see you both."

Luke's face hardened. "Kill one a day, huh?"

Houston nodded. "And so far they're making good on the threat."

"I can see why the women and Henry launched a ferocious attack." Sam wrapped his hands around a tin cup. "They can't relax their guard for a second. One thing I know is Yuma Blackstone's moments are measured. I was ready to hunt him down before for what he did to Lara, but now he's shown plenty more reasons why we can't let him live."

"A man like that doesn't deserve to draw breath." Luke stood and emptied his coffee dregs into the fire. "To threaten an innocent babe has got to be as low as a man can go."

"Yep," Houston agreed. "The two of you get a few winks. We'll start the search for Gus come daylight."

Luke strode to his black gelding and unsaddled the mount.

Sam followed, hollering over his shoulder, "I hope you have a good remuda, Houston. Our horses need to rest for a few days. We about killed them."

"Pick out some fresh ones from the remuda as soon as you can see," Houston answered.

He watched his brothers care for their horses, giving thanks that Stoker had sent them. The tide had turned in their favor. Sam and Luke were tough men who wouldn't stop until they finished the job. Just don't ask them to go up against Lara. His grin returned. His wife was made of stern stuff. No longer would anyone take from her without a heck of a fight. His gaze went to her in the shadows where she stood, comforting Gracie. He rose with a groan and went to them.

"Let me have her for a bit, darlin'. You need to get some sleep."

Lara smiled. "Not much left of this night. I'll have to start breakfast in another hour."

"Just try to rest until then. All right?"

"Are you sure you want to watch after her? I could lay her down next to me."

"Positive." Houston gave her a kiss. "Now scat."

Gracie reached for Houston and he took her. With a yawn, Lara moved toward her bed. Kissing his daughter's chubby cheek, he cradled her close. She grabbed a handful of shirt and gave a shuddering breath. She'd be all right. Her fright had given way to heavy eyelids.

"Go back to sleep, little girl, your papa has you. I'm not gonna let anything happen to you," Houston murmured.

Houston glanced up to find Sam watching him with a big smile plastered on his face. "What's so entertaining?"

"I never thought I'd see you so taken with a babe. Just imagine, my big brother a father. I never thought I'd see the day. Nothing better in life, but it sure takes a lot of work to get it right." Sam moved five paces and took Gracie's hand. "You might as well know. Sierra is in the family way. I'm going to be a pa again."

"Hallelujah! That's great, little brother." Houston knew how happy that made Sam. He and Sierra had adopted Hector after both his parents died. They really loved that boy, and giving him a brother or sister would thrill Hector. No kid should be raised alone, at least in his opinion. "I couldn't be happier for you, Sam."

"Thanks." Sam's gaze went to the chuck wagon. His voice was quiet. "After what happened, I'm sure it's hard for you and Lara."

Houston followed Sam's gaze, thinking of what Lara had shared a short time before. "I sliced Yuma's face tonight, just like he did Lara's, only worse. I brought the knife back across and made a large X on his cheek. He'll remember me every time he looks in the mirror. And you know what?"

"What?"

"It felt damn good too." Deep satisfaction still burned in Houston's chest.

"Too bad it wasn't his throat," Luke said from behind them.

Houston's own throat, the cut hidden under his bandana, throbbed at the reminder. "No, I'm glad it worked out this way. He'll suffer before I kill him. Yuma will know a little of Lara's grief when she goes into a town and people stare." Houston's eyes narrowed to slits. Yes, this was much better than a swift death. And as the light finally began to go out in Yuma's eyes, Houston would spit on him and deliver a harsh kick to his ribs with the toe of his boot. Justice was going to taste so sweet.

"I reckon." Luke spread his bedroll by the fire. "You've got far more patience than I do."

"Or me," Sam said quietly. "If he'd done that to Sierra, I wouldn't rest until I put a bullet in his head."

"It's not that I have patience." Houston shook his head. "The problem is that he's like a damn ghost. One minute he's there and the next he vanishes into thin air."

A dangerous edge filled Luke's voice. "We'll find him. And when we do, we'll make him rue the day he started a war with the Legends. We'll not stop until we spill his blood over every inch of this godforsaken, miserable land."

"For sure. Go ahead and turn in," Houston said. "Tomorrow's going to be a long day."

"Yep." Sam picked up his bedroll from beside his saddle. "And come daylight, we need to make a plan."

A few minutes later, Houston shook his head as his brothers' snores blended with the crackle and pop of the campfire. They hadn't hit the ground before they were asleep.

A plan? Houston had only one—make Yuma Blackstone and his men pay.

He walked to Gracie's crib, laid her down, and tucked a soft blanket around her. For a moment, he looked down at her. When a tiny smile curved her bow mouth, he could've sworn she was only pretending to sleep. The love he felt for the child shook him to the core, making him tremble. He'd move heaven and earth for her and her pretty mama.

They were his whole world, lighting the darkness. Love for them spilled from his heart. No one would take them from him.

No one.

Thirty-four

DAYLIGHT CAME AND EVERYONE JOINED THE SEARCH FOR Gus, but two hours later they had little to show for their efforts except drag marks toward a stamped-down place where four horses had waited.

Luke approached Houston. "Time to talk."

"Yep." Houston sighed and called Sam to join them. They moved a short distance away where they'd have some privacy. He'd hoped Clay would join them but maybe his drover got tied up. "What's on your mind, Luke?"

"A plan. The men are restless, and the longer we stay here doing nothing, the more jittery they get." Luke pushed back his hat. His dark hair glistened in the sunlight. "We need to get this herd to Dodge as fast as we can, while we can protect the men and your family."

"Luke and I respect their loyalty to Gus," Sam added quickly. "We'd feel the same if he was our friend."

"I'm not going off and leaving him behind, and if that's what you think, you don't know me very well." Frustration and anger wound through Houston. "I'm not going to give up and leave him to Yuma. Gus could still be alive. As long as there's a slim chance, I'm going to keep looking."

"I swear, you're all hide and horns this morning." Luke snorted. "Hear Sam and me out. Will you?"

"Speak fast then. I have things to do."

Sam laid a hand on Houston's shoulder. "This has got to be wearing on you, but we may have a plan you'll be happy with."

"I'm listening." At least with one ear. Houston half expected to hear a shout from the drovers that they'd found Gus. Damn, they needed some good news about now.

Luke squatted on his heels and picked up a sharp rock, beginning to draw lines in the dirt. "You and your men push the herd forward as fast as you can. Keep the chuck wagon protected at all times. Sam and I will stay behind and keep searching for your missing drover. When we find him—and we will—we'll join up with you."

"That's a crazy plan," Houston huffed. "Two men alone will be asking for Yuma to take them too. What's to stop him from killing you both?"

"He'll try," Sam growled low. "Doesn't mean he can."

The Texas Ranger in his brother had just come out. Houston allowed a tight smile. It didn't matter that Sam no longer worked for them. The job and what it had taught him was embedded deep in Sam's soul. Houston's gaze drifted to the ugly scar left around Sam's neck. The rope burn marked the time rustlers had hanged him a year ago. Houston still shivered when he glimpsed it. He couldn't imagine the horror that must've been. His little brother was as tough as they came. If Luke hadn't been there and cut him down in time, Sam would've died. Houston didn't want to think about what it would be like now, or ever, if Sam wasn't beside him.

"Two men stand a better chance than a whole group," Luke said, interrupting his thoughts. "We can hide and hit them when they least expect it."

Houston's gaze swept the barren land that was broken only by a few mesas and occasional piles of large boulders. He snorted. "Hide? Are you a lizard, Luke?"

"You'd be surprised at the places I've taken refuge in," Luke answered tightly. "There's a reason why no one's ever caught me. Sam came the closest." The outlaw's strange green eyes flicked to their younger brother.

"I would've, though…eventually," Sam replied. "But by then I'd found out you were kin and it just didn't feel right somehow hauling my own brother to jail."

The admiration in each of his brothers' eyes brought a tightness to Houston's chest. They were all Legends deep down, past their differences, even though Luke still refused to take their name. He wasn't their half brother; Luke belonged to them in every way.

Brothers…Legends…together. That's how it was.

"You've convinced me," Houston growled. "I'll take the herd and my family while you stay behind and look for Gus. If you don't join up with us in three days, mind, I'll come looking for you. If you haven't found him by then, you're not going to. Blackstone isn't going to hide Gus. He *wants* us to find him, wants us to know what he's done. Most of all, he wants to instill terror."

"I agree," Sam said quietly. "I've seen plenty of men like him and they're all full of themselves."

"That only trips up the damn fools every time." Luke rose, glancing at a rider coming toward them.

Clay reined up. "Heard you needed something, boss." The head drover had his hat pulled low and his head turned away from Sam and Luke.

"Wanted to get your thoughts on something. Climb down for a minute." Houston had the feeling Clay was trying to avoid his brothers, but didn't know why.

The saddle leather creaked as the drover swung from the horse. He stood next to Houston. Luke stared long and hard.

"We've decided on some things," Houston said and filled him in. "You and the men go on. Lara and I will break down the camp and catch up."

"The drovers ain't gonna like it one dadgum bit," Clay warned. "But I think it's a wise move. We gotta think about Miss Lara and sweet pea."

"At least we agree. Also, Lara and I are going to send Henry home if the Ledbetters will take him," Houston said.

"Good idea. The boy's scared out of his mind," Clay said quietly.

"I want to send Lara and Gracie too. I tried to talk to her, but she won't hear of it." Houston pushed back his hat and pinched the bridge of his nose. "Things are about to get real bad. But I hate like hell to just up and tell her she has no choice. She deserves a say."

"You can't let her stay. If you love her, get her out of danger." Luke's mouth settled into a grim line. "Do what you have to do, brother, or you'll bury her here."

Luke's words chilled Houston down to his bones. He refused to consider the thought, even though he knew it was a definite possibility. Even with all the drovers and some of the best guns around, Yuma's group was still picking them off one at a time. Houston and his men couldn't protect her. That was a proven fact.

"He's right," Sam said, laying a hand on Houston's back. "If you love her, send her to Texas."

If he loved her? What he felt was sure close to it if it wasn't. Houston knew to lose her would rip out everything inside him. First he had to focus on the immediate problem—*then* he could think about the notion of love.

"There's no guarantee she'll be any safer with the Ledbetters," he pointed out.

Sam lifted his hat and raked his hands through his hair. "Take steps to see to it."

"Yeah, I'll see if the Ledbetter women can loan her some of their strange clothes. With those and one of their bonnets, I think that will disguise her. Anyone will think she's just one of the group." Houston felt better. He didn't want Lara to hate him for making her go. But neither did he want to bury her. That was a definite possibility if she stayed.

"Looks like you got your work cut out for you, boss. Glad I ain't in your shoes." Turning, Clay strode to his horse.

As they started to go their separate directions, Luke spoke. "Hold up a minute, Clay."

Clay frowned and mumbled, "Got work to do."

"Only take a second." Luke fell into step with him.

Houston watched as the two moved away. Clearly, Clay was not happy at Luke's insistence. Houston wished he was a fly on Clay's shirt—something told him they had a lot to talk about.

Shooting them a final glance, Houston reminded himself he had work to do. Whatever was between the two had nothing to do with him. He turned toward camp.

Lara's glance held a question as she met his eyes. Henry sat next to her, holding the babe.

"Hi, Houston," Henry said, grinning. "I'm teaching Gracie how to whistle."

"Is she learning how yet?" Houston asked.

"Just about."

"That's good. Keep after it." Houston turned to Lara and spoke low. "I'm going to speak to the Ledbetters."

"Okay. I'll get ready to roll out."

Still plagued by a nagging worry that this was the wisest course, Houston strode to the tidy camp. If Yuma figured out that Henry and Lara were no longer with the trail drive, he'd go after the Ledbetters. And Houston wouldn't be there to protect them. Stoker had once told him that when faced with two bad solutions, take the one that left room for doubt. Houston knew for damn sure the danger that lay ahead on this cattle drive. The choice with the Ledbetter family left room for hope. His mind was made up.

It didn't take much convincing. Hiram said they'd make room for not only Henry, but Lara and Gracie too. All that was left was telling his wife, and Houston didn't relish that chore. Telling Lara could possibly destroy everything they'd managed to build in their short marriage.

At least the camp was empty at the moment, so he wouldn't have an audience to witness the end of his chances.

Within minutes, he'd relayed the news to the boy as gently as he could. Big tears filled Henry's eyes and his lip quivered. Houston felt like he'd kicked a homeless puppy.

"No! I won't go. I'm staying." The boy swiped angrily at fat tears rolling down his face.

Lara put her arm around him. "I'm sorry, honey, but it's too dangerous. I want you safe."

"Go gather your things, Henry." When the boy let Lara take Gracie and moved toward the chuck wagon, Houston steeled himself and pulled Lara away from listening ears, to some degree of privacy at least.

"I have something else. The Ledbetters are taking you and Gracie as well. You're all going back to Texas."

Green eyes blazed with fury. "That's a dirty, low-down trick. We never spoke about this. You went behind my back. All your big talk of trust and being partners was a bunch of hot air. And what about your promise to never force me to do anything? What about that?"

She lobbed the angry words like missiles. He winced, knowing she spoke the truth. He'd messed up, but dammit, he had to protect her.

"I did it like this because I knew you wouldn't want to go." Houston reached out, only to have her jerk away.

"You guessed right." Anger darkened her eyes. "And you know what else? I'm *not* going."

"Lara, listen to reason. It makes me crazy with worry to have you here. I need to focus on protecting the men and taking these cows to Dodge, and getting you and Angel away from danger. Don't you see this is best? You're a distraction I can't afford."

"A *distraction*?" Her voice rose. "Is that all I am to you?"

"You know it isn't. That was a poor word to use. Try to be reasonable." He reached for her again only to have to move back.

"Here's some reason for you, cowboy." She took a few steps then stalked back and jabbed his chest with her finger. "You need me. Who'll feed the men, dig bullets out…dig graves?" Her voice quavered as a tear ran down her cheek. "Keep you warm at night? Who? I'm your wife and my place is at your side in peaceful times and in danger. I belong with you. We're partners and"—she took a deep, shuddering breath—"and damn you! I love you, Houston Legend."

Thirty-five

LARA'S UNEXPECTED DECLARATION STRUCK HOUSTON WITH the force of a ten-ton locomotive. She loved him? A grin spread across his face. Lara loved him. He took Gracie from her arms. Setting the baby down, he picked Lara up and swung her around.

"Stop it unless you want me to throw up. You're making me dizzy," Lara protested.

Stopping, he hugged her to him. "I never thought I'd hear those words. Are you sure it's not duty or obligation that makes you say you love me?"

"I'm positive, and I'm not taking it back either." She gave him a mulish tilt of her chin. "I realized last night that what I feel for you is love. You complete my world. I can't imagine going through life without you by my side. You anchor me and give me strength to face what comes."

Ever since she'd finally gotten everything in the past off her chest, she'd become a different woman. Maybe being released from that burden had given her newfound confidence and courage. He didn't know, but he liked it.

Very gently, Houston placed his lips on hers. Raw energy went through him. The instant contact melded them together, body, mind, and soul. The kiss stole his breath, taking every thought but one. He had to say what was in his heart.

His hunger for her went beyond the physical. He hungered in a way that was difficult to explain. He hungered for the need to know she desired more than his money, position, and his name.

He wanted her to want *him*. Just him. Nothing more.

When their lips parted, she spoke softly. "I haven't given you much of a reason to love me back. You were tricked into marrying me and I deeply regret that. I've kept my heart locked for so long, using my fear almost as a weapon."

"You had good reason."

"No, please let me finish." She touched his face and met his eyes. "You have so much to offer, more than I ever dreamed. But you could be a pauper with nothing, not even a sheltering roof over your head, and I'd still love you. I want *you*, Houston Legend—only you."

Trembling, he knew he would remember this moment for the rest of his life.

He was finally free to speak his thoughts. Free to be the man he wanted.

"I love you, Lara. I didn't allow myself to care for so long, afraid you'd finish what Becky started, afraid to trust again—afraid to trust myself. I finally realized my feelings for you that night on the porch at Dr. Mary's. Even then, I didn't think I had a chance of you ever loving me back."

"Oh, Houston, I made a mess of things, didn't I?" She kissed the hollow of his throat where his blood pulsed. He loved the way she touched him, the way she had of showing him that she didn't regret marrying him.

"I beg to differ." Houston's voice was husky. "A marriage that started as ours did needed time and space for love to bloom. We both had to learn to trust again."

"Will you always want me, even with what happened, even if my scar doesn't fade?"

His voice shook. "Darlin', I'll want you just as you are until the end of time. You're my lifeblood. There is no other for me. Not now, not ever. Not in this lifetime or the next."

She gave him a stubborn stare that seemed to say she knew ways to make his life very miserable. That was true beyond a doubt. "And you won't try to send me back to Texas without you?"

Lord, she drove a hard bargain. His need to have her safe warred with the hunger to keep her with him. Filled with love, he buried his face in her flame-colored hair. "Heaven help me, I find no strength for the task, Mrs. Legend."

"And I have no strength to leave you either." Lara pressed her face against his throat.

"But what about Gracie? I think we should send her with Henry. He'll look after her."

"Sweetheart, I love you for trying to protect us, and if Gracie was older I'd agree in a second. But she'll starve without my milk."

"Can't some of the Ledbetter women…" He paused, searching for how to say it and finally said, "Fill in?"

"The youngest child is Hiram the fourth and he's been weaned. We have no choice. Gracie has to stay with me."

Houston rubbed his jaw. "All right, I see your point."

The sound of riders reached him. Their golden time was over.

"Houston, where are you, brother?" Sam hollered.

"Just a cotton-pickin' minute." Houston smoothed back Lara's hair. "I haven't had a chance to tell you our plans. We're moving out as soon as we can. Sam and Luke are staying behind to try and find Gus."

Worry darkened her gaze. "Are you sure that's wise, leaving them here alone?"

"It's best for all. My brothers know the risks and are glad to take them. Try not to worry." He tasted her lips again. "Go comfort Henry while I do some things. All right?"

"Okay." She pulled him to her by the front of his vest and her arms went around him. "I love you and don't you forget it."

Houston grinned. "How can I, when my heart beats only for you?"

With a gentle tug from her clutch, he stepped from the circle of her arms and strode toward Sam and Luke, where they waited side by side.

❧

Her heart singing, Lara began stowing things in the various compartments of the chuck wagon. She could hardly bear to look at Henry, where he sat clutching Gracie to him.

She knew her own desperation to stay no matter the danger. How could she expect her brother to understand, when she was the one person who anchored him to this life? Pain swept over her each time she caught him staring at her with that lost look.

Still, this had to be the best thing for him.

Finally, she couldn't stand it any longer. She sat down beside him, putting her arm around his shoulders. "You know I love you, don't you?"

Henry sniffled, dropping his face in Gracie's blond curls.

"And you know I'd never do anything to cause you pain if I could help it."

"Maybe."

"No, not maybe. That's the truth. Now and always."

"Then why can't I stay?" He lifted his gaze.

"Because Yuma Blackstone is trying to kill us. I can't let him steal you from me. I won't." Lara took his hand. "This is just for a little while. We'll be together again soon. Can you try to pretend I'm close by at the Lone Star?"

"But you won't be," he wailed.

"Listen, I know you're upset and I'd give anything to let you stay." She kissed his forehead. "Even though you'll be sad and lonely for a while, it will pass. Papa will keep your mind off us here."

"You promise?"

"Absolutely. I'll make sure of it when we all get back to Texas. The Ledbetters are nice and will take very good care of you."

"Okay. I'll close my eyes and pretend you're there." He tried to smile. It lacked warmth but it was a sight better than anger and resentment.

Lara tenderly brushed back his bright-red hair. "How much do I love you?"

"A whole bunch. More than the biggest sky in Texas."

"That's right." She rose, and as she went to pack, she heard him tell Gracie not to cry when he left because it would just be for a moment. Then he told her to be real good for her mama. Though she felt better about the decision, her heart still ached. Blackstone bore all the blame for the need to send Henry away. One more thing to hate him for.

She dropped a cast-iron skillet, barely missing her foot.

Houston strode back into camp and picked up the heavy utensil. He gently took her hands. "You're trembling. I'll help you."

Lara rested her forehead on his chest. Her heart ached for her little brother.

"What's wrong, darlin'?"

"Henry. Gracie. Gus. Yuma. Sam and Luke. Just take your pick." She burrowed into the folds of his shirt and vest. "Your brothers alone are no match for Yuma and his cutthroats. I'm worried about leaving them behind."

Her need to protect everyone from the man who stalked them brought an ache.

Houston must have seen the guilt she carried. He tipped up her face with a finger and pressed his lips to hers. When he broke the kiss, he stared into her worried eyes and caressed her cheek. "You don't know my brothers. I've never known two more capable men. They have a toughness that few do. Whoever crosses them won't live long. I can guarantee that."

"I hope you're right."

"I am. One more thing I'm sure of, pretty lady—you didn't bring Yuma to us, so forget that crazy notion. He'd have followed us no matter what because he wanted this herd, so stop blaming yourself." He shot a glance toward Luke and Clay. They'd finished their conversation and Clay sat astride his horse. With a laugh at something Luke said, the head drover galloped off. Judging from that and Luke's smile, the tension between them was gone. "Let's get this wagon packed. We need to roll out soon."

Henry hollered to Luke, "Wanna hold Gracie? I think she wants you."

"I kinda doubt that," Luke replied with a chuckle. "What's the real reason, Henry?"

"I got somethin' to do real bad and I can't put her down on account of she eats dirt 'n rocks 'n stuff."

"In that case, I reckon this is as good a time as any to get to know my little niece." Luke lowered himself to a rock next to Henry.

The boy shoved Gracie at him and ran toward a big clump of juniper, disappearing behind it. Houston's gaze drifted back to Luke. His brother made a frown as he held Gracie stiffly at arm's length, studying her.

"She's not an animal to buy, Luke. Or contagious." Houston chuckled. "You can bring her closer to you."

"Ha-ha! Very funny. For your information, I was seeing if she has bowlegs like you."

"Likely story. And don't let her play with your bullets either or I'll have to take away your uncle privileges."

"Dammit, she stuck her finger in my eye!" Luke hollered. "Don't know if I can shoot straight now. Why didn't you warn me?"

"I never heard so much bellyaching in all my born days. Are you gonna let a little girl no bigger than a minute whip your butt?"

"She's not a baby; she's a pint-sized desperada."

"I'm raising my daughter to take care of herself. Have to start early so she won't be sweet-talked by someone like you." Houston grinned, watching the sideshow. For all his hollering, Luke brought Gracie closer and cradled her to his chest, giving everyone who walked by the evil eye.

They might not be able to pry the child away when the time came.

Lara hit his shoulder. "Quit picking on Luke. He's doing okay."

That he was, but Houston wasn't about to tell him that. Nothing sent a man running faster than being told he made excellent Pa material. Truth was, Luke needed to find a good woman and settle down, raise a crop of ornery kids, and discover the real meaning of family.

Sam strode from a little wash a short distance away with some type of fabric in his hand. Houston's grin faded. A niggling in his head told him it was important. He set down the box of staples he held, told Lara he'd be right back, and went to meet his brother.

"What did you find?"

"A bandana with dried blood." Sam held it out. "Could this be Gus's?"

Houston's breath hung painfully in his chest as he took it and gave the soiled fabric a long stare. "Can't be sure. Never paid much attention to his neckerchief. Pony or Joe would recognize it, seeing as how they ran together." He glanced up. "Where did you find it? We scoured that wash this morning."

"You wouldn't have seen it. No one on horseback would. Someone had stuffed it between two snug rocks. The bandana couldn't have gotten there any other way. With the trail being used by hundreds of cowpokes, it could've been there for a while." Sam glanced toward the herd. Houston could just about read his brother's mind.

The slow trek would take them to another camp, another place to bed down for the night, another chance of an ambush.

"Strange though where I found the bandana," Sam murmured seemingly to himself. "It was left there deliberately."

"Take it to Pony and Joe. I've got to help Lara so we can get moving. Pony's easy to spot. Look for a lanky cowboy wearing a piece of twisted lariat for a hatband. It'll probably

have a playing card stuck in it. The other will have a harmonica in his pocket."

"I swear, Houston, I haven't taken leave of my senses,"
Sam huffed. "They've worked on the Lone Star for years."

"Don't pick a fight with me, little brother," Houston
warned with a growl. "I can count on one hand the times
you've been home in the last five winters, and not that often
before that."

"Yeah, well, I had a job with the Texas Rangers back
then," Sam snapped heatedly. He gave Houston a push.
"Go help your wife. Though if Lara's anything like mine,
she'll tell you you're just in the way. I'll take care of this."

With a chuckle, Houston handed him the bloody
neckerchief and strode to camp. He glanced at the herd
meandering north. With luck, maybe they could get quite a
ways before dark. One thing for sure, it was too dangerous
to stay here. No question, Sam and Luke could be a big help
in holding Yuma and his gang back.

But was Lara right? Was he leaving his brothers to die?

Thirty-six

THE NEXT MORNING, THE LEDBETTER FAMILY WAITED IN THE early light while Lara kissed Henry's cheek and told him to be good. Big tears filled his eyes, until Houston took him aside, giving him his pay in the entire amount promised at the end of the trail. Pride flared in Henry's eyes at being treated like a man. Lara wrapped the money in a cloth and tied it around him beneath his shirt, then Henry hugged them one last time.

Sarah Ledbetter broke from the women and whispered to Lara, "I saw questions in your eyes. Just love your man. Everything else will fall into place."

Lara glanced at Houston, tall beside her with his arm around her waist. "I will." Whatever they had to face, they'd do it together—including any fear at making love.

Henry joined the children, waving his arm off. Lara tried to swallow the lump in her throat but it wouldn't budge. Nor could she until Gracie hollered, reaching for her papa. He took the child, kissing her chubby cheek. Gracie patted his face, chattering like a magpie. Lara walked arm in arm with Houston to the chuck wagon, grateful for the warmth he lent, hoping it would chase away the chill inside that Henry's parting had left.

Kissing her, Houston boosted her up onto the wagon seat. "You and Caroline stay ahead of the herd. We'll be

behind. I'll check on you often. We'll not stop until probably nine or ten o'clock tonight. The men can eat jerky and
hardtack for supper."

Lara nodded. He handed Gracie up and she sat the child
on her lap, giving her a rag doll she'd made to replace the
other. "Please be safe, Houston."

"My thoughts will be on you and tonight when we can
be together."

As she and Caroline slowly moved toward Dodge City,
Lara had anxious thoughts. Each mile took her closer to the
moment when she would be Houston's wife in every sense
of the word. And each kiss deepened their love even more.
She remembered young Caroline's embarrassing questions.

What kind of lover would Houston be? It didn't really
matter if he was fast or slow. What mattered was that he'd
be beside her for the rest of her life. However he made love
would be just fine. They weren't running any race.

She wanted more babies, and watching Houston with
Gracie, it wasn't a far stretch to imagine he did too.

More children.

A smile curved her lips. Gracie needed a little brother or
sister. Or maybe both. Now there was a thought.

More Legends.

She shook the reins at the team. "Get along now and
don't dawdle, you lazy bag of bones. I need to get to Kansas."

Although one eye was always on the chuck wagon ahead
in the distance, Houston went to work with a vengeance.

His body, sore from the fight, reminded him of the cost
of spending the whole day in the saddle, but he wouldn't
complain. He was simply glad to be alive. After Ghost and
Yuma, he wouldn't have taken bets.

Clay galloped up. "I think we'll make good time before
nightfall, boss."

"We're moving at a pretty good clip," Houston agreed.

"Keep it up. We've got to make tracks while we can. My brothers can't hold back Yuma's gang for long."

"At least we won't have to fight that giant," Clay shook his head. "Hell, I still don't know how you survived. Ghost was the biggest man I've ever seen."

Houston would have died without that strange twist of fate, and Yuma's personal need to kill him. "We can add horse thievery to Yuma's list of crimes. I hate like hell to lose that palomino. He was a good piece of horseflesh."

"With luck we'll get the gelding back." Clay rested his arm on the pommel. "We haven't seen the last of them."

"Pass the word along to keep on alert. Just because my brothers stayed behind is no reason to let down our guard. Yuma and his group have shown how slippery they are." Houston uncorked his canteen and took a swig of water.

"Already told the men, boss."

"Damn, Clay, have you taken to reading minds in addition to your other chores?" Houston couldn't have chosen a better man.

Clay laughed. "Not hardly. Just using plain ol' horse sense."

Houston chuckled. "I'm struck by the ones who don't even have people sense. By the way, did you and Luke get your problem straightened out?"

"We never had a problem."

"My mistake." Houston studied the weathered face but saw nothing.

"I need to keep moving, boss," Clay said. "Don't want the men to let the cattle slow."

With a nod, Houston turned and watched him ride toward the back. He couldn't figure the man out but he knew Clay Angelo had something to hide. He'd dismissed it before, but now he wondered. What were his secrets, dammit? One bit of comfort was that Luke knew something. And if he thought Houston needed the information, he'd tell him.

He rode close to some brush beside the trail and something glittery caught his eye. He dismounted for a closer look.

It turned out to be a small mirror that had probably fallen from someone's wagon. Picking it up, he dusted it off. Though Lara hadn't mentioned wanting one, a woman needed something to look in. He tucked it into his saddlebag.

The day passed uneventful with no sign of Yuma or his men. The only people they'd seen had been a group of Cherokee riders in the distance. Night had fallen long before Houston and his men stopped to make camp.

Houston hurried to take Gracie from Lara so she could see to her needs. On and off through the day, the babe had ridden with him and other drovers as well. They had drawn straws for a turn to tote the child around. She did truly belong to each of them.

What was worse…Gracie seemed to know it. Her slobbery, toothless grin couldn't get wider each time a drover would reach for her. Something had to be very wrong with Blackstone for wanting the child dead. Houston looked forward to cheating him out of it.

Everywhere Houston turned, he half expected to find Henry. He sorely missed the boy, but no one missed him more than Lara. The pain she carried for her brother was etched on her face. He cursed Blackstone for creating the need to send him home.

Houston moved toward his wife, cleared his throat so he wouldn't take her unaware in the darkness. Lara was nursing Gracie and staring into the night. She seemed a million miles away.

Evidently hearing him, she swung her gaze to meet his. "Hi there, cowboy."

For a long moment, he stood transfixed at the aching beauty of her motherly love.

"I found something today." He handed her the hand glass. "Now you can see how beautiful you are. You won't have to take my word that your scar's fading."

In reaching for the mirror, the cloth shielding her breast fell away. Instead of panicking as she always had, Lara met

Houston's eyes and smiled as though giving him the right to look.

Her lack of embarrassment took him by surprise.

"I am curious." She held up the little looking glass. Wonder filled her voice. "It is. I can look at my scar without flinching now. Thanks to you and the Cherokee woman's ointment."

"That's good." He brushed her face with a knuckle. "What can I do to help while you feed Gracie?"

Her brow wrinkled in thought. "I hate to feed the drovers jerky after the long day they put in. It's just not right."

"I saw a large covey of prairie chickens nearby. I'll raid their nests for eggs."

"Would you mind?"

"Consider it done." Before leaving, he let his hand slide along her jaw and down across her shoulders, trying to drag himself away. Once he finally managed, he quickly ordered the drovers to stay close and look for eggs.

The night whispered around Houston as he scouted the area with Clay. The breeze brought a stench to Houston's nose.

"Let's see where that's coming from," Houston said.

The two men rode about half a mile into some scraggly mesquite trees and pulled up.

The skeleton frames of burned-out tepees stood like silent sentinels. Destruction lay around them. Blackened bodies everywhere of young and old. Houston slid from the saddle and touched the scorched earth, finding it cool. The carnage had taken place days ago. His mind swept to the scalp hanging from Yuma's belt. This had to be the man's handiwork. Had he ridden ahead and looped back? Or was this the work of another group?

Silently, he and Clay walked among the ruins. As Houston picked up an empty can of beans, icy prickles danced down his spine. Yuma's campsites had shown the same type of litter.

"Dammit, Clay, the bastards ate here after they killed these people."

Clay spat in the dirt as though to rid his mouth of a bad taste. "What kind of sick bastards do that?"

Houston dropped the can and strode to his horse. "The kind who're following us."

They rode back to camp, vowing to return at dawn and dig graves. They talked about when Yuma and his men might've done this and decided it happened before Sam and Luke came. Houston pasted on a smile for Lara, determined not to share what they'd found.

Later, after the last drover ate his fill of scrambled eggs and hot biscuits and the cleanup was done, Houston sat beside Lara, counting the minutes until he could be alone with her. He needed her kisses to wipe those images from his head.

"Do you mind if I play with Gracie a bit?" Caroline asked. "It'll give me and Nick practice. Besides, she's the sweetest little thing. I want one just like her."

Lara smiled. "She would love it, and so would I."

"Footloose and fancy-free, Mrs. Legend?" Houston teased with a waggle of his eyebrows.

"Why, it does appear that way."

"How about a ride?" Houston asked. "We won't go far."

"I'd love to."

He grabbed a blanket and lifted her onto the back of the big roan then settled into the saddle behind her. With his arms around her, they rode north, away from the camp and the carnage of the Indian village.

"Where are we going?" Lara asked.

"It's a surprise. I found it today when scouting." He nuzzled her ear, smelling her fragrance. "You'll like it."

"Do you think it's safe?"

"My brothers will keep the gang bottled up a while. With luck, maybe for good." He slipped an arm around her trim waist. "I'll keep you safe."

They'd ridden about half an hour when they came to the Canadian River. Houston reined up at a tall cottonwood tree standing tall in the moonlight. He dismounted and reached for Lara, groaning as she slid slowly down the length of his body.

Sparks flared into a fire as though she was the friction for his match. His mouth went dry. Whatever happened tonight would determine how to proceed. Lara would either accept him and their marriage, or he'd live alone in some kind of private hell while he waited for her. He knew it could go either way. Though she'd vowed her love, the practical side of him realized she still had a mountain to climb.

Would she be brave enough to turn loose of the past?

Or would the memories keep her always frozen in fear?

Houston ran his hands across her slight back, feeling the delicate bone structure. But there was nothing delicate or weak about the woman who filled his heart.

Thickness formed in his throat. "I'm proud to be your husband. Whatever happens now or in the coming days, I will always love you." The words came out hoarse and raspy.

She pressed her lips to the hollow of his throat, below the cut Ghost had left, and emotion made Houston weak. "If I'm dreaming, I never want to wake up. Let me stay in your arms forever. You're all I need. Love for you spills over, flowing through every part of me."

"Through me too."

As her words filled the empty crevices inside him, Houston continued memorizing her body, soaking up the feel of her. He let his hands roam over her before cupping her rounded bottom.

They fit together so well. How could this not be right?

Their lips met in a hungry kiss. Lara slid her hand around his neck into his hair, drawing him closer to the flame.

Dear God, he went willingly, with an ache inching up his spine and spreading outward into his limbs. Not lightning, a cattle stampede, nor outlaws could stop him.

Lara murmured against his mouth, "The grass and trees are a far cry from the arid land we've crossed."

"A special treat for my lady." Houston remembered the

blanket and reached for it, wondering at his shaking hand. "You'll see it tomorrow when we ford."

He spread the blanket on the wild grass by the rippling water's edge, praying he'd find the right words—do the right things. He wanted this to be perfect and he'd take his lead from her. If she couldn't do more than let him kiss her and talk, that was all right.

He could mark time for however long it took until she was ready. As long as she never left him.

Thirty-seven

A MILLION BUTTERFLIES BEAT AGAINST THE INSIDE OF LARA'S stomach as she dropped to the blanket.

Was she ready?

Lord, she hoped so. She loved this patient man who'd shown her great tenderness. He deserved a whole wife, not someone who could only stand beside him in the daytime. He needed a real partner to help during times of crisis, when the darkness swirled around and tested his strength the most.

She leaned closer, inhaling his familiar scent, letting calm replace her doubts. Giving his hand a tug, she pulled him down beside her. Placing her mouth next to his ear, Lara whispered, "This is the beginning of the rest of our lives. Are you ready?"

Houston ran a finger along her jaw and down her neck. "I was born ready for you, darlin'. We don't have to do anything. We can just sit here and talk."

While she still had fear, talking wasn't what she had in mind.

She laid a hand on the side of his face, pressing a soft kiss to his lips. The butterflies disappeared, replaced with a desire to accept wholly everything her husband offered.

He moved behind her and worked at her braid. "Your hair is too beautiful to put away like this."

While he undid each section of hair, Lara asked, "Houston, are you happy?"

A growl rumbled in his throat. "What kind of question is that? I've never known this kind of contentment. You changed my life, Lara. I never want to go back to the lonely man I was before you came. How about you? Are you happy?"

"I am. For weeks, especially in the beginning, I worried that you wouldn't keep me. That I brought too many problems."

With her hair hanging free, he moved to face her. Moonlight helped her see the burning in Houston's soulful gaze. His voice rasped. "Of course I'm keeping you. You're not a holey sock to toss in the rag pile. Promise never to walk away. I never want to step into that kind of darkness again."

He brushed his lips across her forehead. The kiss was so gentle it brought tears welling up. Love for this man swept aside every other thought. Deep hunger for him rose, making her stomach whirl and dip.

"I promise." She leaned back to stare into his eyes and saw the smoldering passion that darkened the color. "To be separated from you would be the end for me too. Houston, I want to be your wife in every way."

"I've yearned to hear you say those words." He drew her closer, protecting her inside the circle of his arms, and pressed a kiss to her temple. "You know what I call you?" When she shook her head, he said, "You're my wild Texas rose."

The beautiful sentiment brought a lump to her throat and trapped the air in her chest.

"I'll tell you why," Houston continued. "The wild Texas rose is known for resilience and determination. Like you, its roots cling to the soil, no matter how rocky, and the plant puts forth the prettiest flowers. The wild rose survives. So have you. Despite everything life's thrown at you, you've tilted that stubborn chin and thrived."

Conviction in his quiet words brought tightness to her throat. She had survived. To be thought of as his wild rose made her deliriously happy.

"You give me far too much credit."

"No, I don't give you credit enough." His hand slid down her back. "Lie down and let the moonlight worship you. Though I doubt it can match the love I have for my rose."

She stretched out with her arms over her head, gazing up at millions of stars. Never had she felt so liberated or loved. She was free of her pain. Yuma Blackstone had lost his power over her. Houston lay next to her. Moments alone with him were precious few, and these meant more than anything.

To her, Houston Legend was a knight on an Appaloosa with a six-gun on his hip—a dream she'd thought she'd forever lost.

Turning on her side, she rested her hand lightly on his chest. "I don't need pretty words to seduce me. I just need you, but I love being compared to such a flower." She kissed the hollow of his throat where his pulse beat. "Make love to me, Houston."

He knelt above her. "If only we had a wagon with sturdy springs, Mrs. Legend."

Lara laughed. "Indeed. But I like being here next to the earth. It's perfect." She stroked his face, staring into the dark, smoky depths of his eyes. Slowly she unbuttoned his shirt and laid a palm on the hard wall of his chest.

As the water splashed against the riverbank, she closed her eyes. It was time to memorize every note of his body. The tune already played in her head. With the rippling river providing accompaniment, Lara began to hear the song written on Houston's well-formed body.

Anticipation hummed in her veins as she flattened her palms over his brown nipples, feeling them harden beneath her touch. Before this trip, she'd never thought about men having nipples or that they could show proof of desire. She loved that he gave her freedom to explore, to let her hands go where she wished.

His bulge pressed into her stomach and she yearned for the courage to touch him there. But she couldn't. Not yet.

Memories tried to wiggle into her head, and each time, she pushed them firmly away. Tonight belonged to Houston and her, no one else. She kept her thoughts on the here and now, and the future full of bright promise ahead.

Houston's palm slid across her throat and collarbone then into her hair.

Releasing a groan, he covered her lips with his. As with the time before, he slipped his tongue inside her softly parted lips to dance with hers. She liked what he was doing and how each shift, touch, and flick of his magical fingers brought pleasure swirling inside her.

Currents of warmth from a low flame danced along her body, but she sensed much more waiting for her just beyond. The music that had begun slow and soft had turned into a crashing anthem. Hunger for her cowboy rose hot, aching, and needy.

Above her, Houston ran a teasing finger down her throat to the buttons of her dress and traced the curve of each breast.

Dear God, she wanted him…this thing he alone could give.

"I have to know if you're all right with this, Lara. Are you sure?" He spread his hand wide across a swollen breast.

Her nipple distended, straining against the fabric, reaching for his caress. She felt like the wanton saloon girl she'd once seen kissing a lusty cowboy in the alley in Amarosa. The fallen woman had made bold moves and took what she wanted.

A craving she couldn't explain made her breath hitch as she managed, "Never more so." Her voice sounded husky, not like her at all. "Please, I have this fire about to consume me."

"Every wish is my command, darlin'." He worked at the buttons on her dress.

Impatience swept over her. She wished he'd simply rip them off and be done. She had to feel his hands on her, to relieve this ravenous hunger, to find the lost part of herself.

With the buttons undone at last, he rose and pulled her up. As he removed her clothes, the air cooled her fevered skin. She turned to undressing him. Each item she stripped away revealed more and more of his beautiful form. Muscles rippled along his chest and his arms.

So strong. So virile. So handsome.

Finally, he stood as naked as she in the moonlight except for his drawers. With his eyes holding hers captive, he slowly lowered the last bit of clothing.

Trembling from head to toe, she lay back on the blanket. He curled next to her, propping himself on an arm.

"Will it hurt?" she murmured, kissing his chest.

"I will never hurt you."

"And will you put out this fire that makes me so hot?"

He chuckled. "I will do my utter best, darlin'."

"I like when you call me that. It makes me feel as though I'm someone special."

"Never doubt that, because you are." He knelt, leaving a trail of kisses down her body.

Lara trembled as she entwined her fingers in his hair. She loved him, this man who had given her child a name, getting nothing in return except a wife frozen by the past. He was her life, her hope, her salvation.

With each touch, pleasure shot from her core, stronger than anything she'd ever felt. She gasped and rode along with the water of the Canadian as it sang her a song she'd never heard. It was a song of hope, love, and told of a future.

The velvet warmth of Houston's kisses drugged her, searing a path to her stomach where he pressed his lips, making her shudder with desire. Finally, he covered her body with his heat. She felt him tremble and knew he waited in anticipation as much as she did.

This virile man, knowing what he knew, chose her. She was his wife and from now on she intended to do more than pretend. Her fingers tangled in his hair before her hand slid down his back to his waist.

He murmured into the hair at her temple. "Your last chance to back out, my rose."

A laugh sprang up. "I brought my gun. Reach for your clothes and I'll shoot you."

"You're kidding. Aren't you?" His tone relayed teasing doubt.

"Try me, cowboy."

Houston groaned. "I created a jezebel." He smoothed back her hair and gave her a sizzling kiss that made her toes curl. New spirals of desire flooded all her senses.

Her breasts tingled, pressed hard against the solid planes of his chest, and her hunger built. She clutched him to her, holding fast, bracing for the moment she'd feared despite every desire not to.

"Look into my eyes and trust me, sweetheart," he murmured. "If I bring you pain, you can take your little gun and shoot me. This I promise."

But he slid inside and only a melting sweetness came. Their bodies joined and began the dance of love. Passion flowed over her like thick, sweet honey and she embraced the beautiful warmth. Lara dragged in soul-drenching draughts of air, praying the night would never end.

Something told her she was in the hands of a master. He brought her to a wave's crest but pulled back before she could plunge over the top. The sweet, teasing torture let her experience the climb several times, until finally, finally, she shattered into a million stars. They rained down on her in a shower of love and passion.

Only then did he take his pleasure and collapse with a shudder. She lay, trying to force breath into her lungs, marveling at what had happened. Making love wasn't anything to fear or avoid, and she prayed for lots more.

After several minutes, still trying to slow his breath, he moved off her. His voice was ragged when he spoke next. "Lady, I sensed deep passion hidden inside you but I didn't know the half of it."

Lara turned on her side and trailed a finger down his

chest. "I never imagined it could be this way between two people. I'm very glad fate brought us together. You've just proven that you and Nick Vincent are nothing alike."

"Oh?" One eyebrow lifted and he mock-growled, "Pray tell, what have you been doing with young Nick?"

"Relax. Absolutely nothing." She shared Caroline's frustrations over her young husband's quick release.

He laughed, putting an arm around her. "That explains why they spend every spare second testing the springs of their wagon. Will you tell Caroline about our lovemaking?"

"Not even a little bit! I won't share one single thing about you with anyone." She caressed his jaw and kissed him. "You're all mine, buster."

Theirs was one life, one purpose, one unforgettable love.

Thirty-eight

HOUSTON AND LARA RODE BACK TO CAMP IN THE MOONLIGHT. Her quiet strength and courage was a balm for his weary soul. They touched, whispering words of love to each other. Lara brought such peace and completeness to his life. His wife had proven a constant surprise. Just when he thought he had her all figured out, she sent him back to the beginning.

"What time do you think it is?" Lara asked.

He glanced up at the stars. "Must be about ten o'clock."

"Gracie will be asleep by now. I feel guilty for being gone so long. I'm sure Caroline must wonder where we are."

"Relax. Like our young friend said, it's good training for her…and it gave Nick a rest." Houston chuckled. "Poor guy. She's going to wear him flat out."

Lara giggled. "I think they're trying to set a record. I've never seen anyone more…frisky…than those two. And they don't seem to care who knows it either. I would die of embarrassment if everyone knew about what we just did."

They rode into camp and the men sitting around the fire stared.

She groaned. "Oh dear. They know."

"True, but they'll never say a word," Houston assured her. If they did, they'd answer to him, and then they'd be out of a job in nothing flat. He'd have no one talking about his wife. Period.

He dismounted and helped her down. Looking a bit frazzled, Caroline hurried to Lara with Gracie sobbing in her arms.

"I've done everything and she won't stop. Oh, I'm going to make a bad, bad, bad mother," Caroline cried.

Houston took Gracie while Lara quieted the young girl. The babe hushed instantly and gave him a toothless grin before burying her face in his chest.

By the time Lara returned, Gracie was fast asleep. He laid the babe in her crib and stood looking down. Something in his gut turned over as he covered the child. She depended on him to keep her safe. No, she depended on them both.

Could he know more contentment...at least in his marriage?

But he shouldn't get too comfortable. Things had a way of changing on a man in the blink of an eye. A strange noise came from beyond the firelight, snagging his attention. The sound didn't fit with anything else. Houston put his arm around Lara. He cocked his head, listening.

"What is it?" Lara asked, pressing against him.

"Not sure."

Most of the men around the fire had crawled into their bedrolls and were snoring. The two still awake rose and walked toward the noise with their weapons in hand.

Crying...someone was crying. Were they hurt? Then came the fierce growls of coyotes. From the noise, it sounded like an entire pack.

"Wait here," Houston told Lara.

The hair rose on the back of his neck. He slid his Colt from the holster and strode toward the din. Once he'd stepped from the firelight, he made out dark forms. One person was surrounded by a pack of wild animals, the shapes proving he was right about coyotes.

"Help!" cried a male voice. "Help!"

Houston and his drovers opened fire on the vicious animals. He shot one in midleap, and the slight man it was attacking turned and raced toward him. The drovers cut down three more coyotes. The surviving members of the pack turned and bounded into the pitch-black night.

Sobbing, the man kept running. "Houston!"

One of his brothers? No, too young. The voice sounded a little like Henry's but it couldn't be. The boy was safe with the Ledbetters. Was it one of Yuma's tricks? Keeping his Colt aimed at the figure, he waited with the drovers. He wouldn't move a step farther until he could assess the danger.

Whoever it was fell to his knees and sank to the dirt. Sobbing, he lay there, a dark blob on the ground. Finally, he began to crawl, digging his hands into the dirt and pulling himself forward. "Help."

Houston turned to the drovers. "Cover me. I don't think he poses any danger, but you never know."

"Be careful, boss," Pony warned.

With a nod, Houston strode out to the man. The closer he got, the more he could see that it was a mere boy. No, it wasn't possible. But it was.

"Henry!"

"Help me, Houston."

Houston raced to him, picked him up and carried him to camp.

Lara crowded at his elbow. "Henry!"

"Find a place for me to lay him," Houston said. "He looks in bad shape."

She hurriedly spread a blanket by the fire and Houston gently lowered the boy onto it. His face was scratched, his clothes torn, and his hands a bloody mess. Tears had created streaks through the dirt and blood.

The boy whimpered and looked up. "I was scared."

"You don't have to be anymore." Lara smoothed back the hair from his eyes. "You're safe now."

"Bring some water," Houston told the drover standing closest. "I doubt he's had anything since early this morning. No telling what he's been through."

Her gaze met his for a moment and, even though her eyes held worry and fear, he saw her strength. "He'll be all right. Just needs rest. Houston, he still has the money you gave him."

That surprised him a little, but he guessed whoever had attacked had been more interested in the adults.

The drover hurried back with not only a cup of water but also a filled pail so Lara could wash Henry's wounds. While Houston itched to learn what had happened, he had to give the boy time or it could drive him deeper into shock.

Gently, Lara bathed Henry's face and set to work washing the blood from his hands and arms. Slowly, the boy began to come out of it enough to say that outlaws had attacked the Ledbetters. Terrified, Henry had hidden among the dead, silent and still. He heard lots of loud gunshots and other riders came.

"I snuck out and started walking," Henry said with tears running down his face. "Followed the cow poop. Big dogs chased me. I kicked and threw rocks but they wouldn't go away. I thought I was gonna die."

"There, there. You're safe now." Lara tenderly bathed his face and kissed his forehead. "We're not going to let anything happen to you."

Houston squatted on his heels. "Henry, did you ever see any of the outlaws before? Was it Yuma?"

"They killed 'em. Blood. So much blood. Get it off." He furiously scrubbed at his hands, appearing in deep shock. And no wonder. What he'd witnessed would terrify a grown man.

"I'll get it off," Lara said gently, taking his hands in hers.

Dammit. All those women. The kids. Slaughtered by riffraff driven by bloodlust. Who were they? Did Yuma Blackstone's bunch bear responsibility? Why would he attack the Ledbetters when he was so focused on Lara? Or maybe it had been a different group entirely. These were dangerous lands.

Worry rose for Sam and Luke. For all he knew they were both wounded…or dead. They might need him. He cursed low. He couldn't leave Lara and Gracie now.

A sudden thought chilled his blood. If he'd sent them with the Ledbetters, they'd both be dead now.

Thirty-nine

BEFORE FULL LIGHT, HOUSTON LED THE DROVERS BACK TO the burned-out Indian camp to bury the dead. Seeing the scene again hammered home the horror even more. He had to find the ones responsible. This couldn't be allowed to happen again. By the time he and the men rode back, he burned with an even-greater need to exact justice.

Lara waited while he dismounted and then demanded to know what had happened. Holding her tight, Houston told her. Her face drained of color, she quietly gathered Gracie in her arms. Houston knew she was thinking but for the grace of God, she'd be dead.

Despite misgivings about his brothers, in the end, Houston opted to drive the herd forward—into the damn ground if he had to. Sam and Luke had known and accepted the dangers when they stayed behind. They'd wrap a post around his head if he left Lara to go back and check on them.

He remembered Lara's story about the man who tried to do everything for everyone and the end result was only resentment. She was right. He had to trust his brothers to take care of themselves. But dammit, it was hard! Ever since Houston was eight years old, he'd been looking out for Sam. Time to break the habit and accept that Sam was a grown man.

No, Houston's place was with his wife and daughter.

The drovers and cattle forded the Canadian after a late breakfast. The lack of mishaps made him breathe a little easier. He'd paused at the spot where he and Lara made love the previous night, remembering the way she'd made him feel like the richest man in the world.

He still felt that way now. Needing a dose of her big smile, he galloped past the mile-long formation of hide and horns. After telling Clay to squeeze them up and adjust the width to fifty feet across, he rode for the chuck wagon out front. He'd have a word with his lady before he scouted for trouble.

Lara's glance held a special warmth. "Howdy, cowboy. Going my way?"

He pushed back his hat with a forefinger and gave her his best Texas drawl. "I sure am, ma'am. Know if I can steal a kiss sometime?"

"I think I can work that out." She gave him a teasing grin. The sunlight struck her russet hair, turning it to liquid fire. "Show me your hand, gambler, and maybe I'll let you do more."

He let out a long whistle. "You strike a hard bargain, pretty lady. Luckily, I'm holding four aces."

This lighthearted side of her was a welcome change from the frightened bride—hidden behind a thick veil—who'd stood with him in front of the preacher. His wild rose was strong and determined.

Henry shifted on the seat beside her. His face was a mass of cuts and bruises, testifying to his ordeal. He still seemed in shock, staring ahead with unseeing eyes. The boy didn't even seem aware that he held Gracie in his arms.

"How's our boy, Lara?" Houston asked.

"I think we just have to let time work its magic. My heart breaks, thinking of those poor people." Her voice cracked. "Hannah never got to hold her sweet baby, and little Hiram the third and fourth will never grow up."

"I know, darlin'. Life isn't fair sometimes." Not for the Ledbetters and damn sure not for Lara. "Try not to think about it too much."

A driving need to avenge them and the Indians was the only thing that helped him cope. There would be justice coming for everyone, and he'd bet twenty of his best horses on that.

He rode around to Henry's side. "How are you, Henry?"

The boy never blinked. Houston asked again.

Never glancing at him, finally the boy mumbled, "Fine."

Gracie raised a big fuss and reached for her papa. Houston leaned over and plucked her from the boy's lap. "I'll let her ride with me for a while."

Lara smiled. "Bring her back when you get tired of tending her."

Houston nodded and hollered to Caroline in her wagon. "You doing all right, Mrs. Vincent?"

"Doin' just fine. You sure are lucky to have such a sweet babe, Mr. Legend."

"Now, I told you to call me Houston," he scolded, riding up beside her. "Mr. Legend is my father."

Caroline laughed. "My folks taught me to call every adult mister and missus, no matter their age. I can't break the habit. Is Henry going to be all right?"

"Eventually. What he saw will be hard to erase. Gonna take some time."

"I hope so. He's such a kind, gentle boy," Caroline said. "I can't imagine all those people being dead. I just can't picture it. They were so nice."

"Yes, they were." Houston turned the roan he'd chosen for the day, intending to ride over to Clay.

"Mr. Legend," Caroline called.

"Yes, what is it?"

"Do you think those murderers will come this way?"

Houston wished Caroline hadn't asked the question that had crossed his mind more than once. "If they come, they'll have to go through Nick and the rest of us to get to you. I have a feeling Nick would fight like a wild badger and leave us with nothing to do but watch."

The young woman laughed. "I 'spect you're right. We

don't have much in the way of worldly goods, but we've got each other. Anyone who tries to hurt either of us will have the biggest fight on their hands they ever saw."

"For sure." He noticed Clay out of the saddle, waving his hat in the air, and Houston galloped off to see what he wanted.

A few seconds later, Clay said, "Got a puny drover."

Quaid Boone lay on his side on the ground, puking.

"Looks that way." Houston handed Gracie to Clay and dismounted. He squatted down beside the boy, where the smell of spirits nearly overpowered him. "What's wrong, Quaid?"

"I'm"—he hiccupped—"sick."

"Keeps falling out of the saddle," Clay said, batting Gracie's hand away from his eye patch. He wore a grin and winked at Houston with his good eye. "If I was a betting man, I'd say he and Virgil got into some rotgut."

"How about it, Quaid?" Houston asked.

Quaid puked again and wiped his mouth on his sleeve. "Yes…yes, sir." He hiccupped again. "But seeing our brother almost d-d-d…dead that…way, do you b-b-blame us?"

"Think you can crawl onto your horse?" Houston asked. The boy nodded.

"Ride to the wagons. You can lie down until you sober up."

"Y-y-yes sir. I don't f-f-f-feel so good."

Houston helped him to his feet, steadying him while he mounted. Quaid finally made it into the saddle after missing the stirrup three times, but most of the credit went to the big heave Houston gave him.

He swung onto his roan and took Gracie. "Clay, I'll make sure he reaches Lara. Keep a sharp eye out for trouble. The way the hair is crawling on my neck, something's coming."

"My gut's speaking to me too. Don't worry, we'll stay alert." Clay reached for his reins.

"Just curious. How's Virgil? Is he sick too?" Houston asked.

"A little green around the gills but nothing like his brother." Clay chuckled. "Maybe Virgil can handle his liquor better."

"I know one thing: Lara is going to give Quaid holy hell. I wouldn't want to be in the kid's shoes." Grinning, Houston followed Quaid, who was slipping and sliding from one side of the saddle to the other as though someone had greased the leather with hog lard.

Houston caught sight of Henry's blank stare when he got Quaid to the wagon. Some lessons were a damn sight harder than others.

～

Two days later, Houston watched Quaid work, glad the boy had recovered from his experiment with whiskey. Lara had lit into him with a fury and it appeared to have left quite a sobering effect.

They'd reach Fort Supply in another three days. A week and a half had passed since Houston had left Sam and Luke, and concern had grown into full-blown anxiety.

He sat on his horse with his arm resting on the pommel, his gaze following Frank Farley as he took out after a longhorn escapee. Yuma Blackstone's former gang member had turned into a first-class drover. No one worked harder or longer than Frank. Houston had begun to have second thoughts about turning him over to the military at the fort. If the man had entertained thoughts of killing them, he'd had plenty of chances. Yet he seemed genuinely glad to be in their company.

Surprisingly, Frank had even shown quite a deep affection for Gracie. And the little angel thought the sun rose and set in the outlaw. Of course, she took up with anyone who offered a smile. Suffice it to say, there would be no living with the child by the time they reached Dodge City. It would be a pure wonder too if she ever figured out what her legs were for.

The late afternoon sun sat low on the horizon. Twilight would soon come. Houston lifted his hat and used his bandanna to wipe the sweat trickling down his face. The weather had turned unseasonably hot over the last week, which made them look forward to the nights, when they could cool off.

For Houston, nighttime couldn't come fast enough for a different reason.

After feeding the drovers and putting Gracie to bed, he and Lara would crawl onto their blanket to while away the hours cementing their commitment to each other. Although they couldn't fully shed their clothing or make love, they found other ways to show how they felt.

Teasing and caressing.

Kissing until they grew breathless.

Whispering words of love.

As he learned his wife's body, Houston grew bolder. He knew what made her eyes grow round, gave her those excited gasps, and had her whispering his name in that breathless voice. He stoked her need to give him pleasure in return.

Pushing the memories aside, he jammed on his hat. "Dammit to hell! I just want to get to Dodge. Bathe my woman in a steaming bath, make love on a real bed, dress her in fine clothes," he growled into the breeze.

Sighing, he turned the Appaloosa and galloped forward, not slowing until he rode alongside Lara's wagon.

"Howdy, cowboy," she said, grinning. "Haven't I seen you somewhere before?"

"Reckon so, ma'am. I ride in these parts pretty often."

"You remind me a lot of my husband. Would you know him?" She leaned toward him and her dress gaped open, giving him a view of the rounded tops of her breasts.

He had to force himself to swallow before he drooled onto his chin. Lara had started leaving the top buttons of her dress unfastened, but not ever this far before. He hoped none of the men would remark on it, because he'd sure hate to knock their teeth out, what with them being so far from a dentist.

"What does your husband look like, ma'am?" he drawled.

Lara ran her tongue slowly and deliberately across her lips. "Oh, he's tall like you and has big, gentle hands that can swallow a woman. His arms ripple with strength and he loves children and horses."

"You don't say?"

"I most certainly do." She slid a forefinger into the parted bodice and moved it back and forth across her skin.

Houston smothered a groan as his heartbeat quickened. His wife had learned fast how to excite him. And right now, all he could think of was rolling on top and spilling himself into her. The bulge in his pants became uncomfortable.

"Anything else about this husband of yours?" he asked hoarsely.

"Oh, I should say. He knows how to satisfy his wife," Lara went on, pushing her finger deeper into the folds of her bodice. Houston smothered another groan. "He keeps me safe and he can be very tough on those who try to hurt me."

"Sounds like you sort of like this man."

"I love my cowboy with all my heart and soul."

"Do tell?" Houston's grin spread. He loved playing this game with her, seeing her lighthearted teasing.

"Know where I can get a bed for the night?" she asked.

"Meet me by the chuck wagon later and I'll tell you."

Before he said any more, Henry stuck his head from the canvas opening and mumbled, "Hi, Houston."

"Why, howdy, Bones. I wondered where you were." He watched Henry climb out to sit beside Lara. The boy's bruises and cuts had begun to show signs of fading, and in the daylight he appeared almost back to his old self. It was only when night came that he retreated inside himself where no one could follow.

"I was playing with Gracie on account of Lara being busy."

"I'm sure your sister appreciates that. Is she safe in the wagon by herself?"

"Yep."

Just then Gracie let out a deafening squeal and jabbered

as fast as she could. Lara stopped the wagon and leaned through the opening. "Come here, Houston, you should see this."

Wondering what she was laughing at, he dismounted and climbed up beside her. The child sat on the floor, secured to a flour barrel with a length of rope. Henry had wrapped the lariat around and around both baby and barrel. Squirming, yelling, and baby cussing, Gracie was having none of being tied up.

Henry poked his head between Houston and Lara. "I was keeping her safe. If bad men come they won't kill her."

Unsure how to reply, Houston crawled inside. He quickly freed the babe, lifting her out to her mother. While Lara comforted the child, Houston asked Henry to come with him. Three paces from the wagon, Houston put his arm around the boy's shoulders. He was almost as tall as Houston. "Henry, I know you saw some real bad stuff in the Ledbetters' wagon—"

"Blood. Blood on my hands. Blood in my hair."

"I can't imagine how much that scared you and—"

"I was afraid to die."

That statement broke Houston's heart. Young boys shouldn't have to be afraid of dying. Henry should be catching bullfrogs and fishing and taking a ribbing from his brothers.

"You don't have to be scared here. Me and all my men are going to keep you and Gracie and Lara safe."

"They *will* come," the boy said matter-of-factly.

"No, Henry. The outlaws are a long way from here. They don't know where we are. And you know why they don't?"

He shook his head.

"Because my brothers, Sam and Luke, are making sure they won't hurt anyone ever again."

"But they might."

Standing in the last rays of a dying sun, Henry wasn't convinced and Houston couldn't really blame him. The boy had seen a horrific sight that was still lodged in his brain.

Houston pulled Henry close. "If you trust me at all, just know that even if the bad men come, I'm not going to let them hurt you. Not now, not tomorrow or forever."

"Okay."

As they turned toward the wagon, a circling hawk squawked overhead. Two more steps and a coyote's mournful howl sent shivers up Houston's spine.

Henry was right. Trouble rode toward them.

But from which direction?

Blackstone and his gang were out there. Waiting. Watching. Thinking. Houston could almost hear the sound of their breathing.

Wild beasts stalking wary prey.

Forty

GLOOM SHROUDED EVERYTHING IN SIGHT BY THE TIME they stopped for the night. Pushing hard, they'd doubled the miles today. That should've satisfied Houston, but it didn't. He wished they'd made fifty, or a hundred, and put themselves out of range of whatever was coming.

Danger crackled in the air like lightning did right before it struck. He felt it, and he knew by the men's anxious glances and nervous laughter they did too.

Near the campfire, he squatted down beside his horse and picked up a handful of red dirt. Maybe it was this color because of all the spilled blood. Lord knew the lawless territory had seen plenty. The area was nothing but a haven for outlaws and mercenaries—the baddest of the bad.

Men with nothing to lose.

Men who killed for the sake of it.

Men such as Yuma Blackstone.

The pounding of hooves brought him to his feet. He slid his Colt from the holster, staring into the thick black night in the direction they'd come. The hair on his arms rose. Still he couldn't see anything, and whoever it was kept coming. The sound grew louder and louder and his heart thudded painfully against his ribs.

Two riders materialized from around a stand of mesquite, riding straight for him.

"Hold it right there!" Houston barked.

The riders stopped. A voice called out, "Don't shoot. It's Sam and Luke."

Relieved, Houston returned his Colt to the leather holster and watched them walk in. Both appeared dirty and tired. From the looks of them, they'd been in the saddle since daylight.

Dark stains covered their shirts. Appeared to be blood.

"You're a sight for sore eyes," he said, clasping their hands. "I figured you for dead."

Sam glanced at Luke and grinned. "You mean we're not?"

Houston touched Sam's shoulder to assure himself his brother was real. "Looks like you had a time of it. You're about ready to keel over."

From beneath the brim of his hat, Luke's eyes glittered like bits of glass in the firelight. "We fought like hell to get here to warn you. They're coming with a vengeance and they've got killing in mind."

"'Course, they're short by at least six," Sam added. "Wish we could've whittled away a few more."

Clay, Pony, and several other drovers gathered around. Houston watched Clay exchange a nod with Luke.

"Did you find Gus?" Pony asked.

"What there was left of him." Luke accepted a cup of coffee Lara brought him, and she passed the next to Sam.

The drovers waited while Sam and Luke took several sips, letting the hot brew wash some of the trail dust from their throats.

Frank Farley stood apart, watching. Houston saw yearning in his eyes to be included. Yet, one question persisted. Was he really with them, or against them? Was he only pretending to be fed up with Yuma? Houston sighed. He couldn't invite the man to join them until he was sure.

Luke turned to Lara, who stood with Houston. "Thank you, Miss Lara. This hits the spot...until I can find something stronger. Which I hope is sooner rather than later."

Lara laid a hand on his shoulder. "Glad I can help."

"Whiskey's in my saddlebag. Help yourself." Houston slid his arm around Lara and prodded his brothers. "I want to know everything from the time we left. But first, tell us about Gus. The men need information about their friend."

"Miss Lara, what we have to say isn't pretty," Sam said with a question in his voice.

Lara stiffened. "I'm no weak lily, Sam. Of anyone here, I most know what Yuma is capable of."

Before the brothers could go on, loud cries erupted. Caroline rushed toward Lara with Gracie. "She fell trying to pull up to that big rock over there and skinned her leg. I told her she was all right, but she wants her mama."

Taking her, Lara moved away so the men could talk. Houston's gaze followed as she comforted the child. Part of him yearned go with her, to plug his ears to more tales of killing, to simply be a family. But as head of the outfit, he had no choice but to stay.

"Go on, Sam." He dragged his attention back to the circle.

"The day you left, we found the carcass of a dead cow," Sam said. "Someone had skinned it and stripped away the meat. We assumed the culprits were hungry Indians from one of the tribes. Then three days later, we ran across Gus."

Luke took up the story. "At first we thought it was another dead cow. Someone had wrapped the cowhide tightly around Gus and bound it while he was alive. They left him out in the sun to dry. The shrinking hide crushed him to death."

A commotion drew Houston's attention as Gus's best friend, Pony, pushed through the wall of men. Tears trickled down his face. "Those dirty, low-down bastards. They could've killed him without torture! He never did one damn thing to them. I say we hunt down every stinkin' one of 'em."

It would be nice. But Yuma wanted him to leave Lara unprotected so he could get to her.

"You'll ride into a death trap if you go." Sam took the

last swig of coffee and tossed the dregs onto the ground. "They're ready and itching to kill more of us. I've been working as a lawman all my life. I've seen my share of killers eaten alive with bloodlust until it wiped out every trace of humanity, but this bunch is more evil than any I've ever seen."

Luke shifted and stared at Houston. His words had a hard edge. "We've got to stop them from getting Lara and Gracie, at all costs. If they do… Well, just know after a few days with them, you won't recognize her."

The warning drenched Houston like a bucket of icy water. It took great effort to drag his gaze from Luke's cold green eyes. When he did, he glanced at Lara sitting with young Caroline. Blue flames from the fire played across her beautiful features, but the shadows made the long, jagged scar on her face appear deep. He watched her kiss Gracie and hug her tight. The backs of his eyes burned.

If anyone hurt either of them, he'd not rest until he wiped them from the earth.

Houston pried the words from his back teeth. "Don't worry, Luke. They'll have to drain every last drop of blood from my body first, and doing that will take more fighters and strength than they've got."

Murmurs of solidarity went around the circle and he knew they'd protect her and Gracie with their lives.

"We were able to pick off six from a cliff top but the bastards just seem to multiply like a bunch of roaches. Sam and I got back here as quick as possible to warn you. They're riding hard and fast. You don't want to see what this group can do." Luke let out a string of curses.

"We found something to show you." Sam walked to his horse and reached into his saddlebag. "We have another group on our trail."

The former Texas Ranger took about a dozen broken arrows from his saddlebag.

Houston nodded and told his brothers about the burned-out village they'd discovered.

"What's to make them think you didn't do it?" Luke asked.

"Nothing." Not one blessed thing. Houston rubbed his day-old whiskers. They could have the Indians after them too. How would they survive both groups?

Henry climbed down from the chuck wagon and went to sit with the women. Even from this distance, Houston could see the dark circles under his eyes.

"Sam, did you and Luke happen to hear of a raid on the Ledbetters' wagon?"

"We stopped it. Why?"

Houston told them about Henry's ordeal and how he walked all that way to them. "He said the outlaws killed them all."

"So that's what happened to him." Sam glanced toward the boy. "We worried when we couldn't find him."

Luke crossed his arms. "In the dark, it's easy to see how he'd think they'd all been killed. Hiram had told them to play dead if they ever came under attack. That's what they did. They're alive, Houston, but almost everyone, including the children, had bad wounds. After helping Hiram doctor them, we escorted them out of danger and they went on."

"It's a relief that they survived the slaughter." Houston glanced at the boy. "Will you tell Henry? He needs to know."

Maybe, somehow, the boy could find his laughter again.

"Sure." Luke walked to the campfire and dropped next to Henry.

"I want your opinion, Sam." Houston rubbed the back of his neck. "I have half a notion to leave the herd and make a run for Fort Supply. The only thing stopping me is not knowing if we could move fast enough to stay ahead of them."

"Luke and I discussed that," Sam answered. "But we'd risk an attack in the open, where they'd cut us down. I say send the women on with one man and make a stand right here, in the shadow of this rocky cliff. We could hold them up and let the women escape. It seems our best option to me. If they were my family, that's what I'd do."

As long as his family and Caroline were out of danger, Houston would draw a line and stay put. He'd take whatever came: life—or death.

The end of Clay's cigarette glowed when he inhaled. He blew the smoke out slowly. "We didn't bring a lot of shovels, but if we work through the night, the men could dig a long trench. Doubt the gang would even see us until it was too late."

Houston mulled that over. Yuma's force had shrunk by six. The drovers outnumbered them now. With luck, the fight would end fast. "I like that idea, Clay. We can set things around to make it appear that Lara is still here. How far behind are they, Sam?"

"A day maybe but could be less," Sam said, rubbing his eyes. "Say, do you mind if I get some grub? Luke and I haven't eaten since yesterday and my belly's letting me know it."

"Go ahead. We'll talk while you eat." Houston strode to the chuck wagon with his little brother. His gaze went to Henry, who sat with Luke. The boy sniffled and wiped his nose but so far held the tears at bay.

Henry glanced at Houston. "They're not all dead. They're not."

"Good news, Henry. Every cloud has a silver lining."

He just prayed this cloud did.

⁂

Lara lay in Houston's arms under the chuck wagon, listening to the sound of the men digging, hearing each time they struck rock. He'd been out most of the night helping but had come back to seek a little rest with her.

She shifted and glanced over to find him staring at the underside of the wagon. "You're so still I thought you might be asleep."

"Thinking."

The deep rumble of his voice brought comfort. "Perhaps you could explain something."

"Anything for you." He kissed her upturned face.

"You're always so calm. Do you ever get afraid you'll die?"

"Sometimes."

"How do you manage to hide it?"

"Lord knows I fail miserably. Maybe what helps is forcing myself to stare danger in the face and move toward it, even when I want to run." He draped his arm protectively across her stomach and she savored the weight.

Lara snuggled against him, listening to his heart beating. "I'm terrified. Not for me, but for Gracie and Henry. And you."

Hot tears lurked behind her eyes. To lose her husband would banish every bit of sunshine and laughter from the earth. She meant to soak up every second of being in his arms.

Just in case they didn't make it.

He brushed her temple with his lips and the touch was so tender it made the backs of her eyes burn.

"Tell me about this house I'm going to build for you. Anything special in mind?" he asked.

Lara knew he was trying to take her mind off the looming fight and she loved him for it. "I want a wide porch going all the way around. In the mornings, I can sit out there and watch the sun come up, and in the evenings I can see the sunset."

"How big is this house?"

"Two-story. Four large bedrooms upstairs." She absently created circles on his leather vest with a finger. "A bathing room with hot and cold running water and a water closet. Big windows downstairs that let light flood in."

"Anything else?"

The way they spoke in hushed voices, little more than whispers, Lara felt as though they were locked in their own private world.

"A tall flagpole at the corner of the house so we can

fly our own Texas flag. That means a lot to me. That flag honors the men who paid the ultimate price so I might live free." She glanced up and smiled. "This state has seen so much bloodshed, yet we Texans still stand tall. I wouldn't live anywhere else."

"Me either. It's the best place this side of heaven."

Lara glanced at a few men grabbing what sleep they could a few yards away, wishing she could make love to Houston, yet knowing she couldn't.

As though sensing her thoughts, Houston nibbled his way across her lips until he coaxed them open. Lara gave a soft sigh and welcomed his tongue, curling hers around it. His mouth seemed like velvet as he created a seal, locking in the hunger of his kiss.

His rough palm slid along the curves of her body, sending warm waves of pleasure down to her toes. God in heaven, she wanted him. This man had taken her into his heart and she cherished him more than her own life.

Sliding her hand into his hair, she melted into his arms, glad she had come on this cattle drive, remembering making love beside the Canadian River in the moonlight. She was meant to be with Houston Legend. Surely the God who'd brought them together despite the odds wouldn't separate them now. He wouldn't be that cruel.

Houston was hers.

As their lips parted, she murmured against his mouth, "I love you, cowboy. Don't ever forget."

"No chance." Houston smoothed back her hair. "No matter what tomorrow brings, I will always cherish this time with you."

"Looking back, it amazes me how we ever got to the altar. One misstep or changed event and we'd never have met." The magnitude still boggled her mind.

Rising on an elbow, he ran the tip of his finger down her scarred cheek. "You've given me more happiness than I have a right to."

"I'm glad. You have me too."

With a rumble in his chest, he took her hand and brought it to his lips. "When we get to Dodge, I'm going to deck you out in silk. And when you walk down the street on my arm, who do you think they'll be looking at?"

"You," she breathed. "No man ever cut a finer figure."

"Nope. They'll pay me no mind, because you'll blind them with your beauty. And I'll be the proudest man you ever saw."

Lara snuggled against him, soaking up the happiness of being with Houston. She never wanted this to end. But would tomorrow sever them forever? A thickness formed in her throat. If he died, she wanted to die with him. She couldn't imagine a world without him in it.

Heavy silence enveloped them as Lara laid her head on his chest and listened to the sound of his soft breathing.

This man she'd married would never falter or waver from the rules he'd created deep within his soul—things like love, honor, and protect.

She thought he'd gone to sleep until another rumble came from his chest. "Lara, tomorrow I'm going to send you, Caroline, and the children ahead."

A fist closed around her heart. He couldn't ask this. "No."

"Listen to me," he said gently, rising up on an elbow. His touch was tender on her skin. "I can't have you here. It's too risky. No matter what happens, it will end right here."

"I'm staying." Leaving him would kill her.

He turned her head to look into her eyes. "I wish I could let you, but I can't this time. I need you to ride as fast as you can to Fort Supply. Probably take a little over two days in the wagon. Wait there. I'll join you when I can."

"Please don't ask this of me. To leave you will rip out my heart." Her voice was thick with an ache no words could express. He needed her. She needed him.

Houston brushed her ear with his lips. "I'd rather I rip it out than Yuma. Think of Gracie, Henry, Caroline. If they stay here, they'll die. They're counting on you to lead them to safety. Be strong for me."

He asked the impossible. She couldn't do this. What made him think she was strong? She ran from trouble like some whimpering, frightened, pathetic animal.

She'd let Yuma instill fear so deep inside, the sun's warmth couldn't reach it. Even worse, she'd almost let the man break her. How could she ride off and hide where she was safe and let Houston face the demons that rightfully belonged to her?

"You have to, for the children and that young girl," he whispered in her ear as though he'd read her thoughts. "For them, you have to do this. Do it for me."

"I'll do most anything you ask." Lara tried to calm the mass of quivers inside her. "You're my partner, my best friend, my lover. Just don't ask me to bury you, because I can't. We're going to give Yuma Blackstone a whipping he won't ever forget."

Forty-one

By daylight, doubt had crept in that they might not win. After a sleepless night in Houston's arms, Lara quietly pulled away from him to start breakfast. Fighting men needed extra food, a feast to give them strength to defeat the foe.

He reached for her. "Morning, darlin'."

"I hoped you were sleeping." She raised her lips for a kiss.

"Too much to think about."

"Me too. I've got to get the biscuits on."

They rose and she went to prepare a meal. Her heart was heavy and she was hard-pressed to give Henry a smile. He sat in the wagon box, clutching Gracie. That was where she often found her little brother these days. He seemed to feel safest there. To make matters worse, the overcast sky and softly falling rain added to the thick gloom encasing them.

Perfect. Could the good Lord not even give them a little sunshine? The men needed to be able to see the enemy. And their guns needed to be able to shoot.

Lara avoided meeting Houston's gaze for fear that the tears lurking so close to the surface would spill. If she could do little else, she was determined not to add to the burden he carried on his broad shoulders. She bustled around, pretending to be busier than she was, but a sharp-edged sense of Houston's whereabouts hummed under her skin every second.

A memory swept over her from her time in Amarosa. A man there had kept carrier pigeons. The birds had always fascinated her, and she'd always been curious to know how they could return to their roost from anywhere.

Now she knew. They instinctively had some sort of built-in homing ability. Lara did too and it wouldn't let her get lost from the man who'd shown her deep love. Slowly, she relaxed. Worry didn't do much anyway, except give her gray hair. She wouldn't saddle Houston with a gray-haired wife this soon in addition to everything else.

Caroline joined her and they could've made matching bookends. Judging from the girl's low spirits, Nick had told her the plan too. Words were at a premium as they cooked.

After getting the biscuits on, she left the young newlywed to watch the salt pork sizzling in the skillet and went to find Henry, who'd disappeared from the wagon box. She spied him lugging Gracie, following so close on Luke's heels it seemed a wonder he didn't plow right into the tall gunslinger.

"Henry, I need to talk to you for a minute."

Though silent, he glanced up.

"Make sure you have all your belongings packed in the wagon. We're leaving as soon as we eat. Can you do that?"

He nodded. "Is Uncle Luke coming too?"

Worry in his eyes dried Lara's mouth. He too sensed trouble. No wonder, since the same fear was so thick it clogged her throat. She forced a smile and brushed back a lock of red hair from his forehead. When had he gotten so tall?

"He will soon. For now, we have to go in front."

"Yuma's coming," Henry whispered in a loud rasp.

If only she could lie. But he needed the truth—at least partially. "Honey, try not to be afraid."

Henry rocked back and forth on his heels, his gaze glued on the distance. "I gotta find my rock. Help me. Help me."

"Calm down, I'll find one." Though she needed to make gravy, she took time to locate a big rock and put it in his hands. Odd how relaxed the stone made him. Now, if she could only find some easy fix for her fears. But the only thing for that would be seeing Houston ride into the fort unscathed, ready to scoop her up into his arms.

Only then would she be able to breathe.

෴

After breakfast, Houston stood in the rain beside the chuck wagon. He pulled Lara close, feeding his fierce need to feel her heart next to his.

"I love you more than I ever thought it possible to love anyone. Though I was thirty when we wed, I feel like I was just a boy." He cleared the lump from his throat. "You've taught me patience, gentleness, and most importantly, how to love. Whatever happens here, I'll gladly give my life for you and Gracie."

She touched his face as tears broke through her resolute smile. "I wish I could stay by your side, but I'll do what you ask."

"Promise you won't look back. Never back. Always forward."

"I never make a promise I can't keep."

With a hoarse cry, Houston crushed her to him and lowered his mouth. He'd never felt these conflicting emotions that ricocheted through him, bouncing off bone and muscle. God, he didn't want her to go. He couldn't. But he had no choice.

Drinking his fill of the woman who'd changed his life, he cherished every second with her in his arms.

Loud voices broke them apart. It was Nick and Caroline.

"I swear, Nick Vincent, you're the stubbornest man on the face of the earth!" Caroline shouted. "You know I can shoot an' doctor an' cook. You need me."

"Nope. You ain't staying and that's that."

The young girl flung both arms around Nick's neck. "I ain't no good without you. I buried my parents and my four brothers and I'm not burying you. I'm not. I just ain't gonna do it."

Houston spoke up. "Sorry to butt in at the risk of losing my nose. Nick, this isn't your fight. Go with Caroline, find your uncle, and start a family. You don't have to stay."

Nick faced him squarely. "Mr. Legend, you've been real kind to Caroline and me. I've never had anyone treat us so nice. You took a chance on me and I'm not going to run out now." He slid his arm around Caroline and kissed her hair. "I figure if I run from this, I'll be running for the rest of my life. A man needs to stand up and be counted or he can't live with himself. I want our children to be proud I'm their pa. I'll stay and fight right alongside you and these drovers."

Thrusting out a hand, Houston shook Nick's. He liked the strength in the boy's grip. "Glad to have you, son."

"Thank you, boss." Nick turned to Caroline. "Now give me a kiss, wife honey. You and Miz Lara gotta be going."

As the young couple finished their good-byes, Houston slipped his hand into Lara's pocket, searching for the small gun. Relieved to find she still carried it, he helped her up into the wagon box beside Henry. He was pressed in the middle between Lara and Caroline and he held Gracie tightly, staring straight ahead. Houston saw the fear digging deep inside. He could almost read the boy's thoughts: he was being sent away again.

Nick climbed up to give Caroline another kiss. The young woman wiped her eyes.

"Remember, Lara," Houston said. "Ride hard, and don't look back."

"I'm not going to tell you good-bye. I'll see you again after you whip these bastards." Lifting the reins, she set the wagon in motion. Gracie cried, kicking her legs and reaching for him. He swallowed hard and turned away before he could stop them.

Damn Yuma Blackstone to hell! All they wanted was to love each other, live in peace, raise a family.

Caroline leaned over the side to yell, "Nick Vincent, if you die I'll never speak to you again! You better come back to me"—she paused and softened her tone—"sweetheart."

Quaid and Pete moved to Houston, leading their mounts.

"Keep them safe, boys. I'm leaving the best part of me in your hands," Houston said gruffly.

They nodded, stuck their feet into stirrups and mounted up.

Houston turned his thoughts to the fight that lay ahead, praying for a miracle.

Frank Farley suddenly blocked him. "Give me a gun. Let me go in Pete's place. I'll protect your family with my blood."

"How do I know you won't turn and fight with Yuma?"

"You don't and I haven't given you much reason to believe me." Tears filled the hard man's eyes. "I once had an honest life full of promise. Yuma rode in one day, reminding me I owed him. He'd saved my life during the war, you see. When I refused to ride with him, he burned my house and barn to the ground, destroyed my crops. Everything I'd worked for was gone. I need a chance to make him pay. Just one." The man widened his stance. "You need another fighter you can depend on. I'll be that."

The raw emotion that leaked from Frank's heart touched Houston. He told Quaid and Pete to wait. "Your gun is in my saddlebag. But cross me and I'll hunt you down."

"I want Blackstone stopped as much as you do. Maybe more. You won't regret this."

"I pray you're right." Houston told Pete about the switch. "Go help the ones digging."

Once Quaid and Frank had ridden out alongside the lumbering wagon, Houston had a hurried talk with his brothers and Clay. "What do you think about getting a few men up to the top of this cliff?"

Sam tilted his head to glance up at the solid rock wall.

"That's thirty feet straight up. It's too sheer, nothing to hold on to."

"With ropes we can," Luke said quietly. "I'll scale it and pull men up."

"The job'll take two," Clay said. "I'll go with you."

They worked to the bone the next three hours and got four armed drovers and everything they'd need on top of the cliff. Meanwhile, Houston arranged pots and pans by the campfire and scattered clothing all around, so it appeared the women were there. He prayed Yuma wouldn't notice the missing chuck wagon.

Then they ran out of time.

"They're here!" The shout came from atop the cliff. "God almighty, there's a bunch!"

Thick dread knotted in Houston's stomach and drovers scrambled into the trench. He could see Luke rappelling down the cliff, Sam staying with the drovers. This was it. Whatever happened, the fight would end here. Today.

The sudden riders froze Houston, caught in the middle of the herd he'd been weaving through. He shot a hopeless glance at the Vincents' wagon on the east side of the trail, his intended target. He'd wanted to bring it next to the campfire to add to the cozy appearance. Even so, he could've used the wagon where it sat, but that wasn't possible now.

Hope faded of catching the outlaws in a crossfire.

They burst in with a flurry of rifle shots, choking acrid smoke, and war cries. The fact that the lawless group had arrived far earlier than anticipated told him they must've ridden all night.

He knew they couldn't see him in the middle of the cattle, but still he felt exposed.

No wonder. His heart froze at the size of their force. Their numbers were far greater than the dozen or so they'd counted the night Houston and Clay had found their camp. Even with his brothers sending six into an early grave, he estimated at least two-dozen riders coming in.

Where the hell had they picked up the extras? Had Yuma sent up a smoke signal and they all came running? Deep as they were in outlaw territory, Blackstone probably had no trouble finding more. Just turn over any rock.

Hell! At least Houston was glad he and his brothers had worked so hard getting drovers set for the fight. The force's erratic shooting showed they had no idea where the drovers were.

With his rifle to his shoulder, Houston waited. He'd ordered his men not to waste lead, to wait for a target. He didn't see Yuma. So far, all the smoke had come from the outlaws' weapons. Not seeing any drovers, they began shooting the animals.

Houston clenched his jaw, adjusted the sight on his rifle, and placed the crosshairs on the chest of Digger Barnes and his cartridge belts. The sneer curling the man's lip sent rage cartwheeling through him.

"Say hello to the devil, you piece of crow bait. This is for my wife." Houston pulled the trigger.

The shot knocked the man sideways in the saddle, and blood spilled down his sleeve. Digger righted himself and sent a bullet into the longhorn next to Houston. The animal fell, trapping Houston's foot underneath. There was no way to get the dead carcass off him.

Ignoring the pain running up his leg, Houston struggled to pull free. Digger rode slowly toward him, weaving between the bellowing cows.

Ten yards.

Six yards.

A trickle of sweat ran down Houston's face. He yanked on his foot. It wouldn't budge.

Five yards. Houston lifted his rifle and squeezed the trigger but an animal jostled his arm and Houston's shot went wide. Digger dove off into the midst of the frightened herd.

Nervous longhorns pressed around Houston on all sides, pushing against him.

Trapping his rifle at his side.

He had nowhere to go. With eyes full of fear, one of the steers lurched, crushing Houston between it and another.

Struggling to breathe and fearing the weight against him would break his spine, he could only pray to somehow survive. To see Lara and Gracie again. As his life hung in the balance, he strained to see where the hated outlaw had gone but he'd disappeared into the milling animals.

A minute ticked by.

Then another.

Sweat drenched Houston's shirt. It was only a matter of time before Digger either resurfaced or he'd be crushed.

Or the herd would stampede. One way or another, he'd be dead.

The bulging eyes of the cattle told him they were ready to bolt. A ticking clock in his head inched toward the moment when it all would be over. He searched the restless, frightened animals, looking for the hated outlaw.

Around him, men were cursing and shooting. The cattle's loud bellows added to the chaos, the din so loud it made his ears hurt. The noise seemed to reach greater heights with each moment.

Dying cows.

Dying men.

Dying hopes.

Houston expected either a bullet to fly from nowhere and explode into him, or to wind up with every bone in his body shattered by the longhorns. He wasn't ready to die. Not when he'd truly begun to live for the first time in his life. He had a woman who loved him, family, and the kind of marriage few men ever knew.

Please don't let me die this soon, and not like this. Not before he got justice for Lara.

As blackness descended, the longhorns shifted and he was able to gulp air into his lungs and free his weapon. His arm trembled violently as he tried to raise the rifle to his shoulder. Trapped as he'd been between the cattle, his muscles refused to work.

After three attempts, he finally lifted the weapon.

Just as he positioned the Winchester against his shoulder, the sun glinted off of the metal on Digger's cartridge belts and he saw the man's hat.

He squeezed off a shot.

Unsure if he'd hit him or not, Houston renewed efforts to release himself. Excruciating pain in his foot almost took his breath. Finally, using what strength he had left, he shoved the beast as hard as he could. He struggled free just as Digger Barnes sprang from the sea of brown hide and horns. His arm rose over his head.

A long knife glittered in the sun.

Forty-two

HOUSTON SQUEEZED THE TRIGGER BUT NOTHING HAPPENED.

No more cartridges, and no time to reload. No time to draw his Colt. No time to think.

In the instant before Digger plunged the knife into him, Houston mustered every ounce of strength left into his numb arms. He swung the rifle.

The Winchester caught Digger across the chest and spun him around.

The cattle bolted into a full-out stampede.

North. The route Lara had taken.

Needles of fear pierced him as though razor-sharp blades. The animals could easily overtake the slow-moving wagon. He thought again of the wagon he'd seen after being caught in a stampede, the broken bodies underneath.

But Houston didn't have a moment even to pray, for he was left without cover. Injured and dying men lay sprawled on the ground, trampled by the frightened cattle. Spurts of gunfire from the trench and on top of the cliff let him know his drovers still fought.

A sudden eerie quiet filled his head. The moment he'd waited for frozen.

Whatever the outcome, this was it.

Houston faced Digger Barnes, thankful he too was left afoot. "Looks like it's time to show me what you have."

"I got plenty for you, big-shot cowboy with your big Legend name. Unstrap your gun belt, put down the rifle, and fight me with your hands."

With a snort, Houston stared at the wounded outlaw. Digger had to be as crazy as Yuma. The man was hampered by the gunshot, but on second thought, Houston could barely stand on his injured foot. They *were* evenly matched and he'd get greater satisfaction whipping the man with his bare hands, inflicting pain. Shooting him would be over too fast. That wasn't the kind of justice Houston had prayed for.

"I can beat you on your best day, Digger Barnes." Houston laid down his empty rifle and unfastened his gun belt.

A strange light filled Digger's eyes. "You know me, I see."

"If you think those cartridge belts scare me, I'm here to tell you they don't. You're just an evil man who stole something very precious from my wife."

Digger cocked his head, his grin showing rotted teeth. "Ah, she told you. Did she say how much she liked it?"

"Lara only had one thing to say—you're nothing but a girl. Said you're smaller than her pinky finger." Houston lowered his eyes to Digger's crotch. "I see she was right. I'm going to rip you apart and spit on you when you die." Houston held his hands wide, his gaze locked with the man's cold, dead eyes. "Then, before we leave you for the buzzards to peck your eyes out, I'm going to bring her here so she can spit in your face as well. It'll be the only drop of water you'll find where you're going."

Growling deep in his throat, Digger released a string of curses followed by a lightning-quick jab. The fist caught Houston's jaw, spinning him around, twisting his foot. Sharp pain shot through him. Shaking his head to clear it, he braced his feet and delivered punishing blows to Digger's midsection in return.

The series of punches knocked the wind from the outlaw. As he fought for breath, Houston brought his hand hard across Digger's face. The open-handed slap sounded like a rifle shot. It did no damage, but emasculating him inflicted a far deeper injury. One Houston found especially gratifying.

An angry bull blinded by rage, the outlaw lowered his head and rammed into Houston.

Sidestepping, Houston grabbed his foe around the neck. With a lift of his knee, he crushed Digger's face. Bone met bone. Blood squirted from the outlaw's broken nose and mouth. His jaw was probably broken as well, if Houston was to hazard a guess.

Digger bent over, screaming and gripping his face. Catching the man with an elbow to the ribs might've finished him off, but Houston wanted to make sure. Standing over Digger, he brought his elbow down again onto his spine. The outlaw fell to the dirt.

Houston scrambled for his Winchester, reaching for the cartridges. He'd managed to insert only one before a grunt alerted him. He swung around as Digger lunged for his gun belt, pulling Houston's Colt.

In a split second, Houston stared down the barrel as the outlaw fumbled to find the trigger.

One second, one twitch, and his life would be over.

He had only one bullet. He prayed that'd be enough. Jerking the lever down to ratchet a cartridge into the chamber of the Winchester, he fired.

Through the smoke, he watched Digger Barnes plunge backward. The hole in the man's chest told Houston that Digger was dead. He leaned down to keep a promise. He drew up the biggest wad of spit he could muster. The aim was perfect—right between the eyes.

Buckling his gun belt, he quickly assessed the battlefield. Sam was in the midst of reloading, with one of the enemy running toward him. Houston quickly squeezed off a shot, stopping the man before he reached his target.

Another shot wounded one more. The outlaw scrambled behind the Vincents' wagon.

Everywhere Houston looked, men were locked in

deadly combat. Hopelessness wound through him. The outlaws appeared to be winning.

How many of his men would lie dead on this godforsaken land?

A bullet slammed high into his chest just below his collarbone. Houston's rifle fell to the ground as fire swept through him, taking his breath. If he could somehow make it to the wagon, he might have a chance of saving himself.

Except that's where the outlaw had run.

Drawing his Colt and breathing hard, Houston limped over to the wagon and carefully inched around, searching for the enemy who'd taken cover in its shadow.

Fighting nauseating pain, he peeked for a quick look. The man fired. Houston dropped to the dirt and crawled underneath the wagon bed. The outlaw's gaze met his a split second before Houston fired. The man sprawled backward. Scooting back out from under the wagon, Houston removed his bandana and held it to his wound to stanch the flow of blood.

Something rustled and Houston startled. He glanced up, trying to raise his weapon, but didn't make it. Relief flooded him at the sight of Luke.

"How bad?" Luke moved closer as a bullet barely missed him, splintering the wood by his shoulder.

"Enough." The word came from between Houston's tightly clenched teeth. "I don't know if we're going to make it. Maybe the Legends are done for here." The sound of Houston's labored breathing filled the space. "Maybe this is it." Maybe he wouldn't see Lara again.

"If so, we'll go down together, brother." Luke squatted, lifting the bloody bandana for a better look. "Just a scratch." A grin showed his white teeth. "Not worth a doctor's time."

Houston appreciated the lighthearted attempt to ease the tension, but he knew the truth.

Still, he was far from giving up. Wasn't in his blood. He'd often kidded that he'd been raised with wolves. It had felt that way when he was growing up. Stoker made sure his boys had the toughness and will to push past the pain.

He gripped his Colt tighter. "Do or die, Luke. Let's give 'em hell and let the buzzards feast on their carcasses."

"Damn right." Luke got to his feet with his rifle blazing.

Struggling to stand on his wobbly legs, Houston took aim with his Colt and fired at an attacker. He missed, adjusted his aim, and tried again, this time hitting the mark. The bullet only wounded, but he considered even that a victory.

Zigzagging, Sam ran toward the wagon. A galloping rider raised his arm to shoot. His brother wasn't going to make it. Houston clenched his jaw tight, focused on the moving target, and squeezed the trigger. He sent a bullet into the man's gun hand. The weapon flew up in the air and hit the ground, and blood spread across the rider's shirtsleeve.

Sam raced behind the wagon. "Thanks, brother. Thought he had me." His gaze went to Luke at the other end. "Looks like we're all together. Time to do our best fighting."

"Yep. Do or die, Sam. Do or die."

They fought until each was down to his last cartridge. Still the riders came. Houston kissed his last bullet and inserted it into the chamber with shaking fingers.

One bullet between him and the inevitable.

Despair swept through him as sweat blinded his vision. He pictured Lara as she'd lain on the bank of the Canadian, bathed in silvery moonlight, passion in her eyes, her auburn hair spread in disarray on the wild grass.

"I love you, Lara. I will to the last breath," he murmured with a thick voice.

Sam and Luke were quiet as they inserted their last bullets.

"See you on the other side," Houston told them.

"Yeah." Luke cleared his throat. "I'm glad I found my family. I always thought I'd die in a gunfight at twenty paces."

"I'm not ready to quit. I promised Sierra I'd come home to her." Sam released a string of cusswords. "I'll fight the bastards with my bare hands like Crockett and Travis did in the Alamo. I'm not licked yet."

Houston leaned against the wagon, glancing down at his bloody chest. He could barely remember the color of his shirt. His black vest appeared a strange shade of red.

Bodies, animals, and weapons lay everywhere. Other than four drovers that he distinguished by the chaps, he didn't see anyone else moving. They must've all died. Grief for his loyal men washed over him. If he hadn't talked them into staying, they'd all be safe now, and far away from here.

Sudden war whoops split the air. He leaned to where he could see and spotted a dust cloud from galloping riders rising in the east. Surprise and disbelief swept through him. *Indians.*

They weren't close enough for him to make out the nation, but those among the new riders with guns were firing at the outlaws, not the drovers. The others shot arrows toward the fleeing attackers, dropping them into the dust.

"What in the hell is going on?" Sam asked.

"I don't know, but they're a welcome sight." Houston grinned, draping an arm around his brothers. "We're still alive."

Luke grunted. "Unless they turn on us."

One tall, proud man wearing a striking bonnet of eagle feathers rode to them, offering the sign of peace.

Since Sam was more versed in their customs, he stepped toward them with his hand outstretched in friendship. He spoke to them in what appeared to be Cherokee, best as Houston could tell.

Judging by the headgear, the Indian must be a highly esteemed man. He answered back in terse words.

Sam looked back at his brothers. "They're Cherokee. The outlaws raided their camp a few days ago, killing and burning. They tracked the bastards here."

"I ran across the burned-out village and buried the dead. Tell the chief I'm sorry and thank him for the help." Houston sagged. The Cherokees had saved their hides. Only what good was it for him to survive if Lara was dead? He extended his arm to the rider, as did Luke, then glanced around. "Where's Yuma?" Houston hollered. "Has anyone seen him?"

"Nope," answered one of the drovers.

A man rose from the pile of bodies. Blood covered one side of his face. "Boss, he lit out a few minutes ago. I couldn't stop him."

Houston spun toward the north and spotted a dust cloud in the distance. It had to be Yuma. But the cloud indicated more than one rider.

Panic shook his numb body. He had to find Blackstone. A horse—where was a damn horse? He had to get to Lara and he had no time to waste.

A roan trotted up about ten paces away. He limped, staggering toward it.

Luke rushed to his side. "You're in no shape to ride. Let me go."

"She's *my* wife." Houston shrugged free and kept moving.

"Dammit, then at least let me help you."

As Luke's arm came around him, Houston welcomed the support. Reaching the mount, Luke helped him into the saddle. Then he grabbed the reins of another horse and swung aboard.

"I'll stay here and see to the drovers," Sam called.

Houston didn't waste time answering. His spurs touched the roan's flanks, and they flew toward the woman who held his heart and all his dreams.

Please don't let me be too late.

Forty-three

DESPITE HOUSTON'S INSTRUCTIONS TO RIDE HARD FOR THE fort, they'd pulled into a canyon a mile from camp. Lara couldn't make herself go a step farther.

She had to stay near her husband.

Now Lara could only listen to the sounds of war as helplessness lodged inside. Sound traveled a long way on open land, and each burst of gunfire made her cringe and imagine the worst.

The rain clouds from the morning had moved on and the sun blazed down, cooking her and the rest. Henry had taken refuge under the canvas top with Gracie. Caroline huddled next to Lara in the sparse shade against a rock wall, gripping her hand.

"What do you think is happening?" Caroline asked. "I'm terrified for Nick. He's all I've got and I'm not ready to lose him. I can't lose anyone else. I just can't."

"Me either." Lara glanced at Quaid, glad he was safe with her. Her thoughts went to Virgil, who'd stayed back with Houston. He was too young to die. He hadn't lived yet. Hadn't kissed a girl or danced in the moonlight.

Sitting on a rock, Quaid lifted his hat to wipe his forehead. "I'm going back. I need to help Virgil and the men."

"No," Lara said firmly. "Houston told you to stay with us and that's what you'll do. I want no argument."

He huffed and took his gun from the holster. Checked for the tenth time that the cartridge wheel was full.

They'd be all right. No one would find them. And then after the fighting ended, she'd go back to whatever remained of the man she loved.

But then the stampeding cattle thundered past and she gave thanks they'd parked off the trail, or they'd have been trampled.

Frank knelt at a little clear stream that trickled through the narrow gorge. He drank his fill and then dunked his head underneath and shook the water off. Lara, shriveling under the sun's heat, wished she could do that. Desperate for relief, she unfastened the top buttons of her dress as Caroline had done and rose. She found a handkerchief, wet it in the stream, and bathed her neck.

Alarm skittered through her at the sound of hooves striking the ground. She stood, reaching into her pocket for the gun. It wasn't there.

She froze, remembering she'd laid it inside the wagon when she'd fed and changed Gracie.

Quaid and Frank moved beside her, making her feel protected. They'd handle whatever trouble came. But nothing prepared her for the bald man on horseback who rode into the narrow gorge.

"Well, this is my lucky day," Yuma Blackstone crowed. "Knew you wouldn't be far away from Legend." He turned to Frank Farley. "Glad you got free. You can help me."

The spit dried in Lara's mouth as she tried to swallow. She stared at the large X cut into the side of his face. The wound was still angry and seeping blood, and she knew satisfaction, even if she hadn't put the cut there herself. For once, Yuma had gotten a small taste of what he deserved.

She held her breath and glanced at Frank. Whose side would he take? If he chose Yuma, they were done for.

Frank shifted, his gaze shooting from Yuma to her. "Sorry, Blackstone. I ain't going to be no help to you at all. Legend didn't capture me. I gave myself up. And I was happy to be shed of you at last. You'll get nothing from me. These people are my friends and I'm glad to fight with them."

"The hell you say!" Yuma hollered.

Quaid pointed his gun at the hated murderer. "I'm going to kill you."

"And if he misses, I'll get you," Frank said with his weapon raised. "In fact, we may use your sorry hide for target practice."

Yuma yawned and dismounted. "I don't think so." He gave a shrill whistle and an armed accomplice scrambled down from the rocks. "Take their guns," Yuma ordered.

Hate and fear settled in Lara's chest as she watched Quaid give up his weapon. The silent outlaw tossed the gun aside, then cracked the back of her brother's head with his pistol. Lara gave a cry, watching him fall to the ground, only vaguely aware of Caroline pressing against her side.

"I hate you," Caroline screamed. "I hope you rot in hell."

Before the outlaw could direct his attention to Frank, the loyal man got off a shot before he took a bullet. Blood covered his chest as he fell. Lara couldn't tell if he was alive.

Caroline screamed again, the sound bouncing off the walls of the little canyon.

This time would be it. This time no help was coming. And this time Lara would not cower. She lifted her chin and slowly moved toward the man she hated with every fiber of her being.

Houston's words sounded in her head. *Maybe what helps is forcing myself to stare danger in the face and move toward it even when I want to run.*

Lara straightened her shoulders. This time she'd fight with every ounce of strength she had. She told Caroline to stay back then forced herself to march to within two feet of Yuma.

Just then the gunfire ceased. The war Houston and the drovers hadn't sought was probably over. Maybe he was dead—maybe all the drovers had lost their lives.

Because of her. Guilt nearly buckled her knees.

In the deadly silence, she heard her frantic heartbeat, felt it hammering against her ribs.

"I'm not afraid of you," Lara spat. "You're despicable."

"You belong to me, girl. Only me." Yuma's cruel smile curved his mouth, and he smoothed his thin mustache with the tip of a forefinger. His glance went to the buttons undone at the top of her dress and his eyes glittered. "You expected me."

He closed the distance to stand inches from her. Up close, the slices Houston had made to his face were still gaping and wet, hideous. A shiver ran down her spine, but she didn't back away.

"Looks like that hurts." Her voice was oddly sarcastic. "How does it feel?" She watched his look of confusion. His forehead wrinkled as though trying to figure her out.

"Yeah, that's right," she went on. "I'm different. Tougher. Smarter. Braver. You can't hurt me."

"We'll see about that, girly," he snarled.

She spat on him and in his moment of shock, as the spittle ran down his cheek, she brought her hand across his jaw. The slap rang through the canyon like a rifle explosion, bouncing off the rock walls.

Behind her in the wagon, Gracie wailed. The fact that she couldn't comfort the frightened babe pierced her heart.

Yuma grabbed Lara's face, pinching it cruelly between his fingers. "I'm killing that brat and I'm going to make you watch. I put a bullet in that husband of yours too. He's dead. You're a widow now. I'll kill every man who looks at you."

Pain ripped through her, taking her breath. Houston was dead. They'd never share any more kisses in the moonlight or make love on a cushion of grass. She swallowed a sob. Yuma had murdered the man she loved. Though she felt her knees crumpling, she willed herself to remain standing. Gracie's crying filled the silence.

"Kill the brat, I said!" Yuma screamed to his man. "Now."

Yuma's iron grip brought tears to her eyes. Though fear lodged in every part of her, she raised her chin in defiance. "Anyone touches her and I'll scratch your eyes out first chance I get."

"That kid is nothing to me—just a squalling brat."

"You're gutless. You can't do anything yourself. You have to order it done. You're a coward. You shake in fear when confronted by anyone different from you." Lara glanced for something to use as a weapon. All she saw were rocks that littered the ground. He'd release her eventually. But would she have time to grab one?

Where was Caroline? Did the other outlaw have her? Yuma still held her face tight. She tried to look out of the corner of her eyes but saw nothing.

"Those Bible-toters thought they were better'n me. Go around praying all the time, sending folks to hell." He yanked Lara's nose to his. "My men showed them."

"Those aren't the only ones you're scared of," she spat.

The stench of his breath gagged her. Bile rose into her mouth as memories of all she'd suffered at his cruel hand swirled inside her head. Gracie's frightened cries ripped into her. Oh God, her child couldn't die! But the loud wails would only make Yuma more desperate to shut the babe up for good.

"Let my sister go!" screamed Henry. He'd climbed from the wagon and came toward them with a rock in his hand.

Yuma's eyes bulged. "Get back, boy."

Henry threw his rock, striking the outlaw's bald head. Blood trickled from the wound. Distracted for a crucial moment, Yuma released his hold on Lara. She turned to see Caroline inching toward Frank's gun. She didn't see the other outlaw. Where had he gone?

"Get back, I say!" Yuma swore as he staggered.

"No! You'll hurt my friends! You'll kill the baby." Henry drew back and launched another rock.

The second missile hit Yuma's chest with a thud. He shuddered, letting the pearl-handled pistol fall from his hand. Spittle ran down his chin. "The wicked shall be turned into everlasting hell! You're devil-possessed, boy."

Caroline was almost to the gun.

But then Lara saw Yuma's man and her heart froze. The outlaw climbed from the wagon, dangling Gracie by one leg. Oh God! Oh God! Oh God!

"Get away from that gun," the man barked at Caroline.

Gracie's screams of terror seemed to fuel Henry more. Lara had never seen her brother so full of rage. Maybe the traumas he'd survived, the constant fear, had snapped something in his brain. She could certainly understand that. He stalked toward them, picking up rocks and throwing them. A good many struck the hated outlaw.

Yuma growled low like an animal.

The gun he'd dropped glinted in the sunlight.

Could she get it and fire before Yuma pulled the second one hanging in the holster?

Her glance slid to Caroline. Anger glittered in her eyes, tightening the girl's mouth.

"The devil's in the brat too! I said kill her." Madness glittered in Yuma's crazed eyes.

The words froze Lara's heart. She had to act or they'd all be dead.

Without considering the possibility of failure, she darted to the pearl-handled pistol. Regardless of what happened to her, maybe Gracie, Henry, and the others would live.

She yanked it up, thrusting her finger onto the trigger. Rage flooded over her and fear too. Shaking, she jabbed the silver barrel into Yuma's chest. Her next words were for the outlaw dangling Gracie upside down. "Lay the babe gently on the ground or your boss is a very, very dead man." The steel in her voice seemed to spring from a place deep inside.

Maybe it had been there all along. She'd just needed to find it.

"She's bluffing. Shut that goddamn brat up!" Yuma's gaze met hers, boring into the depths of her being. Daring her. "She doesn't have it in her to kill me."

An angry roar filled the inside of Lara's head. Without breaking eye contact, she spoke to the other outlaw. "Hurt my daughter, and trust me, it'll be the last thing you will ever do. As soon as I shoot this piece of filth, I'm swinging the gun to you."

Henry launched another rock, this time striking Yuma's face. "I'll kill you!" the boy screamed.

"Don't worry, Lara!" Caroline yelled. "I have Gracie. And I have a gun on this outlaw. Kill the bastard. Do what you hafta do."

She didn't know whose weapon the girl had, but she knew Caroline would use it. "Be careful—don't look away for an instant."

"I ain't," Caroline replied, then crooned to Gracie to comfort her.

Lara reached for the second pistol in Yuma's holster and tossed it aside. Then she slid the .45 in her hand down and shoved it into the one thing Yuma prized more than any other body part. She jabbed the barrel into his flabby flesh. He winced, staring at her in a mixture of fear and disbelief. She noticed an odd light come into his eyes, and his breathing grew harsh.

Power filled her. No one would ever take from her again in this way.

Her voice grew quiet and she moved closer to his ear. "I'll blow you right into the pits of hell and not bat an eye. That fire is awfully hot. Feel it licking around your legs?" She shrugged. "Of course, there's a chance you won't die. In fact, that might be even better. To live without your family jewels would be most fitting."

But could she settle for that? He'd killed Houston. He should pay the ultimate price.

"My men will be here in a minute," he answered in a strange, faraway tone. "They'll take care of you."

"A pity they won't get here in time. I can't imagine living only half a man, eaten alive with hunger, unable to satisfy the need." Lara smelled his fear.

Sweat rolled down his face and he licked his dry lips.

Her voice lowered to a whisper. "This isn't just about me, you know. I'm doing this for all the women you've done the same thing to, and others you will never get a chance to. You're scum, trash to burn. One of us won't leave here."

Yuma licked his lips again. His eyes darted back and forth and he babbled something that sounded like Scripture, but no verses she had ever heard. He seemed to be slipping into a different person. Yuma really *was* crazy.

Lara listened in stunned disbelief. Frank Farley was right. The man was a lunatic.

"Come back here." She jammed the gun deeper into the soft flesh. "There is no escape for you. None."

"What's going on?" Caroline yelled.

"I'm not sure exactly. Thank you for quieting Gracie."

Sudden yelling came from the girl then Lara heard Yuma's man scream, "Put down that gun or I'll shoot you dead."

Panic swept through Lara. Caroline had Gracie in her arms! Oh God! What was happening? She wanted to turn but she couldn't take her eyes off Yuma.

"Mister, I've just about had enough!" the young girl yelled.

"What's going on, Caroline?" Lara couldn't bear not knowing. "Caroline!"

A loud blast rent Lara's hearing.

A man screamed.

Gracie let out a piercing cry.

Horses snorted.

"Caroline, answer me." But all she got was the sound of a struggle.

"I think you'd best go see, girly," Yuma said, his eyes glittering wildly.

Lara shoved the gun into his privates harder. "You'd like that, wouldn't you? Sorry, I'm not taking my eyes off you for a second."

Just as her nerves were stretched to the breaking point, Quaid spoke. "It's all right, sis. Everything's all right."

"I shot him, Lara. I shot his dumb leg and Quaid came to and tied him up. We're all okay!" Caroline yelled.

Henry appeared to the right of her vision. "Don't worry, sis. Just shoot him!"

Yuma gave Lara a sudden shove and lunged for the twin .45 still on the ground.

Before he could lift it, she fired. The bullet tore into his midsection. Yet he kept coming for her, that mad light in his eyes. With smoke still curling around the barrel, she fired again, and this time the bullet struck a bit lower.

Tears streamed down her face. She kept pulling the trigger until she'd emptied the wheel.

As though from a long distance away, she felt Quaid gently pry the gun from her fingers. "He's dead, sis."

Vaguely, she heard another rider enter the canyon but she couldn't even look. She had no more strength left to fight anyone else. Houston was dead and she'd turned into a murderer.

Henry kicked Yuma's leg. "We did it. He's not gonna hurt us anymore."

"Lara!"

The voice sounded like Houston's. Only it couldn't be. Maybe she'd gone as mad as Yuma.

"Lara, are you hurt?" Arms went around her.

"Houston?" she asked dully, the voice still not registering.

"It's me." He hugged her against him. "I was so afraid I'd lost you. It's over, darlin'. It's all over."

She gazed up into her husband's coffee-brown eyes. Blood smeared the whole side of his face, the trail running down his neck into his shirt. She sucked in a breath. "You've been shot!"

Houston tried to work up a grin but the effort appeared to be too much. "I did my best to stay out of the way of bullets."

"Sweetheart, you talk too much." She rose on tiptoes to press her lips to his.

She barely heard Caroline squeal and yell Nick's name, or

notice Luke manhandling the remaining outlaw, or Quaid tending to Frank, who was thankfully alive. Happiness settled through every inch as Lara molded her body to Houston's. Somehow, through everything, they'd survived.

Without breaking the kiss, Lara slid both arms around her husband's neck and drank in all she'd nearly lost. "I love you, my cowboy," she murmured against his mouth.

Forty-four

Battered but not beaten, Houston and his drovers finally arrived in Dodge City two months after leaving the Lone Star. They'd had to lay over ten days at Fort Supply to let him and his men heal and rest. The lull had given them time to fatten the cattle a bit.

Frank Farley was recovering from his gunshot, and instead of turning him over to the military, Houston had offered him a job. He couldn't repay the man enough for helping them and keeping Lara safe.

The sun hovered low on the horizon when they rode into town. The drovers wasted no time in driving the cattle to the huge stockyards, where milling longhorns stretched as far as the eye could see. The sight, combined with the din of all those bawling cattle, boggled Houston's mind. Growing up on the Lone Star, he was accustomed to large numbers, but the yards held more cattle than he'd ever seen.

Even after the losses along the trail and during the fight, he still had a sizeable herd, taking days to round them up following the battle. Once the herd was inside the gates of the stockyard and counted by the tally man, the drovers scattered like a wad of buckshot. Lara had issued a stern warning to Quaid and Virgil not to let Henry out of their sight.

Now pausing on Dodge's Front Street, Houston steadied

his horse. They'd made it, and in one piece. It was a wonder he didn't drop Gracie. The babe was in perpetual motion, trying to take in all the chaos. She kept her pointed finger very busy, scolding everything and everyone. He breathed a sigh of relief and grinned at Lara beside him on the little mare she'd ridden before.

His last glimpse of Sam, Luke, and Clay found them making tracks into the nearest bathhouse. Nick and Caroline had stopped to inquire about Nick's uncle. Who knew where Pony Latham and the remaining drovers had taken off to? Sorrow washed over Houston. They'd had to bury four following the fight. Of the eighteen they'd left Texas with, only twelve had come through. Leaving the loyal men who'd given their all on the windswept prairie had crushed him. Now he'd have to face their loved ones. And Stoker.

Somehow, he'd have to find a way to live with their deaths. He already knew he'd bear the scars the rest of his life.

The first thing he'd do once he got back was make sure their families got the money due the drovers, including the bonus for making it to Dodge. Though that was precious little at best and couldn't begin to fill the holes those men had left behind. He also meant to see what he could do for the Cherokees who came to their aid and turned the tide. Maybe Clay could suggest the perfect thing.

Pushing away the gloomy thoughts, Houston turned his attention to a hot bath, a good meal, and private time with his lady.

It took some doing to weave through the packed street and he was glad they'd left the chuck wagon parked at the edge of town until they could restock it for the return trip. Adding to the noise, scantily clad women hung over the balconies, yelling their prices to the men below. Nothing about them interested Houston. He had what he wanted right beside him. He moved closer to Lara to keep them from getting separated, aiming the horses toward the Dodge House Hotel. Tying up, he dismounted.

A gunshot erupted from the Silver Dollar Saloon across the street as he swung Lara from the mare. She jumped, staring at him with wide eyes.

"Let's get you and Gracie inside, darlin'." Houston put a protective arm around her. "We'll see if they have some rooms."

"I don't think I've ever been so tired." She wearily raised her eyes to his. Hers were the color of a green field under the morning sun. "And I need to feed Gracie."

Though Lara had said very little about the trauma of killing Yuma, he knew she suffered. Over the past few days, he often caught her crying and staring into the distance. Not surprising, for he knew how much taking a life changed a person. Even one that needed taking.

A sign snagged Houston's attention the minute they walked through the hotel door.

Rooms to let
$1 a night with bedbugs
$3 extra without

He put himself between the notice and Lara and strolled to the clerk behind the registration counter. "We'd like a room."

The balding clerk glanced up and shook his head. "Sorry, we're full up. Wish I had something, for the missus and babe's sake. We don't get many families in here. Mostly gamblers and the like. How long are you going to be in town?"

"Two weeks," Houston replied. Lara had earned a good rest after what she'd been through, and he was going to see that she got it.

"Then I suggest Mrs. Malloy's boarding house over on Oak Street. She runs one of the cleanest places in town. Doesn't allow riffraff and it's real quiet."

"Just what we need. We've had a hard trip." Houston sent Lara a smile and put his arm around her. "Tell me how to get there."

A few minutes later, he led them away from the danger and noise.

At the quiet boarding house on Oak Street, Mrs. Malloy welcomed them with open arms, already smitten by Gracie's smile. "I'll keep this little darling anytime you want to get some rest." The rotund woman with rosy cheeks and sparkling eyes kissed the babe's cheek with gusto. Gracie buried her face against Lara, peeking from between her chubby fingers.

"I'm sure we'll take you up on it." Houston filed that tidbit away. "What we really need is a hot bath, if it's not too much trouble."

Mrs. Malloy said she'd have her hired boy bring a tub to their room and check the attic for a crib for Gracie. Then she led them up a narrow staircase to the second floor that opened into a long hallway. Unlocking the first door on the right, Mrs. Malloy swung it open. Lara gave a soft gasp at the pretty room, already bathed in the purple hues of twilight.

Houston couldn't take his eyes off his wife, and seeing such a simple thing give her pleasure made his chest hurt. He cleared his throat. "Mrs. Malloy, I'm wondering if you'd have one more room for my wife's younger brother. The boy requires supervision."

"Why yes, Mr. Legend, I have a small room at the end the hall. Most guests want something larger, so it sits vacant most of the time. It only has a bed and chest. Will that do?"

Houston caught Lara's quick nod. "It'll be perfect."

"Excellent. I'll have a meal ready in an hour." After giving them a few rules and laying out her schedule, the woman left.

Houston turned to Lara and kissed her temple. "I need to find your brothers and mine and tell them where we're at. I'll bring Henry back with me."

"Thank you, Houston. I worry about him, you know." Lara trailed her hand down his neck. "I'll bathe Gracie and feed her. I expect she'll go right to sleep. This little girl is tired."

"I'll be back soon." He shot a longing glance toward the bed. The soft quilt covering it bore a large star in the center, making him think of home. He couldn't wait to make love to Lara surrounded by that comfort. He reluctantly gave her and Gracie a kiss.

Before he reached the door, Lara called, "I love you, Houston. Please be safe."

                         ∽

Safe and Dodge City didn't go together. Gunshots erupted again the minute he turned onto Front Street. He tied the Appaloosa to the hitching rail in front of the first saloon. He'd work his way down the row of establishments. A café stood three doors down, and that looked like his best bet at finding Lara's brothers. At least he'd better find them there and not sowing wild oats.

His would definitely be in a saloon. He strolled into the Spit Bucket but didn't see them. No luck in the second either. The café did yield the Boone boys. They had only gotten halfway through their meal, so he grabbed a piece of chicken off Virgil's plate, telling them he'd be back.

Houston strolled through six saloons before he spied his brothers and Clay coming from Sassy Sal's. Lights from windows of the watering hole revealed their grim faces. The three paused on the boardwalk while Clay lit a cigarette.

Before Houston could call to them, a man raced from Sassy's. "Clay Colby! Face me like a man and make your move!"

Clay Colby? The gunfighter who'd made a name for himself in Cimarron, New Mexico?

What the hell?

Disbelief and shock swept over Houston. Surely there was some mistake. Luke's hand hovered above his Colt, ready to help. Sam watched through narrowed eyes, the set of his jaw meaning he was ready to do battle also. Houston waited anxiously for Clay to set the stranger straight.

Instead, and without turning to the man behind him, Clay grated out, "I got no quarrel with you, Leon."

"I aim to make you pay. You gunned down my brother outside the St. James Hotel." Shaggy like a wooly bear, Leon stalked to Clay. "Deny it and you'll be a bald-faced liar."

"I don't deny I shot Clive, but, *amigo*, you oughta get your facts straight." Clay calmly inhaled on the cigarette, bringing a red glow to the end. Smoke curled up from his mouth. "Your brother drew on me. A dozen witnesses saw him draw first. Now, if you don't mind, I'm tired, I'm hungry, and I'm out of patience." He pushed past the man and moved toward Sam and Luke.

Livid at being brushed off, Leon shouted, "Noon tomorrow, right here! We'll settle this."

"You're as big a fool as your brother," Clay said and kept walking.

"Coward!" Leon jerked out his six-shooter, aiming it at Clay's back.

Before he could squeeze the trigger, Clay whirled, firing with the movement. The impact carried Leon backward, breaking the window at Sassy Sal's. No one spared the man a glance.

Houston crossed the street. "What was that all about?" he asked Sam as Luke and Clay moved the dead man off the sidewalk.

Sam shook his head. "The crazy fool tried to start trouble inside but Clay refused to take the bait. We left. He followed."

"I watched the last from across the street. Clay did all he could to avoid gunplay." Houston laid a hand on Sam's shoulder. "Did you know he was Clay Colby?"

"Figured it out during the attack when his eye patch came off and he put it on the wrong eye. Houston, he's a good man, no matter if he uses Angelo or Colby."

Within minutes, a deputy marshal arrived and took Clay aside. The lawman listened while the head drover explained the circumstances, then he came to speak to Houston and his brothers.

Clay finally cleared of charges, they crossed to the café. Clay removed the patch. "I'm glad I don't need this anymore. The damn thing itches like crazy." He faced Houston. "I owe you an apology, boss. Didn't mean to deceive you. Just wanted a job and not to be recognized."

"I couldn't have asked for a better hand. I took your measure and saw nothing to make me regret hiring you. Still don't." Houston stared into Clay's lined face—lines that told of an honest man who just wanted to live in peace for however long he could. "I have a feeling you want the money from this drive for something specific."

Clay nodded. "Have my eye on a piece of Texas land down in Hemphill County. I aim to hang up my gun, get married, start a family…if other men looking to make a name let me."

Luke's eyes flashed. "I haven't had much luck myself. But we have to keep trying."

The irony tore at Houston. Two honest men longing for a normal life, yet both wanted by the law. Clay had a price on his head, the same as Luke. He told them he and Lara were at Mrs. Malloy's and he'd meet them back at the stockyards early the following morning.

Houston turned to go into the café when he heard someone call his name. The Vincents' wagon pulled alongside and stopped. Nick and Caroline climbed down.

"Can we have a word?" Nick asked.

"Sure. Did you find your uncle?"

"That's the thing, boss. He's dead." Nick took off his hat and crushed it between his hands. "Someone shot him a year ago."

"The land is gone too," Caroline sobbed, pushing a strand of blond hair from her face. "We got nowhere to go and I don't like it here."

"Mr. Legend, I wonder if we could go back to Texas with you," Nick said. "Maybe I could work on your ranch or something until I save enough for my own land. If you don't have room for us, I'll find other work."

Houston knew the cost to a man pride's when his back was against the wall. He squeezed Nick's shoulder. "Be glad to have you. Texas is a big place. We always have room and opportunities for two more. Have you eaten?"

"Not yet." Caroline sniffed the aroma coming from the café.

"Then go inside." Houston handed Nick some money. "You'll have more in the morning after I settle up my account at the stockyards. There's enough there for a place to sleep."

Tears bubbled in Caroline's eyes. "Thank you, Mr. Legend. We'll buy the food but we already have a place to sleep." Her hand stole to Nick's and she met her husband's eyes, shutting Houston out.

They went inside and, after making sure Quaid and Virgil had a room, Houston collected Henry. On the way back to the boardinghouse, he noticed a light still on in a mercantile. He tapped on the glass of the locked door, and a clerk let him and Henry in.

A low hum vibrated just under Houston's skin.

Tonight he would make love to Lara on a real bed.

And what he had in mind to do first would show Lara his heart.

❧

Houston eased open the door to their room and stared, riveted. Lara was fast asleep with her head resting on the rim of the large, galvanized tub. A small table with remnants of a meal sat by the window. Gracie slept peacefully in the crib Mrs. Malloy had promised.

Lara looked for all the world like an angel who had fallen down from heaven. Freshly washed copper hair burnished with gold curled around her face, spilling to her shoulders. Houston laid down his packages, quietly removed his boots, and stole over. Bending, he placed his lips gently on hers and let his hand slide along her collarbone.

"Who are you, cowboy? Do I know you?" Lara murmured, slowly opening her eyes.

"I sure hope so, ma'am." He touched her cheek and let his hand slide down the column of her throat. Brushing her hair aside, he dropped a kiss on the back of her neck. "I don't deserve you, you know."

Her green eyes darkened with desire. "You'd lose that debate." She pulled him down by his shirt front. Her hungry kiss promised a night of raw passion.

Quickly removing his gun belt, Houston peeled off his clothes. Lara gave a contented sigh when he eased his aching body into the tub beside her. He wouldn't give what he had now for all the money, fame, and fortune in the world. Lara took the cloth from him, lathered it with soap, and set to work on everything in sight, and a few things that weren't.

Houston closed his eyes and let her remove all the grime, tiredness, and heavy sorrow. A deep hunger for Lara had risen the second she'd picked up the washcloth. He no longer felt weary down to his soul.

Tonight belonged to the two of them.

Every soap-slickened touch, every kiss upon his rinsed skin, every careless brush of her breasts against him brought a groan. He gently held them, testing the weight in his hands.

"I sure hope I have enough strength left in these muscles to repay you for all of this, ma'am," he murmured lazily as a fire flamed inside him. "I seem to have turned to liquid. You have magic hands."

"Do tell." Lara's breasts nuzzled his chest as she kissed the angry scar on his throat.

"Oh yes, I surely do." He lifted her palm to his lips and kissed the tender flesh, then moved to each fingertip. Lara's touch moved achingly slow under the water, down the flat planes of his chest and across his belly, then lower still.

Bold fingers.

Lazy, sweet strokes.

Tender whispered words against his ear.

Spirals of pleasure stole Houston's ability to think. He

sucked in a breath, reaching for one of the towels on the floor. Rising, he stepped out and secured it around his waist. "I'm going to carry you to bed, Mrs. Legend, and ravish you until morning. What do you have to say?"

Hunger flared in Lara's eyes. "I thought you'd never ask."

She stood and he wrapped the towel around her, swept her up into his arms, and padded to the bed. He laid her on the Lone Star quilt. "Don't go anywhere. I'll be right back."

He went to the pile of clothes, reached into his vest pocket, and pulled out a small box.

Lara lay with her head propped on her arm, watching. "What are you doing?" Without a reply, he perched beside her on the bed. She sat up and frowned. "You're acting very strange."

He couldn't stop the grin as he handed her his purchase. "I bought something special for you. I hope you like it, darlin'." He enjoyed the surprise on her face, the widening of her eyes as she gasped at the gold wedding band. "Our hurried marriage left no time to shop," he said.

A long silence filled the room. Panic made Houston's heart pound. What if she didn't like it? He leaned closer, trying to read her expression, but her face revealed nothing. She must hate it. He should've gotten something fancier. Maybe she thought him cheap. Finally, she plucked the band from a cushion of velvet and he noticed her trembling hand.

When she held the ring to the lamp next to the bed, a tear slid down her cheek. She glanced up and whispered, "*You're My Forever Always*. Oh, Houston, it's just so…so beautiful. I'll cherish this for the rest of my life. Will you put it on me?"

He slipped it on her finger, thinking how fortunate that the mercantile owner had a side business in a corner of the store, inscribing on the gold he sold. "I went in to buy one with diamonds, but then I remembered what you said about preferring things simple. Besides, the gold sparkle seemed perfect for my wild Texas rose."

Droplets clung to the tips of her long lashes as she stared into his eyes. "Diamonds mean nothing to me. They're simply something a rich man can buy. But this…" Her voice broke. "This came from your heart and that's priceless."

"I also bought us both a new change of clothes…that is, if I ever let you out of the bed," he growled.

"A nightgown perhaps?" She gave him a teasing look. Capturing her bottom lip between her white teeth, she tugged at the towel around his waist.

"You won't be needing such a thing." Dropping his towel, he tossed it aside along with hers. Houston crushed her to him and covered her lips hungrily. He loved this woman. She made his knees go weak and his pulse quicken with a teasing glance.

His fingers slid into her hair as their kiss deepened, tangling in the silky copper strands. Lara returned his kiss with equal passion, her touch fevered on his skin.

Lara broke the kiss with a request. "Lie back, my love."

Curious, he did. She straddled his hips boldly and kissed every inch of his chest and belly. This shy wife of his had become a tigress.

When she severely tested his ability to hold himself in check, Houston whispered, "Thank goodness this bed seems sturdy. We're about to give it a workout."

With a quick roll, he put her beneath him and slid into her warmth. Settling into a rhythm, he left a trail of kisses down the long column of her neck to the hollow where her pulse beat. Lara responded with heated caresses up and down his back before gripping his naked buttocks. His ragged breathing was loud as his racing heartbeat pounded against his ribs. Feeling Lara's muscles contract around him, he hurtled toward heaven. He'd remember this night forever.

Each touch, each kiss, each sound sent him closer to the release he craved.

In the midst of building passion, he whispered words of love in her ear. And when she fell over the edge, succumbing to mindless waves of pleasure, he kissed her, swallowing her cries of joy.

Afterward, they both lay shuddering, trying to breathe. As Lara rested against him, Houston trailed a finger up the curve of her shapely arm.

The long day, combined with his frisky wife, proved his undoing and he dozed off with his arm lying across Lara's stomach. All of a sudden, she startled him with a poke in the ribs. "Are you asleep? We've got to get started."

"I might've missed something but I thought we already did. Started how?"

"On another baby. I want your child to fill me. I want a little Houston Legend," Lara whispered next to his ear as he flattened a palm across a swollen breast. "I want to watch him grow up strong just like his handsome father."

A son? Good Lord, he wanted that. His dream of keeping the Legend name going for generations just might see fruition now. His children would watch over and protect the Lone Star, and each would learn chapter and verse about Stoker Legend, the man who'd founded it.

"We have the rest of our tomorrows, my wild Texas rose. I'm not going anywhere." He was home in her arms. "You're my forever always, and I'll stay in your arms until the end of time."

Just then, Gracie let out a string of babbles.

He chuckled. "Or at least until our daughter wakes up."

Read on for a sneak peek of

THE LAST OUTLAW

The final book in Rosanne Bittner's Outlaw Hearts saga

COMING 2017 FROM SOURCEBOOKS CASABLANCA

JAKE TRAILED HIS TONGUE OVER HIS WIFE'S SKIN, TRYING TO ignore his fear that she could be dying. Her belly was too caved-in, her hip bones too prominent.

She'll get better, he told himself. The taste of her most secret place lingered on his lips as he moved to her breasts, still surprisingly full, considering, but not the same breasts he'd always loved and teased her about, with the enticing cleavage that stirred his desire for her.

He would *always* desire her. This was his Randy. She was his breath. Her spirit ran in his veins, and she was his reason for being. God knew his worthless hide had no business even still being on this earth.

He ran a hand over her ribs, which were too damn easy to count. Sometimes he thought he'd go mad with the memory of last winter, the reason she'd become more withdrawn and had nearly stopped eating.

He met her mouth, and she responded. Thank God she still wanted this, but something was missing and he couldn't put his finger on it. He thought he'd made it all better, thought he'd taken away the ugly. He'd feared at first she might blame him for what had happened, but it had been quite the opposite. She'd become almost too clingy, constantly asking if he loved her, not to let go of her, asking him not to go far away.

He pushed himself inside of her, wanting nothing more than to please her, to find a way to break down the invisible wall he felt between them, to erase the past and assure her he was right here, that he still loved her. How in hell could he not love this woman, the one who'd loved him when he was anything but lovable all those years ago? She'd put up with his past, his bouts of insanity, and all the trouble and heartache he'd put her through. This woman who'd given him a son and a daughter who couldn't make a man prouder and who loved him beyond what he was worth, who'd given him six grandchildren who climbed all over him full of such innocent love for a man who'd robbed and killed and worst of all…killed his own father.

He moved his hands under her bottom, pushing himself deep inside her, relishing the way she returned his deep kisses and pressed her fingers into his upper arms in an almost desperate neediness.

That was what bothered him. This had always been good between them, a true mating of souls, teasing remarks back and forth as they made love. But now it was as though she feared she'd lose him if she didn't make love often, and that wasn't the sort of man he was. It had always been pure pleasure between them. He'd taught her things she never would have thought of, helped her relax and release every sexual inhibition. He knew every inch of her body intimately, and she'd loved it.

This was different. And it was harder now; he was terrified he would break something. She was so thin and small. He outweighed her by a good hundred and fifty pounds by now—she couldn't weigh more than eighty or ninety.

He surged deep in a desperate attempt to convince himself he wasn't losing her. And through it all he was screaming inside. Sometimes he wanted to shake her and make her tell him what else he could do to bring back the woman he'd known and loved for nearly thirty-two years. He missed that feisty, bossy woman, the only person on this earth who could bring him to his knees. He'd faced the worst of men as a lawman in Oklahoma, run with the worst of men the first thirty years of his life. He'd spent four years in prison under horrible conditions. He'd been in too many gunfights to count, taken enough bullets that he had no right still being alive. He'd ridden the Outlaw Trail and defied all the odds. His reputation followed him everywhere, and a reporter had even written a book about him—*Jake Harkner: The Legend and the Myth. Myth* was more like it. And the legend wasn't one he was proud of.

And this woman beneath him—this woman he poured his life into this very moment—she'd been there for most of it.

He relaxed and moved to her side.

"Don't let go yet, Jake."

He pulled her against him. "Randy, I can't put my weight on you anymore. You're too damn thin. You've got to gain some weight back or we'll have to stop."

"No!" She shimmied closer, pulling one of his arms around her. "I like being right here in your arms. Don't stop making love to me, Jake. You might turn to someone else. You're still my handsome, strong Jake. Women look at you and want you."

Jake sighed, the stress of her condition making him want to tear the room apart. "You have to stop talking that way."

"That you're handsome and strong?" She turned slightly. "Since when does the magnificent Jake Harkner hate compliments?"

There it was—a tiny spark of the old Randy in her teasing. Every time he saw that spark, it gave him hope. "I've always hated compliments. You know that. The only thing magnificent about me is my sordid reputation. I'd like to wring Treena Brown's neck for putting that label on me in her letter."

Randy traced her fingers over his lips. "Peter's wife was totally taken by you when they visited the ranch last summer."

"She's a city woman full of wrong ideas about what she

considers western heroes. God knows I'm sure as hell *not* one, and right now your magnificent Jake needs a cigarette." Jake pulled away and sat up. "You okay?"

"Of course I'm okay. You just made love to me. How could a woman not be okay after that?"

Jake took a Long Jack from a tin on the hotel's bedside table. "You know what I mean." She didn't answer as he lit the cigarette. He took a long drag. "Did I hurt you?"

"Of course not."

Jake ran a hand through his hair. "Randy, I mean it about your weight. If you don't start eating, I'm not making love to you anymore. Sometimes when I'm on top of you, I envision every rib breaking. We made this trip to Boulder because it was time you started getting away from the ranch, doing a few things amid strangers without being glued to me."

Be patient. Don't yell at her. She might go to pieces.

He heard a sniffle and it felt like his heart was breaking. He took another long drag before he set the cigarette into an ashtray and turned, moving back in beside her. "Baby, I've done everything I can to help you. When you're like this, it makes me sick with guilt. I should have realized what was happening when that barn caught on fire, the way it burned so rapidly. Lloyd suffers with the same guilt. We shouldn't have left the house unguarded."

"No! No! No!" Randy threw her arms around him. "Don't ever blame yourself. You blame yourself for *everything* bad that happens to this family, but you never asked for any of it, Jake."

He held her close, careful not to use too much strength. "Randy, I want my wife back. The woman I'm holding right now isn't her."

"I will be. I promise. Tomorrow, Teresa and little Tricia and I will go shopping. I won't be quite so terrified without you at my side if I at least have Teresa with me. Thank you for bringing her along."

Jake was grateful for the Mexican woman who was such

a help with the cooking as well as cleaning the big log home he'd built for Randy. It was still filled with noise at meals, all of the family gathering for Sunday meals. Before last winter, Randy had been a vital part of those gatherings—the one most in control, who loved all the cooking, who loved teaching and reading with Evie and the grandchildren. Living on a remote ranch meant no schools nearby, after all.

Randy now left it all to Evie. She was no longer her joyful self at the dinner table, although she put on a good show. He knew her every mood, and he could tell she was still suffering inside.

"Tell me what you need, Randy. How else can I help? You aren't here with me when we make love anymore. I can sense it in your kisses, in the way you respond when I'm inside you. I won't make love to a woman who's doing it out of duty."

She buried her face in his neck. "Jake, I still love it when you make love to me. It's just…" She hesitated again. How many times had he come close to getting out of her what was really bothering her?

"Just what? *Talk* to me, Randy."

She curled into a little ball against him. "That…ugly thing they did. That ugly thing. I can't…get past it. I'm so sorry, Jake."

Jake struggled against insane rage every time he thought about it. His precious Randy. Of all the intimate things he and his wife had done, asking her to perform oral sex on him had never been one of them. She'd never suggested such a thing or made an attempt, and he'd never asked. What they had together was enough for him. His first desire was always to give her pleasure, and that alone gave him pleasure in return. It would be disrespectful to ask this beautiful woman to do something he knew in his gut she wouldn't want to do. She was his wife, and he would not ask her to do something she hated. He still had the blazing memory of his father forcing himself on his mother that way right in front of her sons. Such childhood memories still sometimes made him wake up with screaming nightmares.

It all came down to his father, his ruthless, brutal, drunken father—the man he hated worse than all the dredges of humankind, more than the filth he used to run with when he believed he was the worthless sonofabitch his father always told him he was.

"Don't be sorry." *God help keep me sane.* "We'll work it out."

"Don't stop making love to me."

"I won't stop."

"You do still love me, don't you?"

"Stop asking me that. You know better." He wiped at her tears with his fingers. "Get some sleep, Randy. Tomorrow is a big day."

"You won't ever be too far away, will you, even when I leave you to shop?"

"I won't be too far away."

"You'll watch for me?"

"You know I will." He'd never felt so alone. Ever since he found and fell in love with this woman, he'd always had her to lean on, to keep him from the abyss that always beckoned. Tough and able as he seemed to others, *she* was his strength. And now that strength was gone. The tables had turned, and he had to be strong for her. He secretly begged God to help him remember that. He wasn't sure he had it in him to last much longer this way. "Randy, when you figure out what more I can do, or what it is that will help you get better, you tell me. Don't ever be afraid to tell me *anything*, all right? You know I've seen it all and done it all and nothing surprises me. And I love you. I'll do whatever it takes. Understand?"

"Yes."

"I can tell right now you're keeping something from me—something more than what happened last winter. You tell me when you're ready."

She clung closer, kissing his chest. "I will."

He kept his arms around her because she demanded it, every night until she fell asleep. He closed his eyes against his own silent tears. Without that closeness they'd always shared, it was as though he didn't even exist.

Without this woman, who was Jake Harkner?

About the Author

Linda Broday resides in the panhandle of Texas on the Llano Estacado. At a young age, she discovered a love for story-telling, history, and anything pertaining to the Old West. There's something about Stetsons, boots, and tall, rugged cowboys that gets her fired up! A *New York Times* and *USA Today* bestselling author, Linda has won many awards, including the prestigious National Readers' Choice Award and the Texas Gold Award. Visit her at LindaBroday.com.

The Last Outlaw

FOURTH IN THE EPIC OUTLAW HEARTS SAGA FROM
USA TODAY BESTSELLER ROSANNE BITTNER

The old West is changing—not that rugged former outlaw
Jake Harkner would let that stop him. Setting out on his most
dangerous journey yet, he takes the law into his own hands as
he rides into Mexico to rescue a young girl from a fate worse
than death. All the while, Jake's family and his beloved wife
Miranda are left to worry that Jake's end will come the same
way it began—by the gun.

*"Powerful, beautiful, harsh, and tender stories that take
readers' breaths away with their emotional depth."*
**—RT Book Reviews, 4½ Stars, Top Pick
for *Love's Sweet Revenge***

For more Rosanne Bittner, visit:
www.sourcebooks.com

Last Chance Cowboys: The Outlaw

THIRD IN THE SWEEPING WHERE THE TRAIL ENDS SERIES
FROM RITA FINALIST ANNA SCHMIDT

Amanda Porterfield longs to experience real adventure. So when she's offered a position in bustling Tucson, she leaps at the chance despite unknown dangers—dangers like the mysterious Seth Grover.

As an undercover detective working to stop a gang of outlaws, Seth can't afford the distractions a woman like Amanda inspires. Yet when the fiercely intelligent beauty is thrust into the middle of a heist gone wrong, Seth will fight for a future that may never be theirs…even if it means risking everything he holds dear.

"A feisty heroine and a hero eager to make everything right. What more could a reader want?"
—**Leigh Greenwood, USA Today bestselling author of *To Love and to Cherish*, for *The Drifter***

For more Anna Schmidt, visit:
www.sourcebooks.com

A Match Made in Texas

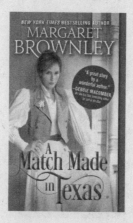

As Two-Time, Texas's first female sheriff, Amanda Lockwood
is anxious to prove herself. She takes down wanted man Rick
Barrett, but there's something special about the charming
outlaw. Common sense says he's guilty…but her heart tells
her otherwise.

Things don't look good for Rick—and they only get worse
when his plan to woo Amanda to his side backfires and he
falls head over heels. Now he must choose between freedom
or saving the woman he loves…and the clock is ticking.

"A great story by a wonderful author."
—#1 *New York Times* **bestselling author**
Debbie Macomber for *Left at the Altar*